TRUTHMARKED

Book Two of the Fatemarked Epic

David Estes

For anyone who believes in magic.

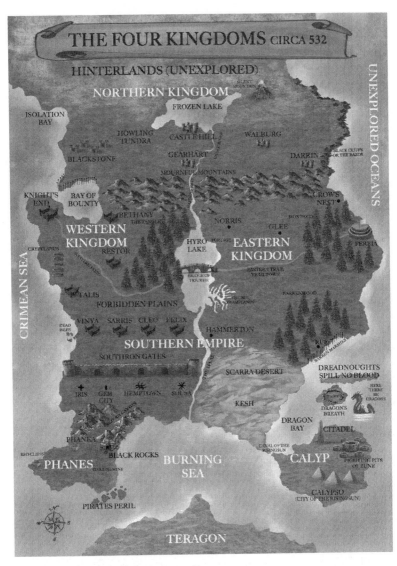

To view a downloadable map online:
http://davidestesbooks.blogspot.com/p/fatemarked-map-of-four-kingdoms.html

The story so far...

The Hundred Years War has stretched over a century, ravaging the nations of the Four Kingdoms. Before the war began, a prophecy was made by a woman now known as the Western Oracle. The prophecy, which promised the coming of the fatemarked, who would bring peace to the lands, has been forgotten by many, while others believe it to be naught but a legend. Still, the truth of the ancient words has begun to come to pass, as there are those being born with strange markings that grant the bearers unusual powers. In some lands, the marked are revered; in others, hated, even put to death.

One of the fatemarked, the Kings' Bane, has his own prophecy: to bring death to eight rulers across the Four Kingdoms, which will usher in a time of peace. His work has already begun—three rulers have been killed in swift succession: King Wolfric Gäric, known as the Dread King of the North, King Gill Loren of the West, and King Oren Ironclad, the Juggernaut of the East, have all fallen. But Bane's task is far from finished, and now he plans to turn his attention to the south...

Little is known of what has been transpiring in the southern empires of Calyp and Phanes, except that the two nations have been embroiled in a civil war caused by the marriage dissolution of the two main sovereigns, Empress Sun Sandes and Emperor Vin Hoza....

In the kingdoms, however, time has marched ever onwards…

To the west:

With the death of King Gill Loren at the hand of the Kings' Bane, his eldest nephew, Jove Loren, attempts to usurp the throne from the true heir, Princess Rhea Loren. To accomplish this, Rhea is charged by the furia with breaking her vow of purity with a common thief known as Grease Jolly, an alias for his true name—Grey Arris. As punishment, a "W" for *whore* is carved on her face, leaving permanent scars. In her mind, her greatest attribute, her beauty, has been stripped from her, leaving her with nothing left but revenge.

When her horror and sadness turn to white-hot anger, she murders her cousin Jove and reclaims her crown, vowing next to win the war and defeat her enemies on all sides…

Meanwhile, Grey Arris's sister, Shae Arris, who is fatemarked, is abducted by the furia and taken south to a chain of islands called the Dead Isles, which are rumored to be haunted. Grey, charged with thievery, has his hand cut off as punishment, but manages to escape Knight's End with some help from Rhea. Grey follows the furia, eventually hiring onto a ship, *The Jewel*, which is headed south. His goal: find his sister and rescue her…

To the north:

After Bane murders the Dread King, the crown shifts to Archer Gäric. However, before he can claim it, his uncle, Lord Griswold, swoops in, accusing he and his mother, Sabria Loren, of conspiring to kill the king. The eldest of the king's heirs, Annise, feels powerless as she watches the execution of her mother. When Archer is brought to be executed, however, the executioner suddenly makes himself known as a famous warrior known as the Armored Knight. They escape through the sewers along with another knight, Sir Dietrich.

While they travel to the southern part of the realm, Annise realizes she has turned eighteen and now has the primary claim on the throne. She refuses to tell her brother, though she confides in the Armored Knight, who turns out to be her long-lost friend from childhood, Tarin Sheary, believed to be dead, but now cursed by the witch's potion that saved his life. They also meet up with their eccentric aunt, Lady Zelda, who reveals that the Kings' Bane is actually their younger brother, who was smuggled from the north immediately after birth.

When the easterners attack Raider's Pass, Archer is knocked unconscious by the Kings' Bane, his own brother, who turns up to try to kill Annise, who is now the lawful queen of the north. However, Sir Dietrich manages to fight Bane off, showcasing his uncanny skills with the blade. Bane, exhausted from the ordeal, vanishes. Annise and the others seize victory from the east, killing King Ironclad and others.

Now, with Annise having declared herself the true queen and with Archer comatose, the Gärics and their allies are marching north toward Castle Hill to reclaim the throne from the usurper, Lord Griswold...

To the east:

When a young man named Roan, who grew up in Calypso, contracts the plague from a mysterious beggar on the street, he's sent to quarantine on an island called Dragon's Breath. There he reveals his own fatemark, called the lifemark, which allows him to heal himself and escape the island, which is guarded by two-headed dragons. Fateful currents pull him to the east, where a chance meeting makes him the prisoner of Prince Gareth Ironclad, who immediately brings him to Ironwood and the eastern capital of Ferria, the Iron City, where humans live in harmony with the Orians, a mystical people who can channel the ore that lies beneath the forest.

With the help of one of the Orians, a fatemarked named Gwendolyn Storm, King Ironclad swiftly learns of Roan's marking, and forces him into helping their armies as they march on Raider's Pass to enact revenge on the north for the killing of the queen. Roan reluctantly agrees, and soon learns that the east has another of the fatemarked, a mighty warrior named Beorn Stonesledge, the ironmarked. Roan also discovers that, as the first-born son, Gareth is "the Shield," which means his life is forfeit, to be given to protect the second-born son, Guy, the true heir to the eastern throne.

Along the way, Roan begins to grow close to both Gwen and Gareth…

At Raider's Pass, the north defeats them, killing King Ironclad, Prince Guy Ironclad, and injuring Beorn Stonesledge. Gareth Ironclad is nearly killed by the Kings' Bane as he tries to protect Guy, but Roan saves him by using his lifemark.

In the aftermath of defeat, Gwendolyn Storm realizes who Roan really is: Roan Loren, prince of the west and true heir to the Western Kingdom. She helps him escape and together they slip away, crossing the border between nations and into the Tangle, the largest western forest, known to be almost impassable…

And now, the story continues…

PART I

Bane ♥ The Beggar ♥ Jai
Rhea ♥ Annise ♥ Raven
Roan ♥ Grey

The warmongers shall resist the flow of destiny, until they are shattered upon sword and shield, sorcery and magic.
Truth, in the end, shall reign.
The Western Oracle

One

The Northern Kingdom, Silent Mountain
Bane Gäric

He was leaving the only home he'd ever known, the little cave high on the western flank of Silent Mountain.

Bear Blackboots was long gone, and soon Bane would be too. He didn't blame the man he'd always known as "Father" for leaving. There was so much blood on both their hands that sometimes Bane felt as if he was drowning in it, a lake of crimson forcing its way down his throat.

He saw the lake in his dreams, too, only it was burning, the waters literally on fire. How it was possible for liquid to burn, he didn't know. When he dreamed about the lake of fire, he could never divert his eyes from the flames, which licked at the bloody lake, an inferno of death and pain and—

Their cries.

He could hear them, too, his victims screaming. *Are they innocent?* he wondered to himself. *Does it matter?*

And in his dream, he would always be drawn to the lake, to the fire, to the cries. He would stumble down the rocky embankment, pulled forward by an irresistible force. He would pause on the precipice of the shimmering waters for a long, naked moment, the heat of the flames washing over him like a summer wind, and then he would fall.

He always awoke before he hit the water. Before the fire could touch him, burn him. Before those he'd murdered could judge him for his sins.

Why, he did not know, but he always felt invigorated afterwards. Ready for what was to come next.

All he knew was that three rulers were dead: His uncle, King Gill Loren of the western kingdom; King Oren Ironclad, the Juggernaut of the east; and King Wolfric Gäric of the northern kingdom.

His father.

What kind of a person kills their own father? he wondered.

He shook his head and cast away the pointless question. What he was didn't matter. All that mattered was the Western Oracle's prophecy, the one he was meant to fulfill. His only purpose.

Eight rulers shall die in the name of peace…

Eight bloody rulers, sent to the lake of fire. Three were dead. Five would follow.

Lost in his thoughts, his hand absently touched the flesh of his unnaturally bald scalp, a place where hair had never grown. He could feel the heat of his fatemark pulsating, hotter in the three sections that had already been filled in with blood.

He bit his lip and then dropped his hand. He shouldered his pack, which he'd stuffed with provisions—melted snow, smoked

12

meat, extra clothing, a knife—though he wasn't certain he needed such earthly things anymore.

Bane was going south, and Death would quench his thirst, and feed him, and clothe him. The knife, yes, he would need the knife.

Something drew him, a dark energy like his own, which was closing in on one of his prey...

No.

Not something. Someone.

I don't have to be alone anymore, he thought, and then vanished.

Two

The Southern Empire, Calyp
The Beggar

He was the Plague. The Plague was him. Even now, as he stood watching the empress's cavalcade, he could feel the disease flowing through his blood, humming along his skin, billowing from his mouth with each exhalation.

He had killed before. *Oh, Mother...* Many times. *Oh, Father...* Countless souls, devoured by what was in him, the evil that trembled along his pale flesh.

The procession thundered past, a long line of horses and the *guanik*, the reptilian creatures with clawed feet and mouths full of fangs, their pink tongues hissing between their black lips. Their riders, the royal guard, or *guanero*, wore dark leather armor bearing the dragon-rising sigil of the kingdom of Calyp. In the midst of their protectors rode Empress Sun Sandes and her trio of daughters, in order of birth: Raven, Fire, and Whisper. The guanik they rode were the largest of the group, towering above the others, giving the crowd a clear view of their leaders.

And their leaders a clear view of the crowd.

Empress Sun was like a ray of light, her hair long and blond, an impressive contrast to her night-dark skin. The juxtaposition was such that her figure appeared to be cut from alternating daggers of sunshine and shadow.

I am ready, the Beggar thought.

He melted into the crowd, almost vaporous in his movements, like a curling billow of smoke. The Southrons called him many things, out of fear—Death's Bastard, Demon Child, and other worse titles—but the name he liked the best was the Beggar.

That wasn't always your name.

He pushed away the thought, because it was an echo from the past, no longer relevant to today. No, that boy was long gone, fading like mist at first light.

I am the Beggar.

For that's what he was. He wasn't a beggar in the classic sense—he had no interest in food or water—but a beggar of forgiveness. Because of his *tattooya*, the mark on his neck—three partial circles, joined in the middle, broken at the edges—most could not really see him. Well, they could see him, but not the real *him*. To any he happened to meet, they would have little memory of him later, and could only describe him as a smudge of shadow wearing a gray hood.

There was one exception to this rule: those who also bore a tattooya. He knew this because once he'd been spotted by one of the empress's daughters, Fire Sandes, the girl who bore the firemark. Her eyes had zoned in on him like a hawk hunting a field mouse, but he'd managed to slip away into the crowd before she could determine whether he'd been real or just a trick of the hot southern sun.

There had been one other, a young man who'd been knocked over by a royal procession, not unlike the one he was watching now, who the Beggar had helped to his feet. A young man who he'd killed by accident, touching him with his plague-infected skin through a tear in his glove. A man who surely must've been marked, because he could see him clearly. *Roan*, the man had called himself.

That man was likely sent to Plague Island, like the rest of the Beggar's victims. Sent to die, quarantined from the rest of Calyp. There were whisperings that the island had been destroyed by dragons. But those were only rumors, of course.

The Beggar wondered what power Roan's tattooya had given him. He also wondered if the poor man had died slowly and painfully, or if he'd found a way to end things quicker.

He was snapped out of his morbid revelry when, suddenly, one of the riders cried out. Horses were commanded to halt, and the guanik, as if by some instinct, skidded to a stop.

I am ready.

The Beggar stepped forward, separating himself from the crowd, which was backing away from the fearsome lizards, which snapped their jaws and clawed in the dirt.

Amidst her protectors, a young woman slid lithely from her guanik's scaly shoulders. Her hair was so dark it was almost blue, plaited down her back where it dangled, snakelike, to her waist.

The Beggar knew her on sight. She was Raven Sandes, eldest daughter of the empress and First Daughter to the Calypsian empire. An eight-barbed whip dangled from one hand, and she wore a black, sleeveless leather tunic that would've made even the most liberal of westerners gasp on sight, as well as a short skirt that left little to the imagination. Her exposed skin was brown, not quite as dark as her mother's, smooth, and seemed to go on forever.

Was she the one who had called out? the Beggar wondered.

"Sister, why did you stop us?" Raven asked, looking over her shoulder.

"I could ask the same thing, Fire," the empress said, though she remained mounted.

Fire Sandes, the Second Daughter, leapt from her scaly steed, flanking her eldest sister. Fire, like both her sisters, was named in the usual Calypsian manner, her physical attributes linked to the natural world. In the princess's case, her tattooya was a firemark, it was said; thus, her namesake. Her skin was a shade darker than Raven's. Her short hair was like a candle flame atop her scalp, lighting a serious expression. She was scanning the crowd intently. Looking for something.

No, the Beggar realized. *Not some*thing. *Some*one. *Me. She's looking for me. That's why she stopped the procession. She caught a glimpse of me.*

And, unlike the last time she'd spotted him, he held his ground, even going so far as to take a step forward, then another.

What am I doing? he wondered to himself. It hit him like a sandstone block to the head.

I want to be caught. I want to be captured. I want to be killed.

I am ready.

He was all alone now, a gray island in an ocean of dust.

The Third Daughter swept beside her siblings. "Can we go? Please," Whisper Sandes said, her voice like wind moving over a desert dune. Four years Raven's junior, Whisper was small and thin, and wore a white flowing dress that nearly reached the

17

ground, rivaling the length of her chestnut hair, which was so long it could be braided and used as rope. Of the three sisters, her skin was the lightest.

"Wait," Fire said, drawing her sword. Flames leapt from her fingers onto the weapon. A sigh of awe rose up from the crowd. The Beggar watched with interest. He'd never seen someone with a tattooya use their power. Well, except for himself, and he had little control over the plague, which seemed as wild as a chest full of snakes. The way she flaunted her power captivated him.

"Wait for what?" Whisper asked. *She can't see me*, the Beggar thought. *Not really. None of them can, save for Fire.*

"Princesses," a man said, striding in front of the sisters. He was garbed from head to toe in leather armor marked with the royal sigil, a silver dragon over a rising red sun. The *shiva*, the master of order in Calypso. His dark eyes roamed the crowd, passing over the Beggar like he didn't even exist. "We cannot tarry here. It's not safe."

"I am only following the empress's orders," Fire said, scanning the crowd once more.

The Beggar didn't wait for her gaze to settle on him, he stepped forward again. Closer, closer. He wanted to say something—*tried* to say something—but his words were swallowed by a sudden wave of emotion that crashed through him.

Relief.

From there, everything happened quickly. Fire leapt forward, her sword blazing. She kicked him in the stomach, knocking him over. The Beggar closed his eyes, waiting for the flames to consume him.

He felt nothing. Something was cast over him, thick and warm. He opened his eyes to darkness. *A blanket*, he realized.

Voices were there, too, but they were like the sound of individual drops of rain in a thunderstorm—impossible to isolate.

Anyway, he didn't care what they had to say about him, not anymore. Soon, he'd be killed.

And then he'd be free.

Three

The Southern Empire, Phanes
Jai Jiroux

None knew of his mark, and it was better that way.

Though those bearing a tattooya were generally revered, almost worshipped, in the south-eastern land of Phanes, Jai Jiroux knew such adoration wouldn't apply to him. No, not when his mark went against everything the current emperor, Vin Hoza, the Slave Master, believed in.

Standing in front of Emperor Hoza now, Jai was acutely aware of the mark on his heel. Though it was hidden, he could see it in his mind's eye, the scales of justice gleaming like a lit candle.

"Master Jiroux," the emperor said, "what do you have to report?" The emperor stroked his dark mustache and goatee, which reminded Jai of an arrowhead. Hoza's face was powdered with the finest sifted chalk dust, a stark contrast to his black hair. His dark, tight braids were piled atop his head in a honeycomb formation. Tied within his hair and beard were diamonds, sparkling in the natural light streaming through an ornate, beveled windowpane. Gaudy jewelry—rings—adorned all ten fingers, studded with emeralds, rubies, and diamonds. The wealth on this man's fingers and hair alone could feed all the slaves in Phanea. As if that wasn't enough, the emperor had jewels sewn into his skin in the typical Phanecian manner—his chest, his arms…even his forehead glittered with two lines of jewels, replacing his eyebrows, which had been permanently removed.

Vin Hoza sat comfortably in a plush chair, leaning back slightly. Behind him were the Great Pillars of Phanea, three black marble columns so wide around it would take a dozen men to surround even one of them. On each was engraved a symbol, representing the Three Great Pillars of Phanes: the Fist; the Sword; the Whip. The Fist was for brothers, used both to settle disputes and to slap one another on the back when the brawl was over. The Sword was for enemies, to cut throats and stab hearts. The Whip was for slaves, its lash a constant reminder. The emperor governed his kingdom by these three tenets, and no others.

Emperor Hoza's eyes generally appeared to be pulled too tight, as if they were incapable of blinking, and yet they did. His mouth was almost always open a sliver, the tip of his pink tongue protruding. Most of his muscular chest was bare, save for a panel of leather secured by two straps. The panel was painted with the Phanecian sigil—the four-eyed lioness. A sleepy spotted *pyzon* lay curled around Hoza's chair, its long sinuous body so thick that no man would be able to wrap his hands around it. Yet, even a pyzon this large was relatively small for the species, which had been known to grow as large as the dragons that patrolled Calyp. Living underground in the desert, there were rumors that some red pyzons could grow as long as the tallest trees in the Tangle. In its sleep, the enormous snake's thin, forked tongue hissed from its mouth intermittently. Several guards stood beside the emperor at attention, but even they were too far away to be of much use.

I could draw the knife from my belt and plunge it through his heart before—

Jai blinked away the thought, for he knew the emperor could enslave him with naught but a touch. After all, Vin Hoza bore a tattooya, too. The slavemark. And unlike Jai, he didn't hide his mark—torches burned all around his chair, illuminating the symbol on his neck and upper chest:

Four lengths of iron chain, linked in the center.

Instead of killing the emperor, Jai said, "Garadia Mine is producing at full capacity." "Diamonds flow from the chutes like a river." *Of course they do*, Jai thought. *Anything less would mean the slaves get whipped, and I cannot allow that.*

"Good. Increase production by ten percent," the emperor said, waving his hand casually, as if to say *Now be gone.*

Jai didn't move, his jaw set. "That's impossible," he said through gritted teeth. He could feel a film of sweat begin to form beneath his own layer of face powder.

He knew it was a mistake to question a direct command from Hoza, but he couldn't help himself. Not when the slaves under his command were already so broken. Not when his justicemark flared at the thought of the injustice of their very existence.

Jai stood, waiting to be punished for his insolence. To his surprise, however, the Slave Master only laughed, his tongue

22

flicking out like the spotted pyzon's. "Master Jiroux, all my life's experience has taught me one thing: nothing is impossible. Once I would've thought it impossible that my wife, the light of my life, could ever leave me, and yet she did, all for a bunch of dogs."

The Calypsian Empress, Sun Sandes, Jai thought. When their marriage union was shattered, civil war exploded in the south. A war that had lasted for a dozen years already. Evidently, Empress Sun was against the use of slaves. *Dogs,* as Vin Hoza liked to refer to them as.

The emperor continued. "I have great power, and I won't waste it. Not when there is land to be conquered, people to be enslaved, wealth to be obtained. Did you know that there is an attempt on my life every day? Sometimes more than one. And it's not because the people hate me, no, nothing like that. It's because there's a superstition that my power will go to the man"—he paused, thoughtfully—"or woman, who kills me. You see? Everyone wants what I have. But I won't die easily. And as long as I am emperor, as long as I bare this mark"—he gestured to his chest—"I will demand the impossible. And I will get it. Especially now, when my enemies are destroying so much of what I've built. The Black Tears are worse than the Calypsian plague."

Jai had trouble controlling his expression. Over the last few years, the rebel group known as the Black Tears had been gaining in strength and boldness. Twice they'd released slaves from their mines. The first group were caught and killed, and now the mine continued to lie vacant, not producing; the second group, however, had disappeared somewhere along the southernmost tip of the Spear. Jai hoped they'd managed to cross the fast-moving river and escape into Calyp, but the emperor was certain they had drowned. *Lost resources,* he called them.

Not much was known of the secretive rebels, except that they were thought to be supporters of Sun Sandes before her feud with her husband. And that they etched permanent markings of black tears on their cheeks, each of which were supposedly meant to represent someone they had killed. A death tally, so to speak. Also, according to rumor, every member of the Black Tears was a woman.

"The Black Tears," Hoza said again, practically spitting the name out in disgust. "May they rot in the Void." The emperor paused again, licking his lips and studying his rings. His gaze traveled sharply back to Jai, and he changed the subject. "I have heard whispers of your methods as a mine master. They are decidedly...unorthodox."

"And yet I get results," Jai said. He'd had trouble with several of his underlings who didn't agree with his methods. Almost certainly it was one of them who had whispered in the emperor's ear.

"Some say the slaves are the masters of the mine, rather than you and your comrades."

Jai didn't like the way this conversation was going, but he remained silent, letting the emperor choose the course.

"What would you say to your critics?" Hoza finally asked, when it was clear Jai would not speak.

Jai clenched his fists at his sides. "That results are results, and the means aren't important. *My* mine is the highest-producing in the empire. Now I know that it's not my slaves who are spreading my secrets, so it must be one of my mine masters. That is unacceptable behavior that must be punished."

The emperor stared at him with eyes as dark as unlit coals. For a moment, Jai feared he'd been too brazen with his words. That his people would suffer as a result.

But then the emperor laughed again, and said, "Indeed. Insolence must be met with strength. Bring him in!"

On command, two bare-chested guards dragged in a man. At first Jai didn't recognize him, such was his transformation in appearance. Wearing nothing but a ripped beige sackcloth, the man was a mess of bruises and cuts. His previously long hair had been shorn to the scalp. His eyes wore a vacant, wild expression. His face was without powder for the first time in Jai's recollection, the skin beneath brown with a hint of orange.

But the man was Phanecian, not Teran, like most of the slaves.

Master Axa, Jai thought. He was one of his most outspoken and violent mine masters. On multiple occasions Jai had to punish this man for beating one of his workers within an inch of their lives. Jai wasn't surprised it was this snake of a man who'd betrayed him.

"What shall I do with him?" Hoza asked Jai now.

"Please," Axa said, dropping to his knees and knitting his hands together. His narrow eyes locked with Jai's, full of fear and something else. A request. For mercy. For forgiveness.

In his current state, Axa seemed penitent, and yet he had plenty of his own small jewels sewn into his skin—a reminder of what he once was, what he still represented.

Violence. Oppression. Arrogance. Wealth.

And yet something about his plea for mercy rang false—Jai's justicemark told him as much. But why would the man lie? Axa really was at Jai's mercy. He considered his options. The emperor respected swift and harsh punishment, but something told him killing the master would be a mistake. Also, it wasn't the way Jai did things. As usual, when faced with a decision such as this one, his justicemark flared on his heel and provided the answer, as clear as a spoken word in his mind. "Give him to me," he said. "His mind, his body, his soul."

"No," Axa breathed. Again, the word itself was false, but Jai didn't have time to consider what that might mean.

The emperor smiled—Jai had chosen wisely. "As you wish." The emperor touched Axa's scalp and the tattooya on Hoza's chest flared to life, shimmering with red and gold and orange light.

Axa screamed and began to shake as a similar marking appeared on his own chest, the chains wrapping around his neck, tightening, releasing, and then settling in. The whites of his eyes turned to darkness, like a sky upon the onset of night.

He stopped screaming. Stopped shaking. Stood stiffly. "What is your command, Master?" he said to the emperor.

Hoza's lips curled up on one side. "I give you to Master Jiroux, from this day forward until I command otherwise. You will obey his every command. Is this clear?"

"Yes, Master."

Though it was what Jai had requested, watching the creation of another slave by the Slave Master himself twisted his stomach into knots. He hated the dark, glazed look in Axa's eyes, the flat, obedient sound of his voice, the stiffness in his movements.

Once more, Hoza flicked his fingers, and this time Jai spun on his heels and departed. Axa trailed behind like a well-trained dog.

One of the emperor's sons was waiting outside. Falcon, the oldest—and meanest—of the Hoza brood. His scalp was shaved to the skin, save for a long stripe of hair down the center, pressed together to look like a blade. On either side of the Mohawk were emeralds sewn into his powdered skin to look like eyes.

Diamond earrings that likely came from Garadia Mine studded each earlobe.

Falcon was known to be a master of *phen ru*, the art of attack, the most popular martial art amongst the Phanecian elite, including most mine masters and soldiers. Like all the masters, Jai had also been trained in phen ru, but it wasn't the style of fighting he preferred. No, his father had taught him *phen lu*, the art of defense, as a child. Now he was a master of both, something no one knew about him.

"Master Jiroux," Falcon grunted.

"Falcon," Jai said. The two brushed past each other without a second glance. It was no secret that Falcon wanted command of Garadia for himself. It was the most valuable mine in the empire, after all. Jai shuddered to think what would happen to the slaves under the future emperor's control.

Then again, with Vin Hoza's decree to increase diamond output by ten percent, it didn't much matter who was the master of Garadia. Worked to the bone, most of the slaves would die anyway.

Unless I do something about it, Jai thought.

He shook his head, ignoring the dark stares of the other two white-faced Hoza brothers, Fang and Fox, as he passed. There was nothing he could do. There were five thousand slaves in Garadia—far too many to escape with. And even if he did, they'd be hunted down and killed for desertion, one by one, along with him.

He wouldn't let them suffer more. He couldn't.

Maybe there's another way, he thought. An idea appeared and then vanished, evading him. It had to do with a story his father once told him. A story about the Southron Gates.

He squinted as he left the palace and emerged into the oven that was the city of Phanea. He'd once heard someone say that the sun was different in the south. Fierier. That the brazen sun rose earlier in the south than anywhere else in the Four Kingdoms, assaulting the horizon like an invading army of fire-bearing warriors.

To Jai, however, the sun was just the sun, an oppressive, sweltering yellow orb.

And there was nowhere hotter than Phanea, which was formed of stone canyons cut in perfect corridors beneath the surface of the desert, creating underground blocks. Although the canyons were straight and narrow, connecting into large squares, it was said the city was built by the gods, not men or nature, cut into the earth long before the Phanecians arrived in these lands.

If so, thought Jai, *the gods are trying to cook us alive*. Although the tall cliffs provided plenty of shade, the stone canyons tended to trap the heat rather than deflect it, creating a superheated box where everything seemed to move slower.

He cupped a hand over his brow to block the sun, and made his way to his chariot, which awaited his return. Along the way, he passed dozens of statues lining the pathway, which was constructed of crushed crystal, scattered underfoot like gravel. The Phanecians loved their statues, which were carved in the images of their past emperors, including Vin Hoza's father, Jin. On the walls of the canyons were even larger statues, cut into the face of the stone wall itself, massive busts of the Hoza dynasty. Jai ignored their stares, which seemed to burn right through him.

When he reached the chariot, a slave driver stood ready, expecting orders.

Jai climbed aboard. "To Garadia," he said, and the driver cracked his whip. He glanced back at Axa, who was trying not to choke on the dust left in the chariot's wake. "You will walk back to Garadia Mine," he commanded.

The new slave began to walk.

Palace slaves toiling in the heat looked up as he passed, but, fearing the lash of their masters, just as quickly lowered their heads. Each were branded with the same chain marking Axa now wore. Most of them were full Terans, having been taken from the southern nation of Teragon, which was located across the Burning Sea. The Teran slaves' skin was red and their black eyes were round. Once they likely had bright blue eyes, but not anymore. Probably never again.

The women had long coppery hair, while the men's hair was shorn to the scalp. Traditionally, it was the opposite: Teran men wore their hair long, usually braided, while the women preferred shorter hair. However, as soon as the Terans were enslaved, the Phanecian slave masters forced them to adapt to their own customs.

Mixed amongst them was the occasional Dreadnoughter, the strange folk from the Calypsian islands, with their broad, flat foreheads and grizzled gray skin. There weren't as many of them, however, as ever since the Southron civil war had begun twelve years earlier, Vin Hoza no longer had naval access to the Dreadnoughts due to the blockade enacted by Empress Sun Sandes.

Jai tried not to think about the slaves, though his heel was on fire.

Ever since he'd been a young boy, Jai Jiroux had known the meaning of truth and justice. It was bred into him, into the mark on his heel, into his head, his heart. He could tell when someone was lying. He could sense when a great inequality was being dealt. In Phanea, in the presence of the slaves, he sensed it all the time.

Void, he'd felt it in his own household, which had had several slaves, including...

Her.

The thought made him grit his teeth and clutch the side of the chariot harder.

After his father was killed, Jai had come up with an insane plan. He'd trained to be a master of slaves, working his way from field lord, to house lord, to mine master. And then, because of his success, he'd been promoted to Master of Garadia.

Miraculously, his plan had worked. He was finally in a position to do something, to help someone, and yet he felt more helpless than ever.

They emerged into the inner city, where the wealthy took up residence in large caverns cut into the rock face. Some of the most lavish living quarters even had water that cascaded down the walls, cooling the caves. In the shade of the narrow canyon, men and women strutted like peacocks on the streets, regaling themselves with mindless chatter used as an excuse to display their finest silk clothes and blood jewelry, much of which was sewn into their faces and skin.

Both the males and females had powdered faces, a Phanecian tradition that had begun when the first Teran slaves were brought across the Burning Sea. It was an attempt by the people of Phanes to differentiate themselves even further from the slaves, though Jai found it rather ridiculous. Most Phanecians' skin was naturally brown, while the Terans' skin carried a reddish hue. Their eyes were different, too, the slaves' wide and round versus the thin, narrow eyes of their masters.

In the canyons of Phanea, the people ate delicacies sold by middle-class vendors with permanent stone platforms that lined the road. Grasshoppers and caterpillars were roasted in oil squeezed from grumnuts, a sweet nut that grew on lush, brown trees that thrived in the shade of the canyons. Smoke rose from a stone pit where a long green pyzon roasted on a spit, a bald Teran slave boy turning it slowly by hand to ensure the rubbery meat cooked evenly.

A group of women practiced the art of *phen sur*, the final of the three martial arts, which was named after the sun goddess herself. Phen sur was considered a feminine art, more like a dance than a way of fighting, and was used mostly in ceremonies and celebrations. The women moved together, aiming high kicks at the sky and lithely springing off their hands.

Jai looked away, because watching the dance of the sun god always reminded him of his mother.

And then the chariot moved beyond, into the outer city, slave quarters flashing by on either side. The slaves, who were primarily red-skinned Terans, lived in tiny cubicles cut into the stone walls, stacked on top of each other like hollow blocks, stretching nearly all the way to the surface. From afar, the slave residences resembled long, gray honeycombs, rolled out along the canyon walls. Those who lived above ground level had to climb narrow, crumbling, stone steps to reach their beds. Sometimes one of them would slip and fall to their death, though their Phanecian masters seemed to care little and less about these unfortunate tragedies. Slaves were easily replaceable, and it would be costly to repair the steps.

Jai trained his gaze firmly ahead, afraid of what he might do if he saw more suffering. More hardship.

No, he needed to be smart when he finally chose to act.

Or maybe he was just making excuses, he wasn't certain anymore.

The canyons of the gods ended and Jai pulled the hood of his cloak over his head to block the harsh sunlight. Yet, despite the heat, he felt cooler outside the city. He felt like he could breathe again.

Without the city, the landscape was a burnt wasteland of imposing plateaus, carved earth, and red buttresses rising against the cloudless sky. Axa would be lucky to survive the journey on foot. Or unlucky, depending on the perspective. Far into the distance was an enormous rock—Garadia Mine, named after the man who discovered the secrets inside it. The wealth beyond measure.

The chariot followed the well-worn path across the rocky landscape, spitting up clouds of dust from its brass wheels.

Lost in the monotony of the desert landscape, Jai's thoughts from earlier came back to him. The memory of a story told by his father, who had fought in several battles against the west along the Southron Gates. How the wall had once crumbled on the eastern side, after being hit by a barrage of projectiles and several battering rams. Evidently, in his haste, the emperor at the time, Jin Hoza, Vin's father, had patched together a repair team that left the inner core of the wall empty, a series of tunnels *through* the wall. By all appearances from the exterior, the wall looked as solid as a mountain, but, according to Jai's father, was a breach waiting to happen.

But how can I use this knowledge? Jai wondered. Even if he could sneak a small group of slaves from the mine, they would still have to traverse the desert from Phanea to the Bloody Canyons, face the rugged terrain and *vulzures* known to nest in the canyons themselves, and then slip past one of the border towns, Sousa preferably, because it was the easternmost city—closest to the rumored weakness in the wall.

Jai knew he'd be sentencing them all to death, both the people he took and the ones he left behind. *Is doing nothing worse? Is a life of hardship and forced labor worse than death?*

"Yes," he whispered.

"Master?" the slave driver said, thinking he'd been issued a command.

"Drive on for Garadia," Jai muttered.

Of course, the slave obeyed.

Four

The Western Kingdom, Knight's End
Rhea Loren

"The red-barbed funnel is the most poisonous spider in the world, did you know that?" Rhea asked.

The red-haired woman was huddled in the corner, her head down. Her hair was tangled and matted, covering her face. She didn't respond. But Rhea didn't care, it was meant to be more of a rhetorical question, a part of her ongoing monologue.

The spider crawled along her palm, repeatedly dashing its mouth against her skin, trying to sting her with the red barbs inside its mouth. The barbs containing the deadliest poison in the world.

Rhea laughed, letting the spider crawl across to her other palm. "So deadly, and yet it cannot use its poison against humans. See?" The spider tried again and again, never giving up its attack. Crawling and striking. Crawling and striking. "Its mouth is too small. Isn't that amusing?"

Again, there was no response from the woman who used to be one of the Three, the Furies that led the *furia*, the righteous warriors of Wrath and servants to the crown. The woman who now appeared as broken as a porcelain plate smashed on the ground.

"See how it strikes again and again, desperate to end me?" She placed her palm against the side of a table, and the spider crawled onto it. "And yet I am the one who holds its life in my hands."

Her fist slammed down with a thud that made the Fury flinch in the corner. When Rhea raised her hand, the spider was crushed, a mushed body and tangle of broken legs. She noticed the Fury's dark eyes staring out at her between a gap in her wall of crimson hair.

"Do you see where I'm going with this? You are powerful, oh yes, a strong warrior, fit to serve a queen. Probably strong enough to *kill* a queen. But you won't, will you? Because if you try, I will crush you." Rhea slammed her fist down again and again, and with each hammer blow the table shook and the Fury flinched.

She stopped abruptly, letting silence fall like a scythe. She stood. Approached the woman, who she had taken to death's doorstep and back again. Reached down, enjoying the way the Fury trembled in anticipation of the blow she thought would come.

But Rhea didn't strike her. Not this time. Instead, she peeled back the hair on one side, tucking it behind the woman's ear. Then she did the same on the other side, until she could see her entire face.

A ragged W was carved in her skin, from temple to chin to temple, and for a moment Rhea admired her handiwork. It was a near perfect match for her own facial scars. At the time her own face was cut, she'd thought it was the end of her life, when, in reality, it had been the beginning. It had opened her eyes to a world beyond beauty, beyond wealth, a world that existed only on *power*, and those who had it.

It had only been a few fortnights ago, but it seemed an eternity since the W on her own face stood for Whore, though that wasn't public knowledge. No, the people of Knight's End, her loyal and adoring subjects, thought the mark stood for Wrath, a symbol of her righteousness and devotion to their deity.

The Fury closed her eyes as Rhea ran the fingernail of her thumb along the scab, which was finally beginning to heal. She traced the W from end to end and then back again, relishing the *feel* of it.

When she was finished, she said, "Whom do you serve?"

The woman's lips moved, but Rhea couldn't make out her words.

"Repeat. Louder."

"I serve the queen," the woman said through cracked lips.

"Be. More. Specific."

"I serve the queen, Rhea Loren, first of her name, Wrath's humble servant."

"Yes. You do. And you will do great things. You have been forgiven of your sins. Now kiss the ring." She held out her left hand and the ring that adorned it, its thick gold band studded with an enormous blue diamond, the only one of its kind, at least as far as Rhea knew. It was the ring of kings, a family heirloom passed down for generations.

36

She'd plucked it from her dead cousin's fingers herself after she'd killed him.

The woman's eyes flashed open, the surprise obvious in her expression. Rhea knew she expected more pain, more torture—not mercy. Which is exactly why she chose now to offer the woman a second chance—because she knew she would take it.

The Fury kissed her ring, the one Rhea had once kissed while her cousin, Jove, the king at the time, had worn it. She'd killed him a moment later.

Rhea knew it was only the beginning.

Not only had the bootmaker given her shelter when she was at her weakest, but he had given her a beautiful pair of boots, the finest Rhea had ever seen.

Now Jordan Vaughn stood before her throne, looking uncomfortable as he shifted his weight from foot to foot. His storm gray eyes darted from the Fury to Rhea and back to the Fury.

"Do you know why you are here?" Rhea asked.

"I, uh, well, no. Not ezzactly. I was hopin' yer boots dinnit need repairs so soon?"

Rhea was surprised when a very real smile creased her face. This gray-eyed old man had showed her kindness when she wasn't certain she deserved it, and she owed him. "No, good sir, the boots remain as perfect as the day you gave them to me." She lifted her purity dress slightly to show him that she was wearing them, and he blushed.

"Good. I—that's good."

"I sent for you for a far more auspicious purpose. I could use your services."

His eyes widened. "'Nuther pair of boots?"

"How about five thousand?"

His jaw dropped and he began licking his lips back and forth. Then his face fell. "I'd have to decline," he said.

"Why?"

"I handcraft all o' me boots. An order of that size would take years. Mebbe me whole life."

"I thought you might say that. What if you created the pattern, and I provided a team of expert leather cutters and seamstresses to manufacture the boots. Would that be fair? I would pay you three Goldens per pair."

"Three Goldens per..." The thought trailed away from the aging bootmaker, and he shook his head. "Aye. I accept, that's more gold than I've ever dreamed of. But why are you doin' this?"

Rhea stood up, floating down the steps toward him. She touched his cheek briefly with her palm and she felt him trembling. Fear, excitement, anxiety...it was all running through him, just beneath his skin. "Because you showed me great kindness once. And I need boots for my army. Your boots will help protect the Wrath-loving people of our great kingdom."

"Thank you, Queen Rhea," he said. "From the bottom of me heart, thank you."

She watched him go, surprised at how warm she felt all of a sudden.

Five

The Northern Kingdom, Gearhärt
Annise Gäric

Annise Gäric never expected to be a queen. *Frozen hell, I never wanted to be a queen*, she thought, sitting by Arch's bedside. No, she'd planned to live out her time as a princess, until her father, Wolfric Gäric, the Dread King of the North, died of old age, and her brother, Archer, as the eldest male heir, took the throne.

However, she was quickly learning that the more you expected something, the less likely it was to happen. Her father had been murdered by the brother she'd thought died long ago, the brother who was now known as Kings' Bane. And then she'd had a name day, leaving her as the queen until Arch turned eighteen, which was still almost two long years away.

Originally, she'd planned to relinquish all rights to the crown to her brother, regardless of his age. But then something had happened. She'd changed. And Arch had been injured in battle.

She'd held vigil by his bedside for days, taking her meals there, sleeping on a lumpy cot brought in by the owner of the tavern they were staying in, *The Laughing Mamoothen*, a formidable broad-faced woman named Netta who also happened to make the best mamoothen stew in all of the Four Kingdom's, at least by Annise's reckoning.

Now, as she stared at her brother's handsome, peaceful face, she wondered whether, when he awoke, he would hate her for stealing his throne. She also wondered if today would be the day he finally opened his eyes. The healer said some people came out of such a condition in mere days. Others took longer, sometimes months, requiring liquid meals and water to be dribbled down their throats to sustain them. Annise didn't want to think about the third group of people, the ones who never woke up.

There was a knock on the door, but Annise didn't look up. It was probably Lady Zelda, her eccentric aunt, once more requesting a queenly decision on strategy. The truth was, Annise wasn't ready to make a decision—not with Archer like this. And yet, she couldn't delay much longer, for the more her uncle, Lord Griswold, sat upon the ice throne and played king, the more the northerners would assume the crown was his.

Annise sighed when there was a second knock. "If you don't have a hot bowl of mamoothen stew, go away!" she shouted.

The door opened slowly, but not all the way. Just a crack. A white piece of cloth fluttered through the opening. "Don't throw anything," a voice called through.

Sir Dietrich. Though he was the best swordsman Annise had ever known and he had saved both hers and Arch's lives during the battle at Raider's Pass, twice they'd argued in the last two days. And yes, she might've thrown a boot at him, which explained his odd request.

"Are you ready to talk about the burn scar on your back?" Annise asked.

"We've already talked about that." More white flag waving. Well, white *shirt* waving.

"Shut the door," Annise said. Dietrich had given her a story about his scar, but Annise was certain it was a lie, or at least only a fraction of the truth.

"Frozen hell, woman," the knight said, pushing the door open the rest of the way and dropping the white shirt. He crossed his arms over his face, presumably to protect himself from projectiles. He wasn't wearing his armor, merely a white cloth shirt tied up the front and sturdy-looking trousers secured with a leather belt. A long sword dangled from a scabbard.

"One—don't call me 'woman.' I am your queen. Two—I'm not going to throw anything at you, so you can stop acting like an unflowered maiden. And three—you don't have any mamoothen stew for me. That perturbs me greatly."

Sir Dietrich's strong arms dropped away from his head, revealing his scarred, but handsome face, and two bright periwinkle eyes that always seemed to contain a hint of mischievousness.

Annise launched the boot she was hiding behind her leg. Dietrich's arms came up, but they were too slow, and also too high, protecting his face. Unfortunately for him, she had aimed for his crotch, and she had excellent aim on account of all the games of Ice Wars she'd played as a child.

He doubled over, groaning and clutching his midsection.

"*Now* are you ready to talk?"

His only response was a groan. He staggered out, his face green. It looked like his breakfast might make a reappearance.

Annise sighed again. What use was being a queen if you couldn't get information out of your subjects? She wondered if her boot-throwing antics could be considered torture, and whether she might eventually earn the title Dread Queen of the North, following in her father's footsteps. She laughed at the notion.

Arch stirred in his sleep, his head rolling from side to side.

Annise froze, watching. Hoping. *Please.*

He continued sleeping, his chest rising and falling with mighty exhalations. *At least he looks peaceful,* Annise thought.

A shadow fell over her as a massive shape filled the doorway. She couldn't hold back a smile as she looked up. Couldn't prevent the loss of breath or the giddy sensation in her chest. But she could hide them. She was a queen, after all, and every queen had to be a master of their emotions. Or at least so Zelda told her, though her aunt was as spontaneous and unpredictable as a winter storm.

"To frozen hell with that," Annise muttered, leaping to her feet and throwing herself at Tarin, who looked confused by both her words and her sudden movement.

Still, he caught her in his strong arms, holding her close. And then he did what would've seemed impossible a mere fortnight ago: He allowed her to lift his black mask, revealing those beautiful dark eyes she'd stared at for days on end while wondering what the rest of him looked like. She pulled down the mesh shield that blocked the lower half of his face. The face which, despite its ghostly pallor and black, bulging veins, no longer seemed so foreign to her. No, she had memorized the lines of his strong jaw, the shape of his masculine nose, the feel of his thick brows.

The taste of his lips, which she tasted again now, pressing her mouth against them so hard she could barely breathe. In this moment, he was her breath. He was the beat of her heart and the blood in her veins. He was her knight in black armor, the only one who seemed to truly understand her.

And when their lips separated it was too soon, was always too soon, and Annise felt as if a part of her had been removed, like a severed limb.

How is this possible? she'd wondered to herself on numerous occasions. *How is* he *possible?* He was her best friend from childhood, a boy who she'd been told was dead from a horrible bone disease, now reborn as a man. Though Tarin Sheary considered the witch's dark magic that had saved his life a curse—the source of his unusual appearance, superhuman size and strength—Annise would only ever think of it as a blessing, a second chance.

"You know, Sir Dietrich might never be able to have children because of your boot," he said. She could feel the rumble of his voice as it rose from his chest, which was pressed tightly against hers.

"Pity," she said, cupping his cheek in her palm.

"He saved your life. Perhaps he deserves a little patience."

"I appreciate what he did, and have thanked him for his courage numerous times. But until he tells the truth, I will not see him."

A look of amusement crossed Tarin's broad face. "I think I've come up with your royal nickname," he said.

Annise didn't think she was going to like it, but she said, "Go on."

"The Stubborn Queen."

She tried to hit him, but he grabbed her hand and held it back and then kissed her again, softer this time, exploring her lips, her tongue. She explored back.

This time, when they broke apart, his eyes bore into hers, and she detected a question in that look. "What?" she asked.

"How?" he said.

"How what?"

"Just...how?" he repeated.

She thought she understood what he meant. "I've asked myself the same question a million times. Remember, I'm not the one who returned from the dead."

"To me you did." His voice had grown gravellier, more serious, sending electricity to every part of her.

"Why, Tarin," she said, "I would've never taken you for a romantic."

His eyes never leaving hers, he carried her backwards, setting her on the edge of her cot, his giant hands roaming down her sides and around her hips. He kissed her once more, quick, stabbing kisses broken up by words. "The reason"—kiss—"Sir Dietrich"—kiss—"came to see"—kiss—"you..."

"Stop talking," she said, clutching the back of his helmet, ripping it off, pulling him closer. "Keep kissing."

He did, and for the next few minutes they fought the urge to do more, an urge they'd been fighting for the last fortnight due to the lack of privacy that came with staying in a busy tavern. Oh, and the fact that her brother was sleeping in the bed next to them and could awaken at any moment.

"There's someone to see you," Tarin finally managed to get out. He was breathing heavily, and so was Annise.

"Lady Zelda?" Annise said, gulping down air.

44

"No. A stranger. An unusual fellow. Calls himself Sir Christoff Metz."

Annise frowned. "And why should I talk to this Sir Metz fellow?"

"He claims he has information on your uncle's army," Tarin said.

Six

The Southern Empire, Phanes
Jai Jiroux

When they finally reached the mine, the sun had long since fallen below the horizon. The temperature had dropped by half, the cold infused in each gust of wind, which sent shivers up Jai's spine.

He stepped from the chariot and said, "You can stay here for the night. You will be given bed and nourishment."

"Yes, Master," the slave said. This man wasn't a Garadia slave, or Jai might've acted very differently. He belonged to the emperor's palace, and thus, Jai couldn't risk treating him the way he longed to: like a person.

He left the man to tend to the horses, striding toward the entrance to the mine, which was as dark and foreboding as a red pyzon's maw. Above the opening stood a towering rock, but the outcropping itself held little value. No, it was what was *beneath* the ground that mattered.

The diamonds.

Though many of the emperor's mines contained an abundance of beautiful jewels, it was the diamonds that Hoza craved the most. They were like an addiction to him, and he was rumored to have entire pools filled with them, in which he would bathe, running the gems over every inch of his body, letting their sharp edges cut his skin.

Which was exactly why every master wanted to be Jai Jiroux, Master of Garadia. Controlling Garadia meant you always had the emperor's ear, so long as you were producing up to his standards. Which Jai was, giving him plenty of leeway as to the treatment of his "slaves."

He entered the mine, pausing just inside the threshold to allow his eyes to adjust to the flickering orangey darkness. Torches were lit along the tunnel, which almost immediately branched off in three different directions. One went toward the masters' quarters, one toward the shafts leading below, to the mines, and one toward the slaves' quarters.

After a long, hard ride, any other master would've gone straight to the lavish quarters they'd been provided with. Jai had a plush, feathered mattress he'd never slept on, a large golden tub he'd never filled with warm water, a broad hearth he'd never lit, and a full larder of foodstuffs he'd never eaten. He allowed his mine masters to use all of his amenities in exchange for their cooperation and silence.

Instead, Jai headed to the left toward the slaves' quarters, where he slept, bathed, and broke bread with his workers. His people. He paused only momentarily to use a small wash basin to clean the white powder from his face. While in the city he was forced to wear it, but never in Garadia, not amongst his people.

Many of the workers were already asleep when he entered the broad cavern where they lived when they weren't toiling in the mines. That was typical. The back-breaking work they did wore on a person, no matter how young or old, how thin or broad, how strong or weak. Slowly, over days or weeks or months, or sometimes years, they were broken, until they had nothing left to give.

Garadia had the lowest death rate of any of the mines, and yet Jai lost at least one soul each and every day, either from accident or fatigue. Some were replaced by new slaves; some were not.

Like the slaves in the capital city of Phanea, Garadia was primarily made up of Terans, though he also had about two dozen Dreadnoughters. The gray-skinned people tended to be taller and broader than the other workers, their hands and feet half again as large. The islanders spoke infrequently, and when they did their voices seemed to rumble up from their bellies. He spotted one of them sleeping off to the side, both his eyes open. Though Jai knew the sleeping giant couldn't see him, it still creeped him out the way the Dreadnoughters slept with their eyes open.

Jai blinked and moved on. The cavern smelled of stale bread and sweat and damp earth. Thousands of workers occupied the cavern at this time of day, most of them sleeping side by side or milling about the washing area—a natural underground stream—or breaking bread in small circles.

Several of the workers who were still awake noticed his entrance and offered him a welcome—three fingers in the air: one for the master, one for the slave, and one for what they'd become, something *other*. It was a sign Jai had come up with, a sign that identified them as one of his. He hated to think of them like that—as *his*—but at the same time, he felt like their lives were his responsibility. When one of them died, he mourned. When one of them cried, he cried with them. When they enjoyed fleeting moments of happiness, he smiled too.

Though their eyes were black and they wore the slavemark like all others ensnared by the emperor's tattooya, Jai had relieved them of their burden of obedience when he'd first been assigned head of the mine. All it had taken was a simple command to be free.

For now, they toiled by choice alone, working for the promise of a better future Jai had offered them. If they wanted to leave, to escape, they could. Jai wouldn't stop them. The other masters would, however, and the runaway slave would likely be killed.

Some chose to leave and paid the price.

Most chose to stay. For now at least.

Although Jai had been tempted on many occasions to teach his people phen lu, he had yet to do so. Training in the defense arts would take many years, and he hoped to escape with them long before that. *It is my destiny*, he thought now. *It has to be.* So instead, he conditioned them for whatever was to come next. Before mining in the morning, the people would run laps around the cavern. After mining they would do more laps. None were exempted, save for those who were with child, too young, or too old to walk.

My people are strong, he thought. *One day that strength will save them.*

His thoughts were chased away when a small boy, as thin as a reed, ran up to him. Though he was full Teran, his skin red and his hair coppery, he'd never seen Teragon, the continent south of the Four Kingdoms across the Burning Sea. No, he was a

49

second-generation slave, his parents captured and forced into bondage years earlier. The boy moved with a limp, the result of being hit by a falling rock weeks ago. The injury lingered, refusing to heal. "Jai!" the boy said. "You're here."

Jai hugged him and tousled his straw-like hair, painted orange in the torchlight. His hair was long, well past his shoulders. As soon as Jai had given the people their freedom of choice, they reverted back to their country's customs of long hair for males and short for females. The boy was wearing the typical garb of slaves: a thin shirt and pants cut from sackcloth. Unfortunately, it was all they had.

"I'm back," Jai said. "How is Emperor Jig, the mightiest miner in all of Phanes?"

Jig giggled, and Jai could almost imagine this was a normal boy, if not for his shadowy eyes and the chain marking circling the red skin of his neck. "Mother says I can't work the mines until my leg heals."

"Your mother is a wise woman."

"I guess," Jig said, sounding unconvinced. "What news from Phanea?"

Jai grinned. He knew the boy was trying to sound like a man, mimicking a standard question he'd heard one of the adults ask. "I saw a pyzon," Jai said.

"You did?" Jig bounced on his toes. He was always eager to hear stories of the outside world; the boy was born in Garadia and had never seen true sunlight, other than a few errant beams that wafted through cracks in the rocks above. "What did it do?"

"Slept, mostly. And stuck out its tongue."

"Oh." Jig sounded disappointed.

"Would you rather it had bitten me?" Jai raised his eyebrows.

50

"No!" the boy said. "But maybe if you fought it and chopped of its head, that would make a good story!"

"Next time," Jai promised with a wink. "Have you had supper?"

Jig went quiet, staring at his feet, which were bare and dirty.

"Jig," Jai said sternly.

"The bread tastes funny," the boy said.

He was never going to heal if he didn't eat, Jai knew. "We'll eat together," he said.

The boy kicked a stone. "Do I have to?"

"Yes."

"Is it a command?"

Jai hated that this innocent boy's entire life boiled down to that one question. It seemed all of Phanes was built upon a foundation formed of that one word: COMMAND.

Just like his own life, his own birthright. His father's words echoed through his memory. *I never commanded her. Not like that.*

Jai shook his head, letting the words vanish. "No," he said. "I will not tell you what to do. But you should listen to your mother. She knows best."

Jig grabbed Jai's hand and pulled him off to the side, to an area somewhat enclosed by a series of large boulders. There, what was left of Jig's family sat cross-legged, huddled around a flat rock set with food. His mother, Marella. His elder sister, Viola. There were two empty spots. One for Jig, and one for his father, who had died in a cave-in a year earlier.

"Jai Jiroux," Marella said. Though Jai refused to let any of them call him "Master," Jig's mother found it difficult to refer to him by first name only. "Please. Sit. Join us."

"Thank you," Jai said.

"You can have Father's seat," Jig said.

51

"No!" Marella snapped. Her tone softened. "I mean, please, we will squeeze in another place for you."

"Yes. Beside me," Viola said, offering a wide smile. Though she was only eleven, the girl was always trying to hold Jai's hand, or hug him. There was no doubt in his mind that she was smitten. The thought made him feel awful inside.

"Of course," Jai said. He wouldn't have felt comfortable sitting in the place of her husband anyway. He slid to the ground between Jig and Viola. The latter immediately latched onto him, holding his arm.

"Jig won't eat his bread," Marella said.

"So I heard," Jai said, breaking off a piece. It was too hard, and beginning to smell of mold. Hence, the funny taste the boy had complained about. Still, it was all they had, the leftovers from the city. He took a large bite, chewing with his mouth open, smacking his lips. "Mmm. It tastes of almond butter and sifted flour." In truth, it tasted sour and earthy.

"Almonds?" the boy said, raising his eyebrows. "I've never tasted those." He took his own piece of bread and bit in.

As Jig munched on the bread, wrinkling his nose and commenting on all the strange tastes he was experiencing, his mother offered a nod of thanks in Jai's direction.

Jai returned her nod, his thoughts drifting to the situation at hand. In the morn, he would be forced to announce the emperor's decree about increasing diamond output. The morale of his people already sat on a knife's edge, and he was afraid this news would push them into despair.

More and more, Jai felt like his life was a fast-moving river, carrying him along at its will and whim, occasionally dashing him against rocks and fallen timber. Every move forward seemed to bring him closer to a precipice, where an eternal waterfall would drop him down, down, down—

No. No. He wouldn't think that way. There had to be a solution, a way to save all of them. Or at least give them a chance.

Yes. It was known that the range of the emperor's control over his slaves only extended to a limited distance. That was one of the many reasons why his slave army hadn't yet invaded Calypso and won the civil war. Doing so would mean the emperor would have to travel with the army, and he wasn't willing to expose himself to the risk. Not yet anyway, though it was only a matter of time.

If I can only get them out of range…, Jai thought. *Maybe we'll have a chance.*

But how far would they have to go? And how would he ensure that the emperor didn't catch wind of their plot until they were far enough away?

These were the questions Jai was trying to answer as he finished his humble meal and lay down to sleep in the midst of his people, Jig's arm across his chest on one side, and Viola's on the other.

He still hadn't come up with a solution, when he heard the first cries rise up, echoing down the tunnels from the mine's entrance.

They were cries of battle.

Seven
The Southern Empire, Calyp
The Beggar

After countless hours spent in darkness, the light was as bright as staring directly into the sun.

The Beggar raised a hand to shield his eyes, but the light had already been lowered, casting a yawning yellow sheen across the sandstone floor. He couldn't see who was there, his vision dancing with spots. A shadow person.

I'm still alive, the Beggar tried to say. *Why?* But nothing came out but a groan, his mouth as dry as dust, his lips as cracked as a sunburnt desert floor.

"You are the bearer of the plague?" a voice said. "The one they call Demon Child?"

No, please. I am the Beggar. Not a demon. Not a not a not a not a...

"Water," was all he managed to croak out.

"An answer first. Then water." The bearer of the lantern angled the light backwards, and he saw who it was.

The empress. Sun Sandes. This close up she was even more spectacular than from afar, her eyes like grey silk, her blond locks waves of crashing sunlight. She wore a light green dress, crisscrossing strands of material that exposed slits of diagonal skin, night-dark in the manner typical of Calypsians.

An answer, the Beggar repeated in his head. *What was the question again?* His mind was fuzzy, shriveled, like a piece of fruit left too long in the sun. *Yes, that is it. The plague.*

"Yes. I am the plague. The plague is me." His voice was scratchy, but at least it was working again. He moved to throw back his hood and reveal himself, but his hand caught only empty air. His fingers searched his body for his cloak, but found only skin as pale as moonlight, dancing with orange light from the lantern. At some point they'd stripped him, left him lying naked in the dark. "My skin," he said, clambering back, away from the empress. "Stay away from my skin." He didn't want to hurt anyone else. Especially not a woman as beautiful and strong as the empress.

Despite his warnings, the empress approached. She handed him a cup of water. "Please. Place it on the ground," he said.

"As you wish." She did, and as soon as she'd drawn back, his hand darted out like a striking cobra and yanked it back, spilling half of it in his haste to drink.

"Ahh," he moaned, the flames in his throat dowsed. He licked his lips. "Thank you. Now, you have to kill me."

"The tattooya on your neck, the three broken circles…it gives you your power?"

Why is she asking me such things? he wondered. *Why is she delaying my fate?*

"I have no power. Only a curse."

"And it turns your eyes as red as hot metal. Curious. Does your skin burn in the sun?"

"Yes," he blurted out, without thinking.

"Can you control whom you infect with the plague?"

What? "Please, just—"

"I'm not going to kill you."

"Why not?"

"You're like my daughter, Fire. Special. Our people believe that all those…like you…have a purpose. I would not waste someone like you, not when you could be the key to the civil war *plaguing* the south." She laughed lightly at her own wit.

"I am No One. I am the Beggar. I have killed hundreds. No, thousands. I deserve to die." *I want to die.*

"I am the Empress of Calyp, and I decide your fate. Now that we have you, we can control you. Plague Island is destroyed and we were forced to exterminate the two-headed dragons that once guarded it. The beasts were old and half-mad anyway, so I won't fault you for that. But now we fear to dump the infected in the ocean as it might contaminate the great waters. But as long as we have you, the plague can be sent far away from Calyp, to Phanes. To my divorced husband, the Slave Master, may he rot in the underworld."

The Beggar couldn't stop the dam from bursting any longer. He covered his head with his hands and wept.

The empress said nothing while he cried, and eventually he stopped. He looked up through blurred vision. "I don't want to hurt anyone. Please don't make me."

"Dear boy," she said. "You can do great things. Things that matter. All you have to do is reach out and touch those I command you to. Pledge yourself to me, and I will help you. I

56

will give you sturdy clothes, thick gloves, a facemask, everything you need to ensure you only come into contact with those you're meant to. How does that sound?"

He wasn't certain exactly, but it didn't sound as awful as he thought it would. Maybe he could still live, in the service of this powerful woman, the Dragon of the South, as she was known. He opened his mouth to answer, but then closed it when the air shimmered on the edge of his vision, almost like a mirage taking shape in the desert.

When he turned his head, he was shocked to find a boy, his scalp as bald as the day he was born, a round mark shining brightly. His eyes burned like fires, a stark contradiction to his snow-white skin and the dark clothing he wore—a cloak, gloves, and boots.

"What in the name of the gods are you?" Sun Sandes said. The light wobbled as she backed away a step. For the first time since she'd arrived, the Beggar thought he could detect fear in her voice.

"I am Bane, and you are marked for death," he said. Then, with a speed and strength that defied explanation, the boy grabbed the Beggar under the arms and launched him at the empress.

He flailed in midair, trying to change his trajectory, but his momentum was too great. His naked body crashed into her, and he immediately felt the buzz of skin on skin, in multiple places.

She screamed, scrubbing at her arms and legs with her hands as she rolled away.

But it was too late. Once touched, it was always too late.

Horrified, the Beggar watched as red pustules rose to the surface of her skin, spreading like a wildfire raging out of control. "No," she whispered under her breath. "Oh, gods, no."

She stood, stepping on the edge of her dress in her haste, the fabric ripping under her trod. Then she turned and ran.

He watched her go, releasing a whimper of regret, tears already bubbling from the corners of his eyes.

She stopped. She turned. Reaching within the folds of her dress, the Empress of Calyp extracted a knife. The expression she wore was calm—almost too calm. "I must protect my daughters," she said. And then she raised the knife, the point aiming back toward her chest.

The Beggar looked away, not wanting to watch.

But he could not stopper his ears from the squelch of broken flesh, and the muffled thump of her body hitting the floor.

"She was going to *use* you to make war," the boy said, taking a step closer. The one who called himself Bane. He'd heard the rumors—everyone had—of the marked boy wreaking havoc on the rulers of the north and west and east. The Kings' Bane. And now he was here, in the south. And he'd killed again.

No. It wasn't him. It was me. I killed her. Me me me me me

"Oi." The boy grabbed him by the chin with his gloved hand and steered his gaze around, until their eyes met. The flames had gone out, though the mark on his head was shining even brighter. Half of it seemed to be filled with blood. "We are alike, you and I. We are the same. Together, we can bring peace to the Four Kingdoms. That woman who called herself empress, she wanted *more* war, not less. I just want the fighting to stop. I want an end to all the death."

The Beggar didn't know what to think, what to say. As much as he didn't want to believe this boy, this killer, he knew he was right. They *were* the same.

"You don't have to decide now," the boy said, slipping off his cloak and wrapping it around the Beggar's shoulders. "Think about it. For now, come with me."

The world spun, twisting with spirals of grey and black and red, and then he lost consciousness.

Eight
The Southern Empire, Calyp
Raven Sandes

Raven Sandes couldn't believe her *maata* was dead.

The empress is dead, she thought, still trying to make sense of the senseless.

Thankfully, it wasn't Whisper who'd found her body two days earlier. It was Fire, accompanied by the current shiva, or keeper of order. In Fire's usual brash way, she'd acted without fear, without hesitation, flinging a flaming blade at her own mother's plague-riddled corpse, burning it to ash and ensuring the disease could not spread. Ordinary fire wasn't enough to eradicate the plague, but Fire's flames were far from ordinary.

It had been eerily similar to how their grandmother, Empress Riza Sandes, named after the City of the Rising Sun, had died.

The man known as the Beggar had vanished after the murder, seemingly into thin air, for none of the guards had seen him escape.

Raven was dimly aware that the Second Daughter, Fire, was speaking, but she couldn't seem to make out the words. *Oh, gods, what are we going to do?*

Her maata's voice answered as clearly as if she was sitting directly beside her, having a conversation. *You will do what the Sandes have always done: fight.*

Her sister's words clarified, took shape, and she caught the end of them. "...am asking, is will you, the First Daughter of Calyp, make a claim for the empire, dear sister?"

Fire was staring at her, her head cocked to the side. She was doing that thing again. The thing Raven hated, where she made tendrils of flames crackle around her face. Her sister might be an arrogant urchin, but she was also intelligent beyond her years. Since they were little girls, the Second Daughter had coveted their mother's position as empress. Now, she was using her tattooya as a show of power, which was the only thing the Calypsians seemed to respect these days.

Well, Raven might not bear a mark of power, but she could be powerful, too, in her own way, and she would not allow her sister to swoop in and steal the seat of the empire out from under her. She glanced at her youngest sister, Whisper, who was staring at her feet, her eyes red from crying.

Raven stood, her dark eyes swooping across the hundreds of guanero in attendance, before boring into her sister's. "I am," she said. "And all those who oppose me will find themselves lacking."

Fire smirked—she'd always loved a good challenge. "I, too, as the Second Daughter, will make a claim." She turned

61

purposefully toward Whisper, her mouth opening to speak again. She paused, and Raven saw the brief hesitation—for all her sister's faults, Raven knew Fire loved their sister deeply, protectively. Seeing Whisper in pain was clearly affecting Fire. However, she recovered quickly. "Whisper, as the Third Daughter of Calyp, will you be making a claim for the empire?"

Whisper looked up, blinking rapidly. She'd only recently passed her fourteenth name day. Had the empress died a fortnight earlier, she wouldn't have had a claim at all. "What? I— I, no. I will make no claim." Raven was proud of her youngest sister for faltering only briefly.

"Then it is settled. The rule of the empire shall be mine or Raven's. Shiva—"

"Shiva," Raven said loudly, cutting her sister off. "Prepare the arena."

Fire glowered at her, clearly annoyed that she'd stolen her thunder. Raven ignored her, turning on her heel and meeting Whisper across the dais.

"Are you all right?" Raven asked. She longed to slide her arm around her sister's back to embrace her, but she couldn't, not in front of the guanero. Sandes women were strong and unemotional. They led with strength and loyalty and respect.

And, most of all, they grieved in private.

Whisper shook her head, saying nothing.

Fire caught up to them as they exited into the palace courtyard in the back. The massive three-sided pyramids for which Calypso was known stretched for the sky on each side, casting long triangular shadows across the land, intersecting in the center, where the Unburning Tree stood, its branches eternally aflame. It was said that the moment Fire came screaming into the world, the sacred tree caught fire and could not be extinguished, whether by water or blankets or otherwise. Though the tree was sheathed in flames, it did not burn.

As the sisters marched across the courtyard, several servants slipped in behind them, carrying Whisper's long pale-pink silk dress so it wouldn't drag in the dust. Raven's garb was far more practical, a short leather skirt with matching tunic, fitted with a dozen loops and clasps used to carry all manner of weaponry— her long whips, several knives, three vials of poison, and a black ivory whistle, constructed of the bones of a guanik, which was used to summon and command the dragons.

Fire, in her usual pretentious manner, wore a red dress set with hundreds of guanik scales, making it shimmer in the sun like fire. Almost subconsciously, she summoned flames that began to lick at her heels as she walked.

"Is this really what you want, dear sister?" Fire said. "You know I can lead. Maata always said I was special, because of my tattooya." Raven's sister never missed an opportunity to remind her siblings of her mark, as if they could ever forget about it.

"I do not doubt your ability, or your leadership, but I fear you would lead Calypso into a war we cannot win." Raven had harbored doubts about their mother's plan to use the plague-bearer against their enemies, while Fire had been in full agreement. In the end, Raven wished she'd been wrong.

"We are already at war," Fire snapped. "And you would allow our dearest Faata to control the south?"

"No. But I would be patient and wait for the dragons to mature."

The dragons were a major point of contention amongst the sisters. While Raven was determined to give them more time and training, Fire would fly off into battle with them at this very

63

moment, if she could. Whisper, on the other hand, was content to keep them as valuable pets.

Fire huffed in frustration, and fire rolled down her neck. "Oh, gods, not this again. If it were up to you, Faata will have tripled the size of his slave army before we attack."

It was common knowledge that Vin Hoza had begun a breeding strategy for his slave army years earlier. Every two years or so a new batch was ready for battle. Each batch was comprised of five-thousand expertly trained and completely controllable slave warriors.

"Slaves are no match for dragons."

Fire went silent, and Raven wished she hadn't spoken. At least there was one thing they were in agreement about: killing the innocent slaves controlled by their father was a necessary evil both of them wished they didn't have to do.

When they reached their personal residence within the palace, Fire said, "May the gods be with you," and stuck out her hand.

"And with you," Raven said, clasping her hand and sliding her fingers to her sister's wrist. She recoiled sharply when Fire's skin heated up rapidly, burning her.

Fire laughed and hustled into her rooms before Raven could retaliate.

Whisper tried to smile, but failed miserably. "Perhaps you should just let her have the empire. I've never seen her so determined."

"I will die before I submit to her," Raven muttered, sucking on her burned fingers.

"Don't say that!"

The look on her sister's face made Raven's anger melt away. "I'm sorry. I didn't mean—I miss her too." Raven tugged Whisper gently into her rooms, letting the wall of tied-together guanik bones dangling from the entrance fall back into place behind them, clanking softly in the breeze.

Whisper fell into her arms, sobbing into her chest. Raven's leather tunic was soon slick with tears. "Oh, sister," she said. "I am here. Always."

"I miss her too much. Like rain in the desert," Whisper said, craning her head back to look into Raven's eyes.

Her sister had always been an emotional sort, crying at the loss of one of the dragon brood, collecting sunflowers in the garden, decorating her sisters' rooms. But now, this time, Raven thought she understood exactly what her sister was feeling. It was like a gaping hole had opened in her chest, filling with sand where her heart should be. It was so painful it almost doubled her over, and it took all her strength—the strength given to her by both her parents—to remain upright. She had to be strong for her youngest sister, for the empire, and she would.

"Come," Raven said. "I will draw you a cool bath. It will help."

While Whisper sat on the edge of her bed, Raven dried the tears from her sister's sun-kissed cheeks, smoothed her chestnut hair back behind her delicate ears, and began to prepare her bath.

She didn't request help from the palace servants. Some things you had to do on your own.

On the morrow she would enter the arena to face her own sister in a battle for the future, but tonight she would think of nothing but the past.

Hours later, after Whisper was bathed and dressed in nightclothes, and the sun had dipped so far beneath the horizon that the pyramids became shadowy, spiked mountains, Fire slipped into the room without a word. The three sisters huddled under the covers and spoke of memories of the woman who raised them, trained them, and never failed to tell them what they were worth.

They laughed and cried and remembered everything there was to remember.

And then they slept, all in a row, until morning came upon the City of the Rising Sun.

Nine

The Southern Empire, Phanes
Jai Jiroux

With a hissed warning to Jig and Viola to remain behind with their mother, Jai sprinted for the tunnel entrance. He hurdled several groggy miners who were sitting up and rubbing their eyes, dashed past a woman carrying two babies in her arms, and pushed between several of the larger miners, who had made their way to the front of the cavern, presumably to defend the others, if necessary.

The clank of metal on metal echoed down the tunnel, punctuated by cries of determination and pain—it was hard to tell one from the other.

The mine is under attack, Jai realized. *But by whom?*

The emperor, was the first thought that struck him. Jai's methods had been determined to be too radical, too wild, regardless of the results. He and his mine masters would be struck down and replaced, as quickly and easily as ants in an anthill. Falcon Hoza would get his wish, and all Jai's work to get to this position would be for naught.

Worse, the slaves would be punished for his sins, he knew.

"Stay here!" he commanded the cavern full of people, and he knew they would obey, because they had to. Unless...

He shook his head as he raced down the tunnel, his shadow growing and shrinking as he passed each torch mounted to the wall.

He emerged from the tunnel into chaos. Shadowy shapes moved all around him. A wash of green moonlight spilled through the mine entrance, glancing off the silver edges of weapons—swords and whip-barbs and knives—flashing like fireflies in the dark.

It was hard to tell friend from foe, but then—

Thump. Thump. Thump. Thump. Thump.

Bodies fell, almost in unison, hitting the ground with a vicious finality. How many? Half a dozen? And on which side? Besides him, Jai only had a dozen mine masters in his employ.

"Master Jiroux," an unfamiliar voice said, stepping forward from the gloom, carrying a torch. It was a woman's voice, and there were no women masters, a requirement laid down by Emperor Hoza himself.

Jai shielded his eyes from the light, squinting, trying to see the torch bearer. His body instinctively fell into phen lu defense position, his knees bent, parallel to each other, his hips level, his back straight. His arms ready to block an attack if one came. "Who are you?"

"For you? The angel of death. The reaper. The end."

Jai had no weapon—he'd never even carried a whip the way the other masters did, because he was more likely to turn it on the masters than the slaves. He was his own weapon.

"You are a master of phen lu?" the woman said, sounding surprised.

He nodded. "And phen ru." Though true, it was a blatant attempt to give her pause before she attacked.

"An unusual combination. And yet you settle into the defense position first."

"It was the first I learned. My preference."

He took a step back, maintaining his stance, but she'd already cut the distance between them by half. More shadows crowded around her, shoulder to shoulder, blades emerging from the gloom like spikes from an enormous mace. The women wore tan form-fitting trousers and tunics, their belts teeming with weapons.

He realized something: *They dispatched my mine masters, all of whom were masters of phen ru. These women must fight like wildcats.*

"Please," Jai said, but it was not a plea for his own life. "Don't hurt the people. Give them a chance to escape."

"Escape?" The word seemed to confuse the woman so much that her hand danced aside for a moment, the light stretching its fingers across her face.

Jai sucked in a breath. Her skin was covered in black markings.

They were tears.

"You are the Black Tears," Jai said, remembering the tales of what they'd done to the other two mines, how they'd helped the slaves escape. And now they were attacking Garadia, the emperor's most prized possession. Jai shook his head, unable to

69

keep a thin smile from creasing his face. The brazenness of their attack was inspiring. He straightened up, falling out of stance.

"And you are dead, *master.*"

She handed the torch to another woman, who was clearly Teran, her red face also dotted with night-dark tears, and strode forward, raising her sword. Jai didn't want to die, but at least he would go knowing his people had a chance.

Noises behind him made him half-turn. A small form emerged from the tunnel, racing toward him. Jig hugged him around the leg, squeezing hard. His eyes were huge as he stared at the woman with her blade held high. "Don't hurt him!" the boy shrieked.

More forms moved forward, slipping around him like river water around a rock. Viola. Marella. Other miners, too: Gorrin the Dreadnoughter, and Hans and Patrella and Nance and Hominy and dozens of others. Jai didn't know how it was possible. They'd come to help him, despite the fact that he'd given them a direct order not to. *Perhaps my prior command giving them free will took precedence,* he thought. He was no student of the complexities of slave command, since he rarely used the power bestowed upon him by the emperor.

Past them, Jai could barely make out the woman's surprised expression as she lowered her sword. "You would protect your master, the one who has enslaved you?" she asked, her voice echoing in the mine atrium.

"The emperor enslaved us, not Jai Jiroux. And yes, we would protect him to the death," one of the men answered. A man named Carp, whom Jai had broken bread with on numerous occasions. A man untrained in combat, and yet willing to fight for him. Die for him.

70

"Has he commanded you to do this?" The woman was frowning now. Clearly in her past mine attacks she'd never had a situation where the slaves defended one of the masters.

"No," a woman said. Sharma. She was big with child—her first. Her husband was a burly fellow named Burnis whose long braid nearly reached his feet. They were hoping for a girl.

As more and more of the people chimed in, Jai was surprised by how many of them he knew personally, how many he'd shared a story with, how many he'd eaten with, laughed with. He wanted to save them, but instead they were protecting him. It didn't seem fair.

"How is this possible?" the woman said.

Jai said to Jig, "It's fine now. Thank you," and detached the boy's fingers and feet from him one at a time. He stepped forward, his people parting for him as he made his way toward the front.

The woman had regathered her torch and was shining her light across the people. She had jet-black hair braided in back, smooth brown skin, and fierce, narrow green eyes that sparkled as if studded with emeralds. Her eyes gave her away as a Phanecian. She wore a tan leather vest, leaving her shoulders and arms bare. "They are not injured," she commented. "No whip marks, no bruises, no scars. I don't understand."

Jai scanned the women in front of him. They were as different from each other as the stars in the sky. While the leader was clearly of Phanecian descent, as was one of the others, two of them were red-skinned Terans, and two were Dreadnoughters, their broad, flat foreheads gray and rough. However, despite their differences, they all bore black tears beneath their eyes, but some had more than others, and none more than their leader, the woman in front. *The number of people they have killed*, Jai remembered. At least according to the whisperings in the city. There were only six of them, a fact that awed him. Six women had taken a mine defended by twice that many masters. Then again, each of them wore the face of a warrior, with the lean, strong bodies to match.

"I can explain," Jai said. "This mine is run by the people, not the masters."

"You mean the slaves?"

Jai shook his head. "To the emperor they might be slaves, but to me, they are my friends. My family. My people."

The woman's narrow eyes narrowed further. "You commanded them to be free? But the emperor..."

Jai said, "What is your name?"

"Anguish. Sorrow. Regret. Destiny. I have many names, and all of them are laced with sadness for the souls I've lost."

Gods. Her words seemed to slash open a wound in Jai's gut. He was intimately acquainted with those names. They were his past. They were his present. And, he knew, they were his future.

She continued. "But the name given to me at birth was Sonika Vaid."

"Sonika," Jai said, trying it out. By his estimation, the name was fit for a warrior, and suited her well. "I am Jai Jiroux. Please do not call me master, whether out of mockery or spite, because I loathe the title as much as you. Unfortunately, I could not command these people to be free, as you have suggested. The emperor's influence roams far, and yes, reaches well past Garadia. But I have given them free will within the confines of this mine, and so long as they meet their quotas the emperor will not intercede."

"The emperor is a pyzon," Sonika hissed, sounding much like a snake herself.

"I cannot disagree with you," Jai said. "But that doesn't mean we can ignore his power."

"Damn his power and his quotas into the Void." Though the anger was clear in her voice, Jai could sense the frustration behind it. This was a woman trying to carry out a rebellion against an enemy who was almost untouchable because of his tattooya.

"Where are the other mine masters?" Jai asked, though he'd already guessed their fate.

Her lips curled into a sneer. "Dead."

"How? They were all masters of phen ru."

"We are masters of a higher art."

"Phen lu?"

She laughed. "Foolish man. Phen sur is the highest of the martials arts, though none but the women seem to realize it."

Confusion roiled through him. Phen sur was a beautiful art form, but he'd never seen it used for violence. He could hardly comprehend it. "You killed my men with a…dance?"

"Yes. Would you mourn them?"

Jai shook his head. "No." He wouldn't mourn his lost masters. Yes, they had allowed him to manage the mine in his own way, but it wasn't out of kindness. No, it was because he gave them an easy life of luxury. They were as guilty as the emperor himself. "But I have to count them. To make certain none escaped to report back to the emperor."

Sonika blinked, as if surprised by his response, but then stepped aside to allow him to pass. Jai turned back to the mine workers. He felt a flutter in his chest, like a bird was trapped within his ribcage. He knew this was it—his one opportunity. Another would not come easily. *My destiny.* "Return to the cavern. Gather your things. Capture as much water from the stream as possible. Bring all the food we have. We are leaving."

The people didn't move, their eyes set on him, their lips falling open a crack. Blinking, blinking, not understanding. Not truly. *When someone has been kept in the dark for so long, how can you convince them to step into the light?* Jai wondered. He raised his hand in the air, forming it into the three-fingered salute. "You will never mine another diamond again!" he shouted.

Burnis clapped his hands together. "Now that's a tempting proposal. Come on, lads, come on, lasses, tonight we leave this filthy Voidhole forever!"

An almost electric energy seemed to hum through the crowd as they passed the message to turn around to the hundreds still amassed in the tunnel behind them. Jai placed a hand on Burnis's shoulder. "Thank you, old friend. Will you please gather a dozen others and raid the masters' quarters? There will be food and water there, too. Take everything you can carry, and then come back for more. Be quick, we only have a limited window for escape."

"Aye. I will." The thickset man strode off, grabbing other men and women by the arms and relaying the message.

Satisfied that his people would rise to the task of preparing for departure, Jai turned back to the Black Tears, who were watching him intently. He nodded to Sonika, and, after a moment's pause, she nodded back. He strode past her, stooping to inspect the first body. Master Gabon, his dark black mustache unmistakable, drooping well past his lips. He'd been an easy sell, a few years earlier. All he cared about was his own well-being, and the promise of an easy lifestyle had been enough to sway him to Jai's plan. Jai checked for a heartbeat—there was none. *One,* Jai said in his head.

One by one, he checked the others. By the time he was finished, only one was missing, but that didn't concern him. It was Master Axa, who had betrayed Jai to the emperor and been slavemarked as a result. By now he would be more than halfway from Phanea to Garadia, stumbling in the dark, stubbing his bare toes on rocks and cacti. With luck, he'd be bitten by a scorpion and die under the stars, his body eventually picked clean like the carrion he was.

Following behind Jai, the Black Tears were removing each body, carrying them to the masters' quarters and away from the mine entrance.

"That's all of them," Jai announced. "Your warriors are thorough."

"Yes. It seems you're the only master left," Sonika said. Her hand was on the hilt of her sword. "And you have no one left to protect you."

Jai's heart thudded faster in his chest. "Kill me if you must," he said. "So long as you protect my people, and do not call me master."

Sonika drew her sword. Stepped forward, turning the blade slowly to let it catch the emerald moonlight. Said, "Your words ring true, but I want you to swear with your blood."

"I will." Jai held out his hand, palm up. With an expert jerk of her hand, Sonika sliced her blade across his palm. Jai gritted his teeth, refusing to acknowledge the sting of pain sizzling through his flesh. It was nothing compared to what his miners had been through, the pain they felt every day from their labors.

He squeezed his fingers tight against his palm, making a fist, letting several drops of blood drip to the ground. "I swear I will do no harm to these people. I swear I am no master, but a rebel, like you. I swear on my blood that so long as you help my people, I will help you."

The leader of the Black Tears nodded once and then motioned to one of the other women, who provided a thick cloth, wrapping it around Jai's cut hand several times before tearing it with her teeth and tying off the end. The Teran woman had short coppery hair that curled around her chin. Twice she glanced at Jai between long golden lashes before continuing her work, licking her pink lips. As she bandaged him, Jai counted the black tears on her red-skinned cheeks. Seventeen. He wondered how many tears she'd be adding for the men she'd killed tonight.

"Thank you," Jai said when she finished. "What is your name?"

"Shanti," she said. "Shanti Parthena Laude."

A beautiful name, he thought. He knew Teran names held great meaning; he wondered what hers meant, but it wasn't the time to ask. "I'm Jai Jiroux," he said.

She laughed slightly. "I know. You were supposed to be the first to die, but instead we found another in your bed."

With that, she went back to helping her comrades remove the bodies of the masters. "Does everyone want me dead?" Jai said to himself.

Though the question wasn't meant for her, Sonika answered. "If the emperor finds out you're alive, then yes, everyone *will* want you dead. But we will burn the bodies, so it will be harder for them to know whether anyone survived."

"Thank you."

"Now show us the diamonds."

"What?"

"You think a rebellion is cheap? We will need the diamonds as much as the food and water. And they're easy to haul. Have your people squeeze them anywhere they'll fit. In their shoes, in their undergarments, in their mouths if they wish. Bring all the diamonds they can carry."

Jai frowned, although the logic made sense. It just seemed strange to take the diamonds like common thieves. Then again, *they* were the ones who'd broken their backs to mine the jewels for years. If anything, it was back payment for all their hard work. "Fine. But today's haul has already been carted to the emperor's palace."

"Then mine more."

Jai wouldn't ask his people to raise another sledge or pick ever again. He'd never ask them to haul another cart or risk their lives in another unstable mineshaft. No. "I'll go myself."

As it turned out, Jai didn't have to ask anyone to descend into the mineshaft with him. He had a wealth of volunteers, ready and willing, including two strong Dreadnoughters, Gorrin and Orrin, twin brothers with identical gray features. And though on occasion the mine was stubborn, not tonight. It was as if the gods themselves were a part of their escape. Before dawn arrived, they had hauled three heaping carts of uncut gems, shimmering piles of wealth beyond measure.

"Are there more?" Sonika asked, eyeing the carts.

"This mine will produce for another decade or longer," Jai said. "There are always more. But it will take time, and every second we wait is a risk." He was exhausted and sore, but now that the people were emerging from the tunnel strapped with bags laden with food and water, he was anxious to leave.

Sonika said, "Fine. It will have to do."

"Where are the other Tears?" Jai asked, his eyes probing the space for Shanti and the others.

"Preparing a gift for the emperor," she said, a twinkle in her eyes.

Jai didn't know what that meant, but he didn't take further time to ponder. Instead, he instructed each person emerging from the tunnel to gather some of the diamonds amongst their things, and to exit the mine. Many had glittering tears in their eyes, and others wore weary, but determined expressions.

Dozens turned to hundreds turned to thousands, but Jai waited for each of them to pass before joining them outside. The last was the eldest woman in the mine—Mother Ko, everyone called her. Her skin was so wrinkled it looked like a sheet of parchment that had been balled up and smoothed out, over and over again. Her long, hooked nose had so many broken blood vessels it was like a beacon on her face. But her unnaturally dark eyes were still clear and intelligent. From past discussions with her, Jai knew she was as shrewd a person as there was, and her age alone told him much about what she was made of.

She was weighed down with a dozen bags, wrapped around her neck and shoulders and bulging from her body like camel humps. "Here. Let me take a few of those," Jai offered.

She slapped him away with shaking hands. "Help someone else," she said. "I'm no cripple."

Yes, she was as tough as a sledge, but also as stubborn as a mule, a sometimes frustrating combination. Jai followed her out, shaking his head.

When he emerged into the daylight, he felt another flutter in his chest. They were leaving, at long last. To his ears, his heartbeat sounded much like the gallop of a trio of exuberant horses, riding in unison.

For the first time in a long time, he felt a true ray of light-giving hope in the darkness.

The sun was rising in the west, lighting the tops of the red cliffs that bordered the sea, and sending plumes of pink and orange across a sky so blue it might've been painted on.

Thousands of people stood before him, waiting. To one side were Sonika and her Black Tears, holding ropes attached to black horses, sturdy steeds that whinnied and stamped in anticipation. While the rebels rode, everyone else would have to walk. In the light, the black tears on each woman's cheeks were stark reminders of how deadly they were. Jai was glad he was on their side, at least, so far.

The only one missing was Shanti, but soon she emerged, too, hauling a wooden barrel behind her. There was a small hole cut in the side, and a steady stream of gray powder was tumbling out, painting a thin line on the ground, disappearing into the mine. From past experience in other mines that used the substance, Jai immediately knew what it was:

Fireroot.

The roots, which were found attached to gnarled old trees growing, unexpectedly, in the driest parts of the Phanecian desert, could be ground up to make the powder, which was highly flammable. And if there was enough powder in one place at one time...

Jai had seen the power firsthand. Personally, he hated the substance, for he'd seen it kill many slave miners if they were unable to get themselves clear of the blast. As far as he knew, the emperor still used fireroot in several of the older mines, in which the gems were harder to get to, but Jai had never used the gray powder in Garadia.

"You're going to destroy the mine?" he said, approaching Sonika.

"No," Sonika said. "There's not enough fireroot in all of Phanes. But we are going to make it very difficult for the emperor to access his precious diamonds. It will take many months to dig out the mine. By then, perhaps, he will be dead."

So this was the gift she'd spoken of. Jai didn't know why the thought of the mine coming down made him feel a sliver of sorrow. Garadia was a cage, a prison, a place where people were treated like possessions. And yet, it had been his home for three years now, a place where he made friends, where he fought for a better life for a people who'd never been given a life at all.

"Good," he said, pushing his emotions aside. "What is the plan?"

Sonika sighed deeply. "Even I didn't realize how many there were," she said, casting a hand across the people. "I had planned to take them south, to a boat. From there we could sail out of the range of the emperor's slavemark. But there are too many."

"There were rumors that you escaped with others across the southernmost tip of the Spear," Jai said.

Sonika looked away, staring at the cliffs and the rising sun. "Those were only rumors."

Jai tried to catch her eye, but she wouldn't look at him. "Sonika. *Sonika.*" Finally, she turned. "How did you get the others out of Phanes?"

There was something in her eyes. Jai recognized it because he'd seen it in his own eyes before, while staring in the looking glass. Guilt. "We didn't," she said. "We tried, but the emperor's men rode us down like dogs. The first group was killed almost immediately, between the cliffs of the Bloody Canyon. The second was more successful—we could see the Burning Sea ahead of us, glittering in the sun, but the result was the same. I lost many of my warriors and narrowly escaped with my own life. We are all that are left of the Tears."

Jai stared at the ground, considering this new information. Here he'd thought someone had finally freed some of the slaves, but instead the Black Tears had only gotten more of them killed during the attempt.

Were his people destined to die, too?

Was it worth it—the risk? Could he still change his mind, usher his people back into the mine and tell the emperor the story of an attack by the Black Tears, an attack that was fought off by the slaves themselves, only the mine masters perishing before it was over?

He shook his head. No, there was no going back. He could see the hope in his people's eyes, in the way they were squinting into the sun, wearing expressions full of amazement, smiles of happiness. They would press on, not south to Sonika's too-small boat, but north to—

"The Southron Gates," Jai said.

"That's suicide," Sonika said.

"Everything is suicide." Jai told her and the others about what his father had told him, about the way through the wall. With Shanti's fireroot it just might be possible...

"And you believe him?" Sonika's eyes bored into him, searching for a lie.

"Yes," Jai said.

"Why?"

"Because my father loved my mother."

Once they were a safe distance away from the mine, Shanti used a torch to light the gray fireroot powder. Everyone watched the flames travel slowly along the ground, picking up speed when a stiff wind coaxed them from behind. Eventually the flames vanished into the dark tunnel entrance.

Jai held his breath, waiting.

A few moments passed without event, and he exhaled. He said, "Perhaps there was a break in the trail of powd—"

BOOM!

The ground shook, rumbling like an earthquake under their feet. Some of the people staggered, while strong arms shot out to help the children and elderly maintain their balance. A plume of smoke roiled from the entrance as rocks cracked and tumbled from above.

The earth went still once more. Silence returned. The mine was blocked by enormous chunks of stone.

The people cheered, and Jai found himself cheering along with them, as excited as he'd ever been. It felt like the first step to long-awaited freedom.

Everyone was staring toward the mine, so several people let out a high-pitched yip of surprise when a figure stumbled amongst them from behind, collapsing to his knees in front of Jai. "Master," the man said, his voice like coarse sand rubbed across smooth stone. "What is your command?"

It was Axa, his previous mine master. *And the last surviving one,* Jai mused, his life having been saved by his own treachery. His black eyes rolled back in his head and he fell on his face, unconscious, the jewels sewn into his skin sparkling in the sunlight.

Sonika's eyes ratcheted between Axa and Jai, her lips a thin line of distrust. "I thought you said no one called you master. Who is this man?"

"A new slave," Jai said. Hurriedly, he explained everything, from his meeting with the emperor, to Axa's poor decision, to the increase in production quota.

"Then this man should die like the others," Sonika said. "He was a bad man, regardless of the slave mark he wears now."

There were several murmurs of agreement from the crowd, which had gathered around the Black Tears. A few of them spat and kicked dirt in Axa's direction. He'd been hated and feared by many of the slaves.

"It is the people's choice," Jai said, turning away from Sonika to face them. "Would you have me kill this half-dead man? He now bears the slave mark, like all of you. Regardless of what he has done in the past, he is another victim of the Slave Master. He is no threat, but I will do as you wish. He is yours now."

A few shouts of "Kill him!" went up immediately, led by a broad-shouldered man named Joaquin who'd been beaten several times by Axa while in Garadia. Others, however, murmured, "No. Spare him." Pockets of intense discussion ensued, rolling through the crowd. Eventually, each group sent forward a representative.

"What shall I do?" Jai asked each.

Only one of them voted to kill Axa. It was Joaquin, growling the decision. "You have chosen," Jai said. "Now who will help me bear this burden?"

None stepped forward. Joaquin spat in the dirt.

"I shall bear him myself, for a time," Jai said. He dribbled some water onto Axa's lips, tilting his head back so the liquid would slide down his throat. The man groaned, choking and spitting out some of the water. Jai tried again, and this time more stayed down. Axa dozed, even as Jai hefted him onto his shoulders.

As he started to carry him, something hard dug into Jai's shoulders, and he placed the unconscious man back on the ground, feeling about the sackcloth wrapped around his legs. There, hidden in the thick folds of the sackcloth, Jai found a small mirror, its reflective surface dusty and tarnished. His own wobbly reflection stared back at him.

Strange, he thought. Normally slaves didn't have many possessions, though they were allowed to accumulate them if they could. Then again, the jewels sewn into Axa's skin contained more wealth than all of the slaves had combined. Still, a mirror? It was a strange thing to have for a slave, especially a new one. *I'll have to ask him about it when he wakes up*, Jai thought, tucking the mirror back into the folds of Axa's sackcloth.

That's when something occurred to him, something he'd forgotten about in all of the unexpected events of the night and morning. More like some*one*. Someone whose body wasn't amongst those of the dead mine masters, and who he hadn't seen in the crowd.

"The chariot driver," he murmured. "Oh gods."

"What?" Sonika asked, but Jai was already gone, racing back toward the caved-in mine, heading not for the entrance but for the stables, which were off to the side. He dashed inside, leaping a boulder that had crumbled from the side of the mountain during the explosion, leaving a gaping hole in the thatched roof.

The chariot was gone, along with the horse that had drawn it.

Along with the chariot driver.

Ten

The Western Kingdom, Knight's End
Rhea Loren

The people—her people—were gathered before Rhea by the thousands. She was delighted to see how many of them had cut their faces to match her own. According to her spies in the city, more and more did so each and every day. Legions of the righteous pledging their allegiance to their righteous queen and their god, Wrath, holy be his name.

Standing atop the castle walls, she raised her hands to silence them. A hush fell over the crowd, and, still, she marveled at the power she wielded. The power over sound. Over hearts. Over minds.

The thought of power brought a memory to the forefront of her mind. Grease Jolly's—no, *Grey Arris's*, she reminded herself—sister had power, too, provided by the sinmark she bore. *What was her name again?* Rhea wondered, but just as quickly thought *Why do I care?* Grease, Grey, whatever his name was, had left her, just as he did the first time, in the crypts, and now she had only herself to trust.

Then again, she wondered how things would've turned out if he hadn't left, or if he'd taken her with him. She wondered where he was, if he was safe.

Secretly, she'd sent a rider to look for him, which constantly made her think *I'm a fool.*

She realized the people were still waiting for her to speak, their heads raised patiently upwards, some shielding their eyes from the sun. She forced thoughts of Grey away and spoke: "In the west, we believe in seven heavens. The first heaven is for the worst sinners, those who fail to carry out Wrath's will on earth. They will burn for an eternity after they die." She paused, letting them chew on that, though the idea of the first heaven had likely been hammered into their brains since before they could understand what it meant.

She continued: "The second heaven is here and now. This world. It is our chance to prove ourselves to Wrath. Our chance to display our righteousness. I see many of you who are taking that responsibility, that opportunity, seriously. My hope is that you will all pledge yourselves to Wrath."

"Here, here!" someone cried. And another: "All hail Queen Loren the Righteous!" More cheers went up, and for a few moments, Rhea allowed herself to bask in their adoration.

Once they had quieted again, she said, "The third heaven is for the apathetic, who die without caring about anyone or anything but themselves. Those sent there will relive the same, meaningless life again and again, for all of eternity. The fourth heaven isn't much better, except you're given a second chance to follow Wrath and ascend to a higher heaven. The fifth heaven is a cut above, where the righteous go, those who love Wrath, who believe his teachings with all their hearts, but who are too scared to actively carry out his will. It is my belief that most of you will achieve the fifth heaven."

More cheers, which Rhea was glad to hear. It was a calculated risk on her part, telling them they would likely not achieve more than the fifth heaven. She wanted to build them up, but not so much that there was nowhere left to take them.

"The sixth heaven is a near miss, for those who did everything in their power to achieve Wrath's will, but who, inevitably, fell just short, because they were too human. Still, it is a position of honor, a place where you can hear Wrath's voice all the time, even if you can't see our God's Face." She paused again, letting the silence build its own momentum. "And then there is the seventh heaven."

Murmurs raced through the crowd, but they were quickly shushed by the others. Ears craned upward, desperate to hear Rhea's thoughts on the pinnacle of human achievement in the afterlife.

"The seventh heaven is where I long to go, a place where I can look upon Wrath's Face and see our God smile. That is why I cut my face, so I wouldn't obsess over my beauty the way the seductresses to the south do."

She saw the Fury to her right stiffen, but she remained silent.

"Many generations of Lorens have told you the same thing. My father, King Gill Loren, my mother, Queen Cecilia Loren, and their parents, and their parents' parents, have counseled you to seek to reach the fifth heaven or above. They were not wrong in telling you this. And yet Wrath has told me to tell you something else. Something more."

"She heard the Voice of Wrath!" someone cried.

Rhea saw numerous heads shaking in disbelief, so she rushed on. "Wrath spoke not directly to me, but through God's righteous mouthpiece, one of the Three." Rhea gestured to the Fury beside her. The woman, as Rhea had commanded her, said, "It's true. Wrath spoke to Rhea through me."

Astonishment and excitement rumbled through the audience. "What did God say?" several people shouted.

In that moment, Rhea knew she had them.

"That the people of Knight's End are ready. That you are on the verge of something great. That I should counsel you to reach for the seventh heaven, for it stands ready to welcome you with Wrath's open Arms."

More cheers. Cheers of hope from a people who'd recently lost two kings, and were grasping for anything solid to hang on to.

"Our enemies belong in the first heaven. Their sinful ways are an abomination before Wrath. The northerners are corrupt, engaging in behavior more fit for beasts than humans. The easterners have bred with the Orians, who are known to engage in dark, unnatural magic. And the southerners? They are no more than barbarians, dressing like heathens, capturing Teran slaves by the thousands, celebrating vile creatures such as dragons and guanik, pyzons and vulzures. They are the reason the Kings' Bane has risen, murdering our monarchs, murdering my father and cousin."

"But what can we do, Your Righteousness?" an especially loud voice shouted. This individual, Rhea was forced to admit, was a plant, paid to ask that exact question at that exact moment. Rhea even made sure he had a horn to yell into, amplifying his voice. Even from high atop the wall she could almost hear his pockets jingling with gold coins. *You earned your reward.*

"A wise question," she said. "And I have the answer, as spoken by Wrath. Are we so blessed as to be able to hide within our walled city, protected from evil, waiting for the day that we'll be delivered to paradise? I say nay, we are only humans living in the second heaven, five long strides away from reaching our true reward. Nay! We must be *more* than the sinners who seek to tear us down. Nay! We must *do* more. We must cleanse this land from evil, from godlessness, from sinfulness. As humble servants who aspire to reach the seventh heaven, it is our responsibility—nay, our *duty*—to send our enemies to the fiery heaven they've earned and rid the world of their influence, carrying Wrath's word to every corner of the Four Kingdoms and beyond! Anything less and we shall deserve our position in the darkness of the first heaven, where we will be hidden from the presence of Wrath forever."

Silence fell across her people, who stared at her, rapt.

"We do not wish to inflict violence on our foes," she continued, casting her eyes downward. Rhea thought of the moment Grey left her alone with the cobbler, which pushed tears to her eyes. A substitute for the real emotion she felt in this moment: anger. "No. We eschew violence with all of our beings...until it is necessary."

"What would you have us do, Your Highness?"

She scanned her people from side to side, back to front, meeting individual eyes, capturing them in her own sparkling gaze. "Fight, I say." And then, louder: "Fight! And be victorious for our God, for our country, for yourselves and your children and your children's children and all who come after us!"

The crowd's response was a roar, thousands of voices raised as one. Thousands who Rhea now believed would fight—and die, if necessary—for her.

She smiled, waved, and turned her back on them.

With the Fury standing silently beside her, Rhea sat on her throne, thinking about the first time she entered this very room after her father's death.

How weak I was. How naïve. How oblivious.

She wondered if one's life could be defined by a single moment, a single choice, and, if so, what her moment would be. The moment Grey abandoned her in the crypts? Or perhaps the moment she sought revenge on him? Or when she freed him, perhaps? She knew those were all important moments in her life, but not THE ONE.

No. Her moment was a darker one. The moment the Furies took her beauty from her with the edge of a blade? No again. No, no, no.

Her life to this point was defined by the moment she killed her cousin, when she took back what was rightfully hers. The beautiful ring on her finger. The golden crown on her head. The moment she felt the pure power running through her veins. The power to hold a life in one's hand and either let it go or crush it into dust.

The thought made her unbearably sad. It wasn't the moment she would choose, and yet it was all she had.

She was stirred from her revelry when her cousin entered. Not Jove, for he was dead. And not Sai, Wheaton, nor Gaia, for

Rhea refused to speak to any of her cousins who'd failed to care for her in her time of need.

Ennis. The only cousin she'd ever truly liked. Perhaps even loved, if she was being completely honest. Though he was twenty-five years her senior, he'd always paid attention to her, even as a child. And he was the only one who'd come to her after her face had been carved by the Furies.

Now he was her adviser. Her only adviser.

He stepped forward without speaking, unwilling to meet Rhea's eyes. He was angry, she could see. She'd done the very thing he'd counseled against: warmongering. If it was up to him, they would carry on the work of fortifying their defenses, as her father had done, and continue to protect their borders. He didn't understand Rhea's need to attack.

He didn't understand that she'd sat back and waited for life to come to her for her entire pathetic existence. And what had it made her? A scarred orphan.

No more.

Ennis reached the steps and climbed them, but halted when the Fury moved to block his path, her hand resting firmly on the knife at her hip.

Ennis sighed, holding out a limp scroll. "I have a message from the north. The stream only just arrived and the parchment hasn't had time to dry." *Streaming* was the fastest way to send messages across the land, using ink from the strange inkreed plant, which had a tendency to vanish when dipped in water, reappearing in the exact same form in the water where the inkreed was originally harvested from. Then the message could be transferred onto a blank piece of parchment. Hence the soaked page Ennis was now waving around.

"It's fine," Rhea said, although she was enjoying seeing this new side of her red-haired protector. But she didn't fear her cousin. Even if he suspected she'd had something to do with his eldest brother's death, he would never do anything to her. He didn't have it in him. If one of them was a spider and the other was the fly caught in the web, she knew exactly who would play which role.

The Fury stepped back on command, like the obedient pup that she was. Her hand, however, remained on the gilded hilt of her knife.

"It's from the north?" Rhea guessed.

"Yes," Ennis said.

"*Now* Lord Griswold wants to speak," she said. "Interesting that he reaches out after he's amassed troops at Blackstone."

They'd been arriving in droves for the last fortnight, lines of soldiers in gleaming armor, shimmering across the waters of the Bay of Bounty. Ships were being built by the north, too. Hundreds now lay moored in the harbor just south of the northern stronghold of Blackstone.

"It's not from Griswold," Ennis said.

She frowned, momentarily confused, a feeling she hated. "Approach."

Ennis climbed the final two steps and passed her the wet scroll. She scanned the document:

Year of the Four Kingdoms:
Circa 532
Queen Rhea Loren, First of Your Name,

First, I am truly sorry for your loss. Your father, King Gill Loren, was a man of vision, who only wanted the best for his people.

He was also my uncle, though I never had the opportunity to meet him. I am further saddened by the loss of my mother, Queen Sabria Loren Gäric, also your aunt. My uncle, Lord Griswold, who has declared himself king regent under false pretenses, murdered her in cold blood without a true trial. Although I did not witness her execution, my sister promises me that she was courageous and fearless at the end. I can only hope to make her proud as king.

Which brings me to my next point. I hereby declare myself the King of the North, for as long as I shall live. Already, my uncle's forces are gathering at Blackstone to attack the west. I have gathered my own army, which I will use to defend Raider's Pass from the Ironclad's to the east. Once I am victorious I will march on Castle Hill and take back what is rightfully mine. I repeat: I am the king, and all negotiations between our kingdoms will be conducted with me.

I am not my father, who was a brutal, violent man. Nor am I my uncle, who desires to flood the south with his armies. No, all I wish is to maintain the frozen lands north of the Mournful Mountains, and provide my people with the sense of peace they've been starved of for many years. As a new queen yourself, I assume you want the same for the west.

Peace. It's such a strange word these days, but one that is not unachievable. That is what I believe. That is what I hope.

I am not requesting your help in retaking Castle Hill. I am simply extending a hand across the battlefield—a hand I hope you will take in a show of good faith. The alliance once forged by my grandfather can still be achieved if we want it to.

Your Humble Northern Counterpart,
King Archer Gäric
Northern Kingdom

Slowly, carefully, Rhea folded the parchment in half. "Strange," she said. "We've already received streams that the battle at Raider's Pass is over, with the northern rebels victorious."

"Someone must've delayed sending this stream, either by mistake or design. And yet this is wonderful news, Your Highness," Ennis said. "Perhaps the situation isn't as bleak as we once believed."

Rhea held the parchment with both hands, and then ripped it in half.

"What are you doing?" Ennis tried to grab at the paper, but the Fury was quick to block him with her arm.

Rhea continued to tear the message apart, until it was naught but scraps of soggy confetti in her hands, which she let fall to her feet, grinding them under her heel.

Ennis stared at her for a moment, confusion stretching across his face, and then said, "Do you remember our history? The north and the west were borne from the same past. It all started with a Gäric, Heinrich, the first Crimean explorer to reach these lands. His son's son, Verner Gäric, fought against the motherland in the First Independence War."

"Yes, yes, the War of Roses," Rhea said tiredly. As a child, she'd loved hearing the story as told by her history tutor. After the final battle, which took place in Knight's End, it was said the streets were so stained with blood they appeared to be covered in a fine layer of rose petals—hence, the war's nickname. It was a good story, full of valor—blood, yes, but what was a war without bloodshed?—and victory and heroes and villains. "That was four-hundred years ago. What does it have to do with the present?"

Ennis began nodding emphatically, as if he finally believed he had her attention. "The *Lorens* fought alongside the *Gärics* and emerged victorious, don't you see?"

"Perhaps you are the one forgetting our history, dear cousin," Rhea said. "A hundred years later there was the Second Independence War, after the reclusive Gärics had already made their home in the north. Who came to help us then? Not the north, but the east! Should we make peace with them, too, our sworn enemies?"

Ennis sighed and Rhea knew she had won a point. Not that she needed one; she was the queen. "Do you know why the Second Independence War was nicknamed the War of Tears?" her cousin stubbornly asked.

Rhea frowned, wracking her memory. She didn't. "Why should a three-hundred-year-old nickname matter to a queen?" she said instead.

"Because you are Rhea the Righteous," Ennis explained. "Servant of Wrath and leader of the Holy City of Knight's End. It was called the War of Tears because after the final battle, in which there were such tremendous casualties on both sides that the dead far outnumbered the living, rain poured from the sky in sheets. The rainfall lasted a fortnight, flooding the land and washing the blood away. Cleansing the earth so we could start anew. It was our ancestor, Queen Mallorhea Loren, who said the rain was Wrath's Tears falling for our people. She's the one who gave the war its nickname. You were named after her."

Rhea frowned. She'd never heard this story. Was he making it up? "I am the first of my name," she said.

Ennis placed his hand on her arm, but she shook it off. Ever since the Furies had pressed the knife to her face she hated being touched. Ennis took it in stride, continuing. "Exactly. Your parents wanted you to be the first of your name, so they shortened Mallorhea's name to give you yours. But it doesn't change the fact that they wanted you to be strong like her—which you are—*and* righteous like her."

"I *am* Rhea the Righteous," she said. "I wear a sign of my devotion to Wrath on my face, would you deny it?" Rhea could feel the heat flushing her face, the anger needling through her veins.

Ennis remained annoyingly calm, his eyes never leaving hers. "It was Queen Mallo*rhea* who, after the War of Tears, forged an alliance with the north, the same northerners who then helped her drive the easterners back onto their lands when they demanded restitution for the losses incurred during the war. It was Queen Mallo*rhea* who did everything in her power to make peace in the Four Kingdoms for the first time in its long and bloody history, a peace that lasted for a hundred years, long after she'd been embalmed in the crypts."

Rhea scowled at him, hating that he was so reasonable, so logical, even playing to his knowledge that she regularly visited the crypts. What he didn't know was that she went there to meet her paramour, not to mourn the dead. It was there, in the cryptlands, that she and Grey first…

She slammed the door shut on the memory. "I will not use history as an excuse to be weak," she said. "Not when the north has shown time and time again that they cannot be trusted, that they are no better than our enemies to the east and south."

"I don't understand," Ennis said. "Archer Gäric wants peace. Surely you will respond."

"Yes, of course, dear cousin. I will respond immediately. Please send the following reply: There shall be no peace. Not now. Not ever."

Ennis's jaw dropped open and he looked like he wanted to speak but no words came out. His mouth closed, opened again, then closed for good. With a small shake of his head, he left the way he'd come, his head hanging.

When he was gone, Rhea said, "Gather what's left of the furia. I have instructions. There are preparations to make."

"Preparations for what, my queen?" the Fury asked.

"For war."

Eleven

The Western Kingdom, The Tangle
Roan Loren

"I think we're traveling in circles," Gwendolyn Storm said, stopping. Her silver hair fell across the shoulders of her form-fitting armor.

"How can you tell?" Roan asked.

Her yellow, catlike eyes flashed with frustration. "I've seen that tree three times in the last week," she said, pointing to a gnarled oak with enormous roots protruding from the ground at strange angles.

"All the trees look the same," Roan said. "Big and old." He knew he was way out of his element. Being from the hot and dusty south, where you could see the distant mountains and sea on a clear day, he was used to vegetation being sparse. Though he'd grown accustomed to the forest from his time spent riding through Ironwood, the Tangle was a whole different beast. The trees, many of which had poisonous spikes sprouting from their trunks, grew together, like conjoined twins, wrapped in bushes and brambles and vines, all of which seemed determined to block the path of travelers. Occasionally Roan got the eerie feeling that the thorny plants were actually moving to try to stop them, or perhaps steering them in a particular direction. Even the sunlight played tricks on them as its rays fought through the cover of the crisscrossing branches, and they never could tell which way it was moving. At night, the moons and stars were completely hidden and useless for navigational purposes.

"Aye. But I marked this one the last time we saw it." Gwendolyn pointed to a thin cut at the base of the tree.

"You're certain it's the same mark?"

"As certain as I can be of anything in this Ore-forsaken forest."

Roan sighed and slumped onto a rare spot of vacant ground. After fleeing the eastern army's encampment just east of the Snake River—which divided the eastern and western kingdoms—they'd swum across the cold, turbulent waters, entering the protection of the ancient forest known as the Tangle.

His biggest regret was not saying goodbye to Gareth Ironclad. Not being able to explain why they had to leave. *Gods, I don't even know if he's still alive, if I did enough to heal him.*

He could still feel the warmth of the prince's lips on his, the one and only time they'd kissed.

Could still see the anger and surprise in the prince's eyes.

The thought made him sad, which was strange considering the way Gareth—who was now, technically, the King of the Eastern Kingdom—and he had first met, almost as if by fate.

And then, when Roan had saved Gareth from death—the death everyone had expected from him, considering he was born to be the Shield, protecting his brothers from harm—Roan had realized he'd begun to think of Gareth as a friend.

That was a week ago. The first few days they took turns sleeping while the other kept watch, but after three uneventful nights passed, they began sleeping back to back. Each night, Roan had relished the warmth of Gwen's body against his. He couldn't deny his attraction to her, nor to the prince, but now wasn't the time to act on it, especially because the Orian was as likely to stab him as she was to kiss him.

Now Roan could only hope they were further west than before, perhaps even nearing the forest's western border. But each day that passed left them more concerned that they were decidedly and hopelessly lost.

I'm so close to home, Roan thought. *And yet seem further away than ever.* For a moment, he wondered whether he would live out the rest of his days in the Tangle, eating bark and sewing together leaves to use as clothing. They could even invent a new language, comprised of bird chirps and gnawing noises.

"Something amusing?" Gwen asked, easing down beside him. Her arrows rattled in the pouch strapped to her back. Though she'd planned to hunt game in the forest, they hadn't seen so much as an earthworm thus far. She'd brought down several miniscule birds, but they had so little meat on their tiny bones that they almost weren't worth the effort or the potential loss of arrows it took to bag one. Despite his hunger, Roan still couldn't bring himself to eat anything that had once had bones, skin, a heart. Maybe in a day or two he'd feel differently, but he wasn't there yet.

They'd run out of bread two days earlier. The only water they'd had in the last day was gathered from cup-like leaves that had captured rainfall.

Roan hadn't even realized he'd been smiling. "I was just thinking about the future," he said.

"And you found that humorous?"

He pushed his blond locks away from his eyes. He needed a haircut, desperately. "As it stands today, aye. Quite humorous. It involves bark salads, leaf-clothes, and gnawing. Lots of gnawing. Oh, and a little chirping."

Gwen looked at him like he was mad—a look Roan was beginning to get used to—then pulled out a bundle of straight sticks and well-shaped rocks she was fashioning into additional arrows. She began to carve, the sound—*chook chook whick!*—obliterating the silence.

"I'm beginning to think this is a fool's mission," Roan said.

Gwen stopped carving. "Do you want to go back?" There was exasperation in her voice, although less than in the past. She didn't hate him quite as much as she used to, perhaps because he'd saved Gareth's life.

Even if Roan did want to go back, he didn't know if they could figure out east from west. Anyway, Roan didn't want to go back, that was certain. For the first time in his life he was moving forwards, not sideways or backways, and it felt good. He didn't know what would happen in the future, but he felt comfortable with it. He didn't know whether his tattooya—the three-leaf marking on his chest, known as the lifemark—really made him the Peacemaker that the mysterious Western Oracle had prophesied would come to do battle with Kings' Bane, but again, it didn't really matter. All that mattered was that he was doing more good than harm.

Step by step, he was moving toward a destiny that was his and his alone.

"I take your silence for a rejection," Gwen said. "Or have you gone mute?"

Roan huffed out a laugh. Strangely, despite the fact that the Orian known as Gwendolyn Storm had shot an arrow at him, punched him numerous times, and stabbed him in the gut, he was actually enjoying her company. They might have different views on the world, but they were connected by their skinmarks. Somehow. He remembered what she'd told him about the name her father said they used to use for the marks. *Fatemarks. Is this my fate?* he wondered.

"I was thinking about how I'm happy for the first time," Roan said.

Gwen's knife slid clumsily off the edge of the arrow shaft. "Happy? So you *have* gone mad then. Fan-bloody-tastic."

"I'm serious."

"We're stuck in the middle of the most horrible forest in all of the Four Kingdoms and you're happy?"

"You're a forest dweller, shouldn't you be at home in the woods?"

Gwen laughed without humor and went back to carving. "Not in *these* woods. My home is Ironwood. I feel connected to the trees there. These ones all seem to scowl at me."

Roan understood what she meant. More than once he swore the trees were giving him dirty looks. "I've heard legends about the Tangle. Are they true?"

"What legends?"

"About strange creatures made from shadow and light, sometimes as small as a pinhole and other times as large as the tallest trees."

"They're not legends," Gwen said, not too happily.

"So they exist?" Roan glanced about himself, half-expecting to be assaulted by one of the trees.

"The stories exaggerate, they always do. But these woods are inhabited by powerful creatures—at least they were. Nymphs and warlocks and sprites. Though that was a long time ago. The forest has grown thick, so nothing is certain anymore."

Roan didn't like the sound of any of those creatures, though at the same time he felt a strange desire to see one of them. "And that's why you don't feel comfortable here?"

Gwen nodded. "Home isn't always one place, but I know it's not *this* place."

Roan got that. "I was never happy in Calypso. Not truly. Sometimes I wondered about why I'd been born."

Gwen threw down her knife and it stuck in the ground. "You act as if the entire world conspires against you."

"Doesn't it?" Abandoned by his own parents, tormented by his Southron guardian who claimed to be trying to keep him safe, afflicted by the plague, attacked by dragons, captured by Gareth Ironclad, and then marched into battle. *How am I still alive?* Roan wondered. If not for his lifemark, he knew he wouldn't be. He'd be dead ten times over. Roan crinkled his brow. Then he remembered back in Ironwood when Gwen had shown him her treehouse. He remembered the poem carved into the gate.

Gwen said nothing, staring into the woods.

"Tell me about your bondmate, the one who wrote the words on your gate back in Ironwood," Roan said.

Gwen stiffened. "It doesn't matter."

"Those words mattered to you. They *matter* to you." He reached over and touched the back of her hand. For a moment, they both stared at their fingers. "I'm your friend, you can tell me."

And then Gwen pulled away and said, "I don't talk about this for a reason. Just because we are on the same path now doesn't mean we'll be on the same path forever. It doesn't mean we're friends. So let's just get through it, agreed?"

Roan felt a little stung by her words, but he said, "Agreed."

The Orian grabbed her knife and went back to shaping her arrows. *Chook chook whick!*

Suddenly, there was another sound. Gwen stopped carving, her head cocked to the side. Listening. Roan opened his mouth to say something like *What in the name of the ore monkeys of Ironwood was that?* but Gwen stopped him with a finger to her lips. *Don't move*, she mouthed. She mimed putting something in her mouth—food, Roan thought she meant—and then chewing it. She went from carver to hunter in an instant, silently regaining her feet, as graceful and lithe as an orecat, but far faster. Impossibly fast. Sometimes the way she moved—slow, purposeful—made Roan think of spilled ink dripping from a tabletop, while other times she was more like a lightning strike, but without the flash of light.

The sound came again, a rustle of leaves, the scrape of something picking its way through the undergrowth. Whatever it was, Roan hoped it was large enough to feed Gwen for a few days. With their luck, it was probably a tiny brown mouse.

Roan watched as she stole through the forest, her silver hair disappearing behind the old oak she'd marked with her knife a day earlier. A moment passed without a sound, and then another.

"Yah!" Roan heard her cry and then there was a shout. It wasn't Gwen's shout, and Roan had never heard an animal make a noise like that before. He leapt to his feet and rushed around the oak, crashing through the brambles with a complete lack of grace, especially compared to the smoothness and silence with which Gwen had just achieved the same path.

When he emerged into a small empty space, he skidded to a stop. "Gwen?" he said. "Who's that?"

Her back was to him, and she was on her knees, pinning someone to the ground. There was something familiar about his boots, which were fine-looking leather and marked with some kind of a sigil—

Roan froze, his breath catching. It couldn't be—could it?

Gwen rolled off of the person, who sat up. "Ho! Peacemaker! What say you?" Gareth Ironclad said.

Roan stuttered and stammered and then finally settled for "What are you doing here?"

"A pleasure to see you, as well," the prince said. *No*, Roan reminded himself. *Not prince. King. Gareth is the king now.*

The oddest thing was: they had that in common—being kings, or at least heirs to kingdoms—though only a handful of people knew it.

Even bedraggled and travel-worn, he looked unbearably handsome.

"I—you're here. How is that possible?" Roan asked. *And you're alive. Thank the gods.* Gareth was wearing light linens—apparently he'd been carrying his armor, which was now cast aside on the ground.

"All who grow up in Ironwood learn the great art of tracking," Gareth said. "Though you haven't made it easy, I must admit. Walking in circles the last three days? It was a confounding strategy. But it was quite effective. I only realized this morning that going backward was the best way to go forward, if you get my meaning."

Roan didn't. Roan didn't get anything at this point. "But why are you here?"

Gareth clambered to his feet and strode forward, until he was eye to eye with Roan.

And then he hugged him, picking him up off his feet before slamming him back down, slapping his back emphatically. Roan's heart skipped a beat.

Gareth stepped back and said, "To thank you. You know, for saving my life." He patted his chest, over his heart, which was wrapped with a thick dressing pulled tight diagonally from shoulder to hip.

"You followed us for half a fortnight to…thank me?"

"Not only. I'm coming with you, of course. Wherever it is you're going. To Knight's End, I'm guessing. My brother was adamant in his belief that you're a Loren and the rightful heir to the western throne, though I'm still skeptical on both of those points. I told him you're a Southron bastard with a rude mouth and a tendency to get himself in trouble."

Gwen cut in. "You're not coming. You're going back immediately. You are *the king* now. You can't just run off and follow us halfway across the Tangle and expect—"

"Halfway? By my estimation you're naught but a fraction of the way through. Not with all the walking in circles. I'm not going back, and I'm not the king. I relinquished that honor to my brother, Grian." Roan started to object, but Gareth spoke over him. "It was never supposed to be me. You understand that, aye? I don't want it."

Roan finally got a few words through. "This is our chance at peace, don't you see? At least between the east and west. If I can get to Knight's End and speak to my sister…we'll have a chance. You and I can change things."

Gareth put a hand on Roan's shoulder and, once again, his touch felt electric. Roan forced himself to remember the prince's reaction when they'd kissed. "You're the Peacemaker, whatever that means. Not me. I am the Shield who failed to shield my own brother. My people will shun me."

Roan shook his head, unwilling to believe it. "They won't. The easterners are reasonable, unlike everyone else in this mad land. You can explain what happened. They'll listen."

Gwen said, "He's right," and at first Roan thought she was agreeing with him, but then he realized she was talking to him. "You didn't grow up in the east, Roan. Neither the Orians nor the humans will respect a failed Shield. He cannot be king."

"So you would have him go west, toward his enemies?" Roan felt like shouting at the insanity of it all. He hadn't saved Gareth only to deliver him to the rival kingdom.

"No one will know it is me," Gareth said. "I mean, my handsomeness will certainly draw attention, but we can concoct a disguise to make me ugly if we must..."

Roan wasn't in the mood for japes. He turned away, a mix of emotions flooding him. Relief that his friend was alive. Anger and frustration that he had chosen this path. A flutter in his chest at being reunited so unexpectedly.

"You're a Loren," Gareth said. "You can protect me."

Roan shook his head. He wasn't anyone. It wasn't like he could just show up and expect to sit on the throne. It would take time, explanations. Wounds would need to be healed. And anyway, he didn't know if he wanted to be king. More than anything, he wanted to get to the Western Archives and search for information on the fatemarks. *I want to know who I am.* "I don't know," he finally said.

"Please. I have nowhere else to go."

Roan turned to find that Gareth's mask had fallen away for the second time since he'd known the prince. The first time was on the eve of the battle, when Gareth knew he would die. *The night I kissed him.* And now...now he looked lost and uncertain, a castaway from a ship in a sea of turbulent waters. He wanted to embrace him, to comfort him.

Still, the prince had put him through a lot in the short time since they'd met. Roan waited five long seconds, counting them off in his head, before responding. "Fine. You can come with us," he said.

The prince rushed forward and hugged Roan again, and then turned to hug Gwen, but she used the speed provided by her mark to dodge him easily.

"C'mon," Roan said. "We need your help to figure out how to get out of the Tangle."

"Excellent," Gareth said, his mood quickly changing back to normal. "Where are we going again?"

Twelve
The Northern Kingdom, Gearhärt
Annise Gäric

"What information could a knight possibly have about my uncle?" Annise asked.

Tarin said, "I love when you act all queenly."

Annise hid her amusement. "Just answer the question."

"Sir Metz said he wouldn't tell anyone but the king. We told him there is no king at present. But there is a queen. That's when he requested to see you."

"So you sent Sir Dietrich to deliver the message?" Annise almost felt bad for hitting him with the boot. Almost. "Send him in. Not Sir Dietrich; this Sir Metz fellow."

"As you wish." He untangled his body from hers, and she instantly missed his warmth. A flood of memories from their time spent camping in the snow rushed back. It felt like a lifetime ago, not a month.

Tarin donned his helmet, pulled his mesh face cover back up, and clamped down his eye mask before departing.

When he left, Annise attempted to make herself look more queen-like, smoothing her unruly dark hair and blotting the sweat from her face with a dry cloth. Her long blue dress was full of wrinkles from her *activities* with Tarin, but she did her best to press them out with her palms.

While she worked, she heard Tarin's heavy footsteps descending the stairs, and then the sound of them returning, along with other footsteps. Tarin entered first, followed by Sir Dietrich, who, to Annise's delight, was still walking slightly hunched over. The third to enter was a tall fellow with straw-like hair and rosy cheeks. His gait was stiff, almost as if he was marching. He was dressed in pristinely polished silver armor, and carrying a helmet under his arm. Presumably, the scabbard at his hip had once held a sword, but either Tarin or Dietrich had likely confiscated it before allowing him to enter the tavern. *Netta is making a lot of exceptions to her women-only policy these days*, Annise mused.

Bringing up the rear was Lady Zelda, her short pear-shaped stature out of place amongst the tall knights that preceded her. She was holding a bowl and spooning brown liquid and chunks of meat into her mouth. The aroma of the soup instantly made Annise's mouth water. Zelda winked at Annise before taking another bite.

"I am Queen Annise Gäric, rightful heir to the northern throne," Annise said to the newcomer. "My men tell me you have information on the Imposter King's army?" 'The Imposter King' had been Zelda's idea, a way of twisting public opinion in their favor. They'd paid three-score runners to disseminate the nickname for her uncle across the north, from Darrin to Castle Hill to Blackstone, and everywhere in between. They'd also sent a hundred streams with the nickname to the most populated towns in the realm. Annise wished she could've seen her uncle's face when he first caught wind of what the people were calling him.

"Yes," Sir Metz said, his voice a monotone. He stared at Annise, blinking occasionally.

Annise frowned, waiting for him to continue. He didn't.

"And?" she said.

"And what?" Sir Metz replied.

Perhaps this was what Tarin had meant when he referred to the knight as unusual. "And what information do you have?"

"The majority of Lord Griswold's army has been relocated to Blackstone, and will soon attack Knight's End."

"If that is all you know, then you have come a long way for nothing," Annise said. "That information reached us here a week ago via message stream."

"That is not all I know."

Again, Annise waited for him to continue, but he remained silent. She prodded once more. "What other information do you have?"

"About what?"

Annise almost screamed, her patience stretching to its limits. "About the Imposter King's army," Annise growled.

"I know the exact number of soldiers guarding Castle Hill. One hundred. Well, now there are only ninety-nine, because I escaped."

"Wait. You are a soldier in my uncle's army?"

"*Was* a soldier. I escaped, like I said."

"Why?"

"Because he's not the king."

"And you thought my brother was?"

"Yes."

"And now that you know he's not, and that the north is ruled by me, a queen, what will you do?"

"Serve you for the rest of my life or until you die, whichever comes sooner. It is the oath I took as a knight."

Annise almost laughed at his declaration. Luckily, she was able to hold back her amusement because his face was dead serious. "Then I shall consider it fortunate to have a loyal knight such as you in my service. What else do you know?"

"About what?"

Frozen hellfire and brimstone. She took a deep breath, trying to control her temper. "About the army at Castle Hill."

"Lord Griswold's potionmaster—"

"Darkspell," Annise said, crinkling her nose. The wrinkled old potionmaster had originally been appointed by her grandfather, King Wilhelm Gäric, the Undefeated King. Annise had always found the hunching bald man creepy, especially because of how he lurked in the shadows when he wasn't in his underground laboratory concocting elixirs and potions to treat anything from a headache to infertility.

"Yes. Darkspell," Sir Metz said, looking annoyed at being interrupted. "At the request of Lord Griswold, Darkspell has formulated a potion for the remaining soldiers at Castle Hill."

This time Annise was ready for a long pause, and quickly cut into it. "What does this potion do?"

"Creates monsters," Sir Metz said.

It was most definitely not the answer Annise was expecting. She opened her mouth, but had no idea how to respond.

Thankfully, Sir Dietrich did for her. "You've seen this?" Was it just her imagination, or was his voice slightly higher pitched than before?

"I've not only seen it, but experienced it," Sir Metz said.

Something occurred to Annise. "The soldiers turn into monsters? Is that what you mean?"

"Yes."

"What kind of monsters?"

"It depends on the soldier. All different kinds. They grow fangs, claws. They grow larger, bigger, faster."

She looked him up and down, searching for any evidence of such changes. "You don't look like a monster."

"The change is temporary."

Annise had no idea whether this man was to be trusted, or whether he might have been sent by her uncle to scare them away from a front-on assault to retake Castle Hill. She glanced at Zelda to see if she was just as skeptical. Her aunt, however, seemed to be ignoring the conversation entirely, throwing back the last dregs of her stew with voracious enthusiasm.

Sir Dietrich chimed in again. "How long does the change last?"

"It depends. Sometimes a day. Sometimes less. Sometimes more."

Tarin's question rumbled out, and it happened to be the very same one Annise was about to ask. "Why wouldn't he give the potion to his entire army at Blackstone? If it's as effective as you claim, they would be unstoppable. He could take Knight's End, and then nothing would be able to stop him from marching all the way to the Southron Gates."

"Lord Griswold is an arrogant man. He believes victory in the Bay of Bounty is a foregone conclusion. And he only has a

113

limited supply of the potion. Darkspell had to travel deep into the Hinterlands to obtain a key ingredient, some kind of brittle stone that must be ground up into a powder and mixed with underground water that has never been touched by sunlight. He only tested the potion once, on ten of us, to conserve the supply. Supposedly he has just enough remaining for a single use for all ninety-nine of his soldiers at Castle Hill."

"Can Darkspell make more?" Annise asked.

"Yes, given sufficient time. And assuming he can locate more of the stone."

Annise considered all of the information, and what it might mean if it was true. "Is there anything else?"

"Like what?" Sir Metz asked. He raised an eyebrow.

"Thank you, Sir. You may go. Sir Dietrich will help you locate the knights' quarters and equip you as needed."

"Thank you, Your Highness," Sir Metz said. He bowed stiffly, turned on his heel, and left, closing the door behind him.

"Go with him," Annise said to Sir Dietrich.

"Annise, if I may—"

"Though 'Annise' is a far cry better than 'Woman', it's still Queen or Your Highness to you, and no you may not. Now go." When Sir Dietrich didn't move, Annise said, "I have another boot, you know." Sir Dietrich scurried away.

Annise could see the amusement in Tarin's eyes. "You are a dangerous woman," he said.

"Of course she is," Zelda said. She finished licking the bowl clean. "She's related to me."

"What do you make of the knight?" Tarin asked.

Annise considered the question. "Like you said, he's unusual. But that doesn't make him a liar."

"Darkspell is a powerful potionmaster," Zelda said. "It is not beyond the realm of possibility that he could have developed such a formula."

"Then what do we do?" Annise said. "We can't stay in Gearhärt forever, hoping my uncle will fall down the steps like my father did."

"True," Zelda said. "How many soldiers do we have at last count?"

"Over eight-hundred, but more arrive every day." Tarin answered. Word of the true queen's claim on the crown had been flying around the kingdom by news bearers and messengers and streams, and hundreds were descending on Gearhärt to offer their support. Then again, she knew she needed to discount the number by half. Many of the newcomers were too young or too old, but Annise was in no position to deny them their right to fight for something they believed in. And yet, even if they were battle-hardened warriors, eight-hundred was a pitifully small number compared to the ten-thousand soldiers gathered at Blackstone.

"My uncle's army is focused on the west. When will we ever have another opportunity to lay siege to Castle Hill?"

"It could be years," Tarin admitted.

"But can a group of eight-hundred ragtag fighters defeat ninety-nine monsters?" Annise asked.

"You are the queen. You decide." Zelda's eyes glittered. Annise knew she'd been backed into the very corner she'd been avoiding ever since she declared herself queen.

She wished Archer were conscious. He'd always had a mind for strategy. She, on the other hand, had more of a mind for pummeling things until they could no longer get up.

"Tarin?" she said, hoping her paramour would bail her out.

"It is your choice, Your Highness."

She closed her eyes. *Archer might never wake up.* The moment she thought it, she knew what they had to do. "Begin making preparations. In a week's time, we ride for Castle Hill, monsters or not."

Thirteen
The Southern Empire, Phanes
Jai Jiroux

The chariot driver had been bound to Emperor Hoza. While it was possible the man had ridden back to Phanea and kept the secret of the Black Tear's attack on Garadia Mine, it was far likelier he was under strict instructions to report any unusual behavior directly to the emperor. And a rebel uprising was definitely in the category of unusual activity.

As Jai had explained all of this to Sonika Vaid, the Black Tear's leader, her frown had grown deeper and deeper. "We have little time to waste," she said.

Jai couldn't argue with that. He'd seen firsthand the merciless speed with which Hoza meted out his version of punishment. "We won't get far." His heart was in his gut. Without the element of stealth, their trek north would be impossible. His people were doomed.

"Perhaps we shouldn't go far," Shanti interjected. The Teran rebel was standing by a cart hitched to her horse, a speckled white mare. The cart was laden with barrels that Jai assumed were not filled with food or water. *Fireroot powder. Enough to blow a hole in a wall, if necessary.*

"Explain," Sonika said.

Shanti squinted out from the cover of her long, coppery lashes. Already the sun was bright and hot, and it would only get worse as it rose toward its apex. Shanti said, "He will expect us to head toward the sea, as that's the closest avenue of escape. However, when his men don't find us, they'll circle back and cut us off to the north."

"We can't exactly stay here either," Jai said. "If that's what you're suggesting."

She shook her head. "No. We have to go somewhere, but not so far that we'll be left in the open."

"You want us to hide?" Jai said. It was a good idea, but where could they hide thousands of slaves?

"Yes. In the Black Rocks. There are safe places there. We've used them before to regroup. Many times."

Jai had heard stories about men searching for treasure amongst the shadowy rocklands to the northeast of Garadia. Some said the rocks were stained black by hot tar that bubbled up from narrow chutes between the boulders. Others said the dark hue was the dried blood of all those who had died amongst the rocks. Occasionally the word *ghosts* was used to describe the perils one would face in the area. But the stories did have one thing in common: they all ended with the treasure hunters never being seen again. Jai pictured all five thousand of his people

118

vanishing from the face of the earth, falling down a hole so deep they'd never reach the bottom. "It's too dangerous," he said.

"Shanti's right," Sonika said. "It's less dangerous than the alternative. And anyway, we've mapped the Black Rocks. We know where to hide. You're just going to have to trust us."

Jai hadn't trusted anyone but the miners of Garadia for a long time, but then again the Black Tears were trusting him, too. "Fine. But we'll have to brush away our tracks. Even the Black Rocks won't be able to hide five thousand sets of footprints in the sand."

The Black Rocks had surrounded them hours earlier, and now seemed to crowd in closer, the paths narrowing, until they were forced to traverse the rocky canyons in single file, an endless train of marching travel-weary refugees.

At the head of the train rode the members of the Black Tears, occasionally consulting a scrap of parchment with scrawled words and lines on it—a map, supposedly, though to Jai it looked more like a child's drawing. How they knew to take the third path from the left or the descending trail over the ascending one would likely always be a mystery to him.

Before they'd departed from the mine, Jai had had the children collect stalks of brittle scrubgrass, which they tied into broom-like bundles, secured with bits of twine and string. The overeager children brought up the rear of the procession, walking backwards and sweeping away the thousands of tracks in the sand. To them it had become a game, and they counted the number of footprints they swept, until they were able to declare a winner. Jig had come in twelfth, which he claimed he was satisfied with, though Jai could see he'd wanted to be first. The wind had done the rest, the ever-changing desert landscape moving and shifting on whisper-soft feet.

Once they were firmly within the maze of the Black Rocks, they ceased the game and moved the kids back into line with their parents or other keepers.

As they walked, Jai prayed to any of the gods who would listen that he wasn't leading them all to their dooms.

Fortunately, the people were no strangers to hard work and harsh conditions, and they uttered no complaint, even as the sweltering sun pressed against their backs and slung daggers of heat upon their cheeks. The men tied their hair into piles atop their heads to stay cool, while the women used sheaves of the broad-leafed caragal plant to fan themselves. They didn't complain even when their inadequate shoes tore and fell away and their feet cracked and bled. Nor when several of the elders collapsed and couldn't get up. They took turns carrying those who still had life in them, while they were forced to bury others in shallow graves in the dust.

Vulzures circled overhead as they walked, and Jai hoped the carnivorous raptors wouldn't become a beacon to the emperor's searchers, who had likely reached Garadia by now. He also hoped the predatory beasts wouldn't attempt an attack on any of the smaller children, which they were known to do. Their talons were as long as fingers and their powerful wings could easily lift the weight of a human, carrying them for long distances, high into their nests built on the sides of the cliffs, where no escape or rescue would be possible.

Jai carried Axa for a long time, until his shoulders ached and his back was bent from the load. Sometimes he wondered why he was doing it. *I could leave him amongst the rocks for the vultures and none would care.*

I would care, he reminded himself, staggering onwards. *I will leave no living slave under my care behind—even one who used to be a master.*

Thankfully, Axa began stirring just as they rounded a curve in the path. Ahead of Jai, the Black Tears had stopped. A brackish river burbled up from a crack in the rocks, slid smoothly past, and then dove back underground. The horses lapped at the dark water greedily.

Jai gently eased the man to the ground, propping him up against a boulder. He cupped Axa's chin, tilted his head back, and dribbled what was left of his water down the man's throat. He choked once, but then swallowed the rest.

"Can you walk?" Jai asked.

The man blinked rapidly and seemed to have trouble focusing. Jai wondered how much of his old life he remembered. Did he know he was a monster? Did he care? Or was he a completely different person now that he wore the slave mark around his neck?

"I can walk," Axa said. "What is your command?"

"I make no command," Jai said.

"Then I shall sit here."

"Why?"

"Because I am aimless."

Jai knew the man wasn't being intentionally difficult. Vin Hoza had given him one command: *To obey me.* That's all he knew, that's all he was, the entirety of his wicked life boiled down to a single goal. Without that goal, he was, as he said, aimless.

Jai knew he couldn't give Axa free will like the others, at least not yet. It was too dangerous, for all of them. He didn't know if

121

Axa would revert back to the man he'd been. That monster. Still, he had to give him a chance.

"You will stay with the group. You will feed and water yourself. You will survive."

"Yes, Master."

"You will not call me master."

"Yes."

He remembered the mirror he'd found on the man. "Why do you have a mirror?" Jai asked.

"To remember myself," Axa said. "I knew what Emperor Hoza would do to me. I wanted to remember who I was."

"How did you get the mirror?"

"I asked for it, in prison. The guards thought it was funny, so they gave it to me. They laughed at me when I stared into it for hours."

Jai hadn't really known Master Axa when he worked for him at Garadia. He hadn't wanted to know his masters, especially not this one, who'd always been particularly vicious toward the slaves. And yet, the man had surprised him with his answers. But he had one more question:

"Did it work? Do you remember the man you used to be?"

"No," Axa said. There was no emotion in his voice.

Jai felt for the mirror, pulling it out and angling it toward Axa, so he could see his own face. "What do you see?"

"Nothing. I see nothing."

Frowning, Jai handed him back the mirror. He walked away, filling his water skin from the gritty stream before following the Black Tears deeper into the Black Rocks.

The sun had long disappeared behind the dark cliffs. Gusts of wind charged through the narrow paths, and Jai felt as if each one swallowed him and spit him out, only to swallow him again with the next blast. He was sweaty, his lips coated with fine grains of sand, his skin filmed with black rock dust.

"Here!" Sonika called from up ahead.

Rock walls rose up on all sides, leaving only a river-like strip of darkling sky above them. The trail was so narrow that the rough walls scraped their skin away, layer by layer. The horses barely fit through several sections, and required a push from behind to squeeze between the rocks.

Jai strode ahead, anxious to see where, exactly, they were.

Sonika and the other Tears were peering into a hole in the rock wall. Jai looked over their shoulders, but all he could see was nothingness, a darkness so complete it was the absence of light. "We cannot send the people in there."

Sonika twisted her head around. "We must. The way ahead is blocked."

Jai peered down the rocky trail, which seemed to go on forever. "How do you know?"

Shanti bumped him from the side. "Because we blocked it." She grinned, her teeth appearing whiter next to the absolute darkness. "Fireroot. My specialty."

Jai knew they couldn't go back, and even if he wanted to, it was a maze. In the dark, it would be impossible to navigate. Once again, he had to trust Sonika and her Tears to lead them to safety. "We should prepare torches," he said.

"We don't need them," Sonika said. She grabbed his hand roughly and pulled it into the inky darkness. She closed his fingers on a rope. "It's not far, and the rope will lead the way. There will be enough light there."

123

"There will be room for everyone?"

Sonika offered a half-smirk. "You're very protective of your people, aren't you?"

Memories of those he'd lost cycled through his mind. Old Hober with the gimpy leg, killed by a cave-in. Simona with the positive attitude, lost while exploring a new area of the mine. Wives. Husbands. Children. Friends. Countless souls.

My mother. Taken away when I was only a boy.

My father. Killed because of my mother.

When would it end?

He realized Sonika was still staring at him, awaiting an answer. "Yes. My people are all I have left."

"Well, now you have us, too."

Voices were starting to rise up behind them, murmurs of confusion along the procession, wondering why they'd stopped. Jai turned to face the curious faces immediately to his rear. "We must walk into the darkness in order to find the light," he said. "There is a rope on the side. Hold onto it. Don't let go until you're through. We'll be safe inside. Pass this message along."

As soon as he'd finished, he heard the others begin to recite his words back through the throng. Each time it was repeated, his words grew a little fainter, until they vanished completely.

"Your words carry the command of a master," Sonika said. The other Tears had already disappeared into the tunnel, leading their horses. "They obey you without question."

He didn't like what she was implying. "They obey because they choose to."

Sonika raised her hands in the air. "I meant no offense. You are no master, not like the others."

Then what am I? Jai wanted to ask. Instead he said, "I will stay here to help my people until they are all through.

"I expected nothing less," Sonika said, and then plunged into the dark.

Fourteen

The Western Kingdom, The Crimean Sea, Somewhere west of the Dead Isles
Grey Arris

The men on the ship treated Grey like a wart on one of their toes, sneering at him, purposely trying to trip him, laughing as he retched over the side of the rocking vessel.

It didn't help that he was useless as a deckhand. His right hand was a traitor, fumbling the ropes, weak, clumsy. *Why did I favor my left hand for so many years?* he often wondered, staring at the infected stump that ended just above where his wrist should've been. The Furies had taken much more than his hand—they'd taken his spirit and self-confidence.

For the most part, he managed to keep his head down and go about his work. He couldn't wait to be off the junker, even if it meant coming face to face with the Fury who'd cut off his hand.

He knew it would all be worth it if he found his sister.

Most of the time, the only job he could do was scrubbing the deck. He had a love-hate relationship with his scrub brush. In a way, the only hours he enjoyed while on the boat were when he could lose himself in his thoughts, scrubbing the rough wood over and over again, the sun filtering through the clouds and warming his skin. It was the time he could think of his sister, Shae, picture her face in his mind's eye, make her real. Make her alive. And yet he hated the scrubbing, because afterwards his muscles would scream at him, his back aching, his knees bruised, his arm as limp as a string of boiled cabbage leaves. And that's when Shae would be taken all over again, by the furia.

For days and days at sea, he'd wracked his brain for answers, trying to figure out why the holy warriors would kidnap his sister. She bore a sinmark, after all, and should've been killed immediately. That was the way of the west. Of course, Grey was glad the fierce red-haired women had chosen to be merciful, but that didn't change the fact that they could be doing *worse* things to her, torturing or tormenting or—

He jammed his eyes shut, biting his lip, trying to erase the awful thoughts from his head.

He opened his eyes. The spot he'd just finished polishing was so clean he could see a faint reflection of himself in it, which, of course, only made the rest of the wooden planks look all the dirtier. His dark hair was long and messy, his eyes tired blue orbs, his cheeks and chin rough with a fortnight's worth of unshaven stubble. "What do they want with you, Shae?" he whispered to his reflection.

"Who's Shae?" a voice said, startling him away from thoughts of his sister.

A set of warm brown eyes peered at him from behind an old fish barrel. The girl's skin was naturally dark, her hair a series of salt-crusted ringlets. She was young, like Grey, perhaps fifteen or sixteen. Grey thought he'd seen everyone on the small ship, but he had most definitely not seen this girl. In fact, she was the first member of the fairer sex he'd seen since they'd sailed from the walled city of Talis.

Grey said nothing, looking away from her and back down at the decks. Whoever this girl was, she was not part of his plan to find his sister.

"Shae's a pretty name. Was she your lover?"

Grey cringed. A bold question. *Does this girl have no filter?* "She is no one. I was just speaking nonsense."

She took the denial in stride, pointing at his left arm. "That doesn't look good. It's infected."

"I know."

"I could help you. I've tended some of the men's wounds before."

Grey stared at the stump, which was once again leaking grayish-green liquid through the bandages. He knew he needed help, or he would lose the rest of his arm. He thought maybe it was already too late. "Thank you."

"Your name is Grey, right?"

Grey honestly didn't know anymore. When he'd been confident to a fault, bordering on arrogant, a smug thief who'd seduced a princess, the name Grease Jolly had felt right. When he lost his hand and his sister and Princess Rhea all in one foul swoop, he knew he would never be that slick city boy again. Did that make him Grey Arris again? Somehow he didn't feel worthy of that name either.

"I guess," he said, biting his tongue. Why was he answering her questions?

"That's a strange answer to a simple question."

"It's the only one I've got."

She closed one eye, as if contemplating him under a magnifying glass, and then nodded to herself. "Aye, you're Grey all right. Did you know the other men mock you mercilessly, even when you're not around?"

Her question was so direct that he almost laughed. As if he wouldn't know. He nodded. "It seems I am the butt of many an ill joke on this voyage."

The girl smiled. "I suppose I should thank you then. You've given me a reprieve."

"How do you figure?"

"They've been so focused on mocking you they've forgotten to mock me!"

Now Grey really did laugh. "I am glad I've served a purpose of sorts. Well, other than cleaning the same decks again and again."

Her smile broadened. "I'm Kyla. Daughter of the captain."

Grey's mouth gaped open as he considered her more closely. By his estimation, this girl looked nothing like the gray-whiskered Captain Smithers, though their skin was a similar shade. "I wouldn't think the sailors would mock the daughter of their captain. Not if they wanted to keep their employment."

Her smile faded. "My father is the worst of all. The last eight months have been...hard."

Grey cocked his head to the side. What was different about the last eight months? She shifted slightly, grimacing, and more of her body was exposed from behind the barrel. Oh. *Oh.* Though she was a small girl with a small frame, her belly was so round and protruding she might've had a small barrel tucked under her gray frock. She was so big with child she looked ready to pop at any moment.

"But who is the father?" Grey asked. As soon as the question left his lips, he knew it was rude.

"'Tis a very good question," a booming voice answered. "But mayhaps ye shuldn't ask the lyin' whore-child."

Grey whipped around. Captain Smithers stood over him, holding a long wooden staff he never seemed to be without. Grey flinched back when the captain feigned a blow and then laughed.

The captain turned his attention to his daughter. "Girl, why are ye above decks? I thought I made meself clear ye were not to parade yerself around like a festival sideshow."

The girl's—Kyla's—statement came back to Grey: *My father is the worst of all.* "She was only making conversation," Grey said. "No trouble at all. I'll just be on my way. Got more decks to clean before the day is done." Awkwardly, he tried to push himself to his feet with one hand; he still hadn't quite gotten the hang of it. The captain stuck his staff between Grey's legs and he toppled over, banging his knee and shoulder, crying out in pain.

Suddenly, Smithers' face was right next to Grey's, so close he could see the tobacco stains between the captain's teeth. "Don' speak to me daughter agin, ye hear?"

"Father," Kyla said, but he shoved her away.

Grey didn't want to speak to her again, especially not if it made trouble for both of them. "Yes, Captain."

"Aye, Captain!" Smithers roared.

"Aye, Captain," Grey repeated.

"And ye stay below decks or I'll chain ye to the brig!" he hollered at Kyla, stomping over to her and grabbing her by the hair. She cried out as he pulled her away.

Grey just watched, hating himself more and more for not helping the poor pregnant girl. Then again, maybe she'd created her own problems, just as he had, and now she had to live with her decisions. Still, he felt sorry for her, and wished he could do something.

But he couldn't risk it. If he helped her now, the captain might decide he didn't need Grey to scrub the decks anymore. And then Shae would have no one to come and find her.

So he gritted his teeth, breathed deeply, and went back to scrubbing, until the sun turned red on the horizon, the waters darkened, and Grey's palm was so raw it burned.

It had been three days since the incident with the captain's daughter. Already, the memory had grown fuzzy around the edges, falling into the category of *Things That Don't Matter.*

Right? This voyage was all about finding his sister. And anyway, he had no right to intercede in relations between father and daughter.

And yet every time Kyla's memory began to fade, Grey would find himself thinking about the way her belly had protruded like a ripe melon, how she'd been the first one on the ship to smile at him, to ask about his sister, to seem to *care.* Then he remembered the way she'd cried out in pain as her father dragged her away by the hair, and how he'd ignored it, pretended it wasn't happening.

He realized he was no longer scrubbing the deck, but banging the wooden back of the brush against it. *Thud! Thud! Thud!*

"Oi! Cripple! Keep it down, will you!" one of the seamen hollered. He was doing real work, lashing the sails to a pole, angling the billowing canvas so it would catch the wind just right. Helping to move the ship closer to where his sister had supposedly gone, to the Dead Isles.

Grey muttered an apology and went back to scrubbing.

His infected stump was getting worse, throbbing and stinging.

Another three days passed before he saw Kyla again. He was passing by the captain's quarters, heading for the bunk rooms, when the door flew open with a bang. "Don' test me, girl!" the captain shouted.

Inside, someone was crying, and Grey could just make out a round form hunched on the floor, her face covered by her hands.

As if Grey didn't exist, the captain slammed the door shut and stormed past, muttering, "Her ma wuld roll over in her grave…aye she wuld…"

Grey stood stock still for a moment, listening to the muffled sobbing. Slowly, he raised the heel of his hand to his head, pressing it into his skull. *Keep going. Just keep going. Not your problem. Not your fight.*

He took a step away, and then stopped. *Godsdammit. I must be the biggest fool in the Four Kingdoms…*

He turned and opened the door, hissing, "Kyla," before stepping inside.

The girl's crying stopped and she turned, her wet eyes peering between curled locks of brown hair. Her hands immediately went to her belly, rubbing it through her clothes. It was like some kind of an instinct. "Grey?" she said.

"I—I wanted—I wanted to—" Why couldn't he get the words out?

Don' speak to me daughter agin, ye hear?

If he finished this sentence, was he risking his sister's life? If the captain found him in his quarters now, Grey knew it wouldn't matter either way. He'd already crossed a line, and he might as well take advantage of it.

"I wanted to make sure you were unhurt."

"You did?"

"Aye."

"Thank you. And I'm not hurt. He didn't touch me, not with his hands. Only with his words."

"What words?"

"Whore. Charlatan. No good lass."

Grey was sorry he'd asked, though he was puzzled by one of the insults. "Why charlatan?"

The girl flinched, as if the word was a wasp that had stung her cheeks. "He says I'm no longer his daughter, that I'm an imposter, a fraud. That his daughter died when my mother…"

She blinked away tears, dashing the few that escaped her eyes with the back of her hand. "Thank you for coming here, Grey, but you should go. If he finds you talking to me again…he will think the worst."

What did she mean? What was the worst? It dawned on him. Oh. Gods. He would never. She was younger than him, and eight months pregnant, and—

"If you ever need anything, come find me," he said.

He left, closing the door behind him. He stood there for a moment, breathing, just breathing, mentally berating himself for making such a foolish offer.

Thankfully, another week passed without him seeing the captain's daughter. *Perhaps she forgot about what I said, or didn't take it seriously. Perhaps she isn't a fool like me. Or maybe she just doesn't need me.*

He tried to forget about her, cleaning out his wound thrice a day, but it didn't seem to make a difference. Pus kept leaking out. It was hurting more and more each day, and he was finding it harder to perform his scrubbing duties.

Then, one day when he'd finished his work, he was looking over the bow of the ship at the endless sea of blue, gnawing on a hunk of crusty brown bread and nibbling on pickled sardines. The sea was a mirror, as calm and glassy as he'd ever seen it. The sky, the clouds, and the sun were all reflected in the blue-gray waters, and Grey could almost imagine that if he jumped, he might fall either up or down, the probability in equal proportion, like the flip of a golden coin, tumbling end over end, never landing. He was just contemplating what that might mean, when he heard a voice. "Psst! Grey!"

At first he couldn't figure out where the whisper was coming from. He looked up, at the crow's nest, but his gaze only drew a well-aimed wad of spit from the watchman in the tower.

As he wiped the spittle from his cheek with his shirtsleeve, a melodious giggle arose, not from above but from below. He stared down into the churning white-capped ocean, wondering whether the infection in his stump had traveled to his brain, addling his mind.

"No, you buffoon! Down here!"

Grey leaned over further, his gaze traveling down the curving wooden planks of the barnacle-riddled bow, to the figurehead at the front, a rusting sea-green statue of a naked woman with a long fishtail.

And perched atop the statue's head, her legs crossed underneath her, was Kyla, the wind whipping through her curls, billowing her gray frock all around her, revealing a large portion of her smooth brown thighs.

Grey immediately feared for her. Being big with child, surely her balance would be thrown off. At any moment she could topple over, and then she'd be gone, lost beneath the waves. And yet she seemed perfectly at ease, both hands resting lightly against the side of the ship.

"Give me your hand," Grey said, reaching down. "I'll help you back on deck."

"Why did you offer to help me?" Kyla asked.

Grey didn't have an answer, because he didn't truly know himself, but he replied, "I'll tell you after you're safe on deck."

"I like it better down here. Down here I don't have to be me."

The words were like knives piercing Grey's chest. Not because of how awful they were, but because he understood them. It was why he'd changed his name and disappeared into a big city like Knight's End. To start over. To be someone else.

"What happened to your mother?" Grey asked. Again, the words were out of his mouth before he could consider whether it was rude of him to ask such a personal question.

Kyla looked away, her stare trained out at sea as the wind whipped her hair and dress around her. Grey was sorry he'd asked, fearing he'd made her cry.

But when she looked back up at him, her eyes were dry, her expression fierce. "She died and my father died with her."

Before he could consider how to respond, or if he should respond, she clambered over the side of the statue, vanishing into a hole in the hull.

Grey and his family—his ma, his da, and Shae—were living in Restor at the time, a traveler's town on the western road, halfway from the Bridge of Triumph to Knight's End. One day the Furies themselves rode through the town, their red robes flowing behind them, their long silver swords flashing. A young boy, Grey was enamored by their energy, how they seemed to command attention from all who looked upon them.

His parents were scared. "Get inside," they said to Grey and Shae. "Hurry."

They peeked through the windows as the Furies went house to house, looking for something...or someone. Five houses away. Four. They were carrying torches, though it was not yet dark.

"Son," Grey's da said to him. "Protect your sister above all else."

"I will, Father," Grey said, although he didn't really understand what was happening.

"We need to show you something," his ma said, using tongs to extract an ember from the hearth. "Give me your hand, Shae."

Shae didn't hesitate. At only five, she already wasn't scared of anything. Her mother brought the ember close to the palm of her tiny hand, which immediately bloomed with golden light. A strange shape took form, the lines curling into a crown and then extending to a spindle, which was broken at the end.

His sister's eyes were huge as she stared at the glowing mark. Grey felt a shiver of fear race through him. No! *he wanted to scream.* Not her. Why her? *In that moment he knew exactly what sort of people the Furies were looking for. They called those that bore sinmarks demons, and now Grey knew his sister was one of them.*

But he didn't see it that way. She was a pure spirit, his best friend. And she was only a child, while he'd had his eighth name day and was becoming a man grown. His da's words pulsed through his skull. Protect your sister above all else...all else...else...

"We have to leave," Grey said, suddenly understanding.

"Yes." His ma nodded, tears shimmering in her eyes. That's when Grey knew she wasn't coming with them.

"Through the back window," his da said. "We'll follow just behind you."

It was the only lie his da ever told him.

The only thing that followed them was the sound of the Furies breaking down their door and the shouts of a struggle. And then nothing.

Grey awoke screaming, thrashing at the knotted sheets tangled around his body. His stump was pounding like a blacksmith's hammer on an anvil. A hand burst through the dark, snapping across his face. "Shut yer crippled trap!" a voice said. "Some o' us are tryin' to sleep." It was one of the deckhands, leaning over the top bunk.

Grey stopped shouting before the sailor chose to hit him again. "Sorry," he muttered. "I need some air."

He untangled himself from the sheets, balling them up and stuffing them next to his pillow. Then he stumbled above decks, where the salty ocean air immediately stung his nostrils. He stared up at the sky, which was clear and dark, speckled with more stars than he'd ever seen in his life. He wondered whether the western belief in the seventh heaven was real, and if so, whether his parents were there now, looking down on him from the red, green, and gold stars.

He hoped not; because if so, they would know of his failures, his weaknesses. They would know that his only friend was a pregnant girl and that he'd broken his promise and been unable to protect Shae.

The longer he stared at the night sky, the more the stars seemed to form shapes, most of which were random patterns and designs, until he saw it: a mark. A golden crown, connected to a shiny, narrow spindle, which extended outwards...

Though he'd only seen it once, the memory of Shae's mark was etched in his mind forever. Her mark ended partway along the spindle, almost as if it had been cut off before it could be finished.

To this day, neither Grey nor Shae knew what power her mark gave her, a fact that had never really bothered him until now.

But now he could see the rest of the mark, formed by the stars above.

The spindle continued further, ending when a rectangular piece stuck from the bottom. Grey's breath hung in the air, his unblinking eyes stinging. The mark wasn't a crown and spindle at all. No.

It was a key.

A key for what?

I'm just being a fool, like usual, Grey thought as he walked along the deck. He'd finished his work for the day and was too tired to be hungry. And too hungry to be tired. It was certainly one or the other.

But neither hunger nor weariness mattered right now. All that mattered was what he'd seen in the stars.

I saw nothing, he reminded himself. *I'm no star-reader. Shae's mark could be a key, but it could also be some kind of a scepter, or a hairpin, or a pointless trinket given to a child.*

And yet he couldn't get the key out of his mind, how it sparkled with possibility.

A scream shattered what was left of the day, freezing Grey in his tracks. It had sounded like a girl's scream, and there was only one girl Grey knew of on the ship.

Kyla.

The scream had been muffled by wood and distance, arising from somewhere below decks. Grey rushed toward the stairs, jostling for position amongst the other seamen, who were doing the same thing. "Watch it, cripple!" one of them warned.

The scream fell away, and now there was a lower, different sound, somewhere between a groan and moan. Grey tried to push through the men, who were packed shoulder to shoulder.

"Pathetic girl," someone said.

"Wrath is punishing her for her sins," another decided.

Grey's heart was in his throat, but still he fought his way forward. Some of the men were already turning around and heading back up top, even before the captain's booming voice rang out. "Let this be a lesson to ye all: Yer sins will always bury ye in the end. Now move along. Leave the whore-child be."

More men turned, elbowing and shouldering Grey as they passed, but he barely felt the hits.

And then, abruptly, he was alone in the narrow corridor, staring into the captain's quarters. The captain's frame filled the doorway, but Grey was looking past him, through the narrow gap. The first thing he noticed was Kyla, collapsed on the floor. The strange guttural, almost animal-like noise was coming from her.

The second thing he noticed was all the blood.

Fifteen
Unknown Location
The Beggar

He awoke to whispers, which were, at first, as unascertainable as the sound of the wind, but which slowly came into focus:

"Four dead. Four dead. Four left. Four. Only four. Then peace. Death, then peace. My fate. Mine alone. Mine mine mine minemineminemineminemine SILENCE!"

The last word was the roar of a lion, echoing through the darkness and making the Beggar flinch.

And then: "Are you awake?"

The Beggar said nothing, wracking his brain for anything that might explain his current plight. It all came back to him in a rush: being captured by the Empire; Empress Sandes coming to him, plotting to use his plague against her enemies; and then the unexpected appearance of the shadowy boy, who grabbed him, who pushed him, who made him *kill her.*

Oh gods, what have I done? the Beggar thought. But it wasn't a thought, he'd spoken the words aloud.

"Not you," the voice said. "Me. You were just a tool. I am the Kings' Bane. But you can help me."

"How?" The question came out before he could stop it.

The bearer of the voice shuffled closer. The Beggar blinked, his eyes adjusting to the murk, which was turning gray. He was garbed in a thick cloth—*the boy's cloak,* he remembered. He could just make out the curve of a hairless, pale scalp and the young boy attached to it. The boy seemed to be shaking slightly, his entire body trembling.

"Don't come any closer," the Beggar said. "I'm dangerous."

Bane ignored his warning and moved closer still. "You're not the dangerous one," he hissed. "The kings and queens and emperors and empresses are the dangerous ones. Their pointless wars result in thousands of deaths. I only want eight, and then the violence can stop. We can have peace."

"But how do you choose?" The Beggar had never been able to choose. Death came to him like flies on feces.

"The ruler in each kingdom must die, as well as their true heir."

The Beggar frowned in the dark, rocking his body to sit up. Pale orbs stared at him, too close for comfort. He crab-walked back three paces. "But what if the ruler isn't a warmonger? Or what if their heir wants peace?"

"They are all warmongers!" Bane screamed.

The Beggar was so shocked by the force of the outburst that he fell backwards. "What do you want from me?"

Bane staggered and then fell to his knees, shaking even harder. He breathed deeply for a few moments, as if trying to gather his strength before responding. "I want you to be my partner. I want you to be my friend." The boy's tone had changed. He sounded so...young. So innocent. Not like the killer he was. Then again, the Beggar heard a bit of himself in the boy. Bane crawled closer, still shaking. "I don't fear you like the others. We could be brothers. On my own, I can cleanse the kingdom of those who would destroy it, but it will be a slow process. I grow weak each time I use my powers. Exhausted. I sleep for days, sometimes weeks. But you...if you help me it will change everything. Peace will dawn upon the Four Kingdoms before winter comes. Here. Take my hand."

The Beggar shrank back from the ghostlike fingers that darted through the gloom. "No. You'll die." Wait. Wait. Perhaps that would be best. Yes. He could kill this murderous boy and then die himself. Would that redeem him? *No*, he knew, but still, it would be better.

"I'm wearing gloves. Thick ones." The gloved hand grabbed his before he could squirm away. The fingers squeezed, and Bane's face eased closer, until he could feel the boy's breath on his face. "Now we are one in purpose. Swear it."

"I—I—" Even through the gloves, Bane's hand felt warm in his. The human contact was like nothing he'd ever felt. For once, there was no fear, no shame, no regret. Just a connection between two people. Two would-be strangers. Was this boy really seeking peace? And if so, could he truly be a part of something so important, so noble? He had nothing left to live for; except perhaps this. "I swear it," he said.

"On what do you swear?"

The Beggar didn't worship the gods, not really. He had no friends, no possessions. But he had a past. He'd once had a family. A mother. A father. An aunt. A name. "I swear on my mother's memory."

"Who was she?" Bane asked.

An enormous chasm opened up in his chest, sucking everything into it. His heart. His soul. His past, his present, but maybe not his future. "The first person I killed," he said.

It was the first time he'd said the truth out loud.

It was warm and dark and quiet. Bane was sleeping, his steady exhalations as soothing as a mother's lullaby. And yet the Beggar didn't feel tired at all.

His mind was moving too fast, like thunder rolling over the open water. Occasionally lightning flashed, splitting his head in two.

Two more deaths, and then it would be over. That was one option. *Touch Bane and then kill yourself.* Quick. Easy. In the dark, he crept toward the first person to ever call him friend, brother. The first one to consider his mark a talent rather than a curse.

If you help me it will change everything...

Peace will dawn upon the Four Kingdoms before winter comes...

He stopped. He'd sworn on his mother's memory that he would help Bane. And the boy's cause was important, grand, real. Peace. It was true: The Four Kingdoms were never going to stop fighting. Thousands more would die. What if he could help stop it? What if he could do something good for once in his life?

But did killing really bring about peace? Shouldn't it be the opposite?

His hand hovered over Bane's face. He could feel the plague humming along the surface of his skin, probing, searching, hungry for another victim. Hungry for human flesh and blood and bone to feast on.

Just touch him. Simple. And then be free.

Closer, closer.

End him. End him! END HIM!

A tremor shook his hand and he almost brushed Bane's cheek, his fingers so close he could feel the heat coming off the boy's pale skin.

He pulled away, breathing heavily, shivering despite the warmth. No, he wouldn't kill his only friend. His new brother. "Where are we going?" he said to himself. "What are we doing?"

Bane shifted in his sleep, but his eyes remained closed. His lips parted. "The Southron Gates," he murmured. "We have an army to infect."

Sixteen

The Southern Empire, Calyp
Raven Sandes

The arena was nestled between the three pyramids. At the apex of each pyramid a single blue eye was painted, and seemed to stare down on the gathering, like silent god-like spectators. They represented the three most powerful Southron deities, Aero—the sky goddess—Ocea—the sea god—and Crag—goddess of the land.

The arena itself was a circle of empty dust ringed by a tall, thick wall meant to keep the action in a confined area and protect the Calypsians, who sat on the stone steps that rose a hundred high in every direction. Thousands had thronged to the arena earlier that morning. It had been eight years since the rule of Calyp had been decided in the arena, and they weren't about to miss it.

Now the sun rose high and hot overhead, and most of the spectators wore hooded cloaks to keep the heat off of their skin, fanning themselves with thick sheaves of parchment or caragal leaves. They were growing antsy, and most were ready for blood.

Raven stood in the exact center of the arena with the shiva, waiting. It was just like Fire to be late, forcing her to look like the fool, standing under the sweltering glare of the sun goddess, Surai. Beneath Raven's black battle leathers, she sweated profusely.

Last night they were sisters in grief, today they were rivals in battle.

A cheer rose up as a figure rode from one of the gates forged into the wall. Fire was garbed in her battle leathers, painted red with flames. Her crimson hair was spiked to a point atop her head. She raised her hand in the air, letting tendrils of flame stretch up to the tip of her sword. The enormous guanik she rode didn't even flinch—he was her usual mount and was used to her fiery antics.

Gods, Raven thought. *If the battle could be won before it was fought, I'd be waving a white flag.*

Fire did a full lap around the arena, milking the crowd for all it was worth—and it was worth quite a lot by the sounds of their roars and whistles. Even if Raven won, they'd clamor for Fire afterwards.

Raven began clapping slowly as her sister finally approached. "Good show, sister," she said.

"I'm just giving our people what they want," Fire said. "Perhaps you should try it yourself."

"You think they want war? You think they want to die in the desert?"

"I think they want to be strong. I can show them the way."

147

Raven shook her head. There was no arguing with Fire, and anyway, there was no point. Only one of them would rule, and today's spectacle would decide whom.

"You can still retreat with grace," Fire said with a smirk. She coaxed her guanik right up to Raven, until their noses were practically touching. The beast opened its mouth to reveal several sets of razor sharp teeth. It roared with such force that Raven's braided hair shifted behind her.

Raven didn't move, refusing to let her sister get the best of her in front of her people. "So can you," she said into the guanik's mouth.

The reptilian creature snapped at her, but then backed away upon command from its rider. Fire laughed. "You are a worthy opponent, sister, but it won't change the result. I shall be empress, and you shall obey me."

Leaving Raven with that to chew on, Fire turned away as the shiva raised a hand to silence the crowd. The raucous applause ceased, and the multitude of voices died down to a muted rumble. Before the shiva could begin the ceremony, Fire's guanik roared once more, which made the audience flare up in pockets of excitement.

Raven knew it was no accident. Nothing her sister did was an accident.

The shiva finally spoke. "On this day in the 532nd year since the Crimean invaders reached our western shores, the rule of Calyp shall be decided in combat." More cheers, the excitement palpable, crackling like lightning. "The contest shall be between Raven Sandes, the First Daughter of our beloved Empress Sun Sandes, and Fire Sandes, the Second Daughter. May the worthiest Sandes emerge the victor!"

The crowd whipped itself into a frenzy. Fire riled them up further by tossing her fiery sword from one hand to the other. Raven just stood there, watching it all, waiting for the shiva to clear the field of battle. He climbed a ladder over the wall, and then pulled it up behind him. Once the battle began, none would be able to escape the dust bowl until it was over.

Fire turned toward her. Her guanik pawed in the dirt.

Raven said, "You would fight mounted while I am on foot? A cowardly move, sister."

"Victory is victory," Fire said, and then she charged.

Raven didn't move, watching as the powerful beast galloped closer and closer, its scaly skin undulating as its muscles flexed and released. Fire's jaw was set, her blade at the ready. Raven had seen that look of determination many times in training, and rarely did she lose.

Get ready, Raven thought.

The guanik raced toward her and Fire swung her blade. At the last possible moment, Raven dove to the side. She felt the wind from the beast's body as it swept past, felt the heat of her sister's sword as it narrowly missed her leather-padded shoulder.

She rolled once, letting her momentum carry her back to her feet. Drawing her own weapon, a black, barbed whip, she whirled around to follow her sister's guanik as it skidded, turned, and charged once more.

That's when she felt the heat on the back of her neck. She grabbed her braid and snuffed out the fire with her fingers, but she'd already lost almost a quarter of her hair from Fire's flaming sword. Her hand was burned and charred black, but Raven forced herself to ignore the pain throbbing in her palm.

She snapped her whip with deadly precision, letting it uncoil to its full length, wrapping around the guanik's two front legs.

With a jerk of her wrist, she yanked it back as hard as she could. When the barbs sank deep into the huge creature's flesh, its momentum was almost enough to rip Raven's shoulder from its socket, but she managed to dig her feet into the dirt and hang on.

The creature's legs snapped together, and the guanik stumbled, tripped, and fell, howling headfirst into the dirt. Fire spun in the air, tucking into a somersault, still clutching her sword, which rotated in a fiery arc.

With incredible grace, she landed lithely on her feet, grinning. "Well played, dear sister. It seems we are on equal footing once more."

The guanik groaned, and Raven felt bad for the poor beast. She tossed her whip aside. It would take time and effort to unbury the barbs from the reptile's skin and muscle. Fortunately, she was prepared, uncoiling another whip from her belt. She had two others, if necessary.

As the sisters faced each other, the shiva stood high on the wall and shouted, "Prepare!" It was the standard command for such an event, and basically meant *Get ready for something that's going to try to kill you.* Although the main goal of this event was to defeat her sister, it wouldn't be just her she was fighting. No. Not even close.

Beneath their feet, metal clanked as spiked chains emerged from where they'd been hidden beneath the dust. Raven danced back, but she was too slow—one of the spikes grazed her leg, tearing through her leathers and drawing a thin line of blood across her calf. Pain shot through her, but it was a mere flesh wound—she would survive to fight on.

Fire had avoided the initial chain trap, but had gone in the wrong direction—now the moving chains had her surrounded, tightening their spiked noose as she whirled around, trying to find an exit where there was none.

Raven said, "Do you submit?"

Fire laughed, which didn't surprise Raven one bit. Her sister hated to lose more than anything else. Nothing but death or unconsciousness would end this contest if Raven were to win.

The chains whipped closer, their spikes narrowly missing Fire's face. She ducked one, jumped another, and then did a front handspring away from the danger. Defeated, the chains were drawn back across the field of battle by whomever was controlling them, and settled against the wall.

A dull roar of appreciation arose from the audience.

Raven slung her whip forward, but Fire made no effort to avoid it. Reaching the end of its length, the barbed end cracked a mere fingerbreadth in front of Fire's face before retreating. *Of course*, Raven mused, *Fire knows exactly how long each of my whips are. I'll have to be more creative.*

The next time she slung her whip, she released its handle, letting it slither through the air like a flying snake. Fire recognized the change in tactic a moment too late, but managed to turn her head and take the blow in the shoulder, the barbs sinking deep into her leather guard, and also catching a bit of unprotected skin. To her credit, she didn't cry out, only gritted her teeth and ripped the whip away, blood dripping from the barbs as she tossed it to the dust. "Clever," she growled.

Raven casually yanked out her third whip, hoping she wouldn't need the fourth. Fire circled toward the left, slowly shifting her flaming sword from side to side.

"Prepare!" the shiva yelled again.

One of the heavy iron gates groaned as it was cranked open. For a split-second, nothing happened, both sisters training one eye on each other and the other on the deep shadows inside the wall.

With a hundred roars, a herd of guanik poured from the opening, spreading across the arena as they fled some hidden enemy. Raven lost sight of Fire as the huge reptiles swerved around them, brushing past on all sides. One collided with her shoulder, knocking her over and then barely missing her with its flat, clawed feet. She fought back to a standing position just in time to see that another beast was bearing down on her. This one wouldn't miss.

There was only one option.

She jumped, reaching out with both arms as the animal slammed into her. It squealed as the whip barbs sunk into its neck. Raven clutched with her opposite hand on the other side, digging her own nails into its flesh. The frightened guanik snapped at her, but couldn't quite reach, even with its long neck.

Kicking out, she clambered around its neck and straddled it. She was now above the fray, which gave her the chance to look for Fire. Her eyes darted back and forth, strafing the stampede, which was beginning to thin out, but there was no sign of her sister. She spotted a cluster of fallen guanik, which were in obvious pain, grunting and snapping their jaws at the air. Smoke curled from the midst of them, and the air held the distinct smell of burning flesh.

A sword burst from the mound of reptiles, flames dancing along its tip. It was soon followed by a hand and then an arm, and then the whole of Fire, who was covered in green guanik blood and bits of charred flesh and scales.

If the crowd was loud before, they reached a crescendo now. Calypsians, who, of course, made annual trips to the fighting pits of Zune to watch the sport of death, thrived on violence and battle as much as their Phanecian enemies to the west.

Fire leapt from the top of the pile of dead guanik, landing in a crouch in front of Raven and the beast she was now riding. The smell alone was enough to make Raven ill, but she maintained a straight face. "You always have to make an entrance," she said.

"They got in my way," Fire shot back.

What a waste of guanik, Raven thought.

That's when the real challenge came: the thing the reptiles had been running from.

Long, black, hairy legs scurried from the gate. The arach was so large it was forced to duck its head before emerging into the sunlight. All twelve of its eyes squinted for a few seconds, adjusting to the change.

Gods. Why does it have to be an arach? Raven thought. She hated all spiders, both the small ones and the big ones. This was most definitely a big one, its bulbous head towering over them, staring down with all its dark, beady eyes. Its eight legs were the width and height of trees, ending in blade-like feet that could skewer a guanik from head to tail. And that's just what the arach did, leaping forward and thrusting downwards, slashing through two reptiles at once, the stragglers squealing once, twice, and then releasing their last breaths. Victorious, the arach unleashed a cry of its own, high-pitched and awful, its black maw opening wide to reveal a single row of knives.

Another hole flashed open, and white, silky material dropped over the spider's victims. It used its legs to tie the material around them, creating cocoons of preserved flesh. *Dinner for later*, Raven thought. *Hopefully I'm not the dessert.*

"It's too big for either one of us," Fire said. "We'll have to take it together."

Raven knew she was right. "Don't tell me you're scared of a little spider," she said, dismounting from her guanik. The animal would give her no advantage in this particular fight, not now that the arach had showed up. The guanik didn't need further urging, fleeing to the opposite end of the arena.

"You're the only one who fears them," Fire retorted. Raven still remembered the time she woke up to hundreds of eight-legged creatures crawling all over her. Fire had collected them over the course of many days in order to play the prank on her elder sister. Raven had had trouble sleeping for months afterwards, sometimes waking up screaming and brushing invisible spiders off her body.

"Not anymore," Raven said, though that was a lie. "On three?"

"One," Fire said.

The arach turned toward them, extracting its legs from the cocooned guanik.

"Two," Raven said.

The arach screamed, and Raven couldn't stop the shiver from rolling through her.

"Three!" Fire cried. As one, they charged the spider, which charged them in turn. Fire swung her sword high and hard, slashing through one of the legs before it could impale her. The hairy appendage tumbled and rolled, and Raven leaped over it while simultaneously snapping her whip.

The barbed end traveled straight into one of the arach's eyes, which exploded outwards with blue goo, like a popped membrane filled with paint.

At that point, the arach went mad. It leapt and slammed its legs down again and again. It snapped its deadly round mouth at anything that moved. Raven hung onto her whip, getting yanked around, rolling across the dust. She pulled back hard, trying to dislodge the barbs, but they had sunk deep into the soft ocular cavity, holding fast.

Fire fared slightly better, managing to dismember another two legs before getting knocked over by yet another of the spider's legs. It tried to step on her, but she rolled just out of range, the edge of her leather tunic getting skewered in the process. She tried to squirm away, but the arach had her pinned to the ground. Somewhere along the way she'd lost her grip on her sword—which was no longer sheathed in fire—and it was now just out of reach.

Raven couldn't have helped her even if she wanted to, because she was in her own kind of trouble. The beast had managed to get the whip wrapped around one of its legs, and it was using it like it used one of its webs, spinning the cord in circles, pulling Raven closer and closer. Finally, she was forced to relinquish the weapon and dive away.

She only had one whip left, which she extracted from her belt. With only five legs, one of which couldn't move because it was pinning Fire to the ground, the arach seemed off balance. Dark-blue blood continued to gush from its devastated eye, running down several of its other eyes and dripping into its maw.

Raven knew the only way to finish it off was to pierce its brain. Her skin felt itchy at the thought of getting anywhere near its bulbous head, but she gritted her teeth and ignored her fear, leaping and snapping her whip as high as she could, releasing a war cry that was one part anger, one part desperation.

The barbs flew over the arach's eyes and landed on the crown of its head, piercing its thick, hairy skin. It jerked back in surprise, ripping Fire off the ground and sending Raven flying as she clutched the handle of her whip. As she soared through the air, she was dimly aware of her sister sliding off the spider's bladed foot and diving to grab her sword, which immediately burst into flame.

Raven, however, quickly lost sight of her sister as she landed on the arach's head. The creature bucked and writhed and tried to dislodge her, but she held on tight with one hand while using her other to grab a short sword she had strapped to the side of her leg. She raised it high, preparing to jam it as hard as she could into the arach's brain…

Heat washed over her, pouring in from all sides, angry red, orange and yellow teeth, biting snapping, singeing her hair and burning through her leather armor.

"Ahh!" she cried out, releasing both her knife and whip and launching herself from the arach's head. To the Calypsians in attendance, she must've looked like a flaming bird, soaring for a few quick moments before landing with a bone-jarring thump in the dirt. She was still on fire, so she rolled rapidly, patting at her hair with her palms.

"Uhhh," she groaned, her cheek pressed to the dust, her eyelids fluttering. She blinked slowly, watching the arach writhe and squeal as it burned to death.

Her sister came into focus, smirking, walking toward her. Standing over her. Her entire body was wreathed in flames.

"Show off," Raven mumbled.

"Do you submit, sister?"

Although she knew her sister loved her, she also knew that she would do whatever was necessary to win the empire. Which left Raven with two options: submit or die.

And she wasn't ready to die. "Yes," she whispered.

Fire raised her hands in victory and the crowd roared.

Later that same day, a war council was convened. Though the shiva was master of order in Calypso only, he attended at Fire's request, for his advice and counsel. Several leaders of the guanero were also invited, as well as three dragon masters. And, of course, Raven and Whisper.

Fire sat on the dragon throne, which could reasonably be nicknamed the fire throne now, considering it was crackling with unnatural flames. Raven took a step back, the heat too much for her already burned skin.

Though her leather armor had mostly protected her, in several places—her left thigh, her abdomen, between her shoulder blades—the fire had eaten through and scorched her. Now, despite the cooling balm she'd rubbed on her skin, it felt like shards of glass were being shoved into her flesh. Her palms were badly burned too, wrapped in thick cloth to protect them from further injury. And, of course, her hair was gone. Though the flames had left a few of her lustrous dark locks, she'd chosen to have them shaved off so she could start fresh.

Whisper had cried. Fire had laughed. Raven had done nothing but grit her teeth, as she was doing now. It was partly due to the pain, and partly because she'd let her younger sister claim the empire for herself.

"What are our options against Phanes?" Fire asked the gathered council.

Raven spoke up first. "Be patient. Allow the dragon brood to mature and train. Then, when we are at our strongest, we will attack."

One of the dragon masters, a woman everyone referred to simply as Rider, said, "The dragons require a year. At least." Raven shot her an appreciative smile. She'd known Rider for years and considered her a key ally.

"Any *other* options?" Fire said, not even looking at her. "More worthy options."

Raven clenched her jaw. She didn't expect her sister to listen to her, but she had hoped she would at least discuss her ideas.

The guanero commander, a career warrior named Goggin, said, "We attack the Phanecians now, when they don't expect it. With the empress's unexpected passing"—a lump lodged itself in Raven's throat—"Vin Hoza will believe he has time to grow his slave army. If we hit their capital city now, they won't be ready."

Raven shook her head, which was beginning to ache, either from this conversation or from her injuries. "A quick attack is impossible. We would have to build ships, gather supplies, and the dragons—"

"Forget about the dragons, sister," Fire said. "The dragons will remain here to grow and train, as you suggested."

Raven was unable to mask her surprise. "I—but—then our forces will have no chance against Faata's slave army. Not without the dragons."

Fire sighed in frustration. "First you don't want to bring the dragons, and now you do. Which is it?"

"I don't want you to go to war at all. Not yet."

"We are going to war," Fire said. There was no room for argument in her tone. "It's just a matter of where and when."

"Still, if you mean to cross the Burning Sea and march on Phanea, it will take time. Months, maybe years."

"What if we don't cross the Burning Sea?" Fire asked.

"What?" Raven said.

Goggin patted his barrel-shaped chest, frowning. "Are you proposing we cross the Scarra? The desert would take much out of our forces even before we forded the Spear. And then we would be forced to fight the Southron border cities—Sousa, Hemptown, Gem City—before entering the death trap of the Bloody Canyon. Even if we made it to Phanea, we would face an army of tens of thousands of slaves forced to fight—and die— for Emperor Hoza."

At least the guanero leader is finally making sense, Raven thought. "I agree," she said. "The Scarra is out of the question."

"Nothing is out of the question," Fire shot back. "And I wasn't proposing we take that route. Just the Scarra."

Raven pursed her lips, before asking, "So we cross the Scarra, and then what—raft down the Spear into the Burning Sea?"

"No, sister, we march northwest."

"Northwest?" Raven was so confused she could barely decipher the meaning of the word. "But the only thing northwest is..." She raised her eyebrows, finally understanding what her sister was proposing. Perhaps what she'd been planning all along, since the moment she found their maata's plague-covered body.so

Fire grinned. "Ahh, so now you see? We shall attack the Southron Gates from the southern side."

"To what purpose?" Goggin asked.

This time it was Raven who supplied the answer. "To weaken the Phanecian defenses against the western kingdom."

Goggin scratched his head. "The west hasn't attacked the south in many decades. Why would they now?"

Raven still remembered the stream they'd received from their spies in the west days earlier, when her mother was still empress.

When Sun Sandes was still alive. "Rhea Loren has seized power in the west. It is said she cares more for dancing than ruling. And Lord Griswold has declared himself king of the north and is amassing forces at Blackstone. He will take the west, and then he will march south, toward the Southron Gates. If the Gates are destroyed, nothing will be able to stop him."

"If we destroy the gates," Fire continued, "the north will do battle with the slave army, instead of us."

"And regardless of who wins, we will be in a strong position to claim whatever is left," Raven said. She hated to admit it, but her sister's plan was creative and bold.

It was the last thing their father would expect them to do.

"Prepare our armies for the desert," Fire said, convening the council.

PART II

Jai ⚅ Rhea ⚅ Roan
Annise ⚅ Grey ⚅ Raven

The curse of war will spread, filling the land with
darkness, as it must; for without dark, there can be no
light.
The Western Oracle

Seventeen
The Southern Empire, Phanes
Jai Jiroux

By the time the thousands had entered the tunnel ahead of Jai, the sky was black, almost melting into the black rocks until he couldn't tell one person from the next.

Jai paused a moment, staring at the darkness that had just swallowed his entire world.

"C'mon," a little voice said, and a small hand shot from the dark, grabbing his and pulling him forward. Jig had insisted on waiting with him until the end, but now the boy was anxious to press onward.

Holding the boy's hand tightly, he slid his fingers along the rope. Voices echoed through the tunnel, seeming to take shape in the dark, bouncing off the walls and tumbling around his feet. Jig said, "Will the west be on the other side?"

Jai could almost believe it would be, though he knew the Southron Gates were still a great distance away, to the north, somewhere beyond the Bloody Canyons and the four border towns. "No, but we will be safe for a time."

"How long will Emperor Hoza search for us?"

There was such childlike innocence in the boy's question that Jai knew his heart would break if he told the truth—*forever*—so he changed the subject. "Can you see anything?"

"Not even the person in front of me," Jig said with a laugh. The boy's laughter buoyed Jai's spirits. Growing up in Garadia, this boy learned to embrace the dark, rather than fear it. They all did. He would be fine. Perhaps they all would be.

As they walked, the scenery began to change. The black turned to gray turned to shadows of bodies, scuffling along single file. Rough rock walls appeared on each side, and, ahead of them, the outline of an opening.

And then they were free of the rocky throat, spilling out into an enormous area sheathed in green light, only the edges cloaked in shadow. Though the entire area was surrounded by cliffs, there was no roof, the one half-moon and its army of stars staring down, providing more than enough light to see by. The other moon had risen somewhere out of sight.

The sound of splashing reached Jai's ears, and he discovered a line of people waiting to take their turn in a large natural pool nestled between several large boulders. Other groups had already formed circles, and were fast asleep. Still others were breaking bread and drinking from skins.

The scene was so utterly familiar they might have never left Garadia, but there was one stark, crucial difference.

Now they were free.

Though he was bone-weary, Jai's mind was very much awake, racing with a mixture of fear and excitement for the future. He'd done what he set out to do, at long last, and he had formidable allies to help him.

Jig, Viola, and their mother were all asleep, their deep inhalations and exhalations falling into cadence with each other, like they were three parts of the same person.

Jai stood and slipped away, silently stepping between the hundreds of sleeping bodies sprawled throughout the canyon. He spotted Axa, sleeping, gripping his mirror with fisted hands. There was a circle of space all around him, as if he carried a contagious disease.

Perhaps he does, Jai thought. *The disease of superiority.*

Something drew Jai toward the center of the area, where he craned his head back and looked up at the vast night sky. A dark shape soared overhead, but he couldn't tell whether it was a vulzure or some other less dangerous bird.

He scanned the cliffs, his gaze settling on a shadow.

The shadow moved. Someone was up there.

A slash of fear cut through him, but then he breathed. There was no way someone loyal to the emperor could have followed them this far. It had to be one of their own. The fierce warriors of the Black Tears were sleeping in a group near the water. Sonika's dark hair was spread out around her head like a black veil of mourning. Jai counted their numbers and came up one short. Who?

Shanti, he realized. The Teran with an affinity for fireroot powder.

Jai traced a line from her shadow on the cliff to the ground, planning his climb. Then he started up. There were plenty of hand and footholds, and several ledges where he was able to stop and rest. However, by the time he reached the top, his arms ached and he was wondering whether he should've just stayed on the ground and tried to sleep.

Shanti said, "Look." She didn't turn around, the Teran continuing to gaze across the night-dark terrain, which was spread out like a three-dimensional canvas before them. Jai looked, his chest tightening because of the sheer wonder of the view. The rocks, which were as black as tar in the daylight, were sheathed in dueling moonlit armor, green and crimson forms that were as beautiful as the stars, as if echoes of their light. The stars were like flower buds opening in the sky—red, green, gold.

"It's…" There was only one word for what he was seeing. "Perfection."

Shanti's head cocked to the side to look at him, a smile playing on her soft-looking pink lips. "Yes," she said. "Like the world we live in."

Jai couldn't agree with that. "This world is a horrible place."

"No," she said, shaking her head. "The world is perfect. We're the only ones who make it horrible. And yet there is beauty amongst us, too. Surely you can see it in your people?"

Yes, he could. Despite their scars and disfigurements, both emotional and physical, his people were beautiful. "I fear I risk too much by helping them escape. The road ahead will be hard."

"Freedom is not always easy, but it is always right. But remember: You can't command someone to be free."

Jai considered her words, which, he had to admit, stung a little. What was she saying, that he was just another master? *No*, he thought, inwardly chiding himself for being so sensitive. She was merely saying that they had a long way to go before true freedom was achieved. Jai nodded his agreement. A sudden urge to tell her about his mother, his father, swelled inside him, but he breathed evenly until it melted away. He feared if he spoke of what he'd lost that he would crumble like brittle stone.

"All I want is to give them happiness," he said instead.

Shanti touched his hand. Her fingertips were warm. "You have. I observed them today. They *are* happy—at least as happy as they can be given their circumstances."

"But they're not safe. Not by a longshot."

"They will be." She patted his hand, and Jai wondered if she was a touchy person by nature, or if the gesture was just for him. He found himself hoping it was the latter.

When he didn't respond, she asked, "How did you learn the defense arts?"

"My father." The two words slipped out so easily it was like they were resting on the tip of his tongue.

Shanti pointed up at the green moon goddess, Luahi, for which phen lu had been named. "It is said that a true master can summon the power of the night goddess."

"Yes." He pointed at the red sliver of the moon god that was still visible. "And they say masters of phen ru are powered by Ruahi. But I've never seen anyone do either."

"Me either," Shanti said.

A memory rose to the top of Jai's mind. His mother, dancing phen sur, while he and his father watched. She was so graceful. Beautiful, like water sliding past smooth stones, like a bird soaring across the sky...

"I've seen someone harness Surai's power while dancing," he blurted out.

166

Shanti raised her coppery eyebrows. "Really? The sun goddess shined on a dancer? Who?"

My mother. "I didn't know her name. A stranger." The lie was bitter on his tongue, but he couldn't open this door. Not now.

She looked away, her large blue eyes floating back toward the rocklands, and he took the opportunity to study her face, which was framed by her short hair. Once more, he counted her tears. Still seventeen. "When will you add your tears for the battle at Garadia?" he asked.

She licked her lips. "I have no tears to add tonight." Absently, she withdrew her hand and touched it to her face, tracing her fingers along each black teardrop.

"I would've thought a fierce warrior such as yourself would've killed at least one of the mine masters."

She chuckled. "I killed three, but that is not what the tears represent."

Jai couldn't hide his surprise. "But everyone says—"

"Everyone is wrong," she said. "That's just the rumor spread by the emperor to make his citizens fear us. If they represented those we've killed, all of our faces would be entirely covered in darkness."

It took a moment for that information to sink in. She must've killed hundreds then. They all had. "Then what are the tears for? Why do some of you have more than others?" *Why do you have so many?*

"They are reminders," she said. Her hand dropped to her side, closing over a small rock.

"Of what?"

"Of who," she corrected. "They are memories of those we've lost. The ones we fight for. The reason we kill."

Jai shivered, but not because of the cool breeze wafting over them.

Shanti threw the rock, and they both watched as it rose, arced, and then fell into oblivion.

Down below, a scream shattered the silence of night.

It took Jai longer than Shanti to descend from the cliffs to the ground, and when he arrived on the scene, all of the Black Tears were standing in a circle, blocking his view of a figure writhing on the hard, rock floor.

"Please," he said, and they parted. Sonika's eyes met his, but he couldn't tell what she was thinking.

And then he saw who it was: Axa, his face contorted in pain, several parts of his body bleeding, crimson streams running down his arms, his face, his chest.

The gemstones that had been sewn into his skin had been ripped out, leaving trails of broken flesh. No one moved to help him. "Who did this?" Jai asked.

A form stepped forward, his palms open, glittering with rubies and emeralds and diamonds. Blood dripped between his fingers. "They weren't his," Joaquin said, his black eyes unblinking.

Eighteen

The Western Kingdom, Knight's End
Rhea Loren

The man walked using a gnarled tree branch as a cane, though Rhea suspected it was all part of his act—she detected no limp in his stride.

He stood before her, meeting her gaze with steely gray eyes that never seemed to blink.

"Kneel before your queen," Ennis said. Though her cousin was wholeheartedly against bringing this man here, he was still utterly loyal to her claim on the crown, a fact that continued to delight her.

The man said, "I kneel before none but Wrath."

"You will kneel or you will be made to—" Ennis snapped, but Rhea silenced him with a hand.

She smiled. She liked this man already. His defiance. His fearlessness. "Bold words for an outcast."

They called him the Summoner, which was the same title his father had worn before him. And his father's father. And on and on, for centuries. Somewhere along the lines, one of the Loren monarchs had determined the Furies were the true warriors of Wrath, not these shadowy Summoner men. However, out of respect for their history, they'd been permitted to live, so long as they didn't speak their sacrilegious words in public.

"In Wrath's Eye, I am no outcast," the man replied. "Have you brought me here to kill me?"

History had a way of jading people, Rhea mused. "What would you do if I had? What would you Summon using that legendary power of yours?"

The man dropped his cane and stood tall, his hands extending to each side. His mouth opened wide in a silent howl and his arms shot over his head, palms forward.

Ennis moved to grab him, to stop him from doing whatever it was he was doing, but then the man dropped his hands and began laughing. Ennis grabbed his arm and said, "Watch yourself, old fool. Your games are not appreciated."

Duly chastened, the man stopped laughing and looked back at Rhea. "I do not Summon. Wrath Summons. I am but his mouthpiece, his hands and his feet in the second heaven."

Rhea nodded. "I heard a story when I was a child," she said. "A story about a great monster that lived in the sea."

"Wrathos," the man murmured, speaking the name reverently.

Ennis said, "That vile creature is now known as Demonos, if it ever existed at all."

"It existed," the man hissed. "It *exists*."

"Good," Rhea said. "And you believe it is still loyal to Wrath?"

"Yes, for God created it. Just like me."

"And you can—as Wrath's mouthpiece—Summon it again?"

"Princess—I mean, Queen—no," Ennis said. "That...*thing* is not of Wrath, it is a demon, the spawn of the devil himself. You cannot control it."

"I can and I will," Rhea said. She turned to the Fury, who had watched the entire exchange with mild interest. "Show the Summoner to one of the empty suites. Give him all that he desires."

"I desire nothing but your trust, Your Highness," the Summoner said. He bent down and retrieved his stick, breaking it in half over his knee. "I already have everything else."

"Rhea!" her twin brother and sister cried in unison. They rushed to the bars and pushed their hands between them, reaching for her.

She took a step back. They were filthy from sleeping on the dirty floor. They were thinner, too, which made them look even more like the weasels that they were.

"Rhea?" Leo said again, his eyebrows pushing together. His long, blond hair was greasy and stringy, making him appear as ordinary as a street rat. "Get us out of here! They said Cousin Jove was dead. He was supposed to be the king!"

"Yes," Bea agreed, nodding rapidly. "They said we had to hide down here for our own safety. But we're safe now, aren't we?" Even in such a disheveled, malnourished state, she was utterly breathtaking, her blue eyes like turquoise crystals, her golden locks lustrous, curling around her chin. Rhea hated her perfect, porcelain features. She longed to cut off her curls, to draw lines down her face, to mar her perfection.

The twins looked pathetic, in the dungeons. Once, Rhea might have felt sorry for them, might have offered them a second chance. Been merciful. But not anymore. The memory of how they'd scorned her, mocked her, pointed accusing fingers at her, was seared in her mind. They knew the truth about the W scarred into her face, what it really represented. And they had big mouths. No, there would be no redemption for the sniveling brats that stood before her, pleading.

She said nothing, turning her back on them as they cried for her to return and set them free.

Ennis walked beside her, prattling in her ear. He spouted his usual objections and religious quotes and mentions of Rhea's "best interests" and the "peace and safety of the kingdom."

Rhea ignored him and focused on the citizens of Knight's End, who stopped what they were doing to watch her march through the city, surrounded by furia. She noticed several with the familiar W slashed across the whole of their faces. They were on their knees, their hands clasped together, their lips parted as they whispered silent prayers to Wrath. Rhea kissed her fingers and extended them in their direction. The Devoted, as they were now being casually referred to, instantly collapsed, as if touched by the Hand of Wrath.

Rhea wasn't certain whether her newfound power was actually bestowed by Wrath or whether she'd simply planted that in the people's minds. But it didn't matter. All that mattered was she had it and she would use it to make the west great again.

She caught a few darker, less friendly stares, too. These were the unbelievers, either in Wrath or in her. She knew with an uttered word and a flick of her fingers her furia would punish them, even kill them, if she wanted. But she stayed silent, offering them each a smile and a nod, to which they responded with surprised looks. She knew she would win them over in the end. But if they crossed her…

As she continued her march through the city, more and more flocked to her, surrounding her furia, joining the parade. Children called her name and threw wreaths of flowers. Ennis tried to keep the projectiles away from her, but she caught several and draped them over her head and around her shoulders. The children cheered.

"Today I visit the Furium," she said to the onlookers. "In the attack on the castle that killed my father, the furia's numbers were greatly depleted." It was not true, but they didn't know that. Some of them may have seen the Three riding south with a large contingent of their righteous sisters, but they did not know that most of the red warriors had yet to return. "The Furium is the most important building in our great city, as it is our future. I implore all the young, strong women of Knight's End to accept the honor given to you by Wrath and join the red ranks and earn your place in the seventh heaven."

Though the throng was now hundreds deep, blocking the streets and disrupting the merchants' daily trade, she could hear her message being passed backwards through the crowd, like a ripple in a pond.

Girls of all ages ran ahead of her, laughing and chasing each other as they made their way to the Furium. In some cases, Rhea spied mothers or fathers carrying their daughters, who were kicking and screaming and fighting it every step of the way. Rhea knew it didn't matter. Once inside the Furium, they would be subdued. Broken, if necessary. Recreated in the name of Wrath. Forged anew with strength and loyalty, damaged swords made stronger. In other cases, however, their mothers and fathers tried to grab their children, to stop them, pleading with them not to go. But the young girls were swift of foot and nimble, and they soon vanished into the human tide. Their parents dropped to their knees and wept openly.

"Halt," Rhea commanded. Her furia stopped in an instant, taking no more than an additional half step. Their unquestioning obedience gave her chills. She moved through her lines of red-cloaked women, and they parted like stalks of wheat before a farmer's scythe.

When she reached the wailing mothers and fathers, she knelt beside them and touched their cheeks. They looked up with wet, weary eyes. "Cry no more," she said. "For your sacrifice has earned you a place in the seventh heaven."

And then she stood and turned her back, continuing on while they praised Wrath's grace in her wake.

"You should not promise so much," Ennis hissed at her when she returned to her place by his side.

She laughed gaily. "Shouldn't I? My promises shall stir them to carry out my will."

"And when your promises are broken?"

She frowned at him, not appreciating his tone. "How can you be certain they will be broken? In any case, I will not be there when Wrath refuses them entrance to the heavenly garden of light."

"You give them false hope."

"Hope is our greatest weapon," she snapped back. "Hope will build my army and lead us to victory. And if hope doesn't work, there is always fear."

Ennis shook his head but didn't respond. She wondered how long his loyalty would hold, and when the dam broke, whether he would fade quietly into the night or have to be put down. She hoped the former, for she still loved him, in a shared-history kind of way.

They reached the Furium. If not for its bright-red arching doors, the nondescript building wouldn't have stood out against the neighboring structures. A line of red-clad women guarded the entrance, their blades held in both hands, their points touched to the tips of their noses. Actually, calling them *women* was being generous, for none of them appeared older than Rhea, who was naught but sixteen. And yet they were disciplined, their eyes never shifting from their steadfast gaze forward, even when Rhea walked slowly past them, waving her hand across their faces.

The Fury stood silently, watching.

Rhea turned to her. "These are your best?" she asked.

"We have no best. We are all equal."

"Even you?"

"Yes." There was no hesitation, no lie. This woman believed her words from the depths of her soul.

"And if you die?"

"I shall be replaced by another."

Rhea nodded. "Good." She gazed behind the guards. A crowd of girls were being funneled inside, the new blood Rhea had recruited as she marched through the city. "May I go inside?"

In truth, it wasn't a request, but a command, but Rhea was in public, and she needed to keep the appearance that the furia were separate from the monarchy, an independent law-keeping body.

"Of course," the Fury said. Without being asked, two of the guards stepped aside. Momentarily, the line of recruits was halted so that Rhea could enter the structure.

Inside was a red-painted atrium with unadorned walls, save for a large image of Wrath. As taught by the furia, God appeared as neither man or woman, human or other creature. The form had the face of a human, the arms of a tree, dark clouds bursting with lightning atop the head, pointed blades for teeth, swirling tornados for legs, the eyes of a tiger and the nose of an elephant. God was everything in creation, constantly changing.

Rhea noticed something else: Many of the features were constructed of gemstones, glittering on the wall. Despite the Furium's modest appearance, there was great wealth here. *There's wealth in serving Wrath*, Rhea mused appreciatively. *Wealth and power. A lethal combination.*

"Carry on," she said, watching with interest as the new blood continued to move through the line. First they were stripped naked, every possession they carried or wore taken from them. Some girls protested, but most didn't. Some covered themselves with their hands, but most didn't.

The Fury spoke to them. "We are all naked in the sight of Wrath. We have nothing to hide, nothing to be ashamed of. From this moment forward, you are not beautiful or ugly, not strong or weak, not large or small. Here you simply are. Here we are all sisters. Here we are all kin. Together we will fight, and die if necessary, for Wrath's will."

Next, a pail of water was dumped on the head of each girl. Several of the furia would then descend on them, scrubbing their skin so hard it turned red.

The Fury continued her monologue: "The outside world has made you filthy, even the most righteous of you. We cannot allow the worldly filth to enter this sacred place. You are not clean until it hurts." Some of the girls began to cry out from the pain, while others bore it with gritted teeth of determination.

Once each girl was deemed to be sufficiently clean, she was taken to an area with a large vat filled with a red liquid resembling blood. "Is that…" Rhea said.

"Dye," the Fury said.

Of course. Each girl's hair was then dyed red, including their eyebrows. Finally, they were dried off and given the familiar acolyte's robe, which was half-red, half-white.

Rhea walked along a line of fresh acolytes who were being taught to stand at attention, though most of them flicked their eyes to look at her when she passed. It was strange, how similar they were already beginning to look after only a few changes. The red hair, the robes, the scrubbed skin. *They really could be sisters*, Rhea thought.

"I want to see more," she said.

The Fury hesitated for the first time since Rhea had broken her into a million pieces. Immediately she understood why. The Fury had just explained how nothing touched by the outside world could enter the Furium. She could see the young girls looking at their leader, wondering what she would do.

The moment felt important, a hinge that would either open a door or close one forever.

Rhea offered her an out. "Of course, I will succumb to the standard process of any acolyte," she said. "I am not above Wrath's Law."

She knew she'd spoken wisely when she saw relief flood the Fury's eyes. She said, "You have already taken the mantle of Wrath when you cut your face, like me, which keeps you clean from this world. Follow me."

She turned on her heel and entered the next room. Rhea followed shortly after, and she could hear the sounds of a new group of girls being brought in for cleaning, dyeing, and robing.

The area beyond the atrium was an enormous training yard. Full-fledged furia taught acolytes of various skill-levels the art of killing. By sword, by poison, by hand-to-hand combat—they were learning it all. In one corner, a large group were praying together, their voices chanting as one.

Rhea saw two girls who couldn't be more than five name days old, doing battle with wooden poles. One of the girls dodged the other's attack and then smashed the butt of her stick into the girl's face. The young girl fell back, clutching her nose as blood ran between her fingertips. Tears sprung from her eyes, pouring down her cheeks.

The victor bent down to apologize, to help her up.

The Fury said, "Stop."

The girl froze, her eyes wide with fear. "I hurt her," she said.

"And she will hurt you one day. Would you have her shame you by showing weakness? Would you have her treat you like a suckling babe and not one of Wrath's warriors?"

"No," the girl said.

"Correct. Now leave her. She can pick up her own pieces. She will return stronger the next time."

Already, the injured girl's tears had dried up. She wiped the blood away on the red half of her cloak. Then she stood, a look of determination crossing her face. She grabbed her pole.

The two girls fought again, and this time the girl with the bloody nose got the better of her opponent, tripping her and throwing her down. Rhea was transfixed as she watched the process repeat over and over again, with the girls alternating victories. There were no more tears, though there was more blood drawn.

"You have done well with this place," Rhea said.

The Fury bowed slightly, but said nothing.

"Tell me, where did the other two go? The other members of the Three. They took a girl with them. She was sinmarked. They stole half of the furia." Rhea remembered Grey's strength as he searched for his sister, Shae, his determination. He looked as though he would go to the ends of the world to find her. At first she'd hated him for leaving her to the mercy of the furia, but now, she silently thanked him. He'd set her free, allowed her to become what she'd become.

"Yes," the Fury said. "They wanted to…understand the girl."

Rhea frowned. "Understand?"

"Study. Observe. Discern what power her mark bestowed upon her."

"They didn't already know?"

She shook her head. "And neither, it seems, did the girl. Or so she claimed. Her mark is a mystery."

Rhea noticed that she didn't call it a *sin*mark. Just a mark. It was highly unusual for a woman of Wrath. "Yes, but it shouldn't matter. If she is marked with sin, then she must be killed. Correct? That is what has been taught for decades."

"Yes. It has," the Fury said, but it wasn't an answer.

179

"Then why isn't Shae Arris dead?"

"It's complicated."

"Tell me," Rhea growled. She grabbed the woman by the front of her robe. The Fury flinched. There it was—that fear. Though this woman was a trained warrior and could kill Rhea in any number of ways, she feared her now, like a dog beaten to within an inch of its life by its master.

"What do you know of the Western Oracle?" the Fury asked.

Rhea released her, letting out a breath. "Children told stories about her. She was a witch. A sorceress. Lover of demons and darkness. An outcast. She was burned at the stake."

The Fury shook her head. "No, she was none of those things, save for an outcast and burned at the stake. The rest was a lie told by your great-great-great grandfather. She was no witch. She was once one of the Three. She was the very first Fury."

Nineteen

The Western Kingdom, The Tangle
Roan Loren

"I think the sun rose from that direction," Gareth said, pointing toward a part of the forest that was so dense they couldn't see past the line of gnarled bushes. Then again, every part of the Tangle seemed to be getting thicker, fighting them every step of the way.

Gwendolyn squinted. "I'm certain it rose from there," she said, gesturing the opposite direction.

Roan grimaced, plucking a thorn from his skin. Blood welled up from a pin-sized hole. Dozens of similar holes dotted his arms. "We need to climb a tree. It's the only way."

"You're not scared of the ore monkeys?" Gareth said, an amused look on his face.

"You think this is funny?" Roan said. "We could starve to death in this forsaken place."

"My apologies, Your Highness," Gareth said, smirking. "It was merely a quip, which was obviously in bad taste. I wasn't aware of the thorns stuck up your—"

"Shut it, you fools," Gwen said. "I thought I heard something."

"Like Gareth's sense of humor shriveling up and dying?" Roan said. "And don't call me 'Your Highness.'"

"Am I mistaken? Are you not the heir to the western throne?"

"No more than you're the heir to the eastern crown, *Your Highness.*"

"I'm supposed to be dead!"

"I saved your life!"

"I didn't ask you to!"

Gwen punched Gareth. Hard. He cringed, massaging his shoulder.

Roan started to laugh, but then she punched him, too. Even harder, or at least so he suspected. He was about to protest, but then he heard it, too. A sound, carrying over the rustling leaves and creaking branches. Someone was singing.

"What the bloody hell is that?" Gareth said.

"Someone singing," Roan said. Gareth glared at him. "You ask a dumb question…"

"If you two don't cease your infernal bickering, I will seal your lips with ore the next time we're in Ironwood."

Roan was fairly certain he would never return to the ore forest, but he didn't want to risk it. "Where is it coming from?" The sound rose up again, louder this time. It was melodious, beautiful, full of hope and life and love, but mournful, too, a sadness so deep it seemed to settle into Roan's skin and bones.

Gwen and Gareth, once more, pointed in opposite directions. Roan didn't agree with either of them. He thought the voice was coming from out of the ground, or perhaps from somewhere high above, almost like the sound was all around them. No, *in* them.

"Why would someone be singing in the middle of the Tangle?" Gareth asked.

"I don't know, but I think we should find out who it is," Roan said. As soon as he said it, the idea seemed to take root in his mind, and he could think of nothing else. "This way. We're close." He dove into the brush, oblivious to the spiky branches and thorns that slashed his skin.

He heard Gareth say something behind him, about exploring in a different direction, and Gwen shouted for both of them to "Stop!" but her command bounced off of Roan's ears, which could only listen to the words of the song, which seemed to flood through his soul:

Once there was a maiden in Tanglewood's Keep,
Resting her head on moss and fern leaf.
Wishing for one to sweep her away,
Break her chains and lead her astray.

Where are the valiant, where are the brave?
The handsome king with a maiden to save?
If he passes the test he can have her love,
Tender as a lamb and pure as a dove.

As the song ended, Roan felt as if a piece of him had been hacked off and stripped away, leaving him empty inside. He redoubled his pace, plunging ahead through branch and leaf, thorn and vine, slapping the barriers away, bouncing off of spiky trees, until—

The ground seemed to sink away from his feet, leaving him hanging in midair, tangled in something that gripped his arms and legs. He fought it, not because he was scared, but because he needed to continue toward whomever was singing, needed it like he needed blood in his veins, air in his lungs, water in his throat...

The voice came back to him, closer now, tantalizingly close.

Welcome, handsome king. You are just in time.

The voice was as clear as a burbling spring, as strong as a lion's roar, as melodious as birdsong. Somewhere in his mind, Roan was aware that the voice was not spoken out loud, but in his head, sliding through his skull.

He peered through the gaps in the net, for that's what he was caught in, not of rope, but of vine, as if the trees themselves had conspired against him. But he didn't care, not one wit, because the bearer of the song, of the voice, appeared beneath him.

Her gown was a thousand flowers of many colors, golden threads binding them, like rays of sunlight captured and stitched together. Her face was the green of leaf, her hair a blanket of moss, crowned with a nest of thorns. In the hollow of her throat hung several silver lockets, dangling from a necklace constructed of seeds strung together.

"How can I help you?" Roan asked, despite the fact that it was he who was a captive. He stopped trying to fight through the net, which was no longer of consequence to him, not while this angel of the wood stood beneath him. Not while she spoke his name with such reverence.

Roan Loren.

Distantly, he wondered how she knew who he was, but the concern flitted away on the gentle breeze.

Something crashed through the forest, bursting into the clearing, broken branches and tattered leaves clinging to shirt and trousers. Gareth. *What is that fool doing here?* Roan thought. "Leave us," he said. "*I* am helping her."

Gareth snarled at him. "*I* am helping her!"

The woman laughed, and the sound was like approaching rainfall. Roan felt himself melt into a puddle. *You can both help me. You are both the handsome, brave kings in my song.*

A muffled voice cried from elsewhere in the wood. "Roan! Gareth! You fools! Where are you?"

The voice was familiar to Roan, but sounded rougher, like bark scraping against his ears. He didn't want her to find them. What was her name again? He couldn't remember, but that didn't matter. He wanted only to be here, to be close to the woman of the forest, to be her hero, her handsome, brave king.

The net that held him drifted to the ground, and slowly released him. Gareth strode up to him, drawing his sword. "Back off," he growled.

Though Roan had abhorred violence his entire life, he wanted to dismantle the prince piece by piece. He had no weapons, so his fists would have to do. He swung at Gareth, who ducked, slashing his blade across Roan's midsection. The edge caught a loose bit of clothing, which fluttered to the ground like a wounded bird. Roan aimed another punch...

"Stop!" Gwendolyn commanded, grabbing his arm from behind, holding him back. She twisted Roan's arm behind his back, but he barely felt the bite of pain, because he needed to get to the green-faced woman, needed to be her brave king, needed to—

185

Gwendolyn swung around him and blocked a blow from Gareth's sword with her iron bow, which she then fitted with an arrow, firing swiftly at the woman.

No! Roan screamed in his head, but the woman had already lifted a shield of thick bark, blocking the arrow, which imbedded itself harmlessly in the wood. She extended her hand and vines shot from her fingertips, grabbing Gwen's bow and wrenching it out of her grasp. Gwen tried to flee, but the vines had already wrapped around her arms and legs, too, tightening, circling around her body like cloth around a mummy, until only her face was visible.

In the confusion, Roan saw an opportunity, rushing at Gareth and tackling him to the ground. Gareth lost his sword, but managed to roll, pinning Roan beneath him. "I don't want to kill you, but I will if I have to."

"Not if I kill you first," Roan declared, kicking hard, bucking Gareth to the side. He snatched the sword from the ground, lifted it, and brought it down toward the prince's face.

Stop. Though the word was naught but a whisper, Roan felt its power in the very marrow of his bones. His arm froze, the sword's edge close enough to shave the stubble from Gareth's cheeks.

Gwendolyn muttered something about how they didn't listen to *her* when she told them to stop. Apparently she could hear the woman's voice in her head, too, a thought that made Roan insanely jealous.

My heroes. My brave kings. I think I will keep you both.

"What do you mean 'keep them'?" Gwen said. And then: "Oh ore, you're a wood nymph, aren't you?"

Shut your mouth, Orian! Though it was clear to Roan that the words were spoken in anger, they were as soothing as gentle waves lapping against a sandy shore. *This does not concern you.*

"These are my friends, nymph, so aye, it concerns me."

And yet you have no power here. This is my domain. I have no use for you. However, because I am merciful, I will permit you to return home to Ironwood. Now go or I'll be forced to kill you.

The vines slithered away from Gwendolyn's body, returning into the woman's fingertips. Roan was captivated. Gwen, however, didn't move. "Roan, Gareth, this woman is a liar and a witch. She has cast a spell on you with her song. Fight it. She can't take you if you don't want her to."

But Roan *did* want her to take him. It's all he wanted. "Go," he said. "Leave us. We will be safe here."

"Aye," Gareth agreed. "Return home, as she said. Ironwood is where you belong."

"Well, if that's what you want…" Gwen turned and started to walk away, but then twisted around sharply and flung herself at the woman with inhuman speed, her heromark flaring on her cheek.

Roan and Gareth both dove to stop her at the same time, but were too slow. The woman—the nymph Gwen had called her, whatever that meant—was faster, however, shooting vines upward. They wrapped around a branch and she swung out of harm's way.

Gwen flew beneath her, landing horizontally, her feet planted on the trunk of a tree. She rebounded off, sprinted over to Roan and Gareth, and grabbed each of them by the collar and dragged them from the clearing.

They fought her every step, scratching and clawing and digging their boots into the dirt. "Stop it, you idiots!" she shouted, her cheeks blooming with lines of blood from their nails, as if she'd been clawed by an ore cat. As she manhandled them away, however, trees blocked their path, their trunks bristling with poisonous spikes.

And then she was there, the nymph, her dress swirling around her like a tornado of many colors, the resulting wind so powerful it halted them in their tracks. While they struggled against Gwen, she held them behind her back with strong ironclad arms.

"I recognize you," Gwen said.

Really, young Orian? What would the daughter of the late great Boronis Storm know of me?

"You are Felicity, eldest daughter of Dressara, Queen of the Wood Nymphs."

Yessss. Clever girl. But my mother is gone now, just like your father. Did you know your father loved me once?

"Liar!"

It's true. He couldn't take his eyes off of me.

"Because you beguiled him."

And what do you think love is? He would've been mine, if not for your horrid mother. Talk about a seductress…

"You know nothing of my mother."

And neither do you, it seems. She deserved what she got, just like my dear mother. She was so arrogant she thought she would live forever. But I had different plans…

"You killed her," Gwen said.

Roan could hear the words, but they were meaningless as he struggled against Gwen's iron grip. "Lemme go!"

"Me too!" Gareth shouted.

My mother had her time. Now it is my time. I am the queen.

"You had four sisters," Gwen said. "Did you kill them, too?"

The nymph's laugh was as spectacular as a rainbow. *I would have, but I didn't have to. They gave me their lockets freely, once they saw what I'd done to dear mother. Now they are just another part of the wood, sleeping beauties. My rule over the Tangle is total. Why do you think you're unable to find your way through?*

Gwen reversed, pushing Roan and Gareth deeper into the wood, until the spiked trees were almost touching their backs. Gareth hissed. Roan growled.

Give them to me, the nymph said. *My soul is hungry, and they are mine. You can still walk away, Orian. What do you care for two humans? They are nothing to our kinds. Their lives will fade away long before we are gone.*

"I am nothing like you," Gwen said. She shoved Roan and Gareth back and, once more, launched herself at the nymph. This time the woman was prepared for both the speed and ferocity of the attack. A wall of vines rose up, swarming around Gwen and pinning her. Thorns burst from the tentacles, and Gwen screamed as they bit into her skin.

Something twisted in Roan's gut hearing his friend's cry, but then the woman spoke again and it was all he could focus on. *Come hither, my brave kings*, she said. *And we shall be as one.*

As one. The very thought of being a part of the woman sent Roan into a frenzy.

Apparently it had a similar effect on Gareth, because they stumbled and fought each other like two young boys showing off for a beautiful lady. In the end, they arrived in front of her at the exact same moment. She smiled at them, and Roan found himself smiling back so broadly it hurt. He'd found his purpose in life: pleasing this woman.

Gwendolyn screamed again, and Roan felt that twisting in his gut, but he didn't look back, caught in the nymph's eyes, which were bright green and glowing, piercing him like twin daggers. She reached down and opened one of her lockets. Inside was a small mirror. *Look*, she said.

"No!" Gwen yelled. "Close your—" Her warning disintegrated into a piercing shriek of pain.

Roan and Gareth's heads smashed together as they fought to be the first to look in the mirror, but neither registered the pain, because images were taking shape, twisting and turning and pushing their way into their minds.

Images of human men and women smiling, jumping, performing heroic feats in honor of this woman of the forest. They were happy. So happy. Roan wanted to be like them. He wanted to be one of the many.

Then Roan saw only himself, reaching forward with a hand...

From somewhere that seemed impossibly far away, Gwen was screaming for him to "Fight it, fight it, fight it!" but all he wanted was to take his own hand, to let his reflection pull him into that place where he would be loved by the most spectacular woman he had ever laid eyes on. He would be her brave king. Yes. Yes, he would.

He touched the face of the mirror, and then he was gone, along with Gareth, who'd done the same.

One by one the men and women in the mirror fell, writhing in pain, thorny vines twisting around them. Screams filled the air. The ground opened up and swallowed them, their cries vanishing as dirt filled their mouths.

Only Roan and Gareth were left, blinking, staring at each other across a wasteland.

A voice echoed from the sky, and it was no longer pleasing to Roan's ears. No, it was like a hammer, pounding him from above, driving him like a nail into the ground, making him feel smaller. Smaller than he'd ever felt, a mere shade of the man he once was.

My brave kings. Now you are mine.

Gareth said, "What have we done?"

Roan shook his head. He remembered the way he'd felt as he looked in the mirror, how good it felt, how perfect…

"She enchanted us. We didn't have a choice." Ahead of Roan, there was an enormous glassy surface, shimmering in the wan light. *The inside of the mirror*, he realized. *We're inside her locket.* The realization sent chills down his spine. "Oh gods, we're trapped."

"We could've been stronger. We could've fought her, like Gwen told us to."

Roan knew he was right. They were weak. Just when he thought he was finally moving forward, controlling the direction of his own life, he'd tumbled headlong into a spider's web.

"I shouldn't even be here," Gareth muttered. He took a step forward across the rocky terrain. Cracks formed where he stepped. Mist swirled around his ankles.

"No, you shouldn't. You should be king."

"That's not what I meant." Gareth took another step. More cracks. More swirling mist. "I shouldn't be alive. I was meant to die. This is your fault."

Roan shook his head. "That better be the enchantment talking. I saved your life. If you had died, you still would've been a failed Shield. Guy was *already dead*." Roan was aware of the nastiness in his voice, but he didn't care. This ungrateful prince had crossed the line too many times.

191

"You coward!" Gareth shouted, launching himself at Roan. Roan twisted away and they went down in a heap. Gareth punched him twice in the ribs, and Roan kneed him hard in the gut. Gareth gasped and Roan rolled away, getting to his feet.

"Stop. This is ridiculous. We have to figure out how to get out of this."

Breathing heavily and clutching his stomach, Gareth said, "You're right."

Roan extended a hand to help him up, and Gareth accepted it. Just as Roan started to pull him to his feet, Gareth yanked back, throwing him off balance. He swept Roan's legs out from under him and pounced on top, landing blows to his jaw, his lips, his nose.

Roan snuck an arm between the barrage, shoving his fingers into Gareth's eyes. The prince howled and fell back. Roan used his advantage to press his knees into the prince's chest, wrapping his hands around his neck. Anger coursed through him, flowing from head to neck to chest, and into his arms and hands, which tightened.

Gareth tried to suck in a breath, but couldn't. His arms and legs flopped to either side, trying to gain purchase on Roan's skin, but finding none. His face was red, his eyes wide and fearful.

But then he stopped fighting, and a resigned expression formed. This was what he wanted—this was what he thought he deserved.

Roan hated himself in that moment. He hated the anger inside him, hated the violence he was capable of, just like any other bloodthirsty man in the realm. He should've turned the other cheek when Gareth hit him, should've let him do as he would, until all of his fury was extinguished.

Roan released him and Gareth gasped, coughing, his hands automatically coming up to rub his sore neck, where fierce red handprints were already forming. "No," he rasped. "Don't stop. Please. Finish me. End me."

"No," Roan said, scooting closer. Slowly, tenderly, he cradled Gareth Ironclad's head in the crook of his arm. The urge to hurt him had been replaced by a much more tender feeling. "I saved you because you are worthy of life. More worthy than I. I saved you because you are my friend."

"Let go of me," Gareth said. "We can't—this is unnatural." Oh. *Oh.* Was this why Gareth had rejected him before, because in his world men were with women and women with men? But there was no power behind Gareth's words, all strength leaving him as he nestled further into Roan's arms. He shook his head and bit his lip and wept, sobbing his eyes out until he ran out of tears.

When they finally rose, it was dark, the sky offering nothing more than a dead, moonless, starless stare.

"How are we going to escape?" Gareth said.

Roan slapped him on the back. "The way we always do," he said. Gareth cocked his head to the side, confused. "With sheer dumb luck."

Gareth laughed, and Roan joined him.

As they wandered the unnatural night, Roan swore he could feel his soul being stretched, pulled, pushed and prodded. He could tell Gareth was feeling something similar, because the prince continuously reached up to touch his chest, where he'd been stabbed by the Kings' Bane, rubbing the skin through his shirt.

But Roan knew it wasn't Gareth's injury that was bothering him, it was this place.

Felicity, the Queen of the Wood Nymphs, hadn't spoken to them again, leaving a hollow, empty place in Roan's chest. It was strange, even knowing what she was, what she'd done to them, he still longed for her voice, her touch.

I am weak, he thought. *Just as Gwendolyn always believed.*

They were walking toward the enormous mirror that stretched from barren ground to black sky, but despite the fact that they'd been marching for hours on end, it never seemed any nearer. The desolate place was full of tricks, too, cracks appearing suddenly beneath their feet, spouting fire; snakes appearing from thin air, striking at their heels; nasty flying creatures with leathery wings swarming from above, clawing their cheeks, and then disappearing into the sky.

"Felicity is madder than a six-legged donkey," Roan commented.

"Aye. She killed her own mother and stole her sisters' souls," Gareth said.

"The lockets?"

"Aye. I've heard stories about the wood nymphs. Their souls are kept in their mirrored lockets. Over time, they break down, until they fade away into nothingness. Unless they feed them new souls. That's where we come in."

"Information that would've been useful *before* we looked into her locket."

"I didn't see you helping!"

"I didn't know what was happening."

"And I did? We were practically slobbering over her."

Roan laughed. This was normal. The constant bickering, the finger-pointing.

"Nice shiner, by the way," Gareth said.

"You got in a few good shots. Sorry about your neck." Roan could still see the marks where he'd squeezed Gareth's throat, the purple-blue shapes of his fingers and thumbs.

"For the Peacemaker, you're awfully violent," Gareth grumbled, but Roan could tell it was meant as a jape.

"I didn't used to be like this. Must be *your* influence."

Before Gareth could offer a retort, a snake burst from the ground, springing up and straight for Roan's face. He flinched back, but Gareth's hand snapped out, catching the viper by the throat. "Nasty creatures," he said, tossing it aside like a bad piece of fruit.

Roan breathed again. "You saved my life," he said.

Gareth shrugged it off. "Not necessarily, we don't even know if they're poisonous. Why would the nymph want to kill us right away when she went through so much trouble to capture us in the first place? From the stories I've heard of the woodland nymphs, she'll want to torment us for an eternity before fully sucking our souls dry."

"That makes me feel better. Thank you."

"My pleasure."

"What else have you heard? Is there any escaping this mirror?"

"Well, someone must've escaped to tell these tales in the first place. But if they knew a way out, I've never heard it."

"Fantastic."

They continued on in silence, moving more for the sake of *feeling* like they were doing something than for any other real purpose. Eventually, Roan collapsed. Gareth joined him soon after. They lay their cheeks on the rough ground and looked at each other. Roan asked, "What do you think she did with Gwendolyn?"

Gareth shrugged in the dark. "Probably released her. Felicity won't want to start a war with the Orians."

The thought made Roan feel somewhat better. If it wasn't for him, they never would've set foot in the confounded Tangle in the first place. "I'm bone-weary."

"Aye. Me too."

"I don't want to wake up with a snake on my face."

"We could take turns sleeping. Me first."

"Bastard."

"Speaking of bastards, tell me a bedtime story."

Roan closed his eyes. Opened them. "What kind of story?"

"About your mother. About your father. About what really happened to you."

Roan sighed, deeply. There was dust in his mouth, and he smacked his dry lips. "There's not much to tell, and I only know what my Southron guardian told me."

"Tell me anyway."

Roan didn't like to think about the past, not when most of it felt like someone else's tale. "They discovered my mark when I was a suckling babe."

"You were born in the west. How are you alive?"

Roan shook his head. "My parents saved me. They killed for me. My mother, she died for me, for my family. She killed herself to protect them from a truth that would destroy our house."

"What truth?"

"Me," Roan said simply.

"Why didn't the west change its ways? Why didn't your father change the laws? He was the king."

Roan propped his head up on his hand. "It's not that simple. Hundreds of years of history, of tradition, of fear, cannot be easily undone. And there were the furia to consider."

"The furia." Gareth wrinkled his nose. "The red warriors are strong, I admit. I have seen them in battle, along the Spear. They are fierce. But doesn't the monarchy control them?"

"From what my guardian explained to me about western politics, no. Neither the crown nor the Faith control one another. They are separate bodies, unified only in maintaining peace and righteousness over the realm. If the monarchy was thought to have fallen into sin, the furia would have the power and numbers to overthrow the crown and replace the ruler with another, more benevolent, leader."

"Benevolent meaning someone who would kill those bearing skinmarks?"

"Aye. The *sin*marked. That's how they think of people like me. The spawn of demons, enemies to Wrath."

"So to save you they had to send you away. It was the only choice."

"Aye."

"I'm—I'm sorry."

Roan's eyes met Gareth's, which were full of sincerity. "What about you? You can't leave the east forever. It's your home."

"Not anymore. Now I have no home. And anyway, last I checked we were stuck in a nymph's enchanted soul locket, so…"

"Good point. For a moment I had forgotten."

"You can sleep first," Gareth said.

"You sure?"

"Aye. I'll keep the creepy crawlies away."

"Thank you."

The moment Roan's eyes closed, weariness sucked him under like a black tide, and he slept.

His dreams were full of darkness and pain.

Twenty

The Northern Kingdom, north of Gearhärt
Annise Gäric

The ragtag group of soldiers formed a twisting, turning brown line in the snowfields. Though a makeshift road had been packed down by the lead riders, the going was slow, the surface too slippery for anyone to move with haste.

Arch hadn't woken up during the additional week Annise had given him, so they had departed Gearhärt as planned, with a force that was now well over a thousand. She'd refused to leave Archer behind, and so her brother lay, still sleeping, in the back of a cart drawn by two horses. Packed around him were bags of dry provisions, as well as several barrels of mamoothen stew, a parting gift from Netta.

Hardly a chariot fit for a king, Annise thought. *Or even a prince, for that matter.* But it was the best they could do at this point, and he seemed comfortable enough. Perhaps one of the many bumps in the road would finally wake him.

And yet, in the back of Annise's mind, she wondered whether it was better if he slept for a while longer, at least until they'd taken back Castle Hill. That way he wouldn't have to fight. That way she wouldn't have to explain that she was the ruler of the north now.

Zelda walked beside Arch's cart, refusing to ride a horse. Something about the packed snow being "softer." Her husband, Sir Craig, rode a brown mare beside her, his stout form at odds with his beautiful steed.

A voice drew Annise away from her brother's cart. "May I ask what is on a queen's mind?" Tarin asked, riding beside her. He was mounted on the largest stallion Annise had ever seen, as large as she suspected the giant horses of Phanes might be. Still, the massive beast was breathing hard under its burden. Though it seemed impossible, Annise almost thought Tarin looked even bigger than he had a week before. *Must be all of Netta's mamoothen stew. I've probably gained a quarter-stone, too.*

"You may ask," Annise said.

"But you won't answer."

Annise offered him a wry smile.

Tarin said, "I thought we were past all of our secrets."

"We are, but I still have a right to my own thoughts. What if I asked you of the bloodlust you feel in battle?"

Tarin grimaced. She'd struck a chord, as she knew she would, though it made her feel a little bad. "Fair enough." He rode away, and Annise wished she hadn't broached the topic of what he referred to as "the monster inside." Unfortunately, it was that

200

very monster that had saved them on multiple occasions, and was why he would be such a valuable soldier in the battle to come.

Still, it saddened Annise to think that there was a part of Tarin that scared her, a part of him that scared himself. *I want to love all of you. I want to understand...* The unspoken words whispered through her mind as she watched him ride away.

His presence was quickly replaced by Sir Dietrich, whose mount was a white mare with a chestnut mane. He was once again wearing his full platemail. Though he'd had the chance to obtain a brand new set, he was still in his old armor, with its dents and scrapes and dull sheen. "You're wearing your boots," he said, grinning.

"I can unlace them quickly," Annise shot back.

His smile faded. "You want to know the truth?"

"That's all I ever ask for."

"I bear a skinmark."

Though Annise had suspected it for a while, the revelation still sent an icy zing of energy racing through her. The only other skinmarked person she'd ever known was the Ice Lord, and he was about as personable as an icicle. Of course, she'd seen three other marked during the battle at Raider's Pass—Beorn Stonesledge, the ironmarked; some kind of a healer, though she didn't know his name; and her brother, Bane, bearing the deathmark.

"Let me guess: you bear the swordmark," Annise said.

"That's as good a name for it as any. I was practically born with a sword in my hand, besting youth twice my age and winning competitions across the realm."

201

"And saving the lives of queens?" Annise smirked, glad things were back to normal with the knight. A little truth went a long way.

He smiled back. "No, that was a first."

"I would've had you knighted, but you've already achieved that status."

"A kiss on the cheek will do."

"It'll earn you a punch on the other cheek from Tarin."

"It'll be worth it. Plus, I heard he hits like a girl."

Annise shook her head. Dietrich was a notorious flirt, even with her. "I'm a girl, and I hit pretty hard." She raised a gloved fist.

"She does," Zelda cut in. "She's my niece."

Dietrich ignored her and said to Annise, "No, you're a woman. There's a difference."

"But I was once a girl. And even then I hit hard enough to make the boys cry."

"I would've liked to see that."

"What does this swordmark look like?"

"Like a burn scar," Dietrich said, winking.

"He burned himself to hide the mark," Zelda said. "Now *that* would hurt."

"Is it true?" Annise asked.

He nodded. Annise couldn't imagine doing such a thing, how painful it must've been.

"What did it look like before you scarred your skin?"

"A sword with an ornate handle. The design was quite intricate."

"Why didn't you just tell me?"

"Because I've never told anyone."

"Why not? It would've brought you fame, and a place at my father's side."

"Despite this smile..."—he flashed his white teeth—"...I was never interested in fame. And it was because of your father that I hid my mark."

"Smart man," Zelda said. "My brother was a greedy king. He coveted those with skinmarks."

Annise frowned. She'd hated her father as much as anyone, but there was clearly more to the story. "What did he do to you?"

Dietrich's smile faded. "Nothing. He did nothing to me."

Annise suddenly felt wrong probing into this man's past. She'd gotten the information she was looking for, the information she needed to utilize the knight to the best of his abilities. Any other information was his to offer.

"Fine. And thank you again for saving my life."

The smile was back. "Now how about that kiss?"

Zelda laughed. "Hit him, Your Highness."

She didn't need to be told twice.

Twice Annise had seen the strange knight, Christoff Metz, ride pass, and twice he'd offered her a "Your Highness" and ridden onward. It was like he was pacing the line of soldiers, back and forth, back and forth, back to front, front to back. The only one she'd seen him speak to was her aunt and Sir Craig. The three of them seemed to get on surprisingly well. Or perhaps it wasn't so surprising, given their individual eccentricities.

Now, as Sir Metz passed the third time, she beckoned him over. Tarin hadn't returned since he'd left, and neither had Sir Dietrich, especially after she'd given him the kiss he'd requested—a snowball to the face. The rest of the soldiers treated her with deference, and were always awkward around her, even if she tried to make conversation. Archer had always been so good with the people, his admirers, but such skill had been lost on Annise.

"Yes, Your Highness, how may I serve?" Sir Metz said as his horse trotted up.

Just like the first time she'd met the stiff-looking knight, his silver armor was so well-polished she could see her wobbly reflection in it. His straw-like hair was perfectly combed to the side. His back was straight and his hands in perfect position on his horse's reins.

"Tell me about yourself," Annise said, trying to make conversation.

"Your Highness?"

Annise sighed, remembering how specific she'd had to be with her questions before. She rephrased. "Where are you from?"

"The north," Metz said.

Annise shook her head. Either the knight had a sense of humor as dry as the Scarra Desert or he was as literal as an ice bear. "Which city?"

"Darrin," he said.

She nodded. Darrin was the Northern Kingdom's easternmost city, protecting the jagged cliffs known as the Razor from attack by the eastern stronghold called Crow's Nest.

"And your family?"

"Yes, they were there, too." Annise noticed he had a strange way of not looking her in the eyes when he spoke to her. It was a little disconcerting, and she found herself bobbing her head to try to meet his gaze. But each time he just darted his eyes away from her.

Once more, she rephrased. "Where is your family now?"

"In Darrin," he said.

"So you left, but they never did?"

"Obviously. I have just stated that they are in Darrin, whilst I am here, riding next to you, suggesting that, yes, I left." The words having left his mouth, he snapped his lips shut, before opening them to say, "I've done it again, haven't I?"

Annise didn't know what to say. She'd never been spoken to in such a way in her life. "Done what?"

"Been rude," Metz explained. "I have a tendency to do that. Mother used to say that I couldn't read between the lines. I read the lines and nothing more."

"It's fine," Annise said. "I don't mind. Brutal honesty is a quality I happen to admire."

"Really? But you're the queen."

She changed the subject. "How did you achieve knighthood?"

A smile seemed to want to form on his lips, but it didn't quite make it. "My father is a soldier. As a boy, he taught me how to use weapons. When I held a sword for the first time, I never wanted to put it down again. I even slept with it at night. I have a tendency to…get obsessed with things."

"Like polishing your armor?" Annise had intended it as a joke, but the knight nodded vehemently.

"How did you know?"

"It shines like a crystal goblet."

"Oh." He looked down, as if only just noticing how well-polished it was. "Yes. I guess it does. I shine it thrice a day, more if it gets smudged or if it snows."

"Which *never* happens in the north," Annise said.

"What? Yes, it does. All the time. Almost every day, in fact."
He paused, scrunching his forehead. "Wait. Sorry. That was a
jape, wasn't it? Sarcasm? Mother said japes were wasted on my
ears, and that I was born without a mind for sarcasm."

"I am the one who should apologize. I will try to refrain from
japing, though I must admit it will be hard for me. I wear sarcasm
as well as armor."

"I wish I could appreciate humor," the knight said. "I always
saw other soldiers laughing, but never understood why."

"Back to your knighthood..."

"Of course. I joined the army when I came of age. I was good
at following orders, though my superiors often mocked me."

"Didn't that bother you?"

"No. Yes. I don't know."

"Sorry to interrupt."

"It's fine. Anyway, I saved one hundred and fourteen lives at
the Black Cliffs."

Annise laughed. "That's a precise number."

Metz frowned, but said nothing. Apparently her comment
wasn't worthy of a response.

"I only mean that most people would say they saved many
lives. They wouldn't count them."

"Oh. I count everything. Like how many steps we've taken
since departing Gearhärt—two thousand seven hundred and
eighty-six. Well, those are my horse's steps, and it will vary from
horse to horse, plus a horse has four legs so it's very different for
those on foot..."

"You've been counting your horse's steps since we left this
morning?"

"Yes."

"While we've been talking?"

"It's just something I do."

Annise shook her head. She'd never met anyone as strange as this knight, which was saying something considering her aunt was known as one of the oddest women in Castle Hill. "Like escaping from my uncle and seeking me out?"

"No, that's completely different. And I didn't seek *you* out. I sought out your brother. I thought he was the king."

"Either way. You did what you thought was right. That's a rare thing these days. Especially in the north."

Once more, he frowned, as if her words perturbed him greatly. "I'm a knight. It is my duty to serve the king—or queen—and you are the queen. Not your uncle."

Pride rose inside Annise. Something about this man gave her hope for the future, a hope she hadn't felt in a long time. "Tell me about the potion my uncle made you drink."

"I didn't want to drink it."

"I know."

"Soldiers held me down. They pinched my nose. They forced it down my throat. It burned like fire."

"Then what happened?"

"I don't want to talk about it."

"Please. It is important."

"Is it a command?"

I'm good at following orders. Annise knew that with a simple command he would tell her everything she wanted to know, but the fear in his eyes, the way his lips were trembling...

She couldn't use his obedience against him.

"No. But I would like it if you would tell me."

"I don't want to!" His voice rose suddenly, startling her, almost making her drop the reins. "I don't want to! I don't want to!"

Tarin was by her side in an instant, his horse nosing between them. Sir Dietrich appeared on the opposite side, pulling the knight away as he continued to scream. "Let go of me! Don't touch me! I don't want to!"

"I'm sorry," Annise said, horrified by the reaction she'd gotten. "Don't hurt him, Dietrich."

Dietrich led Metz and his horse away, the knight continuing his fit. Zelda swooped in, saying something to Metz that seemed to calm him.

Tarin placed a hand on Annise's arm. "Are you well, my queen?"

Annise shook her head. "A little startled, but yes. We were just talking and then..."

"His head isn't on quite straight," Tarin said. "Be careful around him."

"I don't think he would hurt me. He's too faithful for that."

"Still. I'll be present for any future interactions with him."

"I don't need a caretaker," Annise said.

Tarin mumbled something that sounded like a curse.

"What was that? Care to share with your queen?"

"I said, 'The Stubborn Queen.'"

Annise laughed. "The Stubborn Queen and the Armored Knight," she said. "Sounds like an awful children's story."

"If by awful you mean riveting," Tarin said.

"Why Tarin, was that a joke? I was beginning to think your sense of humor had frozen and fallen off back on the Howling Tundra."

"Was that before or after your victory over the ice bear?" he fired back.

"You know, you once called me the Bear Slayer. That had a nice ring to it."

"As you reminded me, you never actually *slayed* the bear. Just chased it off with a few snowballs."

"That's true. You were stumbling over a snowdrift at the time, right?"

"Har and double har," Tarin said. He lowered his voice, suddenly sounding serious, using the gruff tone that always made Annise's heart beat just a little bit faster. "You know, even when you were being stubborn and, well, *yourself*, I wanted to kiss you."

"Even back on the Howling Tundra?"

"Even on the first night."

"When you finally took off your armor so we could snuggle?"

Tarin sniffed at the word choice. "I was being honorable, sharing my body heat. I seem to remember you shivering and begging me to."

"Maybe because I'd wanted to kiss you, too."

"Even before you knew who I really was?"

Annise paused. She wasn't certain. She'd felt a connection with him on the Tundra, of that there was no doubt, but whether it was romantic or not was hard to pinpoint.

"Ha! See? You were scared of me, weren't you?"

"Terrified," Annise said, punching him on the shoulder. It made a dull clang. "Ow. I prefer you without armor."

"The day is wearing thin. We should stop and make camp. If you can procure a large enough tent, I'd be happy to oblige your request for no armor."

Annise laughed, but she had to turn away to hide her blush. His words had sent warmth from her chest to her extremities. Regardless of the playfulness in his offer, he was right. It had been a long, cold march, and she could see the weariness in the hunched forms of the soldiers marching behind her.

"I agree," she said. "We will shelter under the trees for the night." Up ahead, the forward units had entered a thick, dark forest. "I will have Dietrich prepare the largest tent we have available. And you *will* remove your armor, that is a command."

Before Tarin could respond, there was a shout from up ahead, and then a scream.

More screams followed, and then the trees began to shift, as if pummeled by a powerful wind, though the breeze was gentle. One of them cracked, collapsing, crushing a soldier beneath it.

The tree began to rise once more, gripped by an enormous gray hand.

Above the fist rose the face of a monster, thrice again the size of Tarin.

By the time Annise and Tarin reached the tree line, a group of archers had formed, unleashing volley after volley at the...*thing*...standing before them.

Thing was one of several words floating through Annise's mind as she tried to describe the enemy they now faced. Other choices included *monster* and *troll*. Its legs were gray and muscular and appeared to be made of stone, as was the rest of it. Tatters of ripped cloth—the remains of its clothing? Annise guessed— clung to its chest and torso, but the shredded material seemed far too small to have ever fit such a giant. Its head was a lumpy boulder, its mouth a cave with large, blunt teeth. Its eyes were bulbous colorless orbs that could've been staring right at her and she wouldn't be able to tell.

The arrows that fell against the stone creature were naught but pesky gnats, and it swatted them away with one hand while swinging the broken tree trunk with the other. The line of archers dove in every direction as the tree swept past, knocking several into the air like the monster was playing a game of stickball, with the soldiers as the balls. One tried to run and the creature used the tree like a mallet, pounding him on the head.

Annise looked away, unable to stomach the explosion of gore.

Tarin said, "Can you distract it?"

"What?" Annise watched as another archer was batted away, smashing into a tree and crumpling to the ground. In only a few bare moments, most of her forward riders had been destroyed.

"Oi. Listen to me." He grabbed her chin and forced her to look directly into his eye slits. "Distract it," he repeated. "Rally the cavalry, use the ground soldiers to keep it busy. Understood?"

She nodded, sticking out her jaw. *I am the queen*, she reminded herself. *These soldiers are my responsibility.* Tarin started to ride away, toward the giant's left flank. "Tarin," she said.

He turned, glancing back, his dark armor even darker in the fading light.

"Be careful."

She swore she could see his grin through his face plate. As he rode away, she whipped her own steed around. "First cavalry! To me!"

Not unlike the easterners, the northerners did not protect their rulers from battle. Kings and queens were expected to be strong, leading rather than cowering. Though Annise loathed many of the northern traditions, this was one she would uphold, as long as she drew breath. *Only risk for others what you would risk for yourself*, she thought, a mantra she'd overheard Arch being taught as a youth, when it was a foregone conclusion that he would be the next king.

211

Two dozen seasoned riders who had fought with Annise and her brother at Raider's Pass rode up, awaiting orders. She searched for Sir Dietrich, who she'd appointed as their commander. He was nowhere to be found. *No time to think about that.* She spoke to all of them at once. "We must harry the beast from all sides. In and out, in and out, like we are one person breathing together. Do not risk your lives if you can help it. Understood?"

"No," one of them said. "We will distract the monster, but our lives are yours. Our queen."

A lump formed in Annise's throat at the loyalty displayed by this man. By all of them. "Then mine is yours," she answered. To another soldier, she said, "You..." His name escaped her.

"Sir Morley," he provided.

"Sir, please instruct the first battalion of foot soldiers to charge the enemy, but to stop before getting within the cavalry's ranks. We want the giant looking in many different directions. Then come join your brothers."

There was a scream and all heads turned in the direction of the sound. The giant had dropped the tree and was now holding a man between his hands, pulling him apart.

Annise ripped her gaze away. "Go, now."

"Yes, Your Highness. What about the rest of the army?"

Annise's eyes were steel. "If we fail, they should retreat." She wouldn't risk any more lives. If this didn't work, then perhaps their foe was impossible to defeat.

The man nodded and rode off, calling her orders to the foot soldiers trailing behind the party of riders. They were the best of the best. She had purposely set them at the front of their marching train, along with the first cavalry—behind them the remainder of the army was less convincing, most of them untrained, too young, or too old.

"And me?" someone else said, riding up. "What are your orders?"

It was Sir Metz, his armor shining even in the waning daylight. There was no hint of awkwardness in him from his earlier fit, as if it never happened. He was part of the second cavalry. "If we are defeated, lead the retreat, Sir Metz. Protect my brother, for he will be the king you thought he was. And Zelda, too, keep her safe."

She could tell by the hard set of his jaw that he wasn't pleased with her command, but his honor wouldn't allow him to contradict it. "Yes, Your Highness."

She addressed the first cavalry once more, raising her own sword in the air. "For the kingdom!" she cried.

"For the kingdom!" they roared in response.

They charged into battle.

The monster was chewing on something, its stone teeth grinding together. Annise refused to focus on that, instead steering her steed toward a spot just to the left of it. She looked for Tarin, but didn't see him anywhere, though she spotted his horse wandering along the edge of the forest, riderless. "Ahh!" she screamed, brandishing her sword above her head, though she had no intention of actually using it against the stone giant.

The rest of her soldiers roared in unison.

The giant spat out a bone and swung a fist with such unexpected speed that, for a moment, Annise was too stunned to react, barreling headlong into danger. At the last second, however, she managed to steer even further left, the breath of the punch whistling past her like a storm wind. One of her men wasn't so fortunate, taking the brunt of the blow on his flank—

her stomach heaved as she heard both his and his horse's bones breaking.

It had barely begun, and already her plan was falling to pieces, the giant stomping into the thick of the cavalry, punching and kicking. Another man was crushed, his scream lost as he was driven a foot into the ground. *Frozen hell*, Annise thought. *What is this creature?*

The foot soldiers arrived, and despite her warning to not get too close, several of them charged between the riders and slashed at the beast's stone ankles. It roared, but not in pain, in anger, grabbing two of them by the necks and smashing them repeatedly together before dropping them. Their broken bodies hit the ground and didn't move again.

The monster lunged for another soldier, but a white form streaked past, arms wrapping around the foot soldier and carrying him out of harm's way. The giant grabbed at the empty air a few times, as if still trying to understand what had happened.

Beyond it, Annise saw Sir Christoff Metz deposit the soldier back on his feet, unharmed.

Blast him! Annise cursed in her head. The knight was supposed to lead the retreat and protect her brother, if it came to it, and now he was in the thick of things.

Tarin! Where are you? she wanted to shout, but she dared not give away his position, wherever it may be.

The monster targeted another rider, stomping toward him. "No more," Annise breathed. And then she yelled: "Here! Over here, you ugly stone mutt! Face the Bear Slayer, you coward!"

The creature turned, its oddly vacant eyes seeming to focus for a second. On her. And then it unleashed a garbled cry and stampeded right for her. That's when she spotted Tarin, who was somehow clinging to the giant's shoulder, gripping it with one powerful hand, while it flung itself toward Annise. Her eyes met his for an instant, and then he disappeared behind the monster's head.

Distract it. Those two words were all Annise could think as she swung her leg over her mount and slid down, slapping the horse on the rump. It didn't need further urging, galloping away and out of danger.

The giant curled its stone fist, the ground shaking underfoot as it stomped toward her, its strides swallowing the distance too fast, too fast—

She dove to the side, landing hard on her shoulder but letting the momentum carry her into a roll and then back onto her feet. Out of the corner of her eye, she caught a glimpse of the creature flying past, skidding to a stop, gravel spitting from its feet.

Tarin was behind its head now, clinging on with both hands, trying to steady himself. The giant had finally realized it had company, shaking its head and swatting at its own skull. Annise held her breath as Tarin dodged the blows, which crashed like thunder, stone on stone. Chunks of rocks broke off, tumbling around Annise like a landslide. She covered her head as several rocks glanced off her arms painfully.

When she looked back, half the monster's head was gone from self-inflicted wounds, but still Tarin clung to it. Strange inky sap—blood?—was running down the giant's neck, shoulders, back, and chest.

The monster stumbled, falling to one knee, but still it continued to hit itself in the head, trying to dislodge Tarin, who clambered over the giant's brow, raised his Morningstar, and shoved the spiked ball deep into the creature's eye.

The glassy orb popped like an inflated sack, spewing out a white, milky substance. It roared, and this time Annise could feel

215

the pain in its bellow as it fell to its side. But still Tarin didn't relent, pushing the barbed weapon in up to his elbow, twisting it around until it emerged from *inside* the monster's head, almost like he was threading a needle through cloth, bursting from its other eye, splattering more white liquid.

And then he ripped himself free, pulling his Morningstar with him, landing on the run and diving out of the way as the monster's arm flapped wildly, slamming to the ground with a thud.

Annise could barely breathe as the giant writhed and flopped for a few moments, scratching at its own eyes before going still. All around the beast, the soldiers cheered.

Tarin, however, stood and stalked off into the woods, his chest rising and falling beneath his dark armor, sappy blood and milky ichor dripping from the spikes of his Morningstar.

Annise was about to run after him, when something even stranger happened. The stone giant began to crumble, the rocky exterior falling away from its sides, its broad chest, its back, its legs, creating a miniature quarry around its body. Until all that was left was…

Annise gasped.

A man.

In death, their fallen foe was naught but a man, naked save for a thin loin cloth covering his midsection. He had the build of a soldier—strong arms and muscular chest, laced with scars—though he wore no armor save for the stone layers that had protected him.

Annise had ordered he be covered with a large sheet, especially because she couldn't bear to look at his mutilated eyes, dark, bloody pits which seemed to stare at her sightlessly. Soldiers milled around the body, inspecting the shattered stones surrounding him.

Tarin had yet to return from the woods.

Zelda stood beside her. Sir Craig, upon Annise's request, had ridden off to check on Archer.

"Frozen hell, how is this possible?" Annise said, a question intended for herself.

But she received an answer, from Sir Christoff Metz, who strode up to her, bowing stiffly. "Your Highness, this is one of the Imposter King's men," he said.

No. Annise didn't want to believe it, because if it was true, then they were doomed. They'd lost twenty-eight men in the battle, and at least that many had sustained serious injuries. And they'd only fought *one* monster. To have any hope of victory against ninety-eight more of them, they would need a force at least five times the size of the one they had, and that was assuming they were all well-trained career soldiers, which they weren't.

"No wonder my uncle sent his entire army to Blackstone for the assault on Knight's End," Annise said, trying not to sound defeated, though she could hear the tremor in her own voice. "Are all his monsters this strong?"

"Their levels of strength vary from monster to monster," Metz said. "As do their skills. Some are fast, some are strong, some more agile. They seem to complement each other."

"Fantastic," Annise muttered.

The knight frowned. "I fail to see how our current situation could be defined by the word 'fantastic.'"

217

Zelda snorted, but didn't comment.

"Sarcasm, Sir," Annise explained.

"Oh. Sorry."

He looked like he was about to say something else, but just then another soldier came jogging up. He was a foot soldier, still wearing his helm and shield, though his face plate was up, revealing a young, clean-shaven man around Archer's age. "Sir, you saved my life," he said to Metz. "I owe you a life debt." He thrust a hand toward the knight.

Metz backed away quickly, as if being offered a severed body part as a trophy. "Don't touch me!" he said, his face aghast with horror.

The young soldier raised his eyebrows in surprise. "Apologies, Sir, I only meant to thank you."

Metz took a deep breath, his fingers curling and uncurling at his sides. "You're welcome. Just...just please don't touch me. I don't like it when people touch me."

Though it was clear the young soldier didn't understand exactly what was happening, he nodded, and said, "I will repay this debt, one way or another."

"I need no gold," Metz said.

The man shook his head and departed.

"You know," Annise said, "he wasn't actually offering you coin."

Metz frowned. "Then what was all that talk of repayment and debts?"

Zelda said, "He didn't mean it literally. Just like when my husband called himself a drunk all the time, he only meant he was clumsy." She chuckled at this like it was the funniest quip.

"Then he should've said what he meant. People should say what they mean."

More and more, Annise was finding herself speechless around the thin, but valiant knight, and yet she welcomed the distraction. "Why did you disobey my command?" she asked him. "You have vowed to serve me."

"I did not disobey," Metz said, unblinking.

"It's true," Zelda said. "I heard your command."

Annise massaged her forehead. Her shoulder ached and the pain was radiating into her skull. Metz's word games were not helping the situation. "I commanded you to lead the retreat and protect my brother and aunt."

"Was your brother harmed? Clearly your aunt is safe." Beside him, Zelda nodded vehemently.

"Well, no, but—"

"I apologize for the interruption, Your Highness, but was retreat necessary?"

"No, because Tarin managed to—"

"Again, my sincerest apologies for the interruption, my queen, but I followed your command very specifically. You were not specific on what I should do in the event that we were *not* defeated, only if we were. I was fully prepared to carry out your command if the battle had turned against us."

"But how could you carry out my command if you were killed?"

"I wasn't killed."

Annise groaned. Having a conversation with this knight was like trying to run circles around oneself. "Why did you save that soldier?"

"He was going to die if I didn't."

"And you always try to save people from dying?"

His next response came a beat slower, his voice softer. "Yes."

"Why?"

219

"I refuse to answer unless you command me to. Specifically."

Annise stared at him. She'd made a habit of prying secrets from people lately, and she wasn't exactly fond of it. And, in this case, whatever secret Sir Metz was harboring wouldn't be likely to affect his performance in battle. "You may go," she said. "But we're not done. We'll need your counsel on how to defeat the rest of my uncle's army."

Metz bowed and departed.

Sir Dietrich appeared, taking Metz's place in front of her. "I can explain," he said.

Zelda said, "This should be entertaining."

Annise sighed. She was tired of explanations and arguments. Was ruling always this difficult? "Explain why, in their hour of greatest need, you were not there to lead your men into battle? Explain why you lost two knights today while you were nowhere to be seen? Please, I would love to hear your explanation."

"Me too," Zelda noted.

"I was making water," Dietrich said.

Annise almost choked. "The whole time?"

"Impressive," Zelda chimed in. "He has a strong flow."

Dietrich said, "I like to stay well hydrated, and nature was calling something fierce. I heard shouts and tried to…finish up as quickly as I could, but by the time I arrived the monster had already fallen."

Annise couldn't wait for this day to be over, considering the strange turn it had taken. But she couldn't exactly fault the man for urinating. It wasn't like they were expecting to be attacked by a monster made of stone. "Please try to be more alert, Sir," she said. "Just because you saved mine and Arch's lives doesn't mean you can shirk your duty."

"I'm sorry. I will learn to relieve myself faster."

Zelda guffawed. "We should include that skill in our training regimen."

Annise didn't have the energy left to chastise the knight further. Also, she had to turn away quickly to hide her own amusement. Why did he have to be so damn charming all the time?

However, her smile was quickly obliterated when she saw Tarin stride from the woods. She knew exactly why he'd fled the scene. She'd seen it before, when he closed himself off from her after killing three soldiers.

She could see it now, in the dark, intense stare radiating through his faceplate.

He might've killed a monster, but another lurked somewhere inside him. And it was one he could not kill.

"Every monster is different," Sir Metz explained. Annise had gathered all of her commanders to listen to him, to ask questions, to prepare. Zelda was also included, and was standing near the back gnawing on a chicken wing.

Annise was pleasantly surprised when Sir Dietrich showed up on time, offering her a huge grin. He was a hard man to stay angry at.

"But they're all made from stone?" the commander of the third cavalry asked.

Sir Metz breathed deeply at having been interrupted. "Please save all questions for the end. But no, they are not all made from stone. There seem to be endless variations, none of them pleasant. Some have claws, others fangs. Although my time while changed by the potion is like a dream, all fuzzy around the edges, one of the other men told me I was a wolf, but ten times the size. They said I tried to escape my cage, but the bars held."

Sir Metz paused for that to sink in before continuing. "The other thing I remember is the anger coursing through me. The bloodlust. It was like a monster had taken over my body, my mind. I hated it. *Hated it.* Losing control is my worst nightmare. But the other soldiers who were a part of the experiment felt differently. They *enjoyed* it. They spoke of how they couldn't wait to drink more of the potion, feel that power again."

Annise glanced at Tarin, but even under the glow of several torches, his eyes were cast in shadow. She wondered whether he felt the same way Metz had, only all the time. She wished there was something she could say to comfort him. His head turned toward hers for a moment, but then shifted away. "How do we defeat them?" Annise asked, turning her attention back to Metz.

"By focusing," he said. "One monster at a time. Every soldier fighting one."

Dietrich spoke. "But won't the other monsters obliterate us while we're doing that? It will be another massacre."

"I don't think so," Metz said.

"But you're not certain."

"Of course not. Certainty is a fool's game."

"Now hold on just a moment, are you calling me a—"

Annise raised her hand for silence. "Sir Dietrich. Let him finish." He closed his mouth, but didn't look too happy.

"I meant no offense, Sir," Metz said politely. "Only that no one—at least until today—has ever fought creatures like these. They're unnatural, potion-created. We can't be certain of anything. But I did see the way they reacted to each other, in their cages. They looked like they hated each other as much as the rest of us. Before I was made to drink the potion, I saw four others drink first. They tried to attack each other through the bars. So if we concentrate on one monster, it may only draw the other monsters to fight each other."

"That could just give us a chance," Annise said, nodding. "This is good information. Thank you, Sir Metz."

"I am only doing my duty," he replied stiffly, bowing.

"How will we coordinate our attack across our forces?" Tarin asked.

Annise was glad he'd finally spoken. She said, "Sir Dietrich will issue the commands. I will rely on the other commanders to spread the word. But as soon as the attack begins, it should be obvious which monster we're focusing on first."

"And if I die?" Dietrich asked.

"Good question!" Zelda offered enthusiastically from the back, holding up a drumstick.

"You won't," Annise said firmly. The strength of her response seemed to surprise the knight, and he nodded. "But if you do, the chain of command shall continue down the line. Most of all, we need to rely on our trained officers to ensure our untrained soldiers don't retreat at the first sign of violence."

"Agreed," Dietrich said.

"Did you really call it an 'ugly stone mutt' and shout for it to 'Face the Bear Slayer'?" Tarin asked, his dark lips curling at the corners in amusement.

As Tarin had requested, they were in a tent large enough for even him to stretch out across. His head was at one end and his feet at the other, brushing the sides. Again, he looked larger than before, like he had grown taller and broader in only a day.

As Annise had requested, his armor lay in one of the corners, leaving his translucent, black-veined skin bare, save for a thin pair of trousers tied with a rope around his waist. She was having trouble not gawking at the way his broad shoulders met his muscular chest met his brick-wall-like abdomen, as if he was wearing another set of armor, this one made to look like skin. The dark, protruding veins were like ropes, tying everything together.

"I do not recall," Annise said.

"Liar." Tarin grabbed her and pulled her into his lap, curling a strong hand behind her neck while kissing her deeply.

She pulled away sharply as images assaulted her mind:

A man being ripped in half.

A soldier smashing into a tree.

Humans crushed. Blood spilt. Bones broken.

Her people. Her army.

"What is it?" Tarin asked, concern unraveling across his face.

"I don't know if I can do this now." The words burned in her throat, because she *did* want to do this, more than anything, more than being a queen and fighting to take back what was rightfully hers. More than anything, she just wanted to love this man the way he deserved to be loved.

Tarin nodded, pulling her into a hug. He was so warm, so safe. Why couldn't she stay like this forever, and forget queens and kings, empires and kingdoms, unconscious brothers and evil uncles?

But she knew her dream of fleeing to the Hinterlands vanished into mist the moment she became queen.

As if reading her mind, Tarin whispered into her ear. "You are the queen now, and their pain is your pain, their sorrow is your sorrow, their deaths are your grief. I cannot begin to understand how hard today was for you."

Annise shook her head, her cheek rubbing against his broad shoulder. How did he know? How did he sense what she was feeling well enough to put into words what she was unable to herself? *How are you real?*

She was also having trouble reconciling the two Tarins she knew. The first Tarin, the one who'd fought the monster, unleashing violence like an uncaged beast, who'd stalked into the woods dripping blood, seemed like a stranger sometimes. Even after he'd returned, he hadn't spoken to her for a long time, going about helping the wounded, setting up camp, collecting firewood, scouting the area for any evidence of other creatures. Then, slowly, little by little, that Tarin had given way to this one, with his quick-witted quips and broad smile and endless chivalry.

It was like the two versions of him were fighting for control. Sometimes she feared who would emerge victorious. What scared her more, however, was that Tarin seemed to fear the very same thing.

"You know," he continued when she didn't respond. "I could've died today. You as well."

Annise frowned. Was he falling back into his hole of despair? His dark, twinkling eyes said otherwise. "I am very much aware of the danger we were in. Is there a point to this topic?"

"Yes," Tarin said, pulling her face toward his once more. His other hand dropped to her hip, resting there gently, rubbing circles with his thumb. "My point is that we should not waste the precious time that we have. Not one moment of it."

And then he kissed her again, and this time she gave herself to it fully, her nightmares chased away as he pulled off her clothes.

Twenty-One

The Western Kingdom, The Crimean Sea, somewhere west of the Dead Isles
Grey Arris

"What did you do to her?" Grey demanded, his eyes boring into Captain Smithers.

The captain laughed, and the sound made Grey's blood boil in his veins. How could he laugh when his own daughter was bleeding on the floor? "I see ye've taken a likin' to me daughter, have ye? Get in line, boy! Ye and ever' other lad 'tween Knight's End and Talis! Me daughter is a self-admitted whore-child, don't ye git that? Damaged goods. I dinnit lay a finger on her. No, I dinnit have to. Wrath is only makin' her pay fer her sins. She's lucky God dinnit deliver her to the Furies! Now git! She needs time to think 'bout what she's done."

Behind him, Kyla's moans had turned into choking sobs.

Grey was seething, every muscle in his body pulled tight like a bowstring ready to release its arrow. He knew what had happened.

What could he do? A captain was the king of his ship. If he challenged the captain's authority now, he could be hanged for treason. Or thrown overboard. Shae would have no one left to save her.

So he took a deep breath, uncurled his fisted fingers, and turned around, leaving Kyla bleeding on the floor behind her father.

And, as he walked away, Grey hated himself more than he ever had before.

Grey took a dozen steps before he turned around.

The captain was watching him with narrowed eyes. "Ya got somethin' to say, boy?"

"Aye," Grey said. "If you won't help her, let me. And then I'll never talk to her again, I swear it."

The captain blinked rapidly, like there was something in his eyes. "Why wuld ye help her?" he asked.

The question took Grey by surprise. He'd expected nothing less than an outright rejection. "Because I can," he said.

Smithers' body stiffened. A few moments passed in silence, and then his shoulders slumped. His eyes closed. Opened. His mouth opened. Closed. Opened again. He said, "Fine. Do as ye will. But don' let yer work suffer." He stomped off, his boots disappearing up the stairs to the top deck.

Grey blinked. *Did that really just happen?* He'd seen something in the captain's eyes before he'd left, something he'd never seen before. Grief? Perhaps, but not only. Regret? Yes, that was there, too. But the thing he thought he saw the most was something else.

Guilt.

Grey approached the doorway, which was still open. Kyla's moaning had grown softer, no more than the aching cry of a dying animal. Except Grey didn't think she was dying.

No, she was mourning.

He peeked around the corner. If she was aware of his confrontation with her father, or his presence, she gave no indication. She was completely and utterly focused on her arms, which held something in a bundle of bloody rags. The something wasn't moving, wasn't making a sound. Quiet and still.

"Kyla?" Grey said. "Are you hurt?"

Her lips pursed together, clamping off the sound. Her voice was a shattered-glass whisper. "It only matters because it hurts."

Grey took a step forward, into something wet. Kyla's blood, sticky, the smell of copper coins flooding his nose.

Kyla's head turned toward him. Her brow was sweaty, tendrils of hair sticking to her smooth, brown skin. "Do you want to see my beautiful girl?" she asked.

A girl. Oh, Wrath. If you exist, fix this. Give her back her child.

"I—I don't know," Grey admitted. The thought of seeing a dead baby made bile creep up his throat.

"Father wouldn't even look at her, his own granddaughter," Kyla said, tears dripping from her chin.

Grey steeled himself. "Let me see," he said. He stepped closer, ignoring the blood. Crouching down, he peered at the bundle as Kyla unwrapped it. For a moment he thought he was looking at a doll. Her face was so tiny, her eyes pinched shut, her nose naught but the size of a button, her little lips thin on top

228

and fuller at the bottom. Just like Kyla's. Her face had been wiped clean, and her skin was a lighter shade of brown than her mother's, her chin narrower, her eyes closer together. She had a full head of hair, brown and matted with blood and birthing fluid.

"She's"—he almost couldn't believe the truth behind his next word—"beautiful. So beautiful." And it was true. Even in death, this child—this baby—was the most beautiful thing in the world.

"Do you think so?" Kyla's lips trembled, her eyes filled with an ocean of tears.

"Yes," Grey breathed. He didn't think about what he did next, wrapping her in his arms, ignorant to the blood soaking his trousers, the tears drenching his shirt. Ignorant to everything but the broken girl and her lifeless daughter they held together.

As one, their shoulders shook.

The other seamen and their captain stayed above decks long into the night. For once, they made no bawdy jokes nor sang rowdy drinking songs. For once, their cruel laughter ceased.

Grey wondered whether the captain had finally put an end to it, or whether it was only a temporary reprieve.

For an hour, Grey helped Kyla clean herself, running up and down the steps, tossing buckets of bloody water into the ocean and then refilling them using the hand crank. He knew the blood might attract large predators, but so long as no one got thrown overboard it wouldn't be a problem. He was aware of the men's eyes following him each time he emerged and raced to the railing, but he ignored them. They didn't matter, not now. Perhaps they never did.

The captain, on the other hand, didn't look once, his back to Grey, his gaze trained firmly out to sea.

Back below decks, Grey used a damp cloth to clean Kyla's feet, her knees, her legs. He turned away so she could clean the rest of herself. He cleaned her baby while Kyla changed clothes, and then he handed her back the child and took her bloodied frock above and tossed it into the ocean.

Once she'd been settled into bed with extra pillows he'd stolen from the seamen's bunks, Grey found a thick, clean towel, and handed it to her. She looked at it, confused. "To catch any more blood," he explained. He tried not to blush but failed miserably.

She shook her head, biting her lip. "Thank you," she said.

He got to work on the floor, scrubbing tirelessly, determined to return the wood to its natural color. His right arm felt strong, his muscles tight from all the hard work over the last few weeks. While Kyla held her baby and watched, Grey scrubbed the bloodstains away, until they might've never existed.

Finished, he rose and went to her side. He held her hand. He stroked her brow. Her face wore a frown. "You don't care that I'm a whore?" she asked.

Grey grimaced, hating the way she used that word so casually to refer to herself, because she'd heard it so much. "I don't know what you are, but you're not what the world thinks you are."

"You are a good man," Kyla said, and kissed the back of his hand.

Grey had the urge to tell her the truth, how wrong she was, but instead he said, "You should sleep. Let me take her."

"No," she said. "She stays with me."

Grey nodded, closing the door on his way out.

Above, the stars pierced the black sky like sparkling yellow coins interlaced with rubies and emeralds. He looked for the golden key amongst them, but it was gone, vanished, like the tiny soul that should've been Kyla's daughter.

Grey stripped down to his underclothes, and got to work scrubbing out the blood from his clothes.

All the men had slept without their pillows and hadn't once complained. Without speaking, they went about their daily tasks. Grey immediately noticed the mainsail was hung at half-mast, not even catching the wind.

The captain apparently hadn't slept at all, and when Grey made his way to the bow, Smithers was still standing there, staring out at something perhaps only he could see.

He didn't flinch when Grey spoke, as if he was expecting him. "If it's what you want, I won't speak to Kyla again," Grey said.

The man didn't respond with words, but his shoulders shook and his hand went to his face as he cried.

Grey left him to his grief and regret and guilt and went to see Kyla.

To Grey's surprise, when he knocked, the door flew open. Kyla threw herself into his arms, clutching him so tightly he thought it might crack one of his ribs. "I didn't think you'd ever speak to me again," she said in his ear.

"Because of your father?" Grey asked, holding her at arm's length, scanning the room over her shoulder. The bed was made, the extra pillows gone. In the center of the bed was a small bump, wrapped in a clean white sheet.

"No. Because I'm not your problem."

A pang of sadness thumped in Grey's chest. The truth was, he'd almost walked away from her last night, when she'd needed him the most.

I didn't, Grey reminded himself. For once, perhaps, he'd made the right choice.

"You're not anyone's *problem*," Grey said. "You're a person. You're my friend."

He didn't intend to make her cry again, but she did, pressing her cheek against his chest. He waited for her to say something, but she didn't, and they stood that way for a long time.

Finally, she pulled away and spoke. "Do you think if I said something to my daughter, that she would hear me?"

Grey's eyes instinctively flitted to the wrapped form on the bed.

"No," Kyla said. "Not her. Not her body. Her soul."

Grey didn't know what he believed, not anymore. A month ago he would've said this life was all they had, and Kyla's daughter was dead for good. Just like his parents. Just like Kyla's mother. But now, even if he didn't believe, he *wanted* to believe.

"Yes," he said, and though it wasn't the truth exactly, it wasn't a lie either.

Kyla smiled, nodding. "I think so too," she said. "Will you listen?"

"Of course."

They sat on the bed, side by side, almost touching but not quite, except for their hands, which were clasped together like two parts of the same being.

"You will always be known to me as Myree," Kyla said. "My Myree." Her voice broke, but she blinked rapidly and swallowed, fighting off the emotion. "I want you to know that life wasn't always like this, so sad, so broken. I want you to know that once I used to awaken to the smell of yeasty bread rising, the sound of your grandmother singing, the glow of sun on the windowsill. I want you to know that once I was happy, and that I always believed you could make me happy again. Life was once better and I never gave up hope that it could be once more. You gave me that hope."

"Can it be better?" The question fell off of Grey's lips like a pebble bouncing off a cliff, breaking and clattering until it disappeared.

Kyla's eyes snapped to his. They were deep pools of brown, and he felt there was something mysterious in them, hidden so deep it could never be reached.

"I know who my daughter's father is," Kyla said.

After she told Grey her story, she insisted on tending to his arm. The pain was immense, but when she was done cleaning, administering a healing ointment, and bandaging the wound, it felt much better.

He cupped her cheek and said, "Thank you," and then went up to the deck.

Grey wanted to tell Captain Smithers what a fool he had been, but seeing the way the man continued to stare aimlessly out at sea, he didn't think he needed to tell him something he already knew.

Kyla's story was a collection of images in Grey's head, flashing past one by one, repeating over and over.

After her mother died, Kyla was forced to go off to sea with her father, who was the lifelong captain of a merchant vessel called The Jewel. Every fortnight they anchored at a new city, loading and unloading the ship, spending a night or two on dry land before sailing once more.

At first, it was a new adventure and the best possible way to get past her mother's death, but soon Kyla grew tired of all of the traveling, and longed to stay in one place. At a particular stop in Talis, she met a dashing young lad, Callum. They fell for each other quickly and completely, as many young lovers do, and she'd given herself to him in every way. Kyla desperately wanted to stay with him in the city, desperately wanted to marry him.

Her father refused, dragging her to the ship kicking and screaming.

A few months later, she was unable to hide her secret any longer: She was with child. Her father demanded to know who the father was, whether it was Callum from Talis. He demanded to have his revenge, threatening to beat the boy within an inch of his life for unflowering his only daughter.

Fearing for her true love, Kyla lied. In an outburst of anger, she said she didn't know who the father was, because she'd taken a lover in every city they'd stopped at over the last few months. It could be any of them, she claimed, so he'd have to beat them all to get his vengeance. She even managed to laugh to sell the lie.

In a fit of rage, he banished her to the lower decks, refusing her the sky and the sun and the fresh air, even when they were at port. He encouraged his men to call her the whore-child, and other names, which Kyla had worn like a badge of honor while protecting her Callum. When they stopped at Talis several times over the next few months, she pretended they were somewhere else, anywhere else. She slept for as many hours as she could, until she felt the ship's anchor being raised and the sails flapping in the wind once more.

One day, she hoped to return to Callum with their daughter in her arms.

Now, that day would never come.

Grey was the only one who helped Kyla prepare to send her daughter into the depths, though the other sailors watched from a distance, as if afraid that whatever killed the babe might be contagious.

First, they secured Myree's cloth wrappings with a tarlike substance used to mend damage to the ship. Then they constructed a miniature boat out of scrap wood. Although Grey's right arm was strong now, it was still uncoordinated, and after a few failed attempts, Kyla took over the hammering. Once the boat was deemed seaworthy, they lashed the cocooned babe to it with thick ropes, letting the excess dangle at each end. Grey helped as much as he could, but it was Kyla who knew the right kind of knots to tie.

When they finished, they both stared at their work for a few moments, unspeaking. The moment their eyes met, they knew it was time. Grey took one side, determined not to drop the little boat, despite only having one arm to lift with. Kyla raised the other end, gritting her teeth.

For an instant, the boat wobbled between them, and Grey almost fell, but then another set of hands appeared on the unbalanced side. Captain Smithers nodded to Grey, who nodded back.

Tears streamed down Kyla's face as the three of them manhandled the boat to the edge. The captain's strong hands gripped the excess rope, his knuckles whitening as he lowered the boat to the churning waves below. While Grey watched, Kyla hugged her father from behind, all the animosity from the past few months vanishing in that single stolen moment.

And then the tiny boat floated, pulled away by a strong current, and Smithers released the ropes, which slapped the water with a splash before sinking out of sight.

Side by side by side, the three of them followed the boat's progress with their eyes, until it was naught but a bobbing smudge in the distance, a speck next to the vastness of the great, blue sea.

"Goodbye, Myree," Kyla said, kissing the tips of her fingers and pointing them toward her lost child. Tears sparkled in her eyes.

The men got back to work, silent as they toiled under the hot sun.

The Dead Isles appeared a day later in the form of black, jagged cliffs against the horizon. The isles, which were the subject of many a dark and scary campfire story, were barely visible through the fine, white mist that surrounded the land, clinging to the rocks like a wet blanket.

"Ye don' hafta leave," the captain said, sidling up to Grey, who had risen from his daily scrubbing when the lookout had sighted land. "The Dead Isles are an evil place. Ye can stay on as a deckhand. Yer the best one-armed worker I's ever had on me ship."

Grey smiled grimly. He was fairly certain he was the *only* one-armed worker the captain had ever hired. "Thank you. But no. My path is elsewhere."

Smithers nodded. "Be careful." He extended a hand. "And thank ye. Fer takin' care of me little girl when I's too foolish to do so meself."

Grey took his hand, squeezing firmly. "Your daughter was only with one man," he said. "And I believe he is a good one. Your daughter chose a good one."

"I know," the captain said. He wiped at his eyes. "I knew the whole time, but dinnit wanta admit it."

"The next time you stop in Talis, permit Kyla to go ashore. Callum is waiting. She'll need his comfort."

The captain nodded again, and then released Grey's hand. "I'm sorry, but we won' sail closer to the islands. Else we might ne'er escape the fog."

"I understand." Grey climbed into the small boat the captain had generously given him. Two men stepped forward and lifted the sides over the railing while two others braced their feet and held the ropes. None of them had called him "cripple" since yesterday.

Grey looked back at the captain. "Say goodbye to Kyla on my behalf." Last he'd seen her, she was sleeping. She'd been sleeping since they sent her daughter off, and Grey didn't want to wake her.

"I wi—" the captain started to say, but his words were lost amidst the sound of pounding footsteps on the deck.

"Grey!" Kyla shouted, her chest heaving as she reached over the edge of the boat to hug him. Her breath was hot on his neck,

237

her body warm against his. Her curls tickled his cheeks. "Must you leave?"

"I'm sorry," Grey said. "My sister needs me."

"Shae?" she said.

Grey nodded. "She's all alone. We only have each other now."

"No," Kyla said, shaking her head. "You have us, too. You have me."

Grey touched her face briefly with his one hand, and then said, "Find Callum. Be happy."

"I will." Kyla blinked rapidly. "And thank you. For everything."

Grey said, "It was nothing." He really meant it. He'd done nothing but clean up a mess, hold her, and listen to her. He had not been brave, not fought a great warrior, not slayed a dragon... He'd done what a mere child would've been capable of doing.

Kyla grabbed his hand and squeezed it fiercely. "No. You're wrong. It was something. It was a *great* thing. Our greatest moments are often unseen and unheard, but they are never unfelt. My mother told me that, once. I felt everything you did."

Grey's first instinct was to continue to let her praise slide off of him. But he knew that wasn't fair to her or himself. He nodded, his eyes as comfortable on her as they'd ever been on anyone, even Rhea.

When Kyla felt her father's hand on her shoulder, she finally pulled away. She stretched her arm around him, and he reciprocated.

A bond broken, a bond repaired, Grey thought. He wondered whether other kinds of bonds could be fixed too. He wondered if he could be fixed.

As his small boat descended to the sea, his eyes never left Kyla's. He would never forget her, and, he knew, she would never forget him.

He only looked away when the waves lapped at the sides of his craft, churning around him. Though he'd been given two oars, he could only use one at a time. He used one to push off from the boat. He began to paddle toward the mist-shrouded rocks, switching sides every dozen or so strokes so he wouldn't row in circles.

Soon, however, he realized he didn't need to paddle. The current pulled him swiftly.

Straight for the Dead Isles.

Something carried him toward the last place in the Four Kingdoms anyone would want to go, and yet it was exactly where he needed to be.

Twenty-Two

The Southern Empire, Calyp
Raven Sandes

Raven stared into the flames of the Unburning Tree, seeking answers where there were none.

Why did her mother have to die?

Why was Raven born without a tattooya while Fire was?

Why did she fail in the arena?

The Unburning Tree made no sound, not so much as a crackle, its stoic branches wreathed in fire.

Whisper walked gracefully across the courtyard and kneeled down next to Raven, not caring that her white dress sank into the dust. She said nothing, watching the flames writhe and dance. Raven's youngest sister wouldn't be riding with them to war; she was the Last Daughter, the one who would be responsible for ruling all of Calyp if both Fire and Raven perished during the battle.

After Whisper, there were only two other Sandes still alive: her aunts, Viper and Windy. Windy was currently in Citadel, along the edge of Dragon Bay, studying history. Raven had always known her to be a gentle sort, like Whisper, more likely to sketch a dragon than ride one. A stream had been sent to inform Windy of her sister's death, but no response had been received thus far. Viper was in Zune, managing the fighting pits. Ever since she challenged Raven's mother in combat for the empire and lost, she and Sun had been feuding. A message had also been streamed to Viper, but Raven didn't expect her to mourn her sister's death.

Finally, Fire emerged from her quarters wearing her red, leather armor. Her sword dangled from a hip scabbard. The distance melted away, and she kneeled between her two sisters, following their gazes to the Unburning Tree.

She spoke: "Maata would've wanted us to be united in whatever comes next, sisters. And we are. We are stronger together. Do you remember when she gave us our names?"

Of course Raven remembered. Sandes women were given their names when they were eight, old enough to understand the words of wisdom passed down by their maata. Before that, they were called "royal child" in order of birth: Raven was *aati*; Fire was *baati*; and Whisper was *caati*.

"Yes," Whisper said. She recited her mother's words from memory. *"You are the voice in the dark, the hushed silence bearing secrets, the voice of reason in the night, the Underestimated Daughter, the vision of beauty that glistens like a mirage in the desert, unreachable. You are the tears in the rain, the voice in the wind, the sound in the silence, the Child of Nature. You are the Third Daughter. You are Whisper."*

Raven went next. *"You are the flap of dark wings behind the clouds, the clever thinker in the branches, the Misunderstood, the sharp claws and sharper beak. You are the bold hunter, the unexpected warrior, the Child of the Sky. You are the First Daughter. You are Raven."*

Fire nodded, and Raven was surprised to see liquid diamonds sparkling in her eyes. She said, *"You are the Unburning Child, the devourer of the weak, the breaker of branches, the licking flames. You are the fierce warrior, the unquenchable torch, the Child of War. You are the Second Daughter. You are Fire."*

"We are the Three Daughters of the Rising Sun," Raven said.

"As one, we cannot be defeated," Whisper said.

"Not today. Not ever," Fire finished.

The ritual completed, they sank back into silence. Whisper's eyes closed. Fire's never seemed to blink, capturing the flames in flickering reflections. Raven stared past the Unburning Tree, to another time, another place.

She loved playing with her faata's long, twisted braids. She was always grabbing them and roping them around her arms. He would grab her and twirl her around and she would scream with delight. Fire would rush to her rescue, sometimes overzealously, her flames creeping down her arms, forcing Faata to dance back, howling at her. Whisper was always the last to join the fray, grabbing Faata's leg and refusing to let go, making him drag her around like a prisoner chained to a metal ball. Her brothers, Fox, Fang, and Falcon would always just watch, too self-important to get involved.

"Oh Faata," Raven said aloud.

"I miss him," Whisper said, opening her eyes.

Fire shot an annoyed look between them. "He is the enemy now. Our brothers too. We rule with strength. He rules with fear. We will give his people a new life, one worth living."

Of course, Raven agreed with her sister on this point—slavery was wrong. Unnatural. One should not control another, not like that. But it didn't change the fond memories she had of him. And the memories didn't change what they needed to do.

The guanik's rough skin undulated beneath Raven. She barely felt its steps, which were so seamless it was almost as if it slithered like a snake rather than walked on four powerful legs. It was the largest they had and her favorite. She called it simply Iknon—The Big One. Her whips dangled from both of its sides, coiled in perfect circles.

The Calypsians lining the sides of the procession didn't make a sound, watching them go with blank-eyed stares. It was no surprise Calypso was known as the Silent City—even war wouldn't rouse them from their heat-induced stupor.

But Raven knew it wasn't lack of passion or sadness that silenced them. No, it was their strength. They were survivors, a people who thrived on duty and honor and victory.

And they would emerge victorious, as they always had, for thousands of years, long before the Crimeans arrived in their warships, back when their enemies were the forest dwellers in the east, the barbarians in the north, the nymphs and sprites of the western woods.

Raven lifted her chin proudly and faced forward, hundreds of guanik ridden by the guanero stomping behind her. Hundreds more marched on foot, bearing sword and shield, whip and club, dagger and spear. They were three thousand strong, a full quarter of the strength of Calyp. The remainder of the army was spread out throughout the southern peninsula, guarding the borders from the constant threat of invasion by their enemies.

Fire led the war party from the city, her sword raised high, sheathed in flame. *Her arm must be growing weary*, Raven thought, but her sister's limb didn't so much as tremble nor falter, not until they'd departed the shadow of the last of the sandstone dwellings. *She is so strong*, Raven marveled. *A little reckless, but strong. Stronger than I.* Perhaps it was better that Fire ruled. Perhaps she would be the one to finally end the twelve-year-long civil war with their faata.

Raven didn't look back at Calypso—couldn't look back knowing her sister was holding vigil at the apex of the tallest pyramid—*Calyppa*—lighting a new candle every day that passed in her sisters' absence. *I will return*, she promised the wind, breathing out and sending her message back to Whisper. In her mind, she pictured one of the candles blowing out, and her sister smiling in recognition.

The first portion of the journey was relatively easy, the dry, dusty landscape flat and firm. The soldiers talked and laughed, their demeanor relaxed. *As it should be*, Raven mused. *We have an entire desert between us and battle.* The wind was warm, but not as stifling as it could be. Raven pushed back the scarf covering her shaved scalp. She ran a palm across her skin, feeling the roughness of hundreds of new hairs poking up.

"Enjoying the ride?" Fire asked, looking back.

"I prefer the wind under me," she said. "But yes. We are fortunate that the weather is mild."

"You and your dragons," Fire commented. Raven's sister had never taken an interest in the dragon brood that had been hatched when they were infants. *Perhaps because you can breathe fire on your own.* Raven, on the other hand, had spent countless days with the dragon masters, interacting with the young *dragonia*, learning their unique personalities, their temperaments, what

244

they liked to eat. Fire didn't understand the dragons the way Raven did—they were like cats, almost humanlike in terms of the differences between them.

Fire saw them only as weapons of war, powerful beasts that could lay waste to their enemies.

Of course, that was true, too. Raven had seen firsthand what they could do, during the annual testing. Though the dragon masters insisted the dragons were not ready for true battle, already their scales were like triple armor plate, their flames as hot as a thousand fires, their claws like whetted daggers.

Give them another year, Raven thought. *They will be unstoppable.*

As usual, the mention of the dragons drove a wedge between the sisters, almost as if they spoke different languages. Silence reigned, and Raven focused on the stripe of deep blue growing larger against the cracked brown terrain.

The distance fell away as the sun boiled overhead, eventually simmering toward day's end. Dusk was announced by the crashing of waves.

Two decades ago, the Scarra Desert was connected to Calyp by a narrow strip of land wide enough for a hundred soldiers to walk abreast of each other. Now, the land masses were separated by a flowing waterway—the Canal of the Rising Sun—which allowed Dragon Bay to flow into the Burning Sea, and vice versa. If the Scarra and the rest of the Four Kingdoms were the body, then Calyp was the head, severed by a watery slash through the neck that took a dozen years and the efforts of a thousand slaves to complete, including the enormous bridge that now spanned the gap.

According to Raven's maata, completing the canal had been her faata's obsession from the moment they married, and a source of great contention between them, particularly because of his use of Teran slaves for the project. Two years after the bridge was completed, her parents severed their marriage pact and civil war erupted in the south.

Originally, Vin Hoza claimed the main use of the canal was to provide a direct shipping lane from the growing city of Citadel to Phanes, but Sun Sandes had soon realized the other, true purposes:

First, to provide an avenue for Phanecian slave traders to travel to the fighting pits of Zune to sell their slaves into a life of combat, and most likely, death; though all of the Sandes knew the fighting pits were a necessary evil in order to punish criminals and maintain peace in their land, none but her Aunt Viper loved them. And second, to offer Hoza another source of slaves—the Dreadnoughts, the large barbarian island that had been conquered by the Calypsians years earlier.

However, despite Raven's hatred of what the bridge represented—slavery—she had to admit it was a true marvel. Supported by enormous stone columns, the bridge spanned such a great distance that Raven could barely make out the opposite side, which faded into the thickening evening murk. The bridge rose on a gradual incline until it reached its center, where it once more descended to near sea level. This "hill" was necessary so that even the tallest ships would be able to pass safely beneath it.

Fire stood next to Raven, taking in the wondrous sight. "If Faata can do this with a thousand slaves, what can he do with an army of ten thousand, or a hundred thousand?" she asked.

"Conquer the world," Raven said. She was beginning to wonder whether her younger sister had been right about attacking now. The longer they gave her father to grow his army, the greater his advantage would be.

Except for the dragons, Raven thought.

246

In any case, it didn't matter now, there would be no turning back once they reached the desert.

"We'll camp here tonight," Fire said. Eager guanero passed the message back through the ranks, and soon their own thousands had erected a makeshift camp, sprawling across the dry land. Leaders like the Sandes' sisters and the other guanero slept in tents, while the rest of the soldiers passed the night under a blanket of red, green and gold stars.

The next morning, wind whistled beneath the bridge, hitting it side on like a slap from the broadside of a sword.

Standing beside the sisters, the broad-shouldered guanero war chief, Goggin said, "We'll be knocked off like wooden thimbles." It wasn't the comparison Raven would've chosen, but then again, Goggin's maata was a seamstress. She'd seen the large man darn a sock, and despite his sausage-like fingers, she had to admit his dexterity was impressive.

"We'll stick to the middle, three astride, save for the guanero, who shall ride single file," Fire said.

Goggin shook his head. "Thimbles," he muttered again.

Raven laughed. "Don't you know how to swim?"

"Aye," he said. "Just like a rock."

Fire said, "Then you can show the rest of us how it's done."

Raven knew her sister had never learned to swim either. As a child, she'd been far too focused on lighting things on fire to appreciate the one thing that could be used against her: water.

Raven, on the other hand, was an excellent swimmer, having spent summers with her Aunt Windy at Citadel, relishing the taste of the salt of Dragon Bay on her lips, the crystal clear waters teeming with beautiful multi-colored fish nibbling the glowing, incandescent reefs. No, she didn't fear the water, but her ability to float would do nothing to save her from a sheer drop that would turn the Burning Sea into granite.

"We should wait until the winds die down," Raven said, surprised to find herself agreeing with Goggin.

"No," Fire said. "The weather masters advised that the Scarra is between storms."

"I know. I was there. But they gave us a fortnight to reach the Spear."

"At the most."

"If half the army ends up in the sea, it won't matter how quickly we reach the Southron Gates."

In the end, Fire went ahead with the plan to cross.

Raven was frustrated with her sister's stubbornness and recklessness, but she was the empress now, and Raven had no choice but to follow her command. But there was something else that worried her more, something in Fire's crimson eyes that she had never seen before. At first she thought it was determination, purpose, but now she wasn't certain.

They started across the bridge, following Fire's orders, though many of the foot soldiers ended up traveling single file. The swirling winds pelted them from both sides, forcing them to stagger crookedly, as if they'd drunk too much simpre. Twice Raven was forced to dismount and coax Iknon forward as the large guanik refused to take another step, snorting and flicking its tongue.

Fire's mount, like her, showed no fear, practically galloping across the bridge, reaching the end far before anyone else.

Eventually, however, they made it across, even Goggin, though his face was as white as the sifted sands of Citadel, his eyes wide and wild. "Within an inch of my life, I swear it," he said as he kissed the sand, his thick lips coming away looking like a powdered pastry.

Behind them, the bridge was an endless train of soldiers, stretching all the way to the opposite shore, where a sizeable number had yet to step onto the stone walkway. Fire cursed under her breath. "We'll lose an entire day at this rate."

In truth, they lost two days, as nearly half the army was forced to wait for sunrise before starting onto the bridge. Led by Goggin, most of the soldiers passed the time fishing and drinking simpre, preparing a great feast to celebrate their arrival on the edges of the Scarra. And feast they did, late into the night, resting their sore feet and telling stories of the shifting sands of the desert, which had apparently swallowed entire platoons of easterners whole.

"The Scarra will allow only the most stalwart of men to cross its flanks," Goggin declared, raising his fist in the air. He'd already polished off four skins of simpre, Raven knew—she'd been counting. After the second one, he'd removed his shirt and begun pointing to each of his dozens of scars and telling stories of where he got them. (He even claimed one—a long thin line across his abdomen—was from a dragon claw, though Raven knew for a fact it had been his ex-wife's attempt to cut him open.) After the third drink, he'd removed his pants and started on the scars running up his legs. That's when Fire had shaken her head in disgust and left. Raven had watched her go, wondering why she was acting so broody. Was it just the fact that they'd lost two days? For some reason, she didn't think so.

Raven stood now, planning to join her sister in sleep. Most of the other soldiers were already asleep, as well as the guanik, resting their chins on their foreclaws, their deep breaths hissing between three rows of teeth. "So only men can cross the Scarra?" Raven said, a parting shot to Goggin, who was sitting on a thin layer of sand in only his underleathers. She knew Goggin was no sexist, but still she couldn't resist.

"Women *are* the desert," he slurred. "Hot and endless and as beautiful as the day is long."

She flung him a tired smile and said, "Get some rest."

She expected to find Fire asleep in her tent, but instead she was lying on her back outside of it, staring up at the stars. Without a word, Raven laid down next to her. One of the red stars shot across the sky.

"A sign from the gods," Raven said.

Fire sighed.

"What is it, sister?"

"Nothing."

"You've been...distant."

"We are all distant from each other. We are like the stars. We can see each other, but only from a distance."

"Not if you let me see you." Raven had never been as close to her sister as she'd wanted to be. The rivalry between them had prevented that. But now, Fire's final victory over her had swept that all away. And yet, she felt more apart from her than ever before.

"That's impossible," Fire said. With a final sigh, she rolled over and crawled into her tent.

Raven shook her head, trying to understand what she was missing. Another star rocketed across the dark sky in a blaze of light.

The next day they entered the Scarra, the hard-packed dust of Calyp giving way to thick piles of sand, as hot as lit coals under the blazing eye in the sky. Raven's reptilian steed galloped up the first dune, its powerful legs churning over the thick terrain. Fire waited for her at the top, and they continued astride, racing down the backside before starting up the next hill.

Unlike the previous night, her sister seemed in good spirits now that they were on their way again.

Fire whooped and flung a fireball at a brittle dark plant known as *morgotha*—deathleaf—which caused asphyxiation when ingested. "Don't want any of the guanik munching on that one," Fire explained when she saw Raven's raised eyebrow.

Raven shook her head. Her sister knew as well as she that the animals were intelligent enough to avoid a plant that would kill them. She also knew her sister enjoyed playing with her fire far too much.

As the sun continued to rise, the day became hotter, the rounded dunes acting as reflectors, sending the hot rays burning in all directions. Raven felt like she was being boiled alive, even when she dipped her shawl in water and covered her bald brown head.

After Iknon clambered up a particularly large hill, she stopped to let the beast rest, offering it some water, which it lapped at with its long snake-like tongue. Fire was already three dunes ahead, her smaller guanik handling the heat and exertion far better than her own. Behind them, the line of soldiers that had appeared so regal, well-trained, and proud in the confines of the city, had been stretched, becoming a ragged tangled thread. Hundreds had fallen well back, struggling in the heat.

Goggin caught up to her, his own guanik nearly as large as Raven's, and yet still laboring under the man's immense weight and dual steel scimitars, which curled like silver waves on either flank.

"It's as hot as the inside of a clay oven," he said.

"I find it to be quite cool," Raven said. "That breeze. Ah." The wind whipping over the dunes was so hot she could almost see the air sizzling.

"What does that word mean—cool?" Goggin joked back.

Raven would've laughed, but her mouth was too dry, her skin too rough with sand, and she was afraid the edges of her lips might crack. They started down the dune, riding side by side.

"Many years have passed since I enjoyed the hospitality of Kesh," Goggin said, determined to make conversation.

"I've never had the pleasure."

"No? I suppose not. Why should the empress take her three daughters across the desert?"

"Tell me about the desert city." Kesh was the only major dwelling in the Scarra, an oasis in the sand, a place to replenish water skins and rest in the shade for a while. The city had saved many lives over the centuries.

"No," Goggin said.

"No?"

"You have to experience it for yourself." He smiled broadly.

Reaching the peak of another dune, Raven could barely imagine there being a city out there: the dunes marched endlessly from horizon to horizon, crashing waves of sand, always moving, always shifting, blown by the hot thrust of the wind.

Staring out across the desert now, she could almost believe that it *had* swallowed people whole in the past.

Fire was five dunes ahead now. Raven had a feeling that if it was up to her sister, Fire would attack the Southron Gates all on her own.

And she'd probably win, she mused.

Finally, she allowed herself a laugh, spurring Iknon forward until she'd caught up to her sister, the warrior empress.

When they camped after the first day in the desert, the mood was weary but upbeat. None had perished, save for one of the smaller guanik, which was bitten by a large black scorpion. The poison acted quickly, leaving most of the meat uncontaminated. They would not waste the beast's sacrifice, so fires were lit and the meat was cooked, spiced with *atmaran* and *sage* and *cintar*, an aromatic mix of flavors known in Calypso as *mixa*. Everyone ate merrily, washing the fiery meat down with guzzles from their waterskins. Though it would take them four long, sweltering days to reach Kesh, they had plenty of water so there was little need to ration. None drank simpre, not even Goggin, for the strong drink was dehydrating.

Afterwards, several soldiers started a song circle, and it didn't surprise Raven to find Goggin at the center of it, bellowing in his deep, gruff voice.

Fire watched everything from just outside her tent, idly passing flames between her fingers.

Raven plopped down beside her, the sand warm and soft through her leathers. "You rode hard today," she said.

Fire flicked her thumb and the flame bounced, landing back on her palm. "I only know how to ride one way."

"Sister," Raven said. Fire didn't look at her, concentrating on making the flame spin in lazy circles. "Sister," she insisted, and when Fire finally met her eyes, she said, "I don't hold your victory over me against you the way Aunt Viper did against Maata. I am with you in this. I hope you know that. You're not alone."

Fire chewed on her lip, paused, and then said, "I've been alone since the moment I was born." With that, she snuffed out the flame between her fingers and crawled into her tent.

Over the next two days, Raven tried to talk to her sister, but Fire grew more and more withdrawn, slipping into long periods of silence, riding far ahead of the rest of the guanero. Perhaps their mother's death had hit Fire harder than she initially showed. Perhaps she was feeling the weight of responsibility on her shoulders in a way she never expected to. Or perhaps it was just the oppressive heat, which was beating down on all of them.

By day three, no one talked when they camped. No one sang, not even Goggin, who rode hunched over, his head lolling on his shoulders. Four more guanik had died. One was the victim of another black scorpion, two had collapsed from exhaustion, and the last stumbled and broke its leg. The meat was not wasted, but it still seemed a great loss.

Two soldiers had also died. One was naught but a boy, two years younger than even Fire, who was only sixteen. He'd gone off to make water, and when he didn't return was searched for. He was found lying face down with two punctures in his neck.

A cobra was discovered nearby, slashed in half by the boy's last act. The other was a grizzled old veteran warrior, who'd simply passed in the night. His end was so peaceful that everyone assumed he was only sleeping in late, until someone tried to rouse him.

On the morning of the fourth day, Raven joined Fire before they started their march. The young empress was staring out across the dunes, searching the horizon. "What do you see?" Raven asked.

"Wastelands," Fire said.

"If not for these wastelands, our eastern foes might've invaded us long ago. Faata's armies too."

"Perhaps. But is this land really worth winning?"

Day by day, Raven's sister was becoming a stranger to her. "How can you say that? This is our home."

Fire shook her head. "No. You are my home. Whisper. Maata was my home. Home is not a place. Home is your family."

Raven had never heard her sister talk like this, so passionately about family. "You surprise me," she said.

Fire laughed lightly. "I know you think I have no heart, sister. I know you think I'm the edge of a blade, made for only one thing."

It was Raven's turn to laugh. "You know my mind better than I do."

"Yes, I have always wanted to be empress, but not for the power, not to control the most powerful army in the south. No. I wanted it so you didn't have to wear the dragon crown, sister. I was born with the firemark, not you. It's my responsibility, my burden to bear. Mine alone."

Raven had no idea her sister felt this way. She'd hidden her heart well, behind a veil of bravado and strength. All these years... "I don't know what to say. Why didn't you tell me this before?"

Fire squinted into the distance, as if searching for the answer amongst the dunes. "I didn't want your pity. I needed you to think me brash, overconfident. I wanted you to bring your best into the arena, so you would judge me worthy of leading."

Raven shook her head. "I always knew you were worthy. I always knew you were strong. But I withheld love so many times. I gave it to Whisper instead, because I thought she needed it more."

"Yes," Fire said. "That's what I wanted."

Raven rested her hand on her sister's arm, surprised that her typically fiery skin was quite cool to the touch. "You are not alone. I will stand by your side for whatever comes."

Fire reached across her body and rested her hand atop Raven's. "Thank you. I could not ask for a braver ally."

Raven nodded. She gestured to the dunes. "We may not reach Kesh by nightfall. Four days is the estimate for one rider. We have many on foot."

"We must," Fire said. "We will. Come on, the day has wings."

Raising her sword in the air, flames danced from her fingers and up the edge of the blade, signaling the start to the day's march.

Raven watched her sister ride down the hill.

Strangely, the heat of the morning seemed to sizzle around her, making her form fuzzy around the edges, until she faded into a fiery smudge against the sand.

Almost ghost-like.

Twenty-Three
The Southern Empire, Southeast of the Bloody Canyons
Jai Jiroux

If the night prior was sheathed in moonlight, the next eve was speckled with starlight. It was almost magical, the harsh terrain. Thousands of *galanzealas* lit the landscape. The abundant desert plant hid from the sun during the day, pulling itself into a crustacean-like brown shell that soaked up the light, turning it into food. At night, its shell opened and dozens of tendrils climbed toward the sky, glowing purple. It was between these beautiful night plants that Jai and the Black Tears now led his people. Jig and the other children ran from plant to plant excitedly, collecting glowing leaves. Jai could tell the adults were equally awed by nature's display, but held back.

Before they'd gone too far, Jai stopped them. Sonika raised an eyebrow, but said nothing, waiting to see what he would do.

He raised his voice so enough could hear him to pass his message back through the throng. "As you know, we are marching to the wall. There, we hope to escape to the west, where we can finally be free." Murmurs of excitement rippled through the crowd, but Jai silenced them with a hand in the air. "However, the way is more dangerous than you can imagine. I will not lie to you. Even if we make it through the mountains, we will face sword and arrow as we cross to the Southron Gates. Many will die, sacrificing themselves so some of us can make it. I cannot promise you safety."

"It sounds like suicide," someone called out.

"It's not," Jai said. "But it's close enough. We hope our unexpected approach will be enough to surprise Hoza's soldiers, but that will not prevent bloodshed."

"What are you saying?" someone else asked. "That we should turn back?"

Defiance coursed through the throng.

"No," Jai said. "I'm only saying you have a choice. You can hide in the Black Rocks or you can attempt to find a way across the Burning Sea on a ship. Or, if you go back to Phanea of your own will, the emperor may see fit to forgive, to welcome you back into his service."

"Into slavery you mean."

Jai nodded. "Yes. Into slavery. But at least you will be alive. I cannot necessarily offer you the same."

"Slavery is the same as death," someone shouted. Murmurs of agreement rose up.

Jai nodded again. "If any choose to turn back, let them decide now. There may not be another opportunity."

Heads swiveled, looking at each other. None moved back. In fact, most took a step forward. "We're with you," someone said.

"Then let us march to freedom," Jai said, offering the three-fingered salute. His people returned it, thousands of hands raised in the dark, lit by moonlight and galanzealas.

Satisfied, he turned back toward the desert. Feet shuffled behind him.

"Nice speech," Sonika said.

"Thanks," Jai said uncertainly, not sure if he was being mocked or complimented. "I am no master."

"You don't have to keep saying that."

"I—I know. I just want them to have a choice. They should always have a choice."

"And that's what makes you a great leader," Sonika said. "Because they follow you of their own free will. Just like my Tears."

As they walked under the protection of darkness, Jai scanned ahead, his eyes adjusting quickly to the murky evening. To the north were the towers of red rocks that surrounded the Bloody Canyons. It was toward those bloody spires that they now headed, as quickly as they could, for they were naked and unprotected on the dustlands, with Hoza's stronghold in the square canyons of Phanea only a day's hard ride away to the northwest, hidden somewhere beneath the surface of the desert.

To Jai's surprise, he longed to return to the maze-like cauldron of the Black Rocks. At least there they were hidden from Hoza's soldiers.

And yet, the further they journeyed across the dustlands, the greater his hope grew. If they could just get to the red rocks, they'd have a real chance, however slim.

Nearby, Axa walked alone, his head down, his back bent. Already he was looking more like a slave than a master. Several bandages hung from his chest, arms and face like peeling flesh. After what happened a night before, when Joaquin ripped the jewels from his skin, Jai bandaged the man up. Now he kept an eye on Axa, just in case Joaquin tried anything else. In one hand, Axa held his mirror, his only remaining possession.

Jai turned his attention away from his former mine master when Sonika Vaid pulled back from the head of the throng to speak to him. "Your people are strong. They move quickly, even the elderly and children. How is this thing possible? How are they not broken?"

"I trained them. Not only did their strength help them mine more diamonds, which satisfied the emperor, but I wanted them to be ready for…well, for *this*."

Sonika shook her head. "You are…unusual. Most masters break their slaves, you strengthen them."

"Yes, and I prefer phen lu to phen ru, and I lived and ate with my people, and I helped them mine, and—"

"I get your point. I'll stop asking."

Jai took a deep breath. "Sorry. I'm overprotective sometimes."

"It's fine. I understand."

"Also, the day of rest did them well." After their long march through the Black Rocks, they'd lounged and slept the heat of the day away, sticking to the shade and drinking plenty of water. No one had complained about waiting for the sun to go down before leaving—not only would it be cooler but the darkness would mask them better than anything else as they traveled across the plains. "And yes, I worked them hard in the mines to sate the Slave King's lust for diamonds, but I treated them as well as I could. A free person toils far better than a slave."

"How did you accomplish this?" Sonika asked. "When your people have escaped Phanes, I will return to the south and use the information to repeat your work."

"You would return?" All Jai had ever wanted was to leave the south with his people, never to look back.

"There are too many others who need us."

Jai felt selfish. He rarely thought of those slaves toiling in the other mines, or even in the cities. He was too focused on those slaves he felt he could help. The others faded into the background, gray figures that vanished like mist, almost ghost-like. *They are ghosts*, he thought. *We all are.*

"You are a good person," Jai said.

"So are you," Shanti said, pulling up on his other side, her cart rattling behind her. Though Jai walked, their horses moved slow enough to stay with him.

His heart did a quick flip at the sight of her, especially after the moment they'd shared high on the cliffs. He didn't know how to respond to such a compliment, especially when he wasn't certain it was deserved. "I am just one man."

"Well I didn't expect you to be two men," Shanti said, raising a light eyebrow. A smile played tug of war with her lips.

Laughing, Sonika dug her heels into her horse and galloped ahead to convene with the rest of her warriors. Shanti, however, stayed behind with Jai.

Jai watched the rebel leader go. "What's her story?" he asked.

"Sonika's? She doesn't talk about her past much."

"But you've been with her for a while now, right? You must know something."

"She had a brother once," Shanti said.

"He died?"

"I don't think so. They were separated somehow. She mentioned him once in passing, but refuses to say anything else. I think it hurts too much. I think they started all this together, but I'm not certain."

"Oh."

"You seem different today," she said. "Like the door you opened last night has been shut and barred with iron."

I have always been a closed door, Jai wanted to say. At least until he spoke with her last night. And yet he'd still held so much back. He'd only just met her; why should he share so much of himself with her? "Things break when left unprotected," he said. "People included."

"Sometimes a bone must be broken and then healed in order to grow stronger."

Jai raised both eyebrows. "Is that true?"

"Honestly?" Shanti said, laughing. "I don't rightly know. I heard the saying once and it stuck."

Jai chuckled back. He felt like he'd already been broken too many times. Once more and he wouldn't be able to heal again. "So besides memorizing nonsensical old sayings and blowing things up with fireroot powder, do you have any other hidden talents I should know about?"

"Rotzoff!" she exclaimed.

"What?"

"It's a common curse word used by the people of Anatoli."

Jai frowned. "First, I don't even know where Anatoli is, and second, why are you telling me this?"

"Anatoli is a small island off the coast of Robunka. And you asked about my talents. I can swear in seven languages, much to my mother's chagrin."

Despite the fact that Jai didn't know where Robunka was either, he burst out laughing. "Fair enough. I suppose multilingual swearing could be considered a talent of sorts."

Shanti said, "Let's play a game. I share something and then you reciprocate."

Jai considered the offer. "I'll play. What does your name mean?"

She smiled. "What you ask is no secret. I'll give you this information for free. Shanti Parthena Laude means Peaceful Maiden of Highest Honor." When she saw his surprise, she added, "Yes, it is a lot to live up to. Sometimes I wish my parents had named me something with lower...expectations."

"Still," Jai said, "it suits you."

She looked at him slyly. "Really?"

"Well, maybe not the 'peaceful' part considering your talent with fireroot..."

"Hey!"

He ignored her protest. "But you are certainly a maiden, and given your focus on freeing slaves I'd say you are of the highest honor."

She blinked. "Thank you."

"You're welcome. Do I get to ask another question?"

"No. This is my game, so I decide the rules. First, choose a tear. Any of them. I will tell you its story." She dismounted and walked beside him, leading her mare.

Jai studied her face, those seventeen tears. Once he would've thought each tear contained an action-packed tale of her prowess in battle, but after last night he knew they were full of sadness, like real tears darkening on her cheeks. Still, the game was a wonderful excuse to examine her smooth red skin, the faint lines in her forehead, the curves of her nose, her jaw, her lips. "The one beneath your right eye," he said.

"I have many tears. Show me." She shifted closer.

Jai's skin grew warmer, despite the relatively cool night air. Shanti's eyes were blue and round in the typical Teran manner, but in the moment when her eyes blinked open there was a flash of silver around the edges that he could see even in the dark. Every time he looked at this woman he seemed to notice something new. Something more spectacular about her. He reached out a hand, extended a shaking finger, and touched the spot he was referring to. The black tear etched on her face was smooth, flawless, a work of art. *Like you*, he wanted to say.

"My first tear," Shanti said, and he retracted his hand. "For my sister. Aliyah."

"I'm sorry, I didn't mean to—"

She cut him off. "It's fine. I speak of my tears freely; they are my best and worst memories, those stories I hold nearest to my heart."

"Still. I'm sorry you lost her."

Shanti nodded her thanks. "My mother was a slave," she started. Jai cocked his head to the side, having not expected her story to start that way, so similar to his own. "It's true. My father, too. Aliyah and I were marked as slaves the moment we were old enough."

"Ten years old," Jai said. It was the same for the children born in Garadia. They all became slaves on their tenth name day. He had personally taken them to Phanea for the ceremony. Only the knowledge that he would return their free will upon returning to Garadia allowed him to suffer through it. But still, seeing their eyes turn black, that stiff expression falling over their young faces...it broke his heart every time.

264

"Yes. I was ten when I was made a slave. My sister, too, though she was two years older than me."

"How are you here? How are you free?" If she knew a way for slaves to gain their minds back, he longed to hear it. By sunset every man, woman, and child in his group could truly have their freedom, not just the temporary reprieve he'd granted them.

Shanti shook her head. "I don't really know. Our master was not a kind man. We were naught but dogs to him, working us from dawn until the dark of night, until we collapsed into bed. When I was twelve and Aliyah was fourteen, our master finally saw my sister."

Jai frowned. "What do you mean?"

Shanti pursed her lips momentarily, but then continued. "As more than a Teran dog. As a woman. She was already flowered and growing more beautiful by the day. Everything's foggy, like I was living in a world of smoke, but I can still remember Aliyah's beauty. It was like a light in a storm." Jai wasn't certain he wanted to hear the rest, but he didn't interrupt. "Our master tried to take Aliyah to his bed. He commanded her. And then something impossible happened."

"What?" Jai was vaguely aware that they had both stopped walking, the rest of the people passing by on either side, some of them glancing in their direction before continuing on.

"My father intervened." She paused, allowing Jai to consider her words.

"But that's..."

"Impossible. Yes. He was a slave. He shouldn't have been able to do anything but follow the commands of his master. Just as it's impossible that your people can make their own decisions."

"No, that's different. As their appointed master, I gave them free will. They are still slaves, just following *my* command rather than Vin Hoza's."

"True. But my father broke the chains somehow." She motioned to her own neck. "His slave mark vanished. He threw himself at our master, trying to protect Aliyah. My father killed him, Jai, with his bare hands. I watched him as he squeezed the life out of that horrible man."

"I—I don't know what to say." Jai pictured all of the slaves across the realm rising up to fight their masters. The thought made him want to unleash a roar of excitement.

"There's nothing to say. It happened. The only trouble was that our master was very rich and had an army of guards. They caught my father. They made him watch while they slit Aliyah's throat. Then they slit his, too."

Jai's heart was pounding in his head and a fist-sized knot had become lodged in his chest.

Shanti pointed to one of the tears beneath her other eye. "This one is for my father. My second tear."

Jai felt real tears welling up. "I'm sorry."

"Me too. He was a good man. Have you heard of the Teran Virtues?"

He nodded. Jai's mother had taught them to him as a child. There were seven of them. "Purity. Selflessness. Faith. Generosity. Courage. Perseverance..." The last one escaped his memory.

"And Patience," Shanti said. "I always struggled the most with that one. But my father didn't. He was a Seven."

Jai remembered what his mother told him about the Terans, how they strove to master each of the Virtues in order to become

266

closer to their god, Absence. "So he was some kind of a holy man?"

She shook her head. "Not a priest, no. He could've been, but he chose to remain a farmer. Until we were taken."

Gods. "I wish I could've met him. And your mother? Has she passed over into the Void, too?"

She shook her head. "She has no tear. Not yet. She has a new master though. They separated us. She now works for Hoza himself, else I would've rescued her years ago."

Jai contemplated the many times he'd been to Hoza's lavish residence. Had he ever seen a woman that resembled Shanti? He didn't think so. He would've surely remembered a woman as beautiful as that. "I would take your pain if I could," Jai said, his own words surprising him. And yet he believed them. He desperately wanted to erase those tears from her skin, turn back time. Save her family. *And my own.*

"Thank you. You are kind."

"But what about you? I still don't understand."

"Like I said, neither do I. It was like my father; I can't explain it. After I lost Aliyah and my father, after my mother was taken away, I felt different. Still numb, but not from the chains marked around my neck. From loss. From pain. I felt...human again. And then, one day I woke up and the slave mark was gone. I—"

She stopped abruptly, biting her lip.

"What?"

"Nothing." He sensed there was something unsaid, just resting on the tip of her tongue. It vanished. She continued, picking up where she left off. "I ran away from my new master and never looked back. Fate brought me to Sonika, and then to

267

the rest of the Tears. They are my family now. Just like these people are yours."

Jai was about to respond, when someone shouted across the terrain. A small, shadowy form raced across the dustlands, his feet churning so fast they were a blur. "Jig, what is it?" Jai asked, steadying the boy with two hands on his shoulders when he skidded to a stop.

"I found something big," he said.

"What?"

"A hole. A massive hole. I almost fell into it."

Oh gods, Jai thought, a similar gaping hole opening up in his stomach.

Jai and Shanti had to push through a thick knot of people surrounding the hole. Sonika and several of the other rebels had already arrived on the scene, peering down the dark shaft with narrowed eyes.

Jai said, "Does it look fresh?" Once he got within a step of the round void, he leaned over and looked into it. The chasm went straight down but then seemed to angle on a more horizontal underground path. He knew only one thing that could make a hole that big.

Sonika inspected the edge of the hole, rubbing the crusted dirt between her fingers, wincing in pain. "The red pyzon's slime is not yet dry," she said. "It's still poisonous." In other words, yes, it was fresh. The tips of her fingers were already red and enflamed from touching the slime, which, though painful when touched by human skin, was primarily used by the pyzon to mark its territory from other predators.

Jai noticed a large section of dried snakeskin dangling from the far side of the hole, fluttering in the wind.

"There's another hole over here!" someone shouted in the crowd. "And here!" a third said. More and more discoveries of holes were announced. And then: "A skin. I found the skin!"

They moved in the direction of the final call. When they came upon a group of people pointing and gawking at a tangled mess of dried red and black snakeskin, Jai's heart sank even further. The skin was impossibly long—even a hundred men lying end to end would not stretch as far.

"We have to move," Jai said. It was known that after coming out of hibernation, the first thing a red would do was shed its skin. The second thing it would do was hunt. He'd never seen a red pyzon, though he had seen their burrows before. The best bet was to turn around and go the other way. Unfortunately, they couldn't go back.

"Not necessarily," Sonika said. "They travel fast. This snake could be a thousand leagues away by now."

"Or right under our feet," Jai said.

"No," Shanti said, shaking her head. "If it was under our feet, we would feel it. The earth would rumble."

"I hear it," a small voice said. Jai noticed that Jig had pressed his ear to the earth, listening intently. His eyes were wide. "Listen."

Immediately, the Tears and Jai did the same, as well as many of the people gathered around. Though it was faint, the slight tremor was unmistakable. Something was moving beneath the ground. Something big. Murmurs of fear coursed through the crowd like the current from a lightning strike.

Sonika was on her feet in an instant. "Move!" she shouted. She leapt back on her horse and swooped her hand in the

269

direction of the red cliffs, which resembled dark spikes in the distance.

The people needed no further urging, shouldering their packs, grabbing their children's hands, and fleeing north. The mounted Black Tears spread out amongst the people, shouting commands and warning them to avoid the holes. Jai snatched Jig's hand and took off, practically pulling the boy off his feet. "Hurry!" he said.

The rumble grew stronger, until Jai could feel it as he ran. He was forced to skid to a stop when a dark void opened up in front of him. For a moment he thought he'd halted his momentum too late, his foot slipping over the edge, but then he fell back, Jig collapsing on top of him.

Cursing, he scrambled to his feet and cut a wide path around the hole, still dragging Jig behind him.

The ground shifted, throwing him off-balance. He jabbed his hand down to the dirt to keep from falling, but the sudden jerk made Jig trip. As the boy tumbled, his hand ripped out of Jai's grasp.

It saved both their lives.

Just where they would've been had they continued running in a straight line, the earth exploded upwards, followed by an enormous line of rubbery flesh painted in alternating lines of red and black. Jai and Jig kicked backwards in tandem, staring in horror as the monstrous beast seemed to take an eternity to fully emerge from the newly formed hole, its body the length of a hundred men, as wide around as one of the Great Pillars of Phanea. Thick slime spewed from its skin, splattering Jai's face, arms and chest as he threw his body across Jig.

Jai howled at the pain from the slime, which was like a dozen flames being shoved into his skin. Gritting his teeth, he rolled, still keeping Jig between him and the pyzon, which flew through the air, opening its giant maw and swallowing several people whole as it plunged back into the earth, opening up a new hole like a knife slicing through butter.

My people are dying. In the dark, it was hard to recognize the victims, but he'd spotted Carp, the friendly barrel-sized man who'd vouched for him back at Garadia when the Black Tears wanted to kill him. He'd seen the man's mouth gaped open in terror, heard his last cry before the monster took him.

Oh gods, what Void have I led them to?

"No!" Jai screamed, fighting off the wave of sorrow that threatened to pull him under, to suffocate him. It wasn't the time to mourn those lost, not when so many were still alive, rushing in droves through the dark, dodging holes and—

Screams rent the night as the pyzon emerged once more, this time farther away from Jai. Those unfortunate enough to be directly beneath the snake were impaled on its teeth, swallowed whole, or thrown roughly aside like ragdolls. *Gardner, Hominy, Nash,* Jai rattled off in his head. There was one of the Dreadnoughters, too—Lonish—who'd always been one of the best miners working in Garadia. There were dozens more, as this time the snake landed with a thump on the hard-packed dirt, its long tail snapping as it slithered from side to side, hissing and biting anyone in its path.

"Jig," Jai said. "Stay here, right next to its hole."

Jig clung to his neck, tears streaking his cheeks. "Don't leave me," he cried.

Jai clamped his hands on either side of the boy's face. "Do you trust me?"

Jig nodded between Jai's hands.

Jai had once heard that a red pyzon wouldn't dig a new hole directly beside an existing one, because then its tunnels would grow unstable. "Stay here. I have to help the others. Don't move. It's safest directly beside the burrow. Do you understand?" The boy nodded again.

Jai clambered to his feet, praying that what he'd heard was true and he wasn't sentencing the boy to death.

All around him were bodies. Some were injured, groaning and writhing in pain. Others weren't moving. Others were whimpering, too afraid to move, hoping the pyzon would simply pass them by.

Ahead, the snake slapped one of the Black Tears from her horse with its barbed tail. The way her body flopped lifelessly, Jai could tell she was dead before she hit the ground. Though he hated himself for the thinking it, in his mind he said *please don't be Sonika or Shanti, please please please.* The way the other women looked to Sonika, Jai already knew she was the heart and soul of the Tears. They needed her. And Shanti...Jai didn't know what she was to him yet, only that he'd felt connected to her from the moment he met her. Perhaps his subconscious had known they both had parents who were slaves.

With a loud hiss, the pyzon vanished, diving into one of its burrows, its deadly tail scraping behind it. Nearby, a horse whinnied in fright as the ground continued to shake. Jai called out, racing for the rider. It was Sonika, who was gathering the rest of her surviving Tears to her. "We have to fight it," she said. "Wound it or kill it. It's the only way."

Jai knew she was right. Given its size, he was certain the pyzon could devour them all and still be hungry. It was known that one of the reasons red pyzons were so rarely seen was that they hibernated for years at a time, only coming out to hunt when their slow-digesting bodies had used up all of its resources. Then they would emerge from their burrows and feast until sated, before returning to hibernation once more.

"What do we do?" Jai asked. Though he'd never used it to fight, Jai pulled his knife from its sheath, gripping it with white knuckles.

"Go for its eyes, its throat," Sonika said. Her horse reared up when there was a fresh rumble, the ground undulating beneath them. "Get ready!"

For a moment, his eyes met Shanti's, which were full of steel, like she'd become a completely different woman to the one he sat atop the cliffs with. He knew to survive he'd have to become a completely different man, the one trained for combat.

For them, he thought. *I can do it for them.*

The snake emerged, scattering Jai's people like dominoes swept off a table by a child's hand. "Go!" Sonika roared, spurring her horse forward.

Jai took off, quickly falling back from the riders, but refusing to give up, leaping over bodies and swerving around those fleeing the beast. The horses pulled to a stop and their riders attacked, throwing knives and shooting arrows. The miniscule weapons bounced off of the pyzon's hard scales as it reared up, its head too high for any of them to reach with their projectiles.

Jai's knife suddenly felt like a toy against such raw power. *What am I doing?* he thought.

But then he saw several of his people, Jahi and Manesh and Job, hunkering next to one of the burrows. *I'm protecting them*, he thought. *And I will give my life if necessary.* Though he'd always known he would die for them, the realization was like a splash of cold water across his face.

He reached Shanti and shouted up to her. "It's not working!"

She had something in her hand, a wrapped package tied with twine. "Remember what I did to Garadia?" she asked. "If we can get close enough to light this and throw it in its face..."

Jai remembered the power of the fireroot. He also knew there was no way they'd be able to light it and throw the weapon fast enough to land a direct hit. But they had to try.

"I'll light it," he said. Jai searched his pockets for his flint, and then used the blade of his knife to get a spark going, but the thread dangling from the package wouldn't seem to light. The snake hissed loudly, and Jai fumbled the flint, dropping it in the dirt. Frantically, he searched the ground, his fingers finally locating it. When he stood up, the snake was charging right for them, rearing up and preparing to strike.

"Hurry!" Shanti cried.

More sparks, several of them charring the thread, which burst into flame, travelling quickly toward the parcel. The snake flung its head down at them, fangs snapping. With a shout, Shanti launched the package.

BOOM! There was a flash of light and the snake recoiled, snapping its head from side to side. It let out a hiss and dove into the ground, only to reemerge a moment later, slightly further away.

Shanti already had another fireroot package in her hands. "We have to get closer. Blind it."

But there was something in Jai's memory, a flash of thought, and then an idea. "Give it to me," he said, as the giant snake slithered closer.

Above them, the pyzon hissed, preparing to strike once more. When Shanti hesitated, he said, "Hurry!"

She handed him the parcel.

Here goes nothing, Jai thought.

274

And then he charged the pyzon just as it arched its back and struck.

Horses and people screamed as the pyzon smashed its jaws into the earth, snapping viciously. Its scales were so close to Jai that he could see his reflection in their glossy, slime-sheathed surface.

With a cry he threw himself onto the snake's flesh, driving his knife in with one hand while clutching Shanti's parcel of fireroot with the other. As the snake bucked and writhed, acid burned through his clothes, scorching his skin, but he refused to let go, pushing off with his feet. The sticky, scaly skin made the snake's body easy enough to climb, though the pain was so fierce Jai grew dizzy. With each step upward, he slammed his knife between the scales, scraping his body a little higher.

And then the slime was gone—he'd reached the pyzon's head, which was covered with pure red scales with none of the sticky excretion. Still, his entire body was coated in the poison, and he felt as if he'd been thrust into a fire. His vision spun and he feared he might pass out, but he managed to hang onto consciousness by focusing on gripping the knife.

Wind whipped all around him as the world flew past, the snake slithering across the terrain with even greater speed than before. Jai held on with everything he had, but his grip was slippery with sweat and slime, each and every nerve ending screaming with pain. One finger slid off.

"No," he growled, pushing off with his feet and regaining his full grip. If he could just get over the crest of the beast's skull...

The pyzon dove downward, and it was all Jai could do not to be thrown off, his body rattling, his teeth clacking against each

275

other as the snake traveled underground through darkness. The top of the tunnel scraped against Jai's head, dirt spilling all around him, threatening to fill his mouth, his nose—

And then they were aboveground again, the pyzon shooting into the air and landing with a thunderous smack. Jai had almost nothing left to give, his fingers stiff and sore from gripping the knife, his arm and shoulder numb from the climb and clinging for dear life.

With a final kick, Jai pushed himself up and over the pyzon's head, tumbling directly onto its face, sucked downward by gravity. One of its red eyes swept past and he had the presence of mind to swipe at it with his knife, missing, only managing to scratch the scale just under it. Still he fell, bouncing over its slit-like nose and then he was airborne.

Fangs as tall as himself gaped apart, ready to snap him in two, surrounding a maw so black and empty it was as if he stared into the Void itself.

If this would be his last act, he would make it a great one, one that might save his people.

He threw the fireroot parcel.

The pyzon snapped at him and he slammed off the broad side of one of its long incisors, tumbling away into a backflip. He landed in the dust, flat on his stomach, the impact pushing all of the air from his lungs with a whoosh. He rolled over, gasping for breath, clutching at his abdomen as if he could coax the air back into his chest.

Above him, the red moon smiled while the green moon stared with an unblinking eye. The pyzon swayed, readying for a final strike...

A muffled *BOOM!* split the night and the pyzon split in two, its enormous head and neck flopping forward while the rest of it tumbled sidelong. Dark flesh and red scales and clear liquid erupted like a geyser, spraying Jai and the area around him as the pyzon's head landed nearby, its twin black eyes boring through him. Its maw released a final snap, the fangs so close that he could feel the air from their movement, and then the beast went still. The rest of the snake continued to squirm and writhe, as if still alive, but blind and incapable of attacking. Yet, by some instinct, it flopped and slithered and rolled until it found one of its burrows, disappearing underground.

Air rushed back into Jai's lungs and for a while he just sucked at the breeze, watching the golden stars glitter, red stars fly past, and green stars explode in the black sky.

Though he felt like a fried side of bacon, somehow, by the will of the gods, he was still alive.

Twenty-Four
The Western Kingdom, Knight's End
Rhea Loren

Rhea stood, looking down from the highest tower in the castle, gazing across the Bay of Bounty, where her enemies were preparing for war.

But her thoughts were elsewhere, taking her back to that day in the Furium, watching the young girls train to be warriors of Wrath, when the Fury had revealed the truth about the Western Oracle and Shae Arris.

Rhea was thinking about lies. She had been lied to her entire life. In fact, all the people of the western kingdom had been deceived. The scary thing was, the lie had come before any of them were born, passed down from generation to generation. And why? Because her great-great-grandfather's father had decided his most prized warrior, his original Fury, was an enemy to Wrath.

He'd made her into the Western Oracle, Rhea realized. *In distancing himself from her, he'd created her legend.*

All because of some prophecies she'd made about the Four Kingdoms being ripped apart by war and the death of eight rulers and other nonsense that a common fortune teller could make up.

Then again, rulers *were* dying. *Wrath, my own father was killed before my very eyes by a monster.*

Coincidence, had to be.

And yet, Rhea couldn't get the rest of what the Fury had told her out of her head. How the Three Furies discovered an old scroll within a hidden chamber in the Furium. How it contained symbols and a map. How several of the symbols matched known sinmarks, including the one discovered on Shae Arris's foot. How the map showed the locations of other hidden documents, books. The Western Oracle's legacy, or so they thought.

There was the mention of peace in the Four Kingdoms, alliances between rulers. The end of war.

"That cannot happen," Rhea had said.

"No, it cannot," the Fury had agreed.

At least they were in agreement on that point, Rhea mused now. She didn't want peace, she wanted a righteous war to wipe out the barbarians to the south, the witches to the east, the godless citizens of the north. She needed her people to believe they were Wrath's warriors, and if the Western Oracle was suddenly exposed as a Fury? Everything would be questioned, including her own devotion to Wrath. After all, she was the queen now, connected to the furia as none other was.

And the girl—Shae Arris. Her mark was important somehow, or so the Furies believed, which was why they'd taken such drastic measures to get her away from Knight's End alive, to study her. Based on the Oracle's drawing on the scroll they had found, the Furies believed she was the key, both literally and figuratively, to all of the others who bore marks. To Rhea, this was a powerful notion, because many of the marked were her sworn enemies: the Ice Lord in the north; Beorn Stonesledge, the ironmarked, in the east; Fire Sandes in Calyp; the Slave Master in Phanes. If Grey's sister could be a weapon against them…

She'd immediately sent furia riders south to bring back news about the Furies' discoveries, as well as the map. It was a fortnight later, and they had yet to return, a fact that troubled her greatly.

How can a dead woman wield such immense power? she wondered. Though it annoyed her, it also intrigued her. Would she ever be able to maintain power even after she'd gone to her grave? The thought amused her, and she laughed.

Ennis, who'd been standing silently beside her the entire time, said, "Do you find your enemy's naval fleet amusing, Your Highness?"

Rhea didn't like his tone. Sarcastic. Condescending. More and more lately, that was how he sounded. A spark of anger burned through her, drying up her laughter, and she had to fight back the urge to push him off the wall.

She forced a smile back onto her face. "Dear cousin, I don't believe I asked for your counsel."

"Then why am I here, my queen? Why do you keep me on as your adviser when my words are wind, my counsel naught but dust under your feet?"

It was a good question, a fair question, and it gave Rhea pause, for she didn't rightly know.

Something swelled in her chest, a balloon of...

Rhea suddenly felt short of breath, her heart beating too fast, her legs as rubbery as boiled chicken.

Ennis's voice changed, growing less haughty with a note of concern, and he addressed her as a familiar. "Rhea, are you ill?" He reached out a hand to steady her.

The balloon pressed against Rhea's lungs and she couldn't breathe, couldn't breathe, couldn't—

"I'm fine," she snapped, pulling away from Ennis, forcing a deep breath into her shrunken lungs.

"Are you certain? Because you look rather pale..."

"I'm certain. Do not question your queen, and do not call me Rhea again, unless you insert 'Queen' before it. Do I make myself clear?"

Ennis frowned at her, his hand still hovering midway between them, but then he said, "Crystal. If there is nothing else you need, I will retire for the evening. We will all need to be fresh tomorrow."

"As you wish, cousin," Rhea said. She pretended to ignore him, though she watched his every move out of the corner of her eye, until he was well and truly gone, disappearing down the staircase.

She shot glares at the two furia who remained, as still as statues. "Leave me," she said.

They obeyed without looking at her, and the moment they were gone, too, Rhea collapsed to her knees, the tears welling up faster than she could blink them away, pouring down her cheeks. She choked on a sob, the moment of weakness making her cry harder. She felt like a crumpled doll thrown in a corner by a child who'd grown bored of it, moving on to newer and more appealing toys.

Because she'd recognized that balloon in her chest for what it was. A feeling that had been lingering on the edges of her for days, maybe longer, perhaps since the moment Grey Arris had walked away from her, leaving her with a kindly old stranger who'd taken her in, made her soup, and cobbled her a beautiful pair of boots fit for a queen.

She felt alone.

And that was the answer to Ennis's question about why she kept him around.

Because he was the only one left who vanquished the dragon inside her. He was her only true friend.

And yet, she was pushing him away, just like all the others.

She hated this feeling, hated it as much as she hated her enemies, hated it as much as her own scarred reflection in the mirror.

She dashed her tears away with the hem of her dress, pushed to her feet, snarled at the wall, kicking it with the heel of her beautiful boots, and flung a curse toward the north.

"I am strong," she said. "I am not alone. I have myself, and that is all I need." *Wrath, I'm losing it*, she thought. *Talking to myself, kicking walls, crying like a baby.*

It was all this talk of war, she knew. All the preparation, all the strategizing, all the hustle and bustle with no real results. The waiting was the worst.

Focus. She had to focus. She unfurled the message she'd received from the north earlier that week via inkreed stream. This time it wasn't from King Archer Gäric, but from his sister, Annise, who'd declared herself Queen of the North, as her brother was unconscious and she'd come of age under northern law. Her cousin stated that she'd received Rhea's message of war, and that she wouldn't try to convince her otherwise. Annise went

282

on to say that in the current situation, she considered Rhea and the west an ally, if only because they had a common enemy in her uncle, Lord Griswold, who was intent on destroying them both. Because of this, she had offered information, gathered by Queen Gäric's spies at Blackstone. The message was clear: Lord Griswold would attack Knight's End with his entire fleet on the morrow, at midday, under the watchful eye of the sun.

Rhea crumpled the message in her fist, and then stuffed it in her bodice. She would use it as kindling in her hearth later. For she didn't need information from Annise, who was technically her cousin, the daughter of her deceased aunt, Sabria Loren Gäric.

Long before she'd received the message from the north, she was ready for war, whenever it came.

No, not ready. *Starved.* Yes, that was it. She was *starved* for war. And it seemed she would have her feast sooner than she expected.

Her tears long vanquished, Rhea felt herself again, taking the stairs swiftly. Noon on the morrow couldn't come soon enough.

Annise Gäric had not lied, which Rhea respected. Maybe her cousin didn't have to be an enemy, after all. She knew it was a child's dream, but still, she liked the thought. Queen cousins forming an alliance to take control of the Four Kingdoms? It had a certain romantic appeal to the girl she once was.

Regardless, whatever came next would have to wait. As the sun approached its peak, Lord Griswold's ships set out across the Bay of Bounty, their sails unfurled like enormous gray wings, each stitched with the cracked-but-not-broken shield of the north.

An ugly sigil, in Rhea's estimation. She much preferred her own, the rearing stallion atop a cliff. It was more majestic, more royal. She loved the way the symbol sparkled on the full set of armor she was wearing. It spoke of battles past, of victory, of defeat, of a rightful claim to the realm.

Beyond the first wave of enemy ships, hundreds more cast off from the northern shore into the bay, moving full wind ahead. Rhea had to admit, they were an impressive sight as they charged across the shimmering waters.

"Wrath be with us," Ennis said from beside her. Despite their brief altercation the previous day, he'd shown up at first light at her quarters. Utterly predictable, like the return of a misbehaving hound. In any case, Rhea didn't begrudge him his sense of honor, allowing him to follow her around like a love-starved puppy all morning. He was wearing light armor and a broad sword but no shield. Rhea had the feeling he would offer *himself* as her shield if it came down to it.

"Wrath *is* with us," Rhea said. She turned to the Summoner, who was on her other side, dressed in a plain gray frock made of sackcloth, despite the armor she'd had custom made for him. Unless it was well hidden, he wasn't wearing the armor. *Will Wrath armor him?* Rhea wondered grimly. "Do I bear falsehood?" she asked the holy man.

His expression was grim, but it wasn't a denial. "Nay," he said. "You do not lie. Wrath's fury shall be unleashed on our enemies this day."

Rhea glanced back, where her most violent pawn stood waiting, watching, garbed in blood-red armor. The Fury looked ready to murder the world, and Rhea wondered whether the

Summoner meant fury or *Fury*. Either course would work for her, so long as she won the day. "See, cousin, we have nothing to fear."

Ennis didn't look as convinced. He laid a tender hand on her armored shoulder, and this time she didn't shrug it off. "There is still the opportunity for you to watch from the wall. Or better yet, from the tower."

They'd already had this argument to death, and thus, Rhea didn't hesitate with her response. "No."

"But—"

"I will not have my men"—she glanced at the Fury, who was standing behind her—"and women, risk that which I am not willing to risk myself." It was a quote from the message stream she'd received from Cousin Annise, one she particularly liked. Though Rhea wore her image as righteous queen like a second set of armor, that wasn't the real reason she wanted to be in the midst of the battle. *No, I want to feel Wrath's power around me, witness it from touching distance. I want to feel alive again, bursting with something beyond this world.* Rhea couldn't explain it, exactly, only that the thought of such raw power at her disposal was like an addiction, a drug she had to have. And she would have it.

And it was better than being alone atop the tower.

As usual, Ennis wasn't displaced so easily. "I know you trust this man…" He nodded at the Summoner, who didn't seem to care that he was being talked about without his inclusion. "…but you have no evidence of what he claims to be able to do."

It was true. Twice Ennis had tried to goad the man into Summoning something, anything, and twice the man had shrugged it off, saying Wrath did not perform like some festival entertainer. For all she knew, the Summoner could be a very effective fraud, and they were all about to die.

So be it, Rhea thought. She wasn't afraid of death, not anymore. Not when she'd stared into the Blade of Wrath and emerged forged by steel and fire. *If I die today, let it be a bloody death.*

But she didn't think she would die, at least not on this day, and she was willing to take the risk for what the outcast said he could offer. And anyway, it wasn't as if they hadn't taken precautions. They'd sought out the best divers in the kingdom, who had been busy for a fortnight, planting spiked metal balls deep under the waters of the bay, stringing them together with long iron chains. They'd recruited thousands of seaworthy men and women, who now filled their ships to overflowing, prepared to give their lives for Wrath's righteous cause. In return, Rhea had promised them a place in the seventh heaven. Every blacksmith in the realm had been contracted to build armor and swords and other weaponry to outfit her growing army. Thousands of carpenters had flocked to the castle practically begging to assist in the war effort, creating contraptions that could fling almost anything nearly halfway across the bay.

Finally, Rhea had charged the furia—save for the three-score who accompanied her as her personal guard—with manning the shores as the last stand. If all else failed, she would have her finest warriors fight in close combat to the bitter end. And if, after all that, her kingdom was taken, then she would die in peace.

She almost laughed at her thoughts. *Peace? There will be no peace, so long as my enemies are alive.*

"I am going with the Summoner," Rhea said. "But you are not chained to me, cousin. You may cower behind the walls like a simpering child if you wish. I will not hold it against you, I swear it." She knew it wasn't a real option, but she offered it simply because she enjoyed seeing Ennis's loyalty spring to the surface each time it was called into question.

"Your Highness, I would ride with you to the gates of the first heaven and back if you asked me to."

"Then ride now," she said, stepping onto the gangplank. The furia who were already on board lined the edges of the finest ship in the fleet, *Wrath's Chosen*, looking outward. Several seamen who had been hand-selected to sail the vessel pretended not to look at the queen, but Rhea felt their gazes flitting on her and away, on her and away, restless and nervous and full of anticipation.

Behind her, Ennis followed, along with the Summoner and the Fury. The sun shone brightly, far too cheerful for a battle. As the men readied the ship for cast off, tossing lines across the decks and handling the sails, Rhea watched the rest of her fleet take form.

The moment the northerners had set sail, anchors had been raised, and dozens of ships with various Wrath-inspired names had responded, setting out from the royal docks. Rhea could make out seamen scuttling like ants across the decks, steel glinting in the sun.

The lead northern vessels were fast approaching the center of the bay. A volley of arrows shot out, and Rhea held her breath as her shipborne soldiers closed ranks and raised shields. One man was hit, tumbling overboard, but most of the arrows deflected away harmlessly.

Rhea found herself turning back toward the western shores, waiting, waiting. Nothing happened. *Why are they delaying? The northerners are in range.*

As if in response to her question, fireballs roared through the air, enormous boulders soaked in torch oil, flung from massive catapults. She counted them as they flew: Seven, one for each of the heavens, just as she had instructed. She knew her soldiers would already be loading the machinery for another volley, even before the first shots had landed.

Everyone on her ship watched the fiery projectiles soar through the air. They arced and then began their downward descent: Three splashed into the water, their aim miscalculated; two hit enemy sails, ripping through the thick canvas, which was splashed with oil and caught fire; and the last two boulders smashed into hulls. Even from this distance, the sound of the fireballs colliding with the northern ships was loud, their wooden guts cracking and splintering.

Northern soldiers leapt from the damaged ships in droves, though dozens were crushed by the boulders, or lit on fire by the gouts of flame that erupted across their decks.

Rhea was mesmerized by the violence, which was so swift and brutal and *captivating* that it took her breath away.

The catapults released another volley, and more enemy ships were destroyed. But there were simply too many, and the remaining vessels continued to charge across the bay, until they were too close to the western fleet for the long-distance weapons to be effective.

Rhea found herself leaning forward, biting her bottom lip in anticipation of phase two. Somewhere deep beneath the water, her divers were unlocking the chains. Spiked balls filled with lighter-than-air gases were drifting up toward the surface, and then—

The first ball struck with such force that the unfortunate ship veered off course, colliding with its neighbor. Unbalanced soldiers who hadn't been holding on tightly enough toppled into the sea. Hundreds of other balls struck, as well as the chains they dragged, which tangled amongst the ships, slowing their progress. Enemy vessels that were further back adjusted their course to sail around the logjam, but many of them were too slow. The catapults redoubled their efforts, shortening the distance of their aim.

Screams filled the air as the ships were destroyed, taking their passengers with them.

Rhea's nails dug into the wooden railing. She licked her lips.

"The battle might be won before we join it," Ennis said hopefully.

Rhea hoped not, but she didn't respond, for the next phase was about to begin.

The surviving northern ships closed in on Rhea's fleet, the two forces on a collision course, neither side willing to slow. *Wrath's Chosen* had moved up the field, using its superior speed to bully its way into the heart of the battle, just before it was truly about to begin.

They were so close now that Rhea could see the whites of her enemies' eyes, the sharp edges of their swords, the angry snarls on their lips. And then—

There was a second of utter silence, like the world had stopped, like a storm was raging all around them and they'd snuck into the Eye. Rhea felt as if, for the first time in her life, she was really alive, really living. Everything that came before was an uneventful dream, a prelude to this penultimate moment.

The moment passed, and ships smashed into ships, ropes and planks were flung across from deck to deck, arrows flew through the air like flocks of birds in formation.

Soldiers from both sides charged across, their swords and shields clashing. The rest of the northern fleet arrived, but they sailed past the battling boats to meet the trailing ships of the western armada.

Thus far, Rhea's captain had managed to expertly steer their enormous craft through the melee, avoiding everything but a mild glancing blow from a pesky warship half their size. Any attempts to board were fought off by the furia. Ennis stood in front of Rhea like a personal guard, daring anyone to get close. Several arrows came near, but missed.

"Wrath is with us," the Summoner declared in a raspy voice. "Shall we call on our God?"

Rhea took in the carnage around her. In front of her, the northern fleet appeared to be winning. There was a flash of fire and one of the western ships was suddenly alight. Soldiers leapt into the water to avoid being burned alive. Hundreds of arrows followed them into the depths. There was no mistaking the crimson hue that spread across the once-blue waters.

Like the westerners, the northerners had plenty of tricks. One ship contained enormous cages. When opened, several mamoothen stampeded out, their thick wooly hides deflecting arrows and sword as they crossed between ships, devastating anything in their path with heavy hoofs and long, curling tusks. Those that died before them barely had time to unleash a final scream.

Many of Rhea's ships were sinking now, joining their enemies on the bottom of the ocean.

At this rate, it appeared the northerners would break through and make landfall.

"Queen?" the Summoner said.

"Wait," Rhea said. A portion of the northern fleet had not yet reached the middle of the bay. Rhea would not settle for a partial victory—no, she wanted total destruction. Which meant sacrifices needed to be made.

Two enemy ships closed in on *Wrath's Chosen*, steering directly into her flanks.

"Rhea!" Ennis cried, but she didn't need his warning. She gripped the railing tightly. Still, the impact of the dual-collision rattled her bones and nearly flung her into the ocean. The smaller vessels tore through the wooden sides, impaling themselves into the abdomen of the mighty warship until it was as if they were a single mutated craft.

Soldiers leapt onto the decks, raising sword and shield to meet the furia.

"Now?" the Summoner asked.

Rhea shot her gaze over the battle to find a few straggling enemy ships still quite a distance off. "Wait," she said. And then to Ennis and the Fury: "Protect the Summoner above all else, even me."

"Rhea?" Ennis said.

"*Queen* Rhea. That is a *command*," she growled, cutting off his argument before it could start. "Disobedience will be considered treason."

Ennis shook his head, but didn't respond. He turned away to face their enemies. Rhea raised her own blade, which had been blessed with holy water by the Fury earlier.

The furia were fighting like wildcats, but they were sorely outnumbered. One by one they fell. A large northerner broke through their ranks, but the Fury leapt forward and beheaded him with a single swipe of her long red sword. Two more slipped through, and Ennis and the Fury paired up to defeat them.

But more were coming.

The Fury dispatched another two, three, four men. Then half a dozen. Then a dozen. She was inhuman in her skill, in her violence, and Rhea watched her with awe. *I unleashed this creature, just as I will unleash another.*

Then, suddenly, the Fury spun around, her mouth opening wide, her breath leaving her lungs with a gasp. A sword pierced her breast, up to the hilt, the tip exiting through her back. Words scraped from her throat. "Now I go to meet Wrath."

And then she died, tossing herself overboard in her final act. Rhea's mouth gaped open in awe at how swiftly a life such as hers could be snuffed out like a candle flame pinched between two spit-moistened fingers.

But she couldn't dwell on the thought, because the Fury's killer had drawn a second blade and was advancing on her. *Let him come*, Rhea thought.

She stepped in front of the Summoner. "Queen," he said. "There is still time."

"Not yet," she growled. Her enemy was twice her girth and half again her height. He smiled a carnal smile and swung his mighty sword. Rhea raised her own blade to meet the blow…

Clang!

Ennis took the slash on the broadside of his own longsword, kicking out the northerner's legs in the process. Her cousin jammed his blade downward, stabbing the man in the chest. He withdrew his blade and immediately wiped the blood on his armor, as if offended by it. Though Rhea had always known her cousin to be a strong warrior in the training yard, she was impressed by the carryover to battle.

But it wouldn't be enough. The furia were dead or mortally injured. The Fury was somewhere at the bottom of the bay. Dozens of northerners closed in.

A ray of sunlight pierced her mind, as she noticed the positioning of her enemy's remaining ships: every last one of them was on the western half of the bay, speeding toward the shores of Knight's End. In fact, several of the lead vessels had already made landfall, crashing right into the royal docks.

"Now," she hissed at the Summoner, who was backed up against the railing.

Without a word, he raised his hands in the air, palms open.

Rhea turned back to face the soldiers. Ennis tried to shove her behind him, but she fought her way to his side. "The Summoner is our priority," she said. "I command you!"

Three men leapt forward. Ennis managed to slash one through the throat, where the soldier's neckguard had already been cracked open. The second, however, ducked Rhea's blow and crashed into her, sending her sprawling backwards into the Summoner.

They went down in a tangle, and when she turned to look at the holy man, his eyes were rolled back in his head, his lips moving over inaudible words. His hands were still raised over his head.

And yet nothing was happening. Nothing except the razor-sharp claws of certain doom closing in.

The large northern soldier's face pressed tightly against hers, his breath reeking of tobacco and garlic. Blood dribbled from the corner of his lips, and Rhea realized she'd managed to stab him in the gut during the exchange.

Behind him, Ennis fought four men at once. Two more stepped around them, one raising his sword to finish off Rhea, and the other to end the Summoner, who didn't even seem aware of what was happening outside of his own mind.

Ennis spun around, moving his sword in a brazen arc, forcing his enemies to back away. With a cry, he launched himself back toward Rhea, flinging his body on top of her. *Not me, you fool!*

Rhea wanted to shout, but the air left her lungs when her cousin landed on her chest with a thump. Silver slashed down like lightning, but she barely saw it, wrenching her blade from the dead man's abdomen, hurling it desperately across the Summoner's body, hearing the clank of metal meeting metal.

Atop her, Ennis writhed, having been slashed across his shoulder, but she was staring at the Summoner, who was still alive, back on his feet, still alive, still alive—

Abruptly, his eyes rolled forward, having turned bright crimson, flecked with gold. "She comes," he said, the words barely above a whisper.

"Die, old man," the soldier whose attack Rhea had temporarily thwarted said, cutting off the Summoner's head with a single vicious swing.

The holy man's body fell, hitting the deck before his head, which seemed to hang in midair for a moment, before following the rest of him. Rhea gasped for breath, trying to fill her lungs, even as Ennis was kicked off of her and she was dragged to her feet.

The deck beneath her lurched. *An errant wave in the typically calm bay?* she wondered.

"Lookie here, a queen!" the man holding her howled. He stomped on Ennis's knee, and her cousin cried out in pain.

Still, Ennis managed to spit at the man's feet. "Have some respect," he said.

"Respect?" The soldier raised his eyebrows, his lips curling in amusement. "I could say the same for you, pledging your life to a child. Then again, if you cover that horrific face o' hers"—the man looked directly at Rhea and mock-shuddered—"with a bag, she might do just fine." He reached up and touched her face lasciviously, running his finger along the edge of her lips.

"Unhand her or die," Ennis said, trying to fight to his feet but stumbling back to one knee.

The soldiers laughed, and one offered his heel to her cousin's stomach. Ennis grunted and collapsed once more.

Again, Rhea felt the decks move beneath her. It felt like something had rubbed against them from below. Something large. No one else seemed to notice, too distracted by the captive queen's predicament.

Rhea said, "I am no child, but a woman grown. Come closer and I will give you what you want in exchange for my life."

The man grinned. "Now yer talkin'. And I don't e'en need that bag, yer ugliness is startin' to grow on me." His tongue extended and he made to lick her face.

"And now you die," Rhea said, sensing what was about to come.

The man stopped in mid-lick, cocking his head to the side, confused.

And then he was airborne, snatched up by an enormous tentacle that burst *through* the deck, shredding wood and nail. His scream, bright and hot for a moment, trailed away like the fading tail of a comet.

Too stunned to react, the remaining northerners just stood gaping up at the sky, where the tentacle released its prey, who fell, screaming, landing face down on the deck in front of them.

"Frozen hell," one of them whispered, the man who had kicked Ennis. It was the last words he would ever utter, because dozens of other tentacles burst from the ship, swiping men aside, picking them up, launching them out to sea.

Rhea staggered back, tripping on her cousin and clinging to the railing, which was swaying from the internal damage to the pride of the western fleet. Her eyes were huge, her mind on fire, her chest coiled with ropes of lightning.

They were alone on a deck that started to crack in half.

And then it broke, and they were falling. Ennis fought to an upright position and grabbed her, pushing off with both feet, flinging them into the sea, well clear of the capsizing vessel.

Warm, salty water rushed over them, but they quickly resurfaced, sucking in air, gawking at the Summoner's final deathbed gift.

"Wrathos," Rhea murmured reverently. As tall as the walls of Knight's End, the giant squid was wrapped around *Wrath's Chosen*, like a spider atop its prey. Its flesh was red, mottled with dark spots of algae and crusted with barnacles. A single round eye the size of ten men standing on each other's shoulders stared out from its head. Beneath the eye was a beaklike maw, gaping open to receive the human forms it dropped from the sky. Hundreds of thick tentacles swarmed out from its bulbous body, attaching themselves to ships, grabbing screaming men like they were naught but tin soldiers, slamming down on wind-filled sails.

"Demonos," Ennis countered. "What evil have we released?"

Rhea glared at him. "The monster is on *our* side," she said. "Victory is ours."

Her cousin went silent. There was no arguing the point, as they watched the impossible sea creature destroy each and every enemy ship in the bay. It left the remaining western vessels untouched—somehow it could discern friend from foe.

Onshore, the furia killed or captured any westerners who'd managed to escape the ships, most of whom dropped their weapons at the sight of Wrathos.

And when it was finished, when blood and floating corpses filled the once-blue waters of the Bay of Bounty, the monster churned closer, closer, closer, until it towered over Rhea and Ennis. Rhea was surprised she felt no fear, no apprehension. "Wrathos! You. Are. Mine," she shouted up at the beast.

Wrathos roared, its beak snapping together with a crunch, several northerners' bodies still impaled on the spikes. "Obey me!"

Tentacles shot forward, stopping a handbreadth from Rhea's face. Her cousin flinched away and tried to pull her back, but she shook him off. She reached up and grabbed one of the tentacles, the flesh slimy, slick with seawater and blood. "Leave us!" she shouted. "Your work is finished, your hunger sated! Return to the depths until I call upon you!"

It roared again, its tentacles slapping the water.

"Rhea," Ennis pleaded. "We must retreat before it's too late."

"Foolish man," Rhea said.

With a final squeal, the squid sank beneath the surface, its tentacles slithering to follow. It vanished, the sea churning, churning, slowing, slowing…and then the waters of the bay were calm once more, as if the creature had never existed at all.

Wreckage bobbed happily in the sunlight.

The western survivors stamped their feet and pounded their chests in victory.

PART III

Roan 🛡 Annise 🛡 Grey
Raven 🛡 The Beggar 🛡 Jai
Rhea

The greatest monsters shall be in the hearts of men
and women seeking power.
It is those who must be destroyed.
The Western Oracle

Twenty-Five

The Western Kingdom, The Tangle,
trapped in Felicity's locket
Roan Loren

Strangely, the night passed uneventfully. As it turned out, Gareth was a poor watchman—when Roan awoke, the prince was sound asleep, snoring, his head tucked against Roan's side. Warmth filled him, and he had the urge to wrap an arm around him.

Instead, Roan watched the sky brighten. There was no sun in this place, just a gradual lightening from ink-black to dull gray. No clouds marred the sky. No birds flitted past. No bats either, for which Roan was grateful. The ground was rough but not cracked, and devoid of snakes. With a fine mist swirling across them, it was almost peaceful.

Roan craned his neck toward the enormous mirror, which stretched from horizon to horizon, from ground to sky. If they could only reach it...

What? We can pound on it? Try to break it with our fists? If escape was that easy, Roan knew the men he'd watched die the day before would've broken out long ago. No, getting to the mirror was merely something to do, a task to complete, a way to avoid thinking about the depressing thought of spending the rest of their lives inside the nymph's locket.

"An ounce of ore for your thoughts?" Gareth said, rolling away from Roan's side. Immediately the warmth disappeared, like it had never been there in the first place.

Roan flinched—he'd been unaware the prince's eyes were open, staring at him. "I don't think you want to hear them. Too depressing."

"It could be worse."

Roan frowned. "How?"

"We could be dead."

"I thought that was what you wanted."

Gareth jammed the heels of his hands into his eyes, rubbing. He let out a groan. "I don't know what the hell I want anymore."

"That makes two of us."

The comment made the edge of Gareth's lips twitch. "Can't you do that thing where your skinmark flares up and saves us?"

Roan chuckled. "It doesn't work that way. I can heal, that's it. If you want, I can finish healing that sword wound of yours. The bruises on your neck, too."

"What about that black eye I gave you?"

"Nay, I think it's an improvement."

"Nothing could improve your face."

300

"Ha. Your wit is slipping. That was a little too obvious, even for you. Let's go."

"Where?"

"Toward that mirror." Roan gestured into the distance.

"What's the point?"

"To get there. To stare at our beautiful faces. I don't know, but that's where I'm going. Join me if you wish." Roan stood and started off. His legs felt like lead, like he was dragging iron balls attached by heavy chains.

A moment later, Gareth caught up.

"Welcome to the party," Roan said.

"I didn't have anything better to do. Also you said I had a beautiful face."

"I lied." *I didn't.*

If getting to the mirror had seemed impossible the day before, now it was almost too easy. They reached the smooth, glassy surface mere moments after they started walking. "Strange," Roan said. "It's like distance has no meaning in this place." He stared at the mirror, which didn't really seem to be a mirror, for he couldn't see his own reflection. And yet it showed the gray sky, the rough landscape. Just not them.

Gareth reached out and touched the mirror, and it rippled. He jerked his hand back like he'd been burned. "It's cold, like ice."

Roan touched it, too, and the surface felt like warm water to him. Strange. His hand slipped through it, disappearing. "Can it truly be this simple?" he muttered. "We just walk through?"

"Can't hurt to try," Gareth said, pushing his own hand through the glass.

"At the same time?"

Gareth smirked. "At least we won't die alone."

They stepped through. Roan felt his body twist and then he was falling, landing hard on his boots, his knees buckling beneath him. He ended up sprawled on his back, staring up at a smooth, gray sky. Gareth was beside him, his face planted in the dirt. "Are we dead?" he asked.

"Might as well be," Roan said. "The mirror spat us back out." He sat up, studying the enormous surface, which was glassy once more. Something caught his attention. "Look!"

Gareth followed his gaze to where something was moving inside the mirror. Or behind the mirror, it was hard to tell. First there was something big and black and...furry? Then there was a flash of silver, there and gone. There again. Side to side, moving with inhuman speed.

Roan tracked the movement, squinting, realizing...

"Gwendolyn Storm," he whispered.

And then the mirror split open down the middle, cracks spider-webbing across its surface. It shattered, shards of glass tinkling around them like summer rain but deadlier—razor-sharp daggers.

The wind picked up, seeming to originate from the green and brown void behind the broken mirror, which looked to be rushing up to meet them.

Thud!

Roan groaned as, once more, he hit something hard, right between his shoulder blades. Above him, branches crisscrossed, leaves rustled in a gentle breeze, rays of sunlight pierced the thick forest.

"Ungh?" he said, trying to ask a question, but feeling only pain rippling through his body.

"Yes. You're alive."

Roan twisted his head to find Gwen sitting on a stump, staring at him.

"Gar?" he said, unable to complete the full name.

"Beside you. Also alive. What happened to your eye? And Gareth's neck?"

"Hit me, strangled him." Roan felt like he was chasing his breath.

"Good. Saves me the trouble of having to beat some sense into the both of you."

"Ungh," Gareth said.

Roan agreed wholeheartedly. "How?" he asked.

"I fought the nymph witch," Gwen said. "I won."

"Dead?"

"Not yet, unfortunately she escaped before I could lop off her head. But without this, she'll eventually die." Gwen dangled the seed necklace from her fingertips, the silver lockets clinking against each other.

"Broken?" Roan remembered the glass shards raining down around him. He inspected his skin for cuts, but didn't find any.

"Yes," Gwen said. "I broke Felicity's, but not her sisters'. I get the feeling she's kept them captive for a long time. And anyway, now that we have their souls"—she clinked the lockets against each other once more—"the forest might be slightly more cooperative."

Roan sat up, rubbing his head, which felt bruised. Beside him, Gareth stretched out his spine. He found his voice. "Thank you."

Gwen nodded. "Saving two kings seemed a worthy enough cause."

"I'm not a king," Roan and Gareth said simultaneously.

"Perhaps, perhaps not," Gwen said. "But I wasn't willing to risk it. Plus, I need you both if I'm going to gain access to the Western Archives."

"How do you figure?" Roan asked.

"I need you because you're a Loren," she said. "And I need Gareth to ransom in case they don't believe you're the long-lost prince of the west."

Gareth looked at Roan. "Can we go back in the locket?" he asked.

Gwendolyn was right. The forest had changed. The trees were further apart and no longer spiked, the undergrowth less thick and thorn-free, and the vines seemed to have pulled themselves higher, dangling from the uppermost boughs of the tallest trees.

For once, they were all in agreement as to which direction the sun had risen from, and thus, knew where to go. Still, that night they slept in a tight circle, just in case Felicity attempted to retrieve her sisters' lockets. According to Gwen, the nymph queen was dying, but it was a long process that could take over a year.

The next morning, they ate blueberries from a bush that had appeared beside them during the night. "The Tangle is most hospitable," Gareth said, purple juice dribbling down his chin.

"Aye," Roan said. "It pays to travel with a warrior of the iron forest."

Roan expected his comment to at least earn him a wry smile from Gwen, but instead she glanced away, looking uncomfortable. Gareth seemed to notice the change in her demeanor as well. "What?" he asked.

"I might've left a small detail out of my story," she said, still refusing to meet either of their stares.

Roan frowned, trying to remember what she'd said to them, what she could've left out. Nothing sprang to mind. "What detail?"

"How I saved you. Well, sort of. I did save you, but I had help."

"Help?"

She nodded. "Yes, from a…a bear. He helped me defeat Felicity."

Gareth chuckled. "Color me amused," he said. "You had me going there. Roan too."

Roan would've thought she was joking, too, if not for the serious expression she wore. "A bear, like an animal?" he said. And then he remembered what he'd seen through the mirror just before he'd realized it was Gwen. Dark fur.

"It's no jest," Gwen said. "I thought maybe I was hallucinating, some final nymph trick—that's why I didn't mention it right away. But now I don't know…" She stared at her feet for a moment, and then her eyes darted up to meet Roan's, then Gareth's. "I think it was real. After we'd smashed the nymph's locket, the bear spoke to me. Well, he wasn't a bear anymore, he was a large man, one of the largest I've ever seen. Even Beorn Stonesledge would've had to look up to meet his eyes. He was half-naked, and his skin was covered in words."

"Words?" Roan said.

"Aye. I was so shocked I didn't have a chance to say much, but I read some of the words. I think…" She trailed away, chewing her lip.

"What?" Roan said. "What did the words say?"

"I think they were prophecies about the fatemarks."

Gareth laughed. "I think I might still be inside the locket, dreaming."

Gwen ignored him. "The man called himself Bear Blackboots."

"I've never heard that name before," Roan said.

"That's because she made it up," Gareth said. "Roan, she's amusing herself at your expense."

"Me neither," Gwen said, continuing to ignore Gareth to focus on Roan. "But he told me something. Something that might be important."

"What?"

"He told me who his mother was."

"Who?"

"The Western Oracle." As quickly as she could, Gwen brought Gareth up to speed on everything she knew about the Western Oracle and her prophecies.

Gareth threw another handful of berries into his mouth, munching loudly. "You actually believe the words you're saying, don't you?"

Gwen nodded.

"Fair enough. So you're not joking. Considering everything that's happened, I'll suspend disbelief. Let's assume the Western Oracle was a real person and not some western fantasy. If so, she's been dead for almost two centuries. How would her son still be alive?"

"I don't know."

"And he was a bear first, right? And then a man? How is that possible?"

"I don't know. Maybe he's some kind of a shapeshifter."

Gareth rolled his eyes. "And why would he have helped you? Why would he have even *appeared* to you? Why do you suppose eight rulers have to die in order for the Western Oracle's prophecy to be fulfilled?" he asked.

Roan had considered that very question numerous times already. "Because the monarchs are the ones causing the war." The more he'd thought about the Western Oracle, the more he believed she'd wanted peace. That thought only made him more eager to learn more about her and her teachings.

"Don't tell me you agree with her."

Roan glanced from Gwen to Gareth. "I don't know anything about Bear Blackboots or whether the Western Oracle had a son, but I trust Gwen."

"Aye, I get that, so do I. But this forest plays tricks on the best of us."

"I *saw* what I saw," Gwen said.

"Right, a talking bear."

Gwen grit her teeth. "The bear didn't talk until—"

"It transformed into a giant man wearing prophecies instead of a shirt, right, I got that part," Gareth said. "So he's the two-hundred-year-old son of the Western Oracle, here to help her carry out some prophecy. But why eight rulers? Why not six? Or four, one from each kingdom."

Gwen said, "It would need to be five now that the south is in civil war."

"Regardless," Gareth said.

Roan chewed on the question. "Perhaps Kings' Bane will kill two from each kingdom. The current ruler, and the primary heir. Perhaps he thinks that will be sufficient to change the mindset."

"Let's assume you're right," Gareth continued. "What happens when Bane fails to kill a monarch, or the king or queen is killed by someone else. Do those deaths count?"

"I don't know," Roan said. "That's what we need to find out. That's why we're going west. For information."

Gareth wasn't finished. "And what about *my* death? I was dead before Roan brought me back, wasn't I? Will he come to finish me off?"

"Gareth," Roan said. "We don't know, but we're in this together. We're not going to let him kill you. All we can hope is that the Archives have the answers."

"And if they don't?"

"We find someone or something that does."

Gareth took his last handful of berries and tossed them away in frustration. He stood and stalked off. "Aye, someone like this Bear Blackboots fellow, right? Maybe we really *are* doomed."

"Gareth," Roan said, and started to get up to follow, but Gwen stopped him with a hand on his arm.

"Let him go," she said. "He has to cope with all of this in his own way."

"Cope with what? I told him we'll protect him. I'll heal him again if necessary."

"Sometimes I think you have rocks inside that pretty head of yours." Roan raised his eyebrows, more because she'd referred to him as 'pretty' than because of the insult. Her hand was still on his arm, her fingers warm against his skin. It reminded him of how he'd felt when Gareth's head was nestled against his side, the prince sleeping peacefully inside the locket. *He'd just shifted during the night*, he told himself. *His closeness wasn't intentional. The prince doesn't want me, but maybe Gwen still could.*

He had the urge to reach out and touch her hand, but he didn't. Gwen said, "He's worried about his brother, not himself. He fears that by giving up the throne he sentenced Grian to death. Grian is the only family he has left."

"Oh," Roan said, feeling foolish.

"Aye. I can relate. I have no family left either."

Roan couldn't hold back any longer—he placed his hand on hers. Gwen's cat-like eyes danced to their hands, then back to his eyes. Roan said, "You have me. You have Gareth, too. You don't have to push us away. Not anymore."

Gwen's pink lips knitted into a firm line, and Roan waited for her usual response: anger, or flight, or a punch in the shoulder. Which was why he was surprised when she rotated her hand until her palm was touching his. One by one, her fingers laced between his. The sensation was like warm water on skin, more powerful than anything he had ever felt, including the pain of being nearly impaled by a dragon's tooth. His chest swarmed with butterflies. Was this really happening?

She spoke: "Why did you question your own existence as a child?" she asked.

He didn't know what he'd expected her to say, but not that. "I—I don't know."

"Tell me."

He was trapped in her gaze, and he knew he would tell her anything in that moment. It was like being enchanted all over again. "I felt alone. I felt abandoned."

Gwen nodded. "I loved someone once."

"The poet?" Roan asked.

Gwen nodded.

He wanted to say *I'm sorry* but knew it wouldn't be nearly enough. "When? How?"

"During the Dragon Massacre. Many years ago," she said.

Roan rubbed his finger against hers. Though he hadn't been alive when the Calypsians and their dragons had invaded Ferria, the southerners told the tale often. They wore the event like a badge of honor, despite the fact that they'd lost the battle. "But it hurts like yesterday," Roan said.

Gwen blinked. "Sometimes. But not always. Time fades the best and the worst. Dulls the pain. But it's always there, lingering, rising up when I least expect it." Her thumb began moving against his, a tender dance.

"Will you recite his poem for me?" Roan asked, holding his breath.

Her thumb stopped moving. "No."

"I'm sorry, I didn't mean to—"

"No, I mean, I don't remember it."

"*Night black, day bright,*" Roan started, recalling the first line from her iron gate.

The words seemed to awaken something inside Gwen, and she squeezed his hand. "*Stars sparkle, moonlight / Leaves rustle, streams flow / Lightning flashes, winds blow / Gleaming ore hawks, a silver dove / So much beauty, but none like you / My love.*"

When she finished, the breath rushed out of her and her eyes sparkled with unshed tears. "Oh Alastair," she murmured.

"That was his name?"

She nodded.

Roan said, "He was a beautiful poet. But then again, he had a beautiful muse."

Gwen let out a surprised laugh, and it felt more real than anything Roan had ever heard her utter, save perhaps for the poem she'd just recited and the name of her lost love. She withdrew her hand. "Don't make me hurt you," she said.

Roan grinned. "I'm not trying to flatter you. My heart is simply on my sleeve—I have trouble hiding it when there's something I want."

"Or someone?"

He nodded, holding his breath. Waiting for the rejection, like with Gareth.

"Everyone I get close to dies."

And there it was:

The reason.

Why she was the way she was. Why not only her body was sheathed in armor, but her heart too. Why she didn't want any friends. Why she wanted Roan to be naught but a traveling companion. He remembered the way she'd been when the man known as Bark was dying, how she'd threatened Roan, pleaded with him, implored him to save Bark before her. But he didn't. He refused her request and saved her instead. And then it was too late to save Bark. Her friend.

He remembered how much it seemed to *break* her.

Everyone I get close to dies.

Yet, as painful as her words were to hear, they were not a rejection. "I'm not going to die," Roan said.

"You can't promise me that. No one can."

"I bear the lifemark. Not plague nor dragon can kill me. I'm invincible. I'm perfect for you."

Gwen smiled again, dashing the tears from the corners of her eyes with her knuckles. "Speaking of which: Aren't you going to heal your face?" she asked.

"I don't think so. Anyway, it makes me look more dangerous, don't you think?"

"If dangerous is a mouse with long blond hair."

"All cower before my meekness," Roan said.

"Aye, you've moved from as dangerous as a turtle to as dangerous as a chicken."

Roan flapped his arms like wings and made a clucking sound. Gwen laughed. Roan stopped, turning serious. "In truth, I need

311

to feel pain sometimes, just like everyone else. The bruises I wear are a reminder that I can hurt friends as easily as they can hurt me."

Gwen's eyes studied his face, as if tracing every mark, every bruise. It took all of his self-control not to shrink away from her scrutiny. "They will heal well enough on their own," she agreed.

Roan was feeling bolder by the second. He reached up and traced her jawline with his thumb. "What say you?"

"I say you're madder than a man trapped in a nymph's locket." But she didn't reach up to remove his hand. In fact, she leaned into his touch, closing her eyes, sighing slightly.

A rustle snapped them apart and Gareth stepped into the clearing. He frowned, his eyes darting back and forth between them, seeming to notice their close proximity. "What'd I miss?" he asked, seeming to sense the sudden awkwardness his presence had created.

"Just Roan being a nutter again," Gwen said, but Roan caught the quick wink she offered in his direction.

"Aye. I bear the foolmark, what can I say?" Roan said.

Gareth's eyes narrowed further, as if he wasn't buying it, but then they widened and he clapped his hands. "Right. Let's move while there's still sunlight."

He turned his back and marched off. Roan stood, and then offered a hand to Gwen. She reached up, pausing a moment before grasping his hand. With a hard yank, she pulled him down, using the momentum to gain her own feet. She grinned down at him. "This doesn't change anything," she said. "I'm still the strong one." With that, she took off after Gareth.

Roan laughed. He couldn't argue with that, nor did he want to. Still, despite her words, Gwen's hand brushed against his as he caught up to her.

A week later, when they finally emerged from the Tangle, travel-weary and hungry, Roan felt like a hood had been torn off of his head. After living in the confines of the shadowy forest for so long, everything was brighter, more vibrant, and larger. Empty rolling hills of brown grass pocked with occasional rock outcroppings stretched from horizon to horizon.

They hadn't seen any sign of man or bear as they travelled through the forest.

"We veered too far north at some point," Gwen pointed out, nodding to the Mournful Mountains, which were far closer than they expected them to be.

"I'll give you three guesses as to why," Roan said. "But you'll only need one."

"Damn nymph and her tricks," Gareth said, but there was little emotion behind his remark. Despite the time they spent together in Felicity's locket, Gareth had been unusually quiet ever since their argument about the bear. Several times Roan had tried to get him to open up again, to no avail. On the other hand, he and Gwen spoke every day, sometimes of the past, sometimes of their hopes for the future, sometimes meaningless quips and banter. It didn't matter what they talked about—her company was enough for Roan, something he never thought he'd say after her harsh treatment of him from the moment she met him.

Yet still he felt slightly empty inside, because of Gareth's silence.

"At least we can navigate now," Gwen said. "The mountain range goes straight west, all the way to the Bay of Bounty."

Roan thought back to the maps of the west his guardian had made him study in his youth. There was only one major western stronghold before they reached Knight's End. "If we follow the mountains, we'll reach Bethany."

"We should avoid Bethany," Gwendolyn said. "If they realize we have an Ironclad, they will imprison the lot of us."

"Nay," Gareth said, staring at the mountains. There was a distant look in his eyes, like he was seeing something else. Some memory. "We should take the easiest route. Head south to the Western Road. There are inns along the track. Places to rest our heads and get a warm meal."

"Too conspicuous," Gwen said, trading a look with Roan. Roan shrugged back. He had no idea what their friend was thinking right now. "We'll travel overland."

"No," Gareth said sharply. He spoke through his teeth, his jaw set tightly.

Gwen frowned and opened her mouth to reply, but Roan stopped her with a hand on her shoulder. *Let me try*, he mouthed. He approached Gareth slowly, trying to catch his eye. The prince merely looked around him, past him. "Oi," Roan said. "Oi!" He grabbed his shoulder, jostling him.

Gareth's eyes snapped to his. "Take your hand off me unless you want a repeat of the nymph's locket."

The look in his friend's eyes was different than anything he'd ever seen. He couldn't define it exactly. It wasn't anger, no, something else entirely. "You mean when you punched me and I almost strangled you to death? When you asked me to finish you off?"

At first, Gareth's shoulders tensed and he looked as if he might actually hit Roan again, but then the fight fell away from him, the distant look returning.

"What is the matter?" Roan asked.

Gareth rubbed his eyes and yawned, though Roan could tell it was an act. "Nothing. I'm sorry. I'm just weary. I'm only saying we could all use a good sleep and a bowlful of something half-edible."

"We don't have the coin," Gwen cut in. "And what we have, we may need as bribes when we reach Knight's End."

"I have plenty of coin," Gareth said. His grin returned, though it didn't feel natural to Roan. It was a mask, and it reminded him of the mask Gareth was wearing when he'd first met him, back when he thought the eldest Ironclad son was naught but an arrogant prince. "I robbed the war chest before I snuck away. Grian is probably cursing my name as we speak."

"Still," Gwen said, "between my eyes and hair and your namesake, we will attract too much unwanted attention."

But Gareth was on a roll now, not to be denied. "You will plait your hair and wear a scarf that shadows your eyes. And I will call myself...Montoya!"

Roan snorted. "What kind of name is that?"

"I dunno. I just came up with it."

Gwen didn't seem pleased with any of it, but Roan was determined to keep the peace. Plus, the thought of a warm bed and food wasn't the worst idea in the world right now. "How about a compromise? Instead of traveling due south, we head southwest overland, cutting off part of the distance we have left, until we hit the Western Road. Then we take the road west all the way to Knight's End."

Gwen sighed, but the fight had left her. "Fine. But we do not stop in any of the small villages, is that understood? We stop in Restor and Restor alone."

Gareth smiled, and for a moment—just a moment—he was the man Roan knew him to be. As they began walking, the smile faded, and Roan saw a stranger once more.

Twenty-Six

The Northern Kingdom,
south of Castle Hill
Annise Gäric

Annise swore the clouds had descended from the sky and melded with the ground, and now she was floating on them. Hiding her smile was no small feat, and yet she knew she had to, for it was not queenly to smile after the massacre the day before.

She couldn't help it. Waking up in Tarin's arms, warm and safe, kissing his lips *first*, before saying good morning, holding his muscled body against hers, helping him don his armor...

She could get used to mornings like this one.

I can't, she thought. Like Tarin had said the day before, every moment was precious, because every moment could be their last. *I can't lose you. I can't. I would rather die.*

The thought startled her, and, subconsciously, she stopped walking. It was the first time she'd ever thought something like that about anyone, even Arch. *Is it true?* Would she rather die than live life without Tarin?

"My queen?" Tarin said, his voice low and gruff. She remembered the way he'd growled the night before, and the memory sent lightning up her spine.

"Yes, I…" She forced a smile back onto her lips, a smile that only a moment ago had come far too easily. "We need to encourage the soldiers."

"Queen?"

"After we begin our march, you will accompany me along the train."

"Yes, Your Highness."

"What about me?" Sir Dietrich asked, striding up.

"What *about* you?" Annise said.

"Your command?"

"Have you made water this morning?"

Dietrich grimaced. "Aye, but I've just drunk a full flagon."

"Strong flow," Zelda reminded her. She was buttering a scone using her finger as a knife.

Annise eyed the sword sheathed in Sir Dietrich's hip scabbard. How could a man as talented with the sword as this knight be such a fool sometimes? "You'll ride with the first cavalry. You'll *lead* them. You'll not leave their side until we make camp."

"Yes, Your Highness, but what if I need to—"

"You'll water your britches."

Zelda laughed around a large bite of scone.

"It's too cold, they'll freeze solid!"

Zelda laughed louder, spitting out crumbs.

"Then we'll refer to you as Sir Ice Trousers," Annise said. Letting a smile curl the corners of her mouth, she turned on her heel and went to see if her horse was ready. Dietrich was far too easy a target, but that didn't take away any of the pleasure.

They'd left the forest well behind them, and were once again on the hard-packed road that would take them all the way to Castle Hill. Lazy snowflakes swirled through a white sky, though most never seemed to reach the ground. Annise, in a show of strength and fearlessness, had begun the march with her foreriders—most of whom were newly promoted foot soldiers replacing those killed by the stone monster. It had been Tarin's idea, which pleased her greatly. *He does not coddle me. Not anymore.*

Now, they pulled back from the front to carry out her "ride of encouragement," as she was calling it. They started with the cavalry. Annise offered small talk to those she knew, and made introductions to those she didn't. She commended the first cavalry on their valor during the previous day's battle, and even managed to bite her tongue when several witty quips at Sir Dietrich's expense came to mind—it wouldn't do to undermine their commanding officer. Tarin mostly stayed silent, his eyes roving the lands on either side of the road, searching for enemies. And yet his presence alone was enough to bring Annise great comfort.

Next, they passed through the lines of foot soldiers. Considering the horrors many of them had witnessed not half a day earlier, they were in good spirits, laughing as Annise offered jokes, and smiling when she complimented them.

Annise felt something she never thought she'd feel, something her brother Archer had felt his whole life: adoration. These people actually believed in her. *No*, she realized, *it goes further than that. They will die for me if necessary, just as the first cavalry had been willing to do.*

The weight of that responsibility pressed on her shoulders. *But I can bear it*, she thought. She'd always wondered why she hadn't been born petite, like her mother, why she was forced to endure endless mockery from insecure lordlings. Perhaps this was why. Perhaps she was destined to need broad shoulders and a strong back to bear the trust of her people.

When they were alone, in between companies, Tarin said, "A coin for your thoughts?"

She smiled. "I'd rather have a kiss."

"Later," he said. "But those are free, my queen."

"Well, my thoughts are my own, at least for now."

"As you wish." Based on the twinkle in his dark eyes, however, she suspected he knew her mind as well as she did. Maybe better.

"Tarin," she said. "Where did you go yesterday? After the day was won?" Last night, she hadn't wanted to spoil the mood by broaching this topic, but now she felt she needed to. If her paramour knew her mind, she must know his.

"Walking," Tarin said gruffly.

"It spoke to you?" She knew she didn't need to specify who *it* was. Tarin called it the monster inside of him, but Annise hated using that word to refer to anything having to do with him.

"It always speaks to me."

"Even now?"

"Even now."

He'd never told her that. She thought it was only during battle. "I didn't know that."

"I never told you."

"Why are you telling me now? Is it because of what we did last night?" The thought should've made her blush, but it didn't. Nothing she did with Tarin ever felt embarrassing.

His gaze rested on her for a moment, almost thoughtful. "No. I don't want any secrets between us ever again."

"Oh. Thank you?" She suddenly felt bad for not sharing her own thoughts with him.

He chuckled. "I'm sorry I disappeared like that yesterday. I'm sorry for what I am."

"A good man? Honorable? A hero? You have nothing to be sorry for. You never asked for any of this."

"Still, I hate that I have to leave your side when you need me the most."

"Why do you have to? You are so strong, Tarin. I know you are stronger than…whatever is inside you."

He shook his head. "I wish it were that simple. But I will not risk harm coming to you."

She stopped her horse. "You would never hurt me," she said.

He stopped a few paces ahead, but didn't look back. "You don't know what I'm capable of." There wasn't anger in his tone, just resignation. Sadness.

She moved forward until she was close enough to rest a hand on his shoulder, though she had to reach up to do so. He flinched slightly, and that hurt her more than any of his words. "Tarin…*Tarin.*" Finally, he looked at her. "Stay with me. We are stronger together. I believe that."

"I know," he said. "I'm trying." Suddenly his words from the night before, about not wasting the precious moments they had

321

together, seemed different. More like a goodbye than anything else.

Frozen hell, when did I get so needy? Annise thought. She brushed away the thought, because Tarin wasn't some childhood infatuation.

"Fair enough," Annise said. "Let's continue."

The next group they came to were not soldiers, though some soldiers moved amongst them. They were tradesmen and tradeswomen. If the soldiers were the heart of the army, these were the lifeblood pumping through its veins. Even as the train moved forward, they worked, sitting on broad carts pulled by horses. There were leather workers and blacksmiths, seamstresses and cooks. One cart was piled high with boots requiring resoling, while another was a mess of shirts and britches needing mending. Annise stopped at each, complimenting the quality of their work, thanking them for their service to the crown, promising them each a permanent position once they retook Castle Hill.

They reached a blacksmith cart. Though it was too dangerous to set up a mobile forge, the blacksmiths were still keeping busy, hammering out dents in armor, polishing weapons and helmets, designing new weapons on long scrolls of parchment held down by rocks.

Annise peered over the shoulder of a rare female blacksmith, who was adding details with an inked quill to the design of a weapon. "It's beautiful," Annise said.

The woman looked back, surprised. Her level of concentration had been so complete she hadn't noticed their approach. A hammer dangled from a loop in her belt. With black hair cut boy-short, intense gray eyes and a small, angular face, she was an attractive woman, Annise noticed, though she was perhaps a few years older than she. The other thing she noticed was the strength in the lines of her arms, no doubt from countless swings of her hammer against anvil.

"Thank you...Your Highness. I'm sorry, I didn't expect such auspicious company."

"This weapon..." Annise said, motioning toward the parchment. The design showed a spiked ball attached to a chain with a leather grip. "I know of one similar, but larger."

"Larger? It would take a powerful man to wield such a weapon."

"Yes. In fact, the knight who wields it is just here."

Tarin approached, but Annise was watching the blacksmith woman, whose mouth fell open. "Frozen hell," she said. "It cannot be."

Annise lifted an eyebrow. "Cannot be what? What is your name?"

"Fay." It was not the woman who answered, but Tarin.

"I thought you were dead!" the woman—Fay—exclaimed. She rose to her feet, balancing on the unsteady cart.

"Not just yet," Tarin said.

Annise's eyes danced between them, trying to figure something out. The obvious answer came to her. "Fay designed the Morningstar," she said.

"Yes," Fay said proudly. "He's the only man I ever met who could actually lift it *and* swing it with enough force to do any damage."

Annise laughed at that. "Aye. I saw him nearly win a tourney using it."

"Nearly?" Fay said. "You mean he was defeated?"

"Hard to believe, I know. But it just so happens we have the best swordsman in the realm commanding the first cavalry. Sir Dietrich. He emerged the victor."

"Ah. I've heard of him. But still. I watched Choose win a dozen tourneys. When I was with him, he never lost."

With him? What exactly did that mean? "Choose? His name is Tarin."

"Oh," she said. "He told us to call him Choose."

"I have had many names," Tarin said, interrupting, "but now I go by the one my mother gave me—Tarin."

"Well," Fay said, "it's a pleasure to finally meet you, Tarin."

"Did you design his armor as well?" Annise guessed.

"Yes. And I'm glad to see the big guy has kept it in good nick. Though it's looking a bit small these days. Once we make camp, I can work on the fit."

So it's not just my imagination…he is *getting larger.*

"He rarely takes it off," Annise said. "Even to sleep. Though last night…"

"You mean he's still self-conscious about his affliction?" Fay asked.

Annise was taken aback. This woman *knew* what he looked like beneath the armor? "Of course you would know," she said. "You fitted his armor."

Fay laughed. "I wouldn't say I *know*. He never let me see him. But I saw enough."

Annise breathed easier. She liked this woman. Her quick tongue, her skill with the hammer, the strength in her body. And if she hadn't seen what Tarin really looked like, there had been nothing between them worth worrying about.

"Enough about me," Tarin said, sounding uncomfortable. "Where have you been all these years?"

"Around," Fay said.

"With Bart?"

"Who's Bart?" Annise asked. It was strange thinking about Tarin having a past, a space in between the years that she had known him. Though he'd told her some of what had happened to him, there were probably thousands of details he'd left out. People like Fay and Bart who must've been important to him in various ways.

"A money-grubbing little weas—" Fay started to say, but Tarin cut her off.

"My first and only tourney sponsor," he said.

"I haven't seen him in many years," Fay said. "But he was a scoundrel anyway."

"Yes, he liked his coin," Tarin said, "and he helped me for all the wrong reasons. But still, I owe him a lot. I owe both of you."

Fay blinked. Though she tried to hide her feelings, Annise could sense the pride there. "Like I told you before we parted ways..." Fay said.

"I know, I know, you were just doing your job. But still, thank you for my armor, for the Morningstar."

"And now you want to forge smaller versions of Tarin's weapon?" Annise asked, bringing the conversation full circle.

Fay shrugged. "I don't know. Perhaps. It's just something I've been playing around with. The weapon loses a lot of its power when made smaller, but a normal soldier can't wield it otherwise."

"Are you saying I'm not normal?" Tarin asked. Annise was pleased to hear that the lightness in his tone had returned.

"A man-beast like you?" Fay said. "Perfectly normal. You'd fit right in with the ice bears of the Hinterlands."

Annise laughed. "That's what *I'm* always telling him."

Fay smiled. "In any case. It was lovely meeting you, Your Highness. And a pleasant surprise seeing you again, Choo—I mean, Tarin. I won't take up any more of your time."

"I want to know everything about the time after you left Castle Hill," Annise said, as they rode back up the line toward the front of the slow-moving train.

Tarin grunted. "The past is the past. We should leave it there."

"I don't like not knowing things about you."

"I thought you were attracted to me because I was mysterious."

"About as mysterious as a tin can," Annise said, rapping her knuckles on his armor. His hand grabbed hers and he held on, riding together for a spell. "Seriously though, your past isn't a mystery to those who were there with you, so why should it be to me?"

"You have much more important things to set your mind to."

"An excuse."

"I have a deal for you. If we retake Castle Hill, I'll tell you the whole story. Every single detail."

Annise considered it. She could keep pressing him for more information now, but he'd probably only pull his head further into his armor, like a turtle hiding from a predator. It was the best she was going to get. "Deal," she said.

The train rode on for another five days without seeing another of Lord Griswold's monsters. Each day, Annise and Tarin rode the line, getting to know the soldiers, trading quips, learning their names. She was surprised how much she enjoyed it. How good she was at it. She'd always thought of Archer as the charismatic one in the family, but perhaps some of his charm had rubbed off on her along the way. Or maybe it had been hiding inside her the whole time, just waiting to come out.

She always made a point to stop at Fay's cart to chat for a few moments. Evidently, while they camped each night, the blacksmith set up a makeshift forge and continued working on what she was calling her Evenstar design, the miniature versions of Tarin's larger Morningstar.

Today, on the fifth day since Annise had met her, Fay had a sample ready. She handed Annise the handle, and she gripped it tightly, relishing the supple leather binding. Even the sample was of exquisite workmanship. "Can I swing it?" Annise asked.

Fay shrugged. "Why not? This one is for testing, and I've heard you are a strong woman."

Tarin said, "Perhaps we should let someone else test it *before* the queen. Let me."

"Is he always like this around you?" Fay asked.

"He used to be worse," Annise said. "And then I beat off an ice bear. Now back off, Sir Worrywart." With a mighty heave she swung the modified mace overhead. Tarin ducked as the Evenstar whipped past. Annise let out a whoop of delight as she cut a round arc in the sky, the spiked ball whizzing past like a red star. She became more daring, altering her swing to a figure eight, and then a quick snap, like a whip, the ball flinging outwards at an imaginary foe.

She lost her grip.

The Evenstar, chain and all, flew through the air, crashing into the side of a cart bearing a half a dozen seamstresses darning thick socks, who screamed at the impact. As Annise watched in horror, the heavy spiked ball splintered the wood, ripping a plank from the bottom of the platform. The two horses pulling the cart spooked, rearing back and almost toppling backwards.

Annise leapt from her mount and raced over, apologies already on her lips. "Are you hurt?" she asked the women, who looked more startled than anything.

After checking themselves, they all confirmed they were fine. Annise offered them the day off, but they politely declined. Tarin opened his mouth to say something, but Annise stopped him with a single word. "Don't."

"I was only going to say it was a nice shot," he said, chuckling, once they were riding next to Fay's cart once more.

Sheepishly, Annise handed her the Evenstar. "I could've killed someone!"

"But you didn't. And you will learn from the mistake."

"Learn?"

"Yes. For the next time."

"Next time?"

"Yes," Fay said, cutting in. "I want you to have the first one. I think it's the perfect weapon for you."

Shocked, Annise accepted the Evenstar back, though she was almost afraid to touch it. She swore it had practically jumped out of her hand the last time. "I—I don't know…I'm usually better with my fists."

"And snowballs," Tarin reminded her.

"I never thought of the Evenstar's potential as a projectile," Fay said. "You demonstrated that very well."

"It was an accident."

"Some of the best inventions are discovered by accident," Fay said.

Annise wasn't certain whether she was just trying to make her feel better, but she did like the feel of that leather grip. "Then I guess there's nothing left to say but thank you."

"You are most welcome, Your Highness."

Annise held up the weapon toward Tarin. "Now we match."

Tarin only shook his head.

They halted the procession two days later. Not at night, but midday.

Because they could see it. Castle Hill, its white walls and ramparts shining in the sunlight through the swirling snow like a beacon.

Home, Annise thought. It felt like a lifetime since she'd been forced to flee with Arch through the sewer tunnels. Then, she had wondered whether she would ever return to the city she grew up in. At the time, she hadn't cared. She'd hated the city, what it represented. She'd longed to leave its bounds and never return.

But now…

Now she was shocked at how much she'd missed it. Tarin said, "It's more beautiful than I remembered."

Annise nodded. She knew the feeling. "I think it was my father that made it so ugly," she said.

"It seems your uncle is trying to carry on the tradition."

Annise narrowed her eyes, staring at the high, thick walls, wondering what monsters lurked behind them. "It's time for this tradition to change. Gather the cavalry commanders. We attack tomorrow, at first light."

Twenty-Seven

The Western Kingdom, the Dead Isles
Grey Arris

When Grey's small craft collided with the shoreline, he tried to jam one of his oars between the jagged rocks to hold himself steady. For a moment it worked, and his boat held firm, but then a wave crushed him from behind, twisting the boat around and throwing him off-balance. His arms wind-milled several times as he lost the oar, which continue to stick from the rocks like an oversized pin from a cushion.

And then, when another wave swept in on a strange angle, his vessel capsized. Black, churning waters closed in around his head, punching him with an icy fist and trying to claw inside his mouth. He came up sputtering, frantically kicking both legs and waving both his hand and his stub. His head cracked against something hard, and he tried to make sense of the darkness that surrounded him.

The boat. He was inside the boat, which was upside down. Waves continued to bash into the wooden sides, which then threatened to break him in half. He needed to get away from his vessel or he would die.

Taking a deep breath that was as much salty seawater as air, Grey dove, kicking hard and trying to put distance between himself and the boat, which scraped past, borne on the swift current.

When he resurfaced, his boat was gone and he was faced with a greater danger: the shard-like rocks that seemed to want to impale him on their hardened spikes. A wave picked him up, carrying him toward the rocks at far too great a speed. He cried out, but his scream was lost amongst the crashing of the waves on the shore. His shoulder slammed against a black rock, shooting agony through the very marrow of his bones, and he tried to hang on, but the stones were slick with wet moss and his only hand slid away.

The ocean inhaled, sucking him back out to sea.

His shoulder throbbed. His knee ached, too, where he must've hit it on the rocks. His lungs heaved, burning with swallowed saltwater.

The ocean's next breath was a great sigh, in unison with his own, sending him back toward the black sledgehammer that would crush him into human paste.

And then he saw it. The oar, still protruding from the rocks. He reached for it, grunting, a zing of fear and thrill sparking inside his gut. His fingers closed around the wooden shaft, even as his body was smashed like a doll slung against a wall by a tantrum-throwing child.

The world flipped but still he clutched the oar, refusing to let go. He tried to shield his head with his stub and his arm, which took the brunt of the blow.

His legs twisted and he felt something pop, but still he hung on.

The ocean retreated and still he hung on.

The oar creaked and bounced, and still he hung on.

And then, as a fine rain began to fall through the mist, he started to climb, scrabbling at the wet rock and fighting for every inch.

Until he flopped, much like a beached fish, onto the unforgiving shore, panting and crying and laughing.

Shae. I'm coming. I'm here.

The wind blew a forlorn reply, chilling him to the bone.

It was like the sun had been taken captive, barricaded behind a wall of thick gray clouds. Mist seemed to attach itself to everything: the rocks, the ocean, even Grey's drenched clothes. Though he had hoped the rain would abate, instead it howled with laughter and fell harder, icy needles pricking his cheeks and the back of his neck. Surprisingly, he missed scrubbing the decks of the Jewel under the heat of the blazing sun.

He couldn't walk quite right, one of his legs hitching with each step. Of course, like every other lad growing up in the western kingdom, he'd heard the ghost stories about this place, but right now, with his amputated hand and lurching limp, he was the only undead creature staggering across the barren landscape.

The thought made him laugh, and for a moment he howled along with the wind, feeling more alive than he'd ever felt in his life. He wondered whether he'd taken a hit to the head, sending him spiraling into madness.

That thought made him laugh too.

Reaching across his body, he pinched himself, trying to get control. Think. He had to think. He'd had a small amount of food and water, but both were lost when his boat was swept away. Water likely wouldn't be a problem, given the incessant rainfall. Food, on the other hand...

He spun in a circle, seeing nothing but bare, black rocks, towering cliffs, and an endless ocean full of whitecaps.

There! He might've screamed the word, but if he did the wind stole his voice again.

A light flickered through the mist, elevated from his current position. *Atop the cliffs? Or is it a star?* he wondered. No. Despite how gray everything was, it was still daytime, there would be no stars. He saw it again, a sparkle of light fighting through the storm.

Someone else was on the island, too.

Everyone had a different opinion as to what, exactly, the Dead Isles were haunted by. Some said it was where children went if they died, transforming into something evil, feasting on the flesh of wayward travelers that were shipwrecked on the islands' shores. Others believed it was the tip of the first heaven, the place where Wrath banished the very worst souls, sticking from the ocean as a warning to all those who would sin. There were even those who claimed the isles themselves were alive, part of a monstrous demon whose hunger was never satisfied, devouring those who were unlucky enough to step foot on its rocky skin.

To Grey, however, it was just a damn dismal place. He hated the thought that Shae might be here, shivering like him.

He hadn't even seen a single ghost. He hadn't seen anything, save for that light, which seemed to get further and further away with each step. Because of this, his initial excitement had faded into the mist, and weariness and depression began to gnaw on his bones like a pair of starving hounds.

But still he soldiered on, grunting and cursing as he clambered over rough, jagged boulders, making his way toward the base of the cliffs, where he hoped to find...something. Best case scenario would be a set of gently winding stairs that he could take to the top. Even a rope would do. However, when he finally reached the cliffs, what he found made him sink to the ground and close his eyes.

A smooth, sheer rock face stared down at him, grinning a devil's grin.

Grey let himself wallow for a few minutes. After all, he'd earned it. He didn't cry—the last thing he wanted on his face was more saltwater. But he groaned, an audible representation of all his frustration and the aches and pains thrumming through his body. Then he slapped himself on the cheek, hard enough to snap himself out of his temporary misery.

He rose to his feet and continued on, skirting the edge of the unclimbable cliffs. *There is a light up there somewhere*, he reminded himself. *Which means* someone *climbed it. If they did it, so can I. And I will.*

He kept repeating those words—*I will, I will, I will*—over and over in his head, which kept his feet moving one after the other.

Eventually, as he made his way around to the perpendicular side of the cliffs, the landscape changed slightly. The face of the cliff tilted, like the back of a giant as he craned his neck to stare at the sky. Further along still, he found a trail of sorts. It was rough, not paved exactly, but hewn into the rocks themselves, switching back and forth up the side of the cliffs.

He pounded his chest with his stump, opening his mouth to drink the rain. It would be a long trek to the top, and he would need to stay hydrated.

And then he started to climb.

Grey felt like a drunk as he staggered onto the top of the cliffs. His legs were jelly, wobbling beneath him. Everything spun with whorls of black, gray, and white. And orange.

The light.

It was at the top of a craggy hill, standing before a stone structure. A torch of some kind, beckoning him.

He paused, taking a moment to steady himself, to drink more rain. He desperately wanted to sit down—better yet, to lie down and sleep—but he resisted the urge. He knew if he went down he might not have the energy to get up again.

He walked on, reeling in the light with each step, watching it grow bigger and brighter in his field of vision, vibrant against the wall of gray.

The light marked the door to the structure, a rusty iron slab with a huge metal hoop for a doorknob. The building was constructed of enormous stone blocks, each so large it would take a hundred men on ropes to lift it. Grey couldn't imagine this barren place teeming with enough men to build this structure.

335

Unless, of course, some of the stories were true, and it was built by the undead, using supernatural powers.

He laughed away the thought, but then went silent when the doors began to groan.

As fast as he could with his injured leg, he hustled around the corner of the building and pressed his back to the wall, breathing. Breathing and listening. The rain fell in a sheet before him, but not hitting him because he was now under an overhang provided by long, cut stones that formed a roof of sorts.

Rainwater dripped from his clothing, from his ears, from the tip of his nose. From his fingertips and from the soaked bandages wrapped around his stump.

With a final creak, the door slammed open.

And then…

Silence.

Grey pursed his lips, waiting for a sound, anything to give him an idea of who or what had opened the door. But there was nothing, just the whistle of wind over the cliffs and the drum of rain on the rocks.

He envisioned himself sticking his head out and having it separated from his neck by a ghostly scythe. He swallowed the thought down, steeled his nerves, and peered around the corner.

Even through the mist, the color of the two figures' robes was unmistakable:

Red.

Holy Eyes of Wrath, I've found them, Grey thought, ducking back behind the corner. The holy warriors were just standing there, like sentinels, staring out into the storm, saying nothing.

He held his breath and peeked out once more.

The furia were gone.

Frowning, Grey stepped out, peering further along the wall until he could see the door, which still stood open. A sound from behind caught his attention and he spun around.

A powerful fist smashed into his head, knocking him backwards, sending him rolling arse over teakettle down the rocky incline. He came to a stop when the back of his head collided with a medium-sized stone.

Stars flashed across his eyes, though his eyelids were closed, fading to blackness and then worse:

Oblivion.

A scream as bright as a flame jarred Grey awake.

He coughed, rolling to the side and spewing up a bitter mixture of seawater and his breakfast from that morning on the Jewel. A soft yellow light illuminated the pool of vomit below him. He hung off the edge of a makeshift bed—stacked stones covered by a thin mattress.

Where am I? The question rolled and tossed through his mind, like a ship lost at sea. The answer broke through the waves in a rush.

The Dead Isles. The cliffs. The furia.

Captured.

And the scream he heard was familiar. Like family familiar.

Shae.

"No," he breathed, struggling against the ropes that he could now feel biting into his ankles and wrist, secured to iron stakes pounded into the stone walls. Only his stump remained free, wriggling like a worm. Some good that would do him.

"Shae!" he shouted, but he was answered only by another scream.

He knew he was only alive because the furia wanted answers. They might remember him, and if so, they'd probably kill him eventually. Even if they didn't remember him, they'd want to know who he was and why he was there. And then they'd likely kill him. Either way, he was up a rutting creek without even a single godsdamn paddle.

"Argh!" he roared in frustration, pulling against his tethers until they tore into his skin, rubbing him raw and letting the warmth of blood flow freely down his arm and legs.

A door creaked open, a backlit shadow filling the entrance to whatever chamber he was being held in.

"I want to see my sister," he demanded.

"Grey Arris," the woman said, stepping into the light. "Or do you still prefer your ridiculous alias, Grease Jolly?" He instantly knew her—that cold, hard expression, those dark uncaring eyes, the long fiery hair—the woman who had cut off his hand.

One of the Three. A Fury. Instinctively, he wanted to shrink away from her, but his ropes held him fast.

"Where's Shae?" he managed to whimper.

"Who?"

The fear was swiftly replaced with anger, roiling through him like a fireball, spewing from his mouth like dragon's breath. "My godsdamn sister, you evil witch! If you've so much as laid a single finger on her, I swear I will—"

"Stop, child," the Fury said.

Grey stopped, her words like steel blades compared to his, which were naught but wooden playswords.

"You are bound and helpless and your threats are just threats. And there is only one God, Wrath, so don't profane him with Southron superstitions."

Grey took a deep breath, calming himself. She was right. Hurling meaningless threats was pointless and wouldn't help him or Shae. "Is she alive?" he asked, hating the submission in his voice, the deep and unassailable fear.

"Yes. Shae is alive."

"I heard her scream."

She made no attempt to deny it. "You did."

"Why?"

"My sister burned your sister's skin with a hot knife," the Fury answered.

"What?" Cold rage pulsed back to the surface, and Grey wanted to scream to release it. "Shae! Can you hear me?"

"Grey?" a voice called out. It sounded weak, trembling, like a raindrop clutching the edge of a leaf, afraid to fall.

"We've been working very hard to uncover your sister's secrets, but now we're running out of time. All we have left are drastic measures."

"What secrets?" Grey said. They already knew she was marked. They already knew she'd been hiding it her whole life, that he'd been helping her. Neither of them had anything left to hide.

"Why, her power, of course, foolish boy. This will all go better and will be less painful for both of you if you just tell me. Your sister has been unwilling so far."

Grey gritted his teeth, growling his words between them. "That's because she doesn't know, and neither do I."

"Hmm." The Fury tapped her teeth with long, red fingernails. "Could she have been telling the truth?"

339

Another scream rent the air and tore at Grey's ears. "Stop it!" Tears were pricking at his eyes now, blurring his vision. He couldn't move, couldn't act, could only beg. "Please. Please. I'll do anything."

"Sister?" the Fury shouted. The scream fell away, until Grey could only make out a soft whimper.

Footsteps approached and then the other Fury entered, standing beside her sister. "You called?" Though her face was as harsh as her sister's, the second Fury had thinner, sharper eyebrows, and fierce green eyes that seemed to burn.

"I don't think they know," the first Fury said.

The second Fury touched the collar of her crimson robe thoughtfully. "That complicates things. But we should make certain they're not lying."

"How?" the first Fury asked.

The second Fury nodded at Grey. "By killing him in front of his sister."

Twenty-Eight

The Southern Empire, the Scarra Desert
Raven Sandes

"We should stop and make camp," Raven said.

Fire's shadowy form was backlit by the green moon goddess, Luahi, who had risen from the west. "We ride on," she said, refusing to meet her sister's eyes.

Raven felt like leaping from Iknon and tackling her sister, using force to persuade her where reason had failed half a dozen times already. Instead, she gritted her teeth and tried again. "Even if the riders reach Kesh tonight, those on foot have fallen well behind. We need to stay together."

Fire wheeled her guanik around. "This is no debate," she snarled. Her reptilian steed hissed its agreement.

Raven watched her sister ride ahead once more, her entire body blazing with unburning flames. All tenderness they'd shared on this journey thus far seemed consumed by the blaze.

Goggin pulled up beside her. "Long have the guanero served a Sandes' empress," he said. "Do not treat us with childgloves."

And then he, too, rode on.

Raven sighed. She knew the man was right. At the heart of it, she wasn't worried about the guanero or the bedraggled army marching behind them. She was worried about her sister.

Ahead of her, Goggin let out a whoop. Fearing he'd been bitten by something poisonous, she charged after him, plunging with reckless speed into a trough and then pushing her guanik to his limits up the next rise.

There Goggin stood, a mountain of muscle and flesh against the silver sky. A smile as broad as the horizon was painted on his round face as he stared into the distance.

Raven followed his gaze to where lights twinkled like fallen stars on the desert sand. Shadows of palm trees rose up amongst the lights, their large fronds shifting in the wind.

They'd reached the oasis. They'd reached Kesh.

Despite the hour, Kesh was alive with activity. According to Goggin, who claimed to have visited the desert city more times than he could count with his boots off, Kesh lived in the night and dozed in the day.

Grudgingly, Raven had to admit that Fire had timed their arrival perfectly.

A throng of men wearing brightly colored frocks and baggy pants greeted them where the dunes met a thatch of thick foliage.

One of them stepped forward and extended a hand to help Fire down from her mount. His arms jingled with brass bracelets as he lifted them. "It is an honor to meet Empress Fire," he said. Motioning to Raven, he added, "And the First Daughter, too. The hospitality of Kesh is at your disposal."

At the entrance to the city there were a dozen torches planted in the sand, blazing happily. A line of torches led the way into a broad space filled with thatched huts and seating areas placed strategically under copses of palm trees.

Ignoring the man's offered hand, Fire leapt down, landing on her feet with a thud. Her guanik snapped its jaws at the poor fellow, who hopped back, chuckling. "Your beast is lively even after a long day's trek."

"You are..." Fire said.

"Guta," the man said, removing a plush purple hat with no brim and a tall dome. "At your service." He bowed with a broad flourish, sweeping his hat low, all the way to the sand.

"Thank you," Fire said. "You received my streams?"

"Two of them."

"I sent six."

"Yes, well, even water communications are confounded by the shifting sands and heat of the Scarra. Two of six is considered quite successful."

Raven dismounted beside her sister. "Then you are aware of our numbers?"

"Three thousand," the man said, peering into the night, as if counting their train. Goggin and his guanero pulled to a stop, sliding off their mounts. The brightly clothed men descended on the animals, steering them over to long water basins. Soon the beasts were drinking while the men rubbed the sand from their rough skin with wet towels.

Goggin stomped forward. "I trust you have simpre?" he asked.

"It flows like water," Guta said. Here in the desert where water was scarce, Raven wasn't sure what that meant exactly.

"Good. Bring ten barrels and—" He sniffed the air. "Is that smoked pyzon I smell?"

Guta grinned. "You have a good nose."

"I have a good stomach," Goggin said, rubbing his belly and licking his lips.

Guta chuckled. "Phanes may have the largest of the snakes, but the Scarra's brown pyzons are easier to kill and have flesh sweet enough for the palette of the gods."

"No gods here," Goggin said. "But we'll eat the god food just the same. Now show us to the simpre."

"No," Fire said.

Goggin frowned. "Should we wait for the rest of the army? They are well behind."

"No," Fire said again. "We will eat and drink water. No simpre. We need our wits about us."

"No disrespect," Goggin said, "but we rode hard today, and those on foot did, too. They'll expect a reward. And we have three days of rest in Kesh before we continue on, so…"

"One day," Fire said. "We have one day."

Raven interjected herself into the conversation. "We agreed on three days at the war council," she said. "The army needs it. We need it." *You need it*, she didn't say.

"We lost two days on the bridge. We're going to make up for that by not tarrying here."

"We have food and drink for three days for your entire force," Guta said. Even his smile was beginning to falter as the mood changed.

"And I thank you for that," Fire said. "We will take as much as we can carry when we depart. The rest you can give to other travelers."

"Fire…" Raven started to say, but stopped when her sister shot a dark look in her direction.

Goggin turned to his men. "You heard the empress. We have one day. Let's make the most of it. And I don't want to catch any of you so much as sniffing the simpre, we need to save it for the return trip, after we're victorious at the Gates."

Raven looked to see if her sister appreciated the response from her war leader, but she was already gone, following Guta toward one of the sitting areas.

Goggin hadn't exaggerated. Kesh was a magical place, full of brightly colored tents, aromatic smells, festive music, and all the water you could drink. Raven took advantage, emptying four wooden cups before tucking into the generous slab of brown pyzon that Guta served to her personally. Fire was already halfway finished with her meat, while Goggin was on to a second helping. The large man seemed determined to consume a full three days' worth of food in a single night.

Raven sighed as she bit into the flesh, which was cooked to perfection. The typically rubbery meat was tender and flaky now, having been spiced and then cooked underground on a bed of palm fronds set over a layer of hot coals. The hole was then covered with more palm fronds, until the meat had been infused with the flavor of smoke. It practically melted in her mouth.

"Thank you," she said to Guta, who never seemed to stop moving, directing a dozen dark-eyed women hither and thither.

The women were also garbed in bright uniforms, dresses formed of red, purple, yellow, and blue squares sewn together. All of Guta's men and women worked seamlessly together, performing their varied tasks with efficiency. The famed hospitality of Kesh was more than living up to its reputation.

They sat on plush, tasseled red, yellow, and green cushions piled atop long wooden benches flanked by huge tables teeming with food and water. As foot soldiers continued to arrive, they were directed to cushions placed on the ground next to huge colorful blankets set with more food and drink. Nearly the entire space was full already, and soldiers kept coming.

Amidst the crowd, six men played an assortment of instruments—guanik-skin drums, bone pipes, and a stringed instrument called a *banjeho*. Goggin tossed down what was left of his meat and leapt to his feet, grabbing one of the servers and twirling her around, dodging traffic. Though at first she looked shocked, the woman recovered quickly, throwing herself into a traditional desert dance known as the Whip, a name Raven had always appreciated. Others joined her, the women using their long dark braided hair like whips, flinging them around and warding off their "attackers," the guanero.

Raven laughed at the spectacle, and she even caught a smirk from Fire, whose stony façade slowly crumbled amongst the festive atmosphere. Her sister's eyes met hers, but then slipped away, back to the dancers and musicians.

Raven considered sliding across the bench to speak with her, but decided against it. Perhaps Fire needed space—the heat and toils of the day had worn on them both. Instead she leaned back and watched the palms rustle softly overhead, blanketed by a sea of stars, twinkling green, red, gold. Several of the red stars coursed across the sky while the green gods seemed to explode,

346

one by one. Luahi, the moon goddess, had been joined by her brother, Ruaho, the moon god, who'd risen from the east. Luahi was nearly full, a brilliant green orb, while Ruaho was just a red sliver, like a crimson smile. Though Luahi finished her cycle from full to sliver in a mere twenty-eight days, her brother was almost twice slower, taking fifty-two days to accomplish the same feat. *Men*, she thought. *Always a bit behind.* The sibling moons' paths approached each other now, but Raven knew they wouldn't cross, not tonight. The brother and sister only met once a year, on an auspicious night when they were both full at the same time, and they were still months away from joining hands in the sky.

Raven wondered whether she and Fire's relationship was taking a similar path.

When she tried to catch Fire's gaze again, her sister was gone, having snuck away, their paths missing once more.

Though she hadn't gone to bed until daybreak, Raven awoke at midday feeling refreshed. The day was hot, but she wasn't sweating; a cool breeze wafted through the palms that shaded her. Additionally, the large blankets that had been used to serve dinner to the masses had been affixed to poles, providing draping canopies for every single soldier.

Raven was shocked to find Guta already up, too, moving amongst a group of early risers, serving them breakfast. The tireless man had been awake when Raven retired for the night, and it appeared he didn't have need of sleep. He seemed to be running things on his own, because Raven spotted his brightly clad women and men sleeping amongst the soldiers. Goggin had his arm draped around one of the women, the dark-eyed beauty

347

he'd initially danced with, her head cradled in the crook of his shoulder.

The sight made Raven laugh. The sound caught Guta's attention, and he beckoned her over, setting a place for her at the table and filling it with a plate of two hardboiled eggs, spiced pyzon links, and half a pineapple, sliced down the middle.

"Thank you," she said. "I trust you have been compensated already?"

His large smile grew even bigger. "Yes. The empress is most generous."

Raven's own smile faded at the mention of her sister. "I apologize for her conduct last night."

Guta waved it away like he was swatting a fly. "She has much weight on her mind."

"All the same. We appreciate your kindness."

He swept his hands across the oasis with a grand gesture. "This is what I live for!" He flashed his teeth.

Raven laughed. "How did you get into the...oasis business?"

"I grew up in the desert," he said. "You could say I am at home amongst the dunes. Kesh has been managed by my family for many generations. My uncle was the last, and he had no children, so it fell to me after he was taken by the sand."

"Well, I'd say you were born to do this."

The compliment seemed to please the small man greatly, his eyes lighting up. He rushed off, calling over his shoulder, "I'll bring more eggs!"

Raven shook her head—she was already overfull. She slipped away from the table and sought to locate her sister, who was likely asleep in one of the thatched huts. No luck. Fire wasn't amongst the sleeping forms in the makeshift structures.

She spotted Guta again and inquired about the empress. "She went to see to the guanik," he said.

Raven made her way toward where the guanik were tethered to metal plugs pounded into the ground. Fire was stroking her guanik's head, feeding it strips of smoked snake meat.

"Surai shines on you this day," Raven said, using the formal morning greeting.

Without turning, Fire said, "Until Luahi and Ruaho meet in the sky."

Raven approached her own guanik, and Iknon nuzzled against her hand, searching it for a treat. She'd saved an egg for him, which he swallowed down, shell and all. Though the guanik were fierce beasts in battle, they were as docile as lambs when given a good scratching and an egg or two.

"Fire, I'm sorr—"

"No," Fire said, cutting her off. "It is I who am sorry, sister."

Raven was taken aback by her sister's apology, as unexpected as it was. "For what?"

"I have been unreasonable. It's just ever since Maata...I've felt...uneasy."

"I know. I feel the same."

"No," Fire said. "I don't think you do. I feel as if an arach is nipping at my heels and if I don't keep moving it will eat me alive."

"Well, considering what you did to the last arach you faced, I don't think you have too much to worry about..." She had intended it as a joke, but Fire only shook her head. Raven approached her sister, whose arms were hanging limply at her sides. There was no fight in them—not now. "I don't understand what you mean."

Fire shook her head in frustration. "Last night felt too…happy. I couldn't handle it. This world is broken. Our family, broken. Our kingdom, broken. We shouldn't be laughing. We shouldn't be dancing. We should be fighting."

Raven shook her head. "No, you're wrong. If we can't laugh, if we can't dance, if we can't be happy, then what are we fighting for?"

"For the chance to be happy. For a people who've never been given that chance. For a future."

"Whisper?"

"Not only her, but yes. Whisper is as soft as a flower petal. She wasn't made for this world. She's not like us." Though Raven was surprised that Fire placed them in the same category, it made her feel warm inside. Fire continued: "She deserves a place where she can be safe, a life where she doesn't have to be scared about losing the people she loves."

"I know. I agree. That's what we're trying to do. But it's not just her that deserves such a world."

Fire frowned. "I know that. Our people deserve that. Faata's slaves deserve that."

"*You* deserve that."

Fire looked away. "I am a weapon, nothing more, nothing less."

"You're wrong. You're my sister. You're caring, you're kind, you're strong. Yes, you're a weapon. But you are so much more."

"You think I'm kind?" Fire almost laughed.

"Well, not all the time. But sometimes. Now you are. The soldiers will trust you when you're fierce, but they'll follow you when you're kind."

"If you're trying to soften me up so I'll change my mind, it won't work."

Raven laughed. "I know. I'm not. We ride out first thing tomorrow. As you have commanded. I respect your decision."

Fire placed a hand on Raven's shoulder. "And I respect your advice. We shall stay in Kesh two days. It's the best I can do."

Raven blinked back the tears threatening to spill from her eyes as she grabbed her sister's hand. "It is good enough."

There was a murmur of excitement through the camp when Fire made the announcement that they were staying another day. Guta smiled even more, until Raven was certain his face had gotten stuck that way. Then again, she was smiling quite a lot, too. Not only had the wall around her sister seemed to have come down, but she'd finally listened to something Raven had said. The words her maata had taught them as children whispered in her mind:

Together we are the rock that cannot be broken.

She also remembered how sad her mother always seemed when someone mentioned her own sister, Viper. She wondered whether her mother had felt broken when Viper had left for Zune.

If so, the thought made Raven unbearably sad.

"I thought this was what you wanted?" Fire said, startling her.

"Oh. It is. I was just…"

"What? You looked on the verge of tears."

"I was thinking of Maata."

Fire said, "Close your eyes."

"What?"

"Close your eyes."

"Fire, I don't know what you're—"

"I command you as your empress."

"I believe that's called frivolous use of power," Raven said, but she closed her eyes.

"See her face. See her hair, like Surai's golden ropes. That's Whisper's beauty. See her corded muscles, her stern jaw. That's me. Can you see her?"

Raven could see her mother in her mind so clearly it was like she'd never left. "I see her."

"Do you see yourself?"

Raven tried to. But she couldn't. She shook her head.

"See her eyes, beaded obsidian. She is fearless. She is caring. She is intelligent."

Raven saw her mother's eyes. Yes, she was all of those things. "I see them."

"Her eyes are yours," Fire said. "She is in us," Fire said. "All of us. And she is with us."

Raven could see it now. When she opened her eyes, her sister had moved off to speak to Goggin and the guanero, her high laughter joining the sound of music playing.

That night, Raven was jarred from sleep by a scraping sound. She blinked quickly, trying to make sense of where she was and what she'd heard. The underside of a thatched roof stared down at her, visible only because of a painted swathe of green moonlight cascading through the entrance to the hut she slept in. Nearby, Fire breathed deeply, fast asleep. They were the only ones in the hut, the rest of the guanero choosing to pass the night under the stars and the watchful eyes of the moon god and goddess.

Except there *was* someone else—a shadow clinging to the wall, moving, creeping, sliding.

Something glinted in the moonlight, the edge of a blade.

Raven moved like a striking scorpion, yelling out as she lunged across the small space.

The knife came down, but she managed to grab the arm of the attacker, stopping the blade a mere fingerbreadth from Fire's face. Her sister's eyes flashed open, her mouth opening in horror at seeing a knife tip hovering overhead.

The attacker grunted, trying to force it down. Raven pushed back, but the blade dipped lower, wildly, just missing Fire as she twisted her head to the side. Raven strained against the force, which then toppled over, somersaulting away and crashing into the side of the hut.

Raven moved to throw herself at the would-be assassin once more, but Fire held her back. "Fire, we have to—"

"Shh. He's gone, sister. You saved me."

Raven searched her sister's face in the moonlight. Past her, the shadowy figure let out a final groan and then went still. Fire released her and she pushed past, crouching down warily. A blade protruded from the attacker's chest, right over the heart. Fire's sword. She must have been sleeping with it on hand.

Raven grabbed the attacker's feet and dragged the body into the moonlight. When she saw who it was, she inhaled sharply.

It wasn't a man.

One of Guta's dark-eyed beauties. The one Goggin had danced with on the first night, cradling her head as they slept.

Twenty-Nine
The Southern Empire, Phanes, warcity of Sousa
The Beggar

Bane touched the Beggar's gloved hand and their dark world vanished, only to be replaced by another world, full of leather plate and steel sword, roasting meat, and platoons of marching soldiers.

"Where are we?" the Beggar asked. They were nestled in a dark alleyway, out of sight for the moment.

"Sousa," Bane said, stepping into the light, his bald head gleaming in the sun. Like this, amongst so many people, the boy looked utterly small and powerless. Having slept for almost four days and nights in a row, Bane now looked wide-eyed and ready for whatever was to come.

Phanes? The Beggar remembered what Bane had said to him a few nights ago. How they were going to infect an army near the Southron Gates. Were these marching soldiers the army he meant?

The Beggar had never been outside of Calypso before, though Sousa didn't seem that different at first glance. Soldiers had often marched through his home city, too, although they wore different armor and often rode guanik. The buildings here were constructed of a different kind of stone—gray granite rather than beige sandstone—but that was a minor difference. The largest difference, however, was the noise.

Calypso had sometimes been called the Silent City for a reason. The people spoke in hushed tones, rarely raising their voices to a shout, except in the grand arena or fighting pits of Zune. In fact, the only other times he'd heard anyone shout were when he'd accidentally infected someone with the plague. He could still hear those sharp voices in his head, cutting deep inside his brain like knives.

Slashing. Always slashing.

Here in the Phanecian warcity of Sousa, *everything* seemed to make more noise. The horses stamped their feet as they marched. The soldiers' footsteps were like cannon blasts. The merchants selling roasted meat and tubs of freshly caught fish from the Spear shouted their prices and haggled with customers. Even little girls squealed with delight as they played some sort of jumping game.

The only ones who were silent were those bearing an identical mark around their necks, a black chain.

The slaves, the Beggar realized.

People in Calypso often talked about the plight of the red-skinned Teran slaves, but until seeing them in the flesh, he'd never really thought about it. They moved silently throughout the city, performing various tasks, rarely speaking unless they were issued a command, in which case they would respond *Yes, Master.*

"They're like me," he said aloud. A slave to their marks. Half-dead already.

"No," Bane said, shaking his head. "You have power, they have nothing."

The Beggar had never thought of his tattooya as a mark of power. Only as a curse.

Bane led him through the heart of the bustling warcity, ignoring the vendors as they shouted offers at them. Twice the Beggar was bumped into by passersby in the crowd, but both times he was careful not to let any of his skin make direct contact with their skin. Still, he felt a jolt of fear each time.

After the second time, Bane squinted at him and said, "You fear your power? Truly?"

There was only one answer, although giving it to his only friend made him feel ashamed. "Yes." Heat rose to his cheeks.

"You need not be embarrassed. I fear mine, too." And then Bane turned away and continued through the crowd, cutting a zigzagging course.

The Beggar was surprised. Ever since he'd come into contact with the boy, Bane had acted so decisively. Without fear. If he really feared his own power, he hid it well.

Tripping over his own feet, he stumbled to catch up to his friend before he lost him in the crowd. However, when the Beggar emerged from a thick patch of people, he found Bane standing alone, without a small gate set in a tall, curving wall that surrounded the city.

The Beggar reached his side and followed his gaze to a wall ten times larger than the one protecting Sousa, so vast that it might have been a mountain had it not been constructed of enormous stone blocks.

The Southron Gates. Everyone in Calypso knew of them, but few had seen them. Unless you were Phanecian, going anywhere near the famed Gates would generally get you killed. And yet here they were, a northerner and a Calypsian, standing within marching distance of the gateway to the west.

The Beggar turned back to look through the entrance into the city, watching the soldiers marching hither and thither. "Is that the army you want me to infect?" he asked.

Bane didn't answer for a long time, peering at the wall under the shade provided by his cupped hand. "Stay here," he said. "Consider what *you* want to do. You are no slave and I am not your master. I am your brother, your friend. Yes, this is Vin Hoza's army, and they reap death everywhere they go."

"But if I infect them, won't everyone in the city die? The plague spreads like wildfire, and the Phanecians are ill-equipped to quarantine those who fall ill."

"Many must die before we can have peace," was Bane's only response. And then he vanished.

Bane didn't return for three long days. The Beggar spent them staring at the people in Sousa, studying them. He watched horrors being committed—a slave beaten to within an inch of his life simply because he didn't complete a task fast enough. And yet he also saw great love exhibited—a little girl, the daughter of one of the soldiers, giving her father a flower. He swung her around and around as she laughed.

Many must die before we can have peace.

Was Bane right? Would infecting this slave city offer peace to the Four Kingdoms? *Is that my true purpose, the reason I was given this cursed tattooya by the gods or whomever?*

The more the Beggar watched the Sousians, the more confused he became, the more torn in half.

When Bane finally returned, looking troubled and weary, the Beggar said, "I have made no decision."

"You will," Bane said. "You will."

Thirty

The Southern Empire, the Red Rocks east of the Bloody Canyons
Jai Jiroux

The day was garbed in sunshine, a seamless cape of light pulled tight across the harsh barren landscape of shattered earth and broken rocks that dotted the terrain behind them. Off in the distance, Jai could just make out the enormous rotting carcass of what remained of the red pyzon—mostly its head, the only part that was unable to slither back underground. Vulzures were already circling, diving and ripping off hunks of its flesh.

We made it, Jai thought, shifting forward to gaze at the red rock spires ahead.

He was reclining on a makeshift gurney constructed from the wood of a gnarled old thatchwhistle, which was known to be a strong and sturdy desert tree, despite its small stature. It was tied at the corners with rope harvested from the skin of the red pyzon, which upon the snake's death had lost its potency. Support branches ran along the bottom, also tied with the knotted ribbons of skin. For comfort, the skin beneath the pyzon's armor-like scales had been cut and layered. It was on this bed of drying skin that Jai now lounged.

Of all people it was Axa who carried him, gripping the front of the hammock with two hands. For the moment his dusty old mirror was tucked somewhere in the folds of his sackcloth skirt. When it was time to depart, he'd stepped forward silently and picked up the gurney before anyone else could. Shanti had offered her horse to two people injured in the battle with the red pyzon, and now carried the opposite end, watching Jai upside down.

Everything hurt. Jai was bruised and scratched, like he'd been in a Phanecian street fight with a couple of thugs and a cat. His muscles screamed with each jostle of the gurney, his bones seeming to rattle in their joints. But that wasn't the worst of it, not by a desert league. No, the worst was the inferno smoldering just beneath his skin, a result of the copious amounts of pyzon slime he'd come into contact with.

The first moments after the pyzon had exploded were still a blur, like a waking nightmare. The stars and moons above. Dozens of his people hovering over him, anxious to help but not knowing how. Sonika taking charge, as usual, ordering fresh water to be pooled together. Shanti, dipping scraps of cloth in the water and washing him. Her touch so gentle, and yet the equivalent of knives piercing every pore in his skin. He'd screamed and had to be held down, but she never faltered, going about the work until it was complete.

For a few blessed moments, he'd felt relief as a light desert breeze cooled his skin.

And then the fires began again.

Still, he was alive, and that was more than scores of his people could say. The final count was determined to be ninety-six souls lost, including two of the Black Tears, and over two-hundred injured. Jai wasn't the only one seriously hurt; a number of other gurneys were being carried by the others, and all of the surviving Tears had given up their steeds for those in greater need.

"You owe me a story," Shanti said, her head bobbing over him with each stride she took. Her bare shoulders and arms were sweaty with exertion, her muscles taut against the inside of her skin. In the daylight, he could clearly see the bands of silver ringing her otherwise blue eyes.

"I've got a good one," he said. "It's about how an ordinary man slew a red pyzon a hundred times his size." He grimaced as the gurney bounced, his entire body screaming at him.

"I've heard that one," Shanti said. "But I did have one question: How did you know the fireroot would ignite inside the snake's belly?"

"I didn't," Jai admitted. "But once in Phanea I saw a group of a hundred hunters who had slain a red. They carried it into the city, parading it through the streets. They cut it open in front of everyone. And when they did, smoke poured out. The inside of the snake's belly was ringed in fire."

Shanti frowned. "I've never heard that before, and I'm usually an expert on anything to do with fire and smoke."

"I'm just glad it worked."

"You risked your life on a theory."

"You make it sound so brave."

"It *was* brave. The bravest thing I ever saw."

Jai shook his head, although he immediately wished he hadn't as pain ripped through him at the movement. "It was a foolish thing to do."

"Perhaps," Shanti agreed. "But it still took courage."

"I have a long way to go before I slay any dragons."

"The red was close enough," Shanti said, smiling.

"Will it regrow?" There were legends about the giant snakes' ability to survive even when chopped in two pieces.

"No one really knows," Shanti said. "But I suspect it will. It is said they must be burned to ash before they are truly dead. In any case, it won't bother us for a while. Though it was a shame we had to leave all that fresh meat. I've heard the flesh of the red is as sweet as crabmeat."

Jai didn't want to admit that it was, because he'd tasted it once, at a feast thrown by Emperor Hoza. "We didn't have time to linger."

Shanti nodded. Tall spires of red rock appeared on either side of her as they entered the elevated lands to the east of the Bloody Canyons. She gritted her teeth under the strain of the first incline. Jai knew it was only going to get steeper.

"You're not planning to carry me all the way to the Gates, are you?" he asked.

"No," she said. "But I'll go as far as I can." For some reason her statement felt like an oath.

"Thank you," Jai said. "For cleaning the poison off my skin. For carrying me."

"It was the least I could do after you saved us all, though I'll take an assist since it was my fireroot." She smiled. "But now, how about that story?"

Jai grimaced, but this time it wasn't from the pain. He was hoping she'd forgotten. Then again, he'd wanted to tell her a couple of nights ago, and she'd opened up to him about her past. And maybe the pain of the telling would help him forget about his physical pain, at least for a while. The incline grew steeper, the red rocks thicker and taller, rising to great points cutting into the blue sky.

"My mother is a slave," Jai said.

Shanti flinched. "That's not funny," she said.

"Sorry, I should've led with another line," he said. "But I wasn't japing. It's true."

"I…don't understand." Her coppery brows furrowed together, a few locks of hair blowing across her face. "You are not Teran. Your skin isn't red and your hair is too dark."

"I'm half. My father was Phanecian," Jai explained.

"That explains your eyes. They are too big for you to be full Phanecian, though your skin is tanned like the slavers."

"My father was a slave owner," Jai said.

"Oh. *Oh.* I'm sorry."

"It's not what you think. My father didn't force my mother, didn't rape her. They loved each other."

Shanti said nothing.

"It's true," Jai insisted. "I'm not clinging to some childhood fantasy."

"How do you know?"

"Because my father is…" The words stuck in his throat—it had been years since he'd spoken of his past. "He's gone. My father is gone."

Shanti licked her lips, a troubled expression working its way from her chin to her eyes, which reflected Jai's own sadness. "I'm sorry. You don't have to tell the rest. It is your story to lock away, if you wish."

"No," he said, reaching up to grasp her wrist, just above where she held the edge of the gurney. The pain that lanced through his arm was fierce, but it was worth it. "I'm ready to tell it. My father was a slave owner, yes, but he never treated his slaves badly. That doesn't make it right, I know, and I don't condone it, but I can't hate him either. Despite her red skin and black eyes, I never even knew my mother was a slave until I was five name days old. I can still remember the agony in my father's eyes when he told me the truth. I wanted to hit him, to run away, to hide and never come out. But I didn't do any of that, I just fell into his arms and cried. Later, after I felt better, he told me he fell in love with her the moment she came into our household. A little later she had me.

"Looking back, it seems so obvious. She looked like all the other slaves, but she had her free will, to do as she wished while in our household. She was an amazing dancer."

Shanti's eyed widened. "Phen sur, right? She was the dancer you were talking about before, wasn't she?"

Jai nodded. "She glowed when she danced. Literally. It was like Surai was inside of her, or a part of her. My father and I couldn't take our eyes off of her when she danced."

"What happened?"

Jai tried to decide where to start the next part of his story. "As a boy, Father never let me leave the house. I didn't mind that much, because he taught me phen lu, which I loved. When company came over, I had to stay in my room. But I was young and ignorant to the ways of the world. Only his slaves knew about me, and they were commanded to keep his secret."

"And yet secrets always find the light of day eventually," Shanti said. Jai could see it in her eyes, she knew what was coming, or at least had a guess. Once you've experienced tragedy, you tend to look for it hiding behind every shadow. Jai knew that feeling all too well.

"Yes. One of the other neighboring household masters realized what was going on, what had happened. He told the emperor about my mother, about me. The day I first laid eyes on Vin Hoza is branded in my mind like it was yesterday. He took my mother away. She didn't fight it, couldn't fight it—not when Hoza commanded her with the voice of her original master—but my father did. He slew four of Hoza's men trying to get to the emperor before they subdued him. Hoza could've stopped him, made him a slave, but he seemed to be *enjoying* watching my father's rage. Afterwards, he killed him for it. That's how I know my father loved my mother, regardless of the slave mark she bore."

Shanti didn't need to say she was sorry again, Jai could see it in her silver-blue eyes. They'd both lost those they loved, regardless of whether he had the black tears to prove it. "What happened to her? To your mother."

Jai shrugged. "I don't know. They took her away."

"She's still a slave?"

"We are all still slaves. Just like my people. I gave them free will, but they are still slaves, at least until we can get them out of Phanes."

"What happened to you after Hoza took her? How did you become a master?"

Jai flinched at the title. "I was taken to a master training camp. I think Hoza thought I was young enough to still be 'rehabilitated' to think the way he did. They taught me and the other boys phen ru. Not to protect, to punish. Sometimes the things I saw in that place gives me nightmares, but it gets better with time. But I never forgot what Emperor Hoza did to my family. Never."

"You want to save these people for your mother?"

"I don't know if I have a specific reason. Only that I must. Only that it's what I'm *meant* to do."

"We all have our reasons for what we do. Revenge. Atonement. Anger, hate, love. A lost brother, mother, friend. A lost soul."

"What is your reason?"

"The reasons don't matter," Shanti said, squinting. "Only the results. I just want the empire to burn to the ground, with Hoza amongst the rubble. Why else would I haul all this fireroot around with me?"

"I understand wanting to overthrow Hoza and set our people free," Jai said. "But this is our home. We can't destroy it."

"We are outsiders, even you with your tanned skin. This was never our home," Shanti said. "We've sent our stories to the gods. Now it's up to us to finish them."

She crested the top of an incline and started down the opposite side. The line of refugees stretched for leagues in both directions.

A day later, Jai could walk again, though each step was painful. Two days later and he didn't hunch nearly as much. On day three his skin began to peel off, flaking away with each breath of wind.

Though his people were weary and saddened by the loss of their loved ones between the Black and Red Rocks, they were fighters, as they had been their entire lives, never wavering as they pushed through the superheated mountain passes. More of the injured died along the way, and they buried them beneath cairns constructed of red stones. It was the best they could do, although it pained Jai greatly to know the vulzures would get to the bodies. The large raptors had been following them ever since the night with the red pyzon, and Jai was certain their long winged shadows wouldn't leave them until they breached the great wall to the north.

On the fourth day, Jai noticed Axa sitting by himself when they stopped for their midday meal. He was holding his mirror and talking into it. *The heat has addled his brain*, Jai thought. When he went over to him, Axa thrust the mirror back into his skirt.

"I wanted to say thank you for carrying me for so long," Jai said. Like Shanti, Axa had refused to pass his burden onto any other, even after his arms began trembling with exertion. Joaquin had taunted the former master for a while, before growing bored of it.

"Yes, Master," Axa said.

"I am not your master," he said. "Not anymore."

"Master?"

"No." Jai shook his head. He said the words he'd said to all the others. "I command you to act of your own free will, to make your own decisions, to walk your own paths. You are no longer chained to me. You will no longer call me Master. You are your own master. Do you understand?"

"Yes..." Axa hesitated, as if the word 'Master' was on the tip of his tongue, like some kind of subconscious reflex, but then he closed his mouth. His eyes were still fully black, because, like the others, he was still technically a slave. If Vin Hoza were to appear next to him and tell him to leap from a cliff, Axa would obey without question. He wasn't truly free, and never would be until they got past the bounds of Hoza's territory.

Jai turned and walked away to find several of his people watching him with narrowed eyes. "Do you remember the time *Master* Axa beat me within an inch of my life?" one of them said, stepping forward. It was Joaquin again, his arms folded across his chest. He was a blunt man with a crooked nose and small, narrow eyes. Jai did remember. It was one of Axa's first days as a mine master in Garadia. From the beginning, Axa had rebelled against Jai's way of doing things. Jai had found Joaquin in a puddle of his own blood, ragged whip marks strewn across every bit of his skin. One of his eyes was swollen shut and he was barely breathing.

"Yes," Jai said.

"And now you set him free, treat him like you treat the rest of us?" His eyes fired arrows of accusation across the space separating them. Several others nodded their agreement with his words. Other turned away, not wanting to get involved in the confrontation, but Jai had a feeling their thoughts would echo Joaquin's.

"No," Jai said. "He's not like you. He's not my family. He's just a broken man in need of a second chance."

"And if he runs away and goes back to his true Master? Hoza will destroy us all. Is that what you want?"

"You know I don't."

More and more people noticed the raised voices, milling toward them to find out what was going on. Sonika Vaid and her Black Tears approached, but Jai waved them off. Like Axa, they were outsiders, too, not connected to his people the way he was.

"We should beat him and leave him for the vulzures," Joaquin said.

"We already decided he could come with us," Jai said.

Joaquin pointed a finger at Jai. "No. *You* decided. After your speech, who was going to vote against you?"

Jai recalled that there was one vote against him—Joaquin's—but he didn't think pointing that out would make a difference. "I won't leave anyone behind," he said.

"Oh no? What about our dead? We left them, didn't we? That man doesn't belong here, and we can't let him go, so that leaves only one other option."

"We're not going to hurt him." Jai remained calm, still hoping he could resolve the situation with words. "Being marked by Hoza changes a man. He's not the master he once was. He never will be again."

"And yet, at his soulless core, that's what he is."

"He carried Jai Jiroux across the desert," a new voice said. Several people looked back, and Jai craned his neck to see who had spoken. The gathered crowd parted and Jig and Viola's mother, Marella, approached. "Master Axa would never have done that. He hated Jai as much as he hated us. Do you not remember?"

Joaquin shook his head. "Do you not remember what he did to me? And I'm not the only one. That filth"—he jabbed an angry finger at Axa, who was ignoring the entire thing, once more whispering into his mirror—"beat us, whipped us, belittled us, spat on us. And we're going to just forget all that because he's finally been given a taste of his own treatment and made a slave?" His words were having an impact, Jai could see. More and more heads were nodding. If he didn't defuse the situation soon, the protests could turn violent.

As it turned out, he didn't need to, because Marella and her two children stepped between them, facing Joaquin. Marella said, "We have trusted Jai Jiroux for many years, and we must trust

369

him still. He has never failed us, has never given us anything but a chance at a different life. A better life. Were you not there on the desert plains when the red pyzon was killing our people? I was there. I saw what Jai Jiroux did. He risked his own life to save us. He did what no one else would, all for a bunch of worthless slaves."

Jai tried to interject, but Marella waved him off.

"My children have no father. That is Vin Hoza's fault alone, but they look at Jai Jiroux like a father. He is my family and he is yours. Trust him and find a better life. He will not let us down. He never has."

Her words hung in the air in a silence broken only by the wind whistling between the red rocks. And then Jig cried, "Aye! What my mother said!"

The boy's unexpected shout seemed to break the spell over the crowd, and one by one they added their agreement, dispersing and returning to their meals, until only Marella, her children, and Joaquin remained.

Joaquin said, "I will never forget the day you chose Axa over me."

"Joaq, come on, that's not what I—" Jai started to say, but stopped when the man turned and walked away.

Jai's chin dropped to his chest. Marella said, "He doesn't mean it. He's just angry."

"I know." And yet the truth didn't make it hurt any less. Joaquin was once someone he could share a meal with, a man who would throw himself in front of a cave-in to protect another slave. A friend. Jai wondered if what he'd said was true; if, in a way, Jai had chosen Axa over him. If so, was it worth protecting someone who'd once hated him?

Jai's justicemark burned on his heel. *Yes*, it told him. *Axa is not the enemy. Not anymore.*

To Jai's relief, there were no additional confrontations as they made their way through the Red Rocks. Two more of the injured from the pyzon attack died, bringing the total to over one hundred. Jai remembered every single one, and was determined to make their sacrifices count.

When they descended the final slope and emerged from the red, blade-like spires they'd known for the last seven days, Jai's heart leapt so high he could feel it in his throat.

Because there they were: the Southron Gates, rising tall and impenetrable in the distance, a final barrier to freedom. To the east, the waters of the Burning Sea sparkled in the midafternoon light. An ocean of desert was spread out before them. Directly ahead, between them and the Gates, were the outlines of structures. A city. The great warcity of Sousa, home to thousands of Hoza's soldiers charged with defending the eastern portion of the wall.

"We'll wait until nightfall," Sonika said, once more astride her horse, a beautiful black destrier she called Chainbreaker. "Then we make directly for the weakness in the wall your father told you about. Let's hope his words were true."

"I know they were," Jai said. A ripple of emotion swelled within him at the thought of breaching the walls. His head wasn't in the clouds, however; he knew many would die during the final leg of their journey. "We will have to be silent on our approach. Tell everyone, the children especially. Those with small children will have to do everything in their power to keep them quiet. We'll pad each horse's hooves."

Right on cue, Shanti's own horse rattled up, pulling its cart laden with several barrels filled with fireroot. "We'll pad the wheels of this rickety old cart, too."

"Good," Jai said, nodding. "Do we have enough powder?" A few barrels had been lost during the pyzon attack, and another cracked open when it fell from the cart while traversing one particularly treacherous mountain pass.

"Enough to crack several large stones," Shanti said. "So it will depend on how thick the first layer of the wall is before reaching the hollow your father told you about."

"It will have to be sufficient," Jai said. "But we also need to save enough to blast through the other side."

Shanti nodded. "Leave it to me. Or did you want to handle the fireroot? After the last time, I think you may have a talent for blowing things up." She grinned.

"I'll pass," Jai said, grinning back. "I'd hate to risk my new skin." Over the last few days more of his flesh had peeled off, leaving his arms, chest, and back patchy and marbled.

"Back into the rocks," Sonika said. "We need to rest and prepare for tonight."

As the Tears spread out through the people to pass along the orders and the plan, Jai gazed at the point where the Burning Sea met the longest river in the Four Kingdoms, the Spear. Just beyond, he swore he saw a ray of sunlight glint off of something metallic. But then it was gone. *A trick of the eye*, he thought. *Nothing more.*

He turned and followed Sonika and the others back up the path to the cover of the rocks.

Once more, he would offer his people the choice to turn back, to hide or return to Phanea or take whatever they thought was the best course. He suspected none would accept his offer, a thought that thrilled and terrified him.

On the morrow, many would die.

The sacrifice for freedom, he thought.

Thirty-One
The Western Kingdom, Knight's End
Rhea Loren

Rhea the Righteous wasn't just the title her people had given her. No, it was more than that. It was her legend, her mark, a name that would follow her after death into the annals of history. Songs would be sung about her. Stories would be told, molding and changing and becoming even more wondrous than the already-wondrous truth.

Though she was far from death, she knew she would never really die, a thought that pleased her more than anything else.

To spur her legend on, Rhea released twelve northern prisoners, each of whom looked ready to piss in their britches just looking at her. They were given safe passage across the bay to Blackstone, where they would tell their tale, moving through the kingdom until they reached Lord Griswold at Castle Hill, where they would inform him of the destruction of his entire force. No streams would be sent. No, she wanted the news to move slowly, methodically, like a painful disease. She wished she could be there to see the look on his face.

Additionally, Rhea enlisted the help of western messengers, who would ride south and east, spreading the news of her pet sea monster and the north's demise. She would use fear like a spear, striking the first blow on her remaining enemies' hearts from a distance. And then she would come for them to take their heads.

But first she had a distasteful, but necessary, task to attend to.

The dungeon master opened the door for her as she approached. Ever since Wrathos' Revenge, which is what the battle had been named by the bards, whom were already singing of her glory, Rhea had worn her battle armor whenever in public. She didn't want her people to think one victory—regardless of how decisive it had been—was the end of the war. She even refused to have any of the metal cleaned or polished, using the bloodstains as a reminder that she had been there like any of the other soldiers, that she was one of them, willing to die for Wrath's righteous cause.

Now, she said nothing to the grisly old dungeon master, for he didn't have any ears to hear it. She simply nodded at him and continued onward, her boots echoing down the corridor. She wrinkled her nose when she remembered the last time she'd entered the dungeons—to see her twin siblings. Thankfully, she wasn't here to see them today. No, she was here to visit another family member.

Ennis lifted his chin when she stopped before his cell. "My queen," he said.

Wrath, Rhea thought. *My cousin is a fool, yes, but an unflinchingly loyal fool. Shame I can't keep him around.*

"Dear Ennis," she said. "How I've missed you." It wasn't entirely a lie. The truth was, she missed her never ending arguments with her cousin, his constant attempts at chivalry, and even his misplaced sense of honor. She missed her whipped dog, too, the Fury, but she could eventually be replaced. Not Ennis.

Once he was gone, she wouldn't have a single cousin left in Knight's End—apparently Ennis's three living siblings had fled the castle moments before the battle with the north had begun, expecting the north to win.

She pushed aside the sadness and loneliness that was always there, on the fringes of her heart, waiting to clamp down.

"And I, you, Rhea." The way he said her name was too tender, too familiar, considering he was the one behind bars. His voice scraped against her nerves.

"You still love me? Even after I've had you imprisoned for a fortnight?"

"I will always love you, cousin. I *have* always loved you, since the day you were born. Even with your faults."

"Didn't you hear? I have no faults." In addition to the numerous titles bestowed upon her—the Righteous, the Brave, the Pure, the Guide—*the Faultless* had been added by her people.

"We all have faults," Ennis said. "Mine was being too weak to convince you otherwise."

"And treason. Don't forget that one," Rhea mused, drumming her fingernails on one of the iron bars. Her cold exterior was the only true armor she had left.

I can't lose you too, Ennis, why oh why did you have to disobey me in battle?

"If treason is protecting one's queen from certain death, then I am the greatest traitor in the realm," Ennis said.

Wrath, does he always have to make things so difficult? "You disobeyed a direct command from your queen. You almost cost us the battle. If not for my actions—"

"We would never have lost half the fleet, would never have sacrificed thousands of lives to satisfy your need for destruction, would never have summoned *a demon* from the depths of the sea."

Rhea clucked her tongue, anger pushing away the sadness. "*Now* you decide to grow bold, cousin? It's too late. Your words are chaff in fields that have already been harvested. And your soul is lost to me."

"I fear it was always lost to you."

It wasn't. It isn't. "Perhaps," Rhea said. "But I tire of this conversation. I am giving you a choice, Ennis, only because I care about you still, even when you are like this."

"What choice is there in death?" he asked, and for the first time the fight had gone out of him, his shoulders sagging, as if the weight of his own thoughts were too much for him to bear— the weight of the world. Rhea felt sorry for him, but not as sorry as she felt for herself, for having to do this. He spat the next words out the same way he'd spat at the feet of their enemies on the deck of *Wrath's Chosen* before their last stand. "Guillotine or noose? Blade to the heart or to the head? Whatever I choose, I go to meet my maker in whatever heaven Wrath sees fit to honor me with."

"Unless you choose life," Rhea said. Ennis blinked in surprise. *Good, let him be shocked.* She remembered another name given to her: the Merciful. It was one of her favorites, even if it was a lie. She wasn't given mercy under the Fury's blade; why should she offer it herself?

"What life?" her cousin asked.

"Banishment. To Crimea or the Hinterlands or Teragon. Or even the unexplored oceans to the east, if you can survive the trek through enemy countryside. As long as I am alive, as long as I am queen, you will not set foot in the Four Kingdoms again."

He stood, gingerly, favoring his right leg, his arm and shoulder still heavily wrapped. Walked over to the bars. Reached through, taking her hand with tender fingers, like she was as delicate as glass.

"I choose death," he said.

Despite all her bravado and bluster, Rhea's heart sank.

Rhea's command had been simple:

Bring me everything you can find on the Western Oracle from the Archives.

Though the archivists' jaws had dropped open, they'd scurried away to do their duty. However, what they came back with was disappointing. Two books, three scrolls, and a half-burned section of parchment that was nearly illegible.

Still, Rhea was glad for the distraction after her meeting with Ennis hadn't gone as planned. She opened the first book, an abridged history of the fourth century after the Crimean discovery of the Four Kingdoms. The archivists had been thorough, identifying the pages of interest with white ribbon and using a removable gray chalk to highlight the relevant passages.

Only two pages had ribbons. Only one passage on each page was marked. They were frustratingly brief. *Circa 350: A woman who later became known as the Western Oracle prophesies of the 'coming of the fatemarks,' which will return peace to the Four Kingdoms.* The first passage, while short, was odd. Everyone knew that the Hundred Years War didn't begin until the fifth century. Before then, there was relative peace in the Four Kingdoms. Which, in a way, meant the Oracle had predicted the war fifty years before it began. It said nothing of her being one of the original Furies, however, like she'd been told.

The next passage was equally short. *Circa 352: Western Oracle is charged with heresy and sorcery after the first marks appear on newborn children, giving them strange and unnatural powers. She is sentenced to death, as well as those who are marked.*

Rhea noticed a subtle distinction. The Western Oracle was sentenced to death, but there was nothing about the sentence being carried out. Maybe it was nothing. And even if she wasn't executed, that was nearly two centuries ago, so she'd have died of natural causes already. Still...

Rhea opened the next book, which only had one passage marked: *A prophecy by the Western Oracle: The fatemarked shall arise, and one marked with Death, the Kings' Bane, shall bring about the death of eight rulers, cleansing the realm. And then the Peacemaker shall come, and with him, Life.*

Kings' Bane. The demon who'd stalked this very castle, murdering guardsmen at will, eventually slitting her father's throat. Rulers *were* dying. Her father. The Dread King in the North. King Ironclad at Raider's Pass. There were even rumors being streamed that Empress Sun Sandes had been killed under strange circumstances in Calypso. One ruler was nothing. Two? A coincidence. But four, all within a short time period?

She slammed the book shut and unfurled the first scroll, which contained a series of quotes scribed during a trial. *The*

Western Oracle's trial, Rhea noted. Again, the relevant spot was highlighted with gray dust. She'd have to commend the archivists later.

'*For I am but a Servant of the All Mighty, our Lord and God, Wrath, who is of Many Names, including the Teran name, Absence, who I have communed with on my travels. They call me a Witch. They call me a Sorceress. They call me the Western Oracle. But I am Nothing. I am a Woman. I am a Servant. I Create what I am told to Create.*'

Rhea breathed in. The Western Oracle hadn't just claimed to know of the coming of the marks. *No. She claimed to have created them.*

Rhea reread the passage, and then slowly rolled up the scroll, tying it carefully with the ribbon. *Why doesn't anyone talk about this?* She knew the answer. If people thought the Oracle had created the marks in the name of Wrath, or at least claimed to, they might begin to question whether the marks were truly evil. The furia and the Loren king at the time had declared them sinful, given them the name sinmarks. Rhea was surprised this scroll had survived. Clearly, based on how few references there were to the Oracle in the Archives, most documents had been destroyed.

Greedily, she untied the second scroll. The entire top portion was wrinkled and damaged, the ink long smudged away, as if it had been immersed in water. Only one passage remained, and most of it was illegible. *The...Oracle's son...not...found, though...certain he...located before...moons next kiss...sky.*

The Western Oracle had a son? Why didn't anyone talk about him? Who was he? Was he executed too? Was he a sorcerer like his mother?

Rhea felt supercharged, like she was closing in on some important truth. Something once lost, hidden behind misinformation and lies. The third scroll felt more precious than gold in her hands as she unfurled it. Disappointment swam like river trout in her stomach. The entire scroll was destroyed, save for one word: *Oracle.*

She didn't take the care with this scroll that she had with the others, crumpling it, tearing it, tossing the remains into the fire. Why would anyone even keep such a pointless scroll? Maybe the archivists weren't as helpful as she thought.

The last document was black and crisp around the edges. Clearly it had been tossed into a fire and then quickly retrieved, the flames stamped out before they could consume the entire document. Still, most of it was unusable. On the top portion, she could just make out who it was addressed to, as well as part of the year. *Circa 37...* Rhea knew there was no way this document was from the year 37, so it must be 37-something, long after the Oracle had been sentenced to death for her crimes. It was addressed to *King Loren* and it began with *Hear my words...* Everything after that was lost, the page eaten through the middle by the flames, leaving it charred and full of holes. There were, however, a few words toward the bottom. *She lives on. She will never die. Will you?* The letter was unsigned.

Something occurred to Rhea. How did the archivists know this letter had anything to do with the Western Oracle if it made no reference to her? She realized something else. After being burned and then nearly two centuries passing, wouldn't the paper be practically falling apart? Instead, it was in reasonable condition, other than the scorched parts. She sniffed it. It smelled like fire, ashy. Wouldn't the scent have worn off years ago?

As she marched into the archivists' office, Rhea was a storm, her armor seeming to spark with lightning, her expression a dark cloud. Crimson raindrops fell around her sides, the furia. "Stop!" she said.

The archivist spun around, the evidence of her sins held in her hands, which were shaking. Smoke poured from the hearth, which blazed with fire, flames licking the sides of a pile of books and scrolls, cresting the top, consuming them.

As her furia grabbed the woman, wrenching the unburned documents from her hands, Rhea wondered where the other archivist was. Then she saw a leg sticking out from behind an old wooden desk. Rhea barely noticed when one of the furia slit the first archivist's throat, her body thumping to the floor, because she was peering around the corner of the desk. The other archivist had a knife buried in her chest, her dead hands gripping it as if she'd tried to pull it out before she died. Instinctively, Rhea knew the woman had known she was already dead, so she'd killed herself.

Why? The question thundered through her chest.

Secrets and lies. All for what? Rhea frowned, half-watching as the furia carried the dead women away. If the marks were known to be created by Wrath, or at least by his command, the Western Oracle would be more akin to a priestess than a dark sorceress, the Fury she originally was. But what would that mean? The facts lined up in Rhea's head. The marks were not exclusive to the Western Kingdom. No, they were pervasive to the Four Kingdoms, appearing in equal measure in each realm. The west simply killed those that bore them. But if the marks and their bearers were known to *not* be evil…then why would Wrath give them to the barbarian Southroners? To the eastern witches? To the godless sinners of the north? And if the furia had been killing markbearers for *no reason*...

Secrets and lies, Rhea thought. *This can't get out or there will be chaos.*

"Bring whatever survived to my chambers," she commanded the furia who remained.

Thirty-Two
The Western Kingdom, the Grasslands
Roan Loren

Roan and his companions soon learned that the grasslands of the western kingdom were not friendly to strangers, despite the numerous farms that dotted the landscape, with herds of cattle and flocks of sheep grazing across the prairie.

The first farmer they spied fled to his dwelling, barring the door and peering out at them through a smudged window. "Go away!" he shouted. "Don't want no trouble."

After they left, Gwen touched the dark headscarf she'd donned at the first sign of civilization. "Is my hair showing?"

Roan started to examine the edges of the fabric, looking for gaps, but Gareth pushed him aside. "Let me," he said.

Roan frowned, but didn't argue. It was the first thing Gareth had said to him since they left the Tangle, so he took it as a small victory. Instead, he focused on the graceful but strong lines of Gwendolyn's face, which was partially hidden beneath the shadow of the scarf. It was like the covering only made her more beautiful, more mysterious. He desperately wanted to reach over and touch her chin, her cheek, run his fingers along her skin, move closer, his lips parting—

"You're covered," Gareth announced, cutting off Roan's thoughts. He blushed slightly when Gwendolyn lifted the scarf and noticed him staring at her. The hint of a smile played on her lips, as if she could see inside his head, which only made his cheeks grow warmer.

Roan wondered how different things might be if Gareth hadn't reacted to their kiss the way he had. Would he still be interested in Gwen? Would he be torn between them both? But that wasn't a problem anymore, and he couldn't dwell on a man who clearly had no interest in him, right? Regardless, he was tired of hiding his feelings, which were like a turtle stuck in a shell, trying to burst free. But he couldn't let them, for he didn't want to further alienate Gareth when he was clearly dealing with his own internal struggles. Also, Roan wasn't certain whether Gareth had ever had true feelings for Gwen, or if his talk of her beauty was merely a long-running jape to him.

Also, despite his attempts to forget about the prince, he couldn't, not when every time he saw him he felt pulled in different directions. Sometimes he felt like a stranger. Sometimes like a close friend. Sometimes like something more…

All those thoughts passed through his mind in a second.

He doesn't want you anyway, so forget about him, he urged himself once more. *He speaks of his conquests of women like victories in battle. And you have Gwen to think about now…*

They continued on, feeling the farmer's eyes watching them until they passed out of sight.

The next farm they came to earned them a similar result. This time, the farmer's entire family was outdoors, working the fields, when they were spotted. The farmer ushered his family inside, dropping tools as they ran.

"We mean you no harm," Roan said through the door. He wondered what sort of travelers passed by that they should be so frightened. When there was no response from inside, Roan turned to Gareth and said, "Do you have only eastern coin?" He was certain the iron Shields of the east would be worth little and less here in the west.

Gareth shook his head, riffling through a large pouch that jingled when he moved it. He extracted a gold disk, unprinted on both sides. Neutral currency, used during periods when the war was at a standstill and inter-kingdom trade was possible.

Roan placed the coin in front of the door, and said, "I'm leaving one Golden for your trouble. And we're taking one of your fat sheep and a basket of vegetables."

Gwen grabbed his arm. "You've overpaid," she hissed.

"It will sustain us until Restor," he said, "so it's worth the gold." Plus, it was only fair considering the farmer didn't exactly agree to the transaction.

They were heading back toward the sheep, when Roan heard the door creak open. The farmer peeked out. "Take a dozen eggs from the henhouse, too," he said.

"Thank you," Roan said.

"Don't thank me. Just don't come back."

The man snatched the coin off the ground and started to duck back inside, but Roan quickly asked, "Who are you so scared of?"

The man paused, frowning. "You're not from the west, are you."

It wasn't a question, and Roan froze. *I'm a fool*, he thought. Asking a question like that in Restor could get them killed. "We have been traveling a long time," he said neutrally.

The man squinted at them, though the sun was hidden behind puffy white clouds. "The west used to be a safe place. The furia patrolled the Western Road. They protected farmers like me. Like my neighbors. But ever since King Gill Loren was killed…we haven't seen one of the furia in a fortnight, maybe longer. Marauders have taken over. They do not fear Wrath. They do not fear anything. They drink and they steal and they use our women."

Roan realized he had stiffened when the man said his father's name. Slowly, he let out the breath trapped in his throat. "I'm sorry. But we are not marauders."

"Still, we don't know you. And two men travelling with a woman"—he motioned toward Gwen—"is most unusual. Be on your way now."

Roan nodded, but the door had already closed.

When he turned back toward Gwen and Gareth, both their mouths were pulled into thin lines. "What does it mean?" he asked. "Why aren't the furia patrolling the west?"

Gwen said, "Isn't it obvious?"

"The west is preparing for war," Gareth finished.

After weeks of nothing but stale bread, boiled roots, and overripe berries, the fried eggs and stewed carrots, onions and tomatoes were the best thing Roan had ever tasted. And, based on the ecstasy on his friends' faces, apparently the meat was equally tasty.

"You still don't eat meat," Gareth commented, his mouth half full. The meal had done what Roan and Gwen had been unable to do: loosen his tongue.

"No."

"But Calypsians eat meat."

"Yes."

"Fine." Gareth took an exaggerated bite of meat, letting juice dribble down his chin. Roan had to look away. "Have your secrets. You've got enough of them." He grabbed a sheep's leg and stalked off.

"What is with him?" Roan said.

"He has demons just like the rest of us," Gwen said. "Give him time."

Roan wasn't certain time was the answer, but he sat and finished his meal, mulling over what Gareth had said about his secrets, wondering if he was referring to his skinmark, his lineage, or something still hidden, like his feelings for Gwendolyn.

It wasn't until after Roan and Gwen laid down to sleep that he heard Gareth return. Roan cracked his eyelids and watched as Gareth snapped the leg bone in half, sucked out the marrow, and then tossed the remains in the fire, before laying down to sleep.

"The Western Road," Gareth declared brightly the next day, when they finally stumbled upon a long, narrow path of smooth stones and dirt, winding its way both to the east and the west.

"I thought it would be more impressive," Roan said.

"You should see the Bridge of Triumph," Gareth muttered, but didn't elucidate further.

They stepped onto the road, gazing along the path. Roan half-expected to spy a cloud of dust moving toward them, a dozen marauders riding full-tilt in their direction. But nothing moved. The road was quiet and empty.

Without a word, they headed west, traveling faster than before on the even terrain.

The first town they came to was shuttered. An untethered horse roamed aimlessly between the wooden structures, nibbling on tufts of grass sprouting up. He was white with black speckles, and though his ribs were starting to show, he was still well-muscled and strong-looking. Roan patted his head and fed him a carrot, which he gobbled up. "Whoa boy," he said. "What happened here?" The horse only sneezed in response.

They found the first body outside the inn.

She was young, perhaps thirteen, maybe a year or two younger or older. Her throat had been cut.

Roan's stomach roiled. Though he didn't want to look too closely, based on the lack of decomposition, she'd been killed recently. "This isn't the west I was told about," he said.

"Who are the savages now?" Gwen said, but there wasn't venom in her tone. Only sadness.

Gareth said, "Every kingdom has bad people. They hide. They wait. And as soon as the rulers begin to unravel, they pounce."

"Even the east?" Roan asked, turning away from the body, trying not to gag.

"Of course," Gareth said. "Our prisons are used as much as any."

There were more bodies inside the inn. The tavern, too. No one was spared. There were broken schooners everywhere. The floors were sticky with ale and blood. Dry goods had been spilled between the pantry and the door. The larder was empty, as was the mead cellar.

"They took everything," Gwen said. "Marauders."

"But why did they have to kill everyone?" Roan asked.

"Why does a wolf hunt a rabbit?" Gareth said. "Because it's what he is."

Roan shook his head. Humans were not wolves. And yet, it was the only explanation for what was all around him. "We should bury them," he said.

"There are too many," Gwen said. "It will take three days."

"We can burn them," Gareth said.

"No," Roan snapped. "No."

Gwen ducked her head to catch his eye. "*We* will do it, Gareth and I. You load that horse up with our bags, water him. We'll take him with us."

Roan hadn't told anyone about the two children his guardian had burned in Calypso, a moment that changed his life forever. And yet Gwen seemed to know exactly what he needed at this particular moment. He nodded. "I can help you with the bodies. Then I'll see to the horse."

"More secrets," Gareth muttered, refusing to meet Roan's eye.

They used a cart to gather the bodies in the center of the dead village, finishing the funeral pyre off with wooden doors and shutters from the abandoned structures. Gwen and Gareth stayed to light the pyre and watch it burn, while Roan took care of the horse. Though he knew little about horses, he was no longer uncomfortable with them, ever since his long ride from Barrenwood to Ferria and on to Raider's Pass.

It was strange how the memory of the journey was already slipping away into a hazy past.

He found a brush inside the stables, and used it to comb the knots out of the mare's pearl-white mane. "You're a clever horse, aren't you?" he said. "They took all the other horses, but not you. You hid from them. Aye? Am I right?" The horse chuffed in response. Next he found rainwater that had gathered in an open barrel. The horse lapped at it greedily. Finally, he slung the bags over its back, tying them with ropes under its midsection. The marauders had left no saddles—they were far too valuable—but Roan located a thick blanket, which he draped over the horse's back. "We're not going to ride you until you get your strength back," he promised. The horse whinnied.

"We should call him Horse," Gareth said from behind.

"Original," Roan said.

"*The* Horse?"

Roan couldn't do this, not right now, couldn't laugh and pretend everything was the same as it had been before the battle at Raider's Pass. The prince had changed too much, was too volatile. "I'm sorry I kept so many secrets from you. Before. I didn't know you. I couldn't read you."

"And now?"

"Now I'm worried about you."

"Don't."

"You're my friend."

"Right. My *friend*. We're all friends here. I only came with you because I had nowhere else to go."

The words were knives, but Roan didn't care. He let them cut him to ribbons, taking a step closer. "After we find the Western

391

Archives and get what we're looking for, we'll return to the east with you. We'll make this right." Until he said it, Roan didn't know he was considering it. *I am. I will.*

But Gareth only mock-laughed. "Right. The king of the west will convince the east to accept their fool-brained prince back into the fold, no questions asked. Thanks, but no thanks."

Roan said, "Gareth," but he'd already left the stables.

Roan stood there for a long time, just breathing, stroking the horse's mane.

At some point, he realized it wasn't only his breath he was hearing. He whirled around, letting out a startled sound. The horse whined beside him, perhaps sensing his unease.

The boy he'd first met at Raider's Pass in the midst of the battle stood before him. The one who'd called him the Peacemaker.

The one who'd killed Guy Ironclad.

The one who'd tried to kill Gareth Ironclad.

"Kings' Bane," Roan breathed. He took a step back. Roan was unarmed, and he could see the flash of a knife as the boy shifted his stance.

"You're a hard person to find. I can't sense you the way I can the others. It's taken me three days. And I travel fast." His words were too light for what he was, what Roan had seen him do.

Roan took another step back. "What do you want?"

"Don't be scared. I only want to talk," Bane said.

"Talk?" The word sounded foreign after what had transpired the last time they'd met.

"Yes. We're on the same side here. We always have been. We're part of the same prophecy. My goal is peace in the Four Kingdoms. And you are the Peacemaker. We are two sides of the same coin. Don't you see?"

Roan didn't see anything but a troubled boy who'd tried to kill one of his friends. "You're killing innocent people," he said.

The boy frowned, his pale scalp wrinkling. "Innocent? No one is innocent these days. Least of all the monarchies that have driven their people to more than a century of war. That man you saved? King Gareth Ironclad? He is a murderer, just like his father was."

"You don't know what he is. He's my friend."

"Friend? How can you make peace by befriending the enemy?"

The question pounded on the core of the ideals Roan had clung to his entire life, as he'd watched the Four Kingdoms tear themselves apart, as the Southern Empire had become embroiled in civil war. "That's the only way to make peace."

"No. You're wrong, friend."

"I'm not your friend."

"Then I'm afraid I'll have to kill you, too."

Roan backed up another step. "I will not fight you," he said. "I am done with violence."

"I didn't mean today." Bane seemed amused by Roan's response to his threat, his lips curling on both sides. "I'm giving you a second chance to do the right thing. If you kill Gareth Ironclad, I won't have to."

"He's already refused to be king. He's not your next target." As the words spilled from Roan's tongue, they tasted bitter. How could he protect Gareth while potentially sentencing his brother to death? And yet he knew he would do the same thing a hundred times in a row if necessary. A thousand times.

"Doesn't matter," Bane said. "He's still the heir. He's still the threat to peace."

Roan thought of his broken, troubled friend. "He is no threat. I don't know if he ever was, but he's not anymore."

"It doesn't change what I have to do. Eight monarchs have to die."

"How many are dead so far?" Roan knew of at least three.

"Four," Bane said. "Sun Sandes is dead."

"What?" Roan knew he shouldn't be surprised by the news, not after having seen what Bane was capable of. And yet, having grown up in Calypso, learning of the empress's death rocked him to the core.

"Do you care that I killed her?"

Roan hated himself for saying it, but... "No. I don't." He despised the Sandes and their rule, just as he despised all the monarchies waging war.

"See? We're not so different." Bane's words were so close to his own thoughts that a shiver of unease rolled down his spine.

Roan swallowed the feeling away, because this was a rare opportunity to gather information. "Are you killing two rulers in each kingdom?"

Bane nodded. "One is dead in each so far. One more to go."

"And in the east?" Roan already knew the answer. He was just delaying, giving himself time to think.

"King Oren Ironclad is dead. Gareth is next in line."

"Then you'll have to go through me," Roan said.

"I thought you were done with violence, cousin?"

"I'm not your cousin. And I'm warming up again."

"Very well. I will see you soon. But first I have other business to attend to."

When Roan blinked, Bane was gone, disappearing like he'd never existed at all.

"His name is *The* Horse," Roan said, when he rejoined Gwen and Gareth out on the road. He looked for some kind of a reaction from Gareth, but got nothing back.

Gwen said, "Whatever you say, Peacemaker."

They started off, with Roan leading The Horse.

"What's wrong?" Gwen asked, after they'd been walking in silence for a while.

"You mean, besides that town being massacred?" Roan said.

"Sorry," Gwen said. "I just thought there was something else."

Roan realized he was doing it again—falling into the lies, the secrets. He'd been to the brink of death with these two and yet he still wasn't willing to trust them? "There is," he said. "I saw Bane."

"What?" Gwen and Gareth said at the same time.

Gareth drew his sword.

"Relax. He's gone."

Gareth frowned, but sheathed his blade. "Did he say anything?" he asked evenly.

"He said we're on the same side. The side of peace."

Gareth scoffed. "He tries to murder me and says he wants peace?"

"I believe him," Roan said. "I think in his twisted mind he believes that killing eight monarchs will bring peace to the Four

Kingdoms. He spoke of a prophecy, and I'm certain he meant the Western Oracle's teachings."

"And you agree with him?"

"Of course not! I'm just saying that *he* believes it."

"Did he say anything else?" Gareth asked.

Roan nodded. "He asked me to…"

"To what?"

"To kill you."

None of them had said much after that. Roan confirmed he wasn't planning on killing Gareth, at least not yet. Gareth thought the idea of Roan killing anyone was hilarious. And Gwen said she had the urge to beat them both senseless, although she noted that wouldn't be difficult since they were both so thin on sense as it was.

Roan told them everything else that Bane had told him, and then all conversation died for most of the day.

By nightfall, they reached the next town, and, to Roan's relief, this one was full of life.

"Restor," Gwen said. "The last major stopping place on the Western Road. Knight's End isn't far now. Two days. Three at the most."

"I still think we should pass it by," Roan said. "It's too risky."

"There are hundreds of travelers here," Gareth said. "None shall take notice of three wayward strangers."

"Two men and one woman?" Roan said. "We shall stick out like a black eye."

"I will arrive separately," Gareth said.

"No," Roan said quickly. "We stay together."

"He's right," Gwen said. "We have to split up. At least temporarily. We will meet by happenstance at the second inn on the right. Gareth, when you arrive, request a room on the top floor, facing west."

The dead village they'd passed through earlier popped into Roan's mind. He said, "This is folly."

Gareth grinned in the green moonlight. The red moon was naught but a bloody sliver, giving the entire night an eerie complexion. "What? You don't trust me on my own? I once commanded entire battalions. I've fought in many battles. I think I can handle a few outlaws."

Roan shook his head, but offered no further objection.

They approached the town wearing cloaks to mask their faces, except for Roan, who, with his blond locks and soft features, would fit in here as well as anywhere in the west. Before they reached the edge of the lights, Gareth broke off to the side of the road, disappearing into some tall grass. Roan and Gwen continued on.

Restor, unlike the previous town, was a bustling waystation with torchlit streets filled with hundreds of people leading carts laden with goods, merchants selling wares, cooks offering hot bowls of stew, and grooms trying to attract travelers to the inns they worked at with "the best stables in town!" People seemed to be haggling over everything. The price of a leather cap. The cost of a bowl of soup. The going rate for a room at the nearest inn. Nothing seemed to be set in stone. Strangely, though he was a world and a lifetime away from his childhood home, Restor reminded Roan of Calypso, where "negotiating" was an art you learned before you could walk. He remembered when his guardian would bring him to the markets. They would take turns trying to get the best price for fruits and vegetables. His guardian had been terrible at it. Roan, however, had taken to it naturally. Once, he'd managed to procure an entire bushel of apples for only a single Dragonmark. Markin Swansea had been so proud.

Aye, he thought. *A lifetime ago.* Now Markin was dead and Roan was in the west, a place his guardian had always warned him was dangerous to someone like him. Someone marked.

Roan shook away the memories, politely declining two offers from inns on the left, as well as the first one on the right, before stopping and pretending to consider the second on the right, the one they'd agreed with Gareth to meet at.

A young groom approached. He had blond, tousled hair and a crooked smile. His front two teeth stuck out, but they only made him appear friendlier. *The innkeeper made a good choice in salesmen*, Roan thought. The boy said, "You are lucky. We have one spot left for your horse. It will be cared for as well as you and your mistress."

"She's my wife," Roan said bluntly. Gwen fired a look in his direction, but he ignored it.

"Oh. My apologies. I meant no offense."

"None taken. How much for room and board for us and our horse?" Roan asked. Gareth had given him some of the coin he'd raided from the Ironclad war chest before they'd separated.

"For you? One Golden or twelve Silvers."

"Do you take me for a fool?" Roan said, though he had no idea what the going rate was. All he knew was that *not* haggling would be more suspicious. He had to go lower by at least a third, but if he offered a price too low the groom might take him for a lost cause and walk away. "Eight Silvers and I'll forget how you twice insulted me and my wife."

The young boy's face reddened. "I…yes, you have a deal. My master will be most pleased to have such an astute traveler under his roof."

Roan handed him The Horse's reins and flipped the groom a Copper. He caught it with one hand and bit it, grinning from ear to ear. Roan suspected he'd still overpaid, but it was better than making a scene. "I will water, feed, and brush your horse. Does he have a name?"

"The Horse," Roan said.

The boy blinked, but then took it in stride. "The Horse it is. Come now, boy, we'll take good care of you." He started to lead the horse toward the stables attached to the inn, stopping only to call back over his shoulder. "My master is Carrington. Tell him the rate we've agreed and he'll get you squared."

"How did you do that?" Gwen whispered, when the boy was gone.

Roan laughed. "In Calypso, haggling is a way of life. Maybe the west isn't such a foreign place to me after all." But still, he felt proud to be able to do something that impressed Gwen. She seemed so capable of doing *everything* herself, better than anyone else. It was what attracted him to her—that free, independent spirit, like a wild stallion galloping across the plains.

"In Ferria, the price is the price," she said.

Roan winked. "Where's the fun in that?" He offered her his hand.

She looked at it, a half-smile curling the edge of her lip. "Wife?"

He shrugged. "The west is a religious place, though it seems the Western Road has descended into chaos. Still, I wanted to be safe. If we're a legitimate pair, it will raise fewer questions."

She took his hand. "He barely looked at me, did you notice?"

Though Roan hadn't grown up here, Markin had taught him much of the west. "It is considered the worst behavior to stare directly at a woman."

"That's helpful," Gwen said. "Strange, but helpful."

Hand in hand, they stepped closer to the light of the inn. *Carrington's* it was called. Roan opened the door, holding it for Gwen. He followed close behind, stepping back in front of her as soon as they were inside. Such behavior would normally earn him an elbow to the ribs or a push, but this time she allowed it.

To his surprise, the atmosphere inside the inn was subdued, the patrons hunched over bowls of soup and talking in hushed tones. A few glanced in their direction, but their gazes didn't linger.

A man of average height bustled past carrying a tray of bowls expertly in one hand. "Be right with you," he said. He had a broad bald head on top, shining in the lamplight, and a ring of salt-and-pepper hair around the edges, descending on either side into bushy sideburns that connected with his beard. He slipped between tables in an effortless manner that suggested years of practice. With a deft jerk of his wrist, the bowls slid from his tray onto one of the tables, alighting almost perfectly in front of each of the hungry men awaiting their suppers. The innkeeper pirouetted like a dancer, returning the tray to a spot beside a door that presumably led to the kitchen. He turned to face them.

"Did Pod get you all sorted out?" he asked.

"Yes," Roan said. "He drives a hard bargain."

The man chuckled. "Indeed he does. My margins have increased by ten percent since I brought him on. But I probably shouldn't be telling you that."

Roan smiled amiably. "We agreed on eight Silvers for room and board, for us and our trusty steed."

The man frowned, as if frustrated, though Roan could detect the lie behind his eyes. "It seems you drive a hard bargain, too."

"Is the rate too low?"

The man seemed to consider, though again, Roan could see the act behind his mannerisms. In his eyes glinted the light of greed. "For you, no," he said. "I will accept it."

"Thank you." He counted out the Silvers, and threw in two additional Coppers, which he hoped was a reasonable enough tip to gain them preferred service. "May I request a room on the top floor, westward facing?"

The man pocketed the coins so quickly Roan barely saw him do it. If the inn didn't work out he had a career as a pickpocket. "I will see what I can do. Right this way."

He snatched a large key from a hook, two lanterns from a platform attached to the wall, and led them to the left, away from the tables, and then up a switchback staircase for three flights. On the landing, they took a door to the right into a hallway, the walls painted warm brown. Several doors down, he unlocked a room and pushed inside. He placed one of the lanterns on a small table. "Will this serve?" he asked.

Roan scanned the small room. There were two small no-post beds and a window facing to the west, though the dark curtains were drawn. "Yes, thank you. Can supper be brought up? We'd prefer our privacy."

"Of course." The man paused in the doorway, as if waiting for something.

Roan made a big show of digging around in his pocket before handing him another two Coppers. "Please allow for one bowl to be free of meat."

The man gave him a strange look, but nodded. As before, the coins vanished, only the softest jingle giving them away in his deep pockets.

"At last," Roan said when he'd shut the door. "We're alone."

"Hilarious," Gwen said. She cast off her cloak, revealing her yellow eyes and silver hair. Her armor was orange in the lamplight. "What?" she asked, noticing Roan's stare.

"You're…"

"Don't say it," she said. "I am not some sprite to be wooed with empty words."

Roan grimaced as Gwen strode to the window, peeling back the curtains a sliver to peer out. "Must you always be so…"

"So what?" She didn't look back.

"Never mind." Roan sat on the end of one of the beds. How had he made such difficult friends?

"Where is he?" Gwen muttered. "Gareth was supposed to follow almost right behind us."

"He's probably just taking his time," Roan said.

If Gwen heard him, she gave no indication.

He came up behind her, placing his hand on her shoulder. She flinched at the touch, but then relaxed, rubbing her cheek against the back of his hand. "I'm sorry," she said. "I know I am as sharp as my sword at times…"

"At times?" Roan japed.

She twisted her head back to give him a dirty look, but he could see she was amused. "Must you always joke?"

"Not always," Roan said. He cupped his other hand against her cheek. His fingertips felt afire. She stood, her face so close he could see the individual flecks of color in her golden eyes. One hand remained on her cheek, while the other drifted down her neck, her shoulder, along the smooth armor protecting her

402

arm, and finally dropping to the swell of her hip, resting there lightly.

He wanted her so badly he felt powerless against the desire burning inside him.

And then she pressed her lips to his and stars exploded across his vision. All the worry, all the fear, all the triumphs and defeats melted away into the kiss, which was nothing but pure sensation shooting through him.

With a gasp it was over and Gwen was pulling away and looking back out the window. Roan stared at her. *What just happened?* he wondered.

"I'm sorry," she said again.

"It's okay," Roan said, though he felt breathless and weak from the kiss being broken off so early. "But I warn you, I will not give up. I promise to make the next kiss so good you shall not be able to withdraw."

To his delight, she laughed, and the momentary tension was broken.

A moment later there was a knock on the door. Roan opened his mouth to warn Gwen but she moved so fast he didn't get a word out before she was cloaked, turned away from the door.

"Yes?" Roan said.

"Supper," came Carrington's voice through the door.

"If you would, please leave it outside the door." Roan wasn't about to let the man swindle him into giving away any more Coppers, lest the innkeeper think him an easy target.

"As you wish." There was a clatter and then the sound of footsteps departing on wooden floorboards.

In an instant, Gwen's cloak was off and she was back at the window. Roan had the urge to go back to her, to rope his arms around her, but thought better of it. He didn't want to suffocate her, not when it was clear she needed space and time. Instead, he opened the door and retrieved the tray Carrington had left. It contained two mugs of water and two bowls of soup, one of which appeared to be free of chunks of meat. A small dish of salt accompanied.

Roan placed the tray next to the lamp on the small table and took his bowl to the bed, leaning back against the wall. He slurped a mouthful from his spoon, cringing at its blandness. He added salt, and the flavor improved. "Aren't you going to eat?"

"Someone has to watch for the king."

"Do you really think he'll ever go back to Ironwood?"

Gwen turned to look at him, and her eyes were thoughtful. "He better. Grian is too impulsive. Guy was somewhat better, but still too quick to wage war. Gareth is a thinker, always has been. He would be the better choice of the three."

"Except he doesn't want to be king. And you said it yourself, a Shield who doesn't fulfill his purpose will receive no respect from his people."

"I know," she said. "But there has to be a way for him to redeem himself."

"Well he can't do it from the west. He needs to go back to Ferria."

"He won't go without a strong reason."

Roan finished his soup and took Gwen's place at the window so she could eat. Now he was starting to get worried, too. Gareth should've arrived a long time ago, unless he'd stopped elsewhere for supper, or forgotten which inn they'd agreed to meet at...

And then he heard a noise, rising above the general bustle of the town. He scanned the main road, searching for the source. His heart sank when he found it.

"Gareth, what are you doing?" he muttered.

"What?" Gwen said, pushing beside him to follow his gaze.

Gareth stood on an overturned crate in the middle of the road, holding a large mug, waving it back and forth like a sword. He wore no cloak, like he'd promised he would, and his strong Ironclad features—his dark, curly hair, his strong, dimpled chin, his pale skin—as well as his armor bearing the eastern sigil, were revealed for every passerby to see.

And, to make matters worse, he was shouting, his voice so loud Roan could make out every word. "Come drink with your enemy, westerners! I am *King* Gareth Ironclad and my weapon of choice is ale. I challenge each of you to a duel. Whoever falls from their crate first is the loser!"

Gareth swayed, tumbling from the crate and spilling the strong drink all over himself.

"For ore's sake," Gwen hissed. "The fool! He will be the end of us all." She swept away from the window and burst through the door. The corridor was already empty by the time Roan gathered up their things and moved to follow her.

He raced for the steps, taking them two at a time, ignoring Carrington's question about the quality of the soup as he passed, bursting through the door and onto the street. To the right and down a ways, Gwen, fully uncloaked, was helping Gareth to his feet while other travelers stared at them, pointing. Roan could see why. Gwen's armor was like a silver starburst, her hair like falling water. Even in the darkness, she was a spectacle the likes of which most of these people had never seen.

Not to mention her eyes…as yellow and bright as twin suns.

Several, rougher looking men crept around the edges, whispering to each other behind their hands. *Not good*, Roan thought, making his way toward his friends.

He boldly walked up to them, raising his voice. "Friends," he said. "I should never have bought you those fake sets of armor or wigs. You make fools of yourselves."

Gwen's gaze darted up to his, and he nodded in the direction of the sinister-looking men. Her yellow eyes narrowed. Roan continued. "And you…"—he grabbed Gareth by the arm—"…should go easy on the drink. Do you remember that time in Talis when you ran naked through the streets? I feared the furia would hang you from your manhood as punishment!"

A few of the people laughed, but Roan was watching the rough men. They said something to each other and then left, off to find an easier, less public target.

Roan exhaled deeply. "C'mon," he whispered to Gareth. "We cannot stay here any longer."

"A shoft bed," Gareth slurred.

"Some other time."

"Hot shoup."

"Later."

Gareth shrugged, a lazy grin flopping across his face. "Fine. Take me home."

Roan raised his voice once more. "We will, Your Highness. We'll get you on the first caravan back to the Ironclad castle in Ferria!"

More laughter from the crowd, who finally started to disperse.

"Nice save," Gwen said. "Your talents grow by the hour."

"Sometimes it takes a fool to save a fool," Roan said.

Together, they hauled Gareth out of town and back onto the Western Road, stopping only once the lights of the city were well behind them.

"We should go back for The Horse," Gareth said loudly.

Roan regretted leaving The Horse behind, but the poor animal would probably be better off without them. The stable boy was a good lad, and would keep him warm and well-fed, which was more than they could promise. And if they set foot in Restor again, there was a good chance they would never leave.

They argued nonstop from Restor to Knight's End. Two days had passed, but each was the same argument, one that had resumed after a brief pause for a midday meal of day-old bread and hard butter that they'd purchased from a passing cart-merchant.

"So I stopped at a tavern for a quick mug of the west's finest ale, who cares? I was just trying to have a good time," Gareth said.

"And lost your cloak somewhere," Gwen said.

"And declared your true identity in the middle of the streets," Roan added.

"And were so drunk you could barely walk."

"And challenged every person you saw to a drinking duel."

"And lost The Horse."

"All right, all right," Gareth said. "What if I said I don't remember any of that, does that help my cause?"

"NO!" they both answered together.

"Then I'm extraordinarily sorry," Gareth said, though he didn't sound sorry at all. "Well, about The Horse anyway. I miss him."

It was, however, the first time he'd apologized, so Roan considered it progress. And he was joking again, though Roan wasn't certain what that meant exactly. The last time Gareth had japed this much he was covering up the turmoil he was feeling inside.

They rounded a bend, curling over the crest of a small rise, and Roan stopped abruptly when he saw it.

Knight's End.

Its high stone walls were tan, framing the city like a giant picture frame. Beyond the walls the city rose gradually, until it reached a hill where a castle stood like a beacon shining in the sun, three round towers stretching to the seventh heaven these people so devoutly believed in. Until this moment, Roan never expected to feel anything when he first laid eyes on the city of his birth. Instead, anger rolled through him like a slow-burning fire. His mother had been forced to send him away from this city with a violent Dreadnoughter because of his mark, something he'd been born with, something he had no control over. How was that fair? How was that right? How did a people who claimed to be holy treat a mere child like some kind of a demon?

"Roan," Gwen said.

He barely heard her, the anger chased away by another feeling:

Sorrow. The sadness was rich and deep, a pool that rose over his head, stealing his breath. It was sadness for a lost childhood, stripped from him before he'd ever really understood why. He'd lost his family at the same time, and now both his parents were dead. He'd never feel their embrace. Never. That word was filled with so much finality he could hardly bear to think it.

"Roan?" Gwen said again. "Are you well?"

"Aye," he said. "I was only thinking about what it will be like to meet my siblings at last."

"We can't rightly march up to the castle gates and declare your true identity," Gareth said.

"No," Roan agreed. "That's *your* favorite thing to do."

Gareth winced, but he wore a smile. "I suppose I deserved that."

Roan shook his head. He knew a fantastic way to chase away his own melancholy. Deflection. He turned to Gareth and said, "When I first met you, you were a brash, arrogant prince standing on high, looking down on the world with a smug grin. Now I know the immense weight you were carrying—the death of your mother, your role as the Shield—but you held that load over your head like it was nothing, a sack filled with air."

Gareth looked away, back toward the city. "I was different then. I hadn't failed."

Roan felt like he could see the weight on his friend's shoulders, a growing load, hunching his shoulders, making it difficult for him to stand.

Gwen seemed ready to say something, but Roan stopped her with a subtle gesture. "You're the same person," he said. "Except now you drag the weight around like an iron plow, and it's pulling you under, burying you alive."

Gareth looked back, and the weight vanished, the familiar cheeky smile returning like it had never been gone in the first place. "As usual, you are too serious, my friend. I only wanted a bit of drink and a good laugh. Yes, I took things too far. I messed up and I'm sorry. It won't happen again."

Roan glanced at Gwen and she shrugged. Gareth did seem to be back to his normal self all of a sudden. "Fine. Good. But we can't make any mistakes in the Holy City. The furia will be here. Getting drunk or causing a disturbance will not go unpunished."

Gareth bowed to him. "Yes, Your Highness. As you command."

Roan rolled his eyes and turned his attention back to the city. They made their way down the small hill to where a there was a steady influx of travelers, as well as lines of merchants departing the city. Those exiting were mostly ignored, while guards bearing the rearing stallion sigil on their chests eyed newcomers, asking questions and searching their belongings for weapons.

The southern entrance to Knight's End was like a peephole into the enormous walled-in city, providing the barest glimpse of the cobblestoned streets and sturdy buildings beyond. This was the third major city Roan had seen, and he marveled at how different each was. Compared to the dusty clay and sandstone streets of Calypso, Knight's End was a fortress, though even the tall castle towers lacked the beautiful symmetry of the Calypsian pyramids. And next to Ferria and Ironwood, Knight's End felt so...open, almost unguarded, if not for the wall that surrounded it.

They fell into the slow-moving line.

Once more, Gwen was cloaked in black, her face hidden in shadow, while Gareth was wearing a simple cloth shirt and trousers. They'd left his armor in a bush off the road. He'd seemed glad to see it go, like it was his final act in relinquishing the crown to his brother. Roan had encouraged Gwen to work her magic to get rid of her own armor, but she refused. Plus, she'd explained, removing ore was more difficult when outside of Ironwood, and once she did, she wouldn't be able to get it back.

Roan hoped the gate guards wouldn't ask to check beneath her cloak. *They shouldn't*, he thought. *A woman's modesty is respected here.*

They approached the gate. "Let me do the talking," he said. Gwen nodded and Gareth smirked.

One of the guards eyed them as they came near. "State your business," he said.

Roan smiled easily. "We are seeking sanctuary and work in the city."

"Sanctuary from what?"

"Birds," Gareth said. Roan fired daggers from his eyes.

"Birds?" The guard's natural scowl deepened.

"I'm only japing," Gareth said. "The Western Road has grown dangerous these last days. Outlaws. Vagabonds. Scoundrels. We fear for the life of our sister." He motioned to Gwendolyn, who bowed rather stiffly.

"Yes," Roan interjected, trying to regain control of the situation. "We are brothers, though many don't believe us."

"What is your trade?"

"Entertainers," Gareth said, once more interrupting. "Puppet shows, mostly. But never fear, good man, our japes are of the clean variety. After all, we are Wrath-abiding citizens."

Roan held his breath as the man stared them down. Then, to his utter surprise, the guard waved them through. "We could use more entertainers in this crusty old city."

When they were out of earshot, Roan said, "That was a big risk."

Gareth shrugged. "Not really. We *are* pretty entertaining, wouldn't you say? And anyway, sometimes a bit of absurdity goes a long way."

Though Roan was somewhat annoyed, the feeling was eclipsed by his relief that Gareth was beginning to act more like his normal self.

Knight's End was like a thousand Restor's stacked on top of and next to each other. The streets were full to overflowing. Sights, smells, and sounds assaulted Roan's senses, and he quickly became overwhelmed. Gareth seemed less so, buying small trinkets and foodstuffs from merchants, trading quips and smiles. He had a way of blending in while still seeming larger than life. It was a quality Roan envied.

Gwen, on the other hand, just seemed bitter. "Look at how the women are dressed," she said. "It must be a thousand degrees. I'm swimming in sweat." Roan *had* noticed the women, most of whom were dressed in what his guardian had called purity dresses, shapeless white frocks that covered all but their hands and faces.

"It is tradition," Roan said.

"Aye, a foolish tradition."

A spike of anger rose up in him. "And they think the Orians are a bunch of godless witches," he said. "So you both think the other's traditions are foolish. And everyone wonders why this war will never end."

Though he couldn't see Gwen's face, he could sense her silently fuming beneath her cloak.

Thankfully, Gareth broke up the tension. "I don't know," he said. "There's something enticing about beauty hidden beneath folds of cloth, don't you think?"

Roan rolled his eyes. Leave it to his charming friend to see something lustworthy in a purity dress.

"And what of *those* women?" Gwen whispered, pointing to a few gathered together, discussing something quietly.

"What about them?" Roan asked. Then the women turned and Roan had to force himself not to stare. Their faces were freshly scarred, deep lines cut into their flesh, forming what appeared to be a W across the whole of their faces.

"Do you think that is a noble tradition?" Gwen asked harshly. "Self-mutilation?"

Roan almost hoped the scars were self-inflicted, the only other option being a much worse one. Still, he'd never heard of westerners carving their own faces. "All I'm saying is we should keep an open mind."

They moved on. Gareth asked a female merchant—whose face was, thankfully, not scarred—where the Western Archives were, and she directed him toward the castle at the top of the hill. "But you need special permission to visit them."

"What's your plan to get into the Archives?" Gareth asked as they walked.

"I don't have one," Roan said.

"Fantastic. My favorite kind of mission, an ill-planned one." The sarcasm was heavy in his voice.

"We could sneak in," Gwen suggested.

"If the Archives are in the castle, they'll be heavily guarded. I'm sure many of the texts are priceless."

"Then how?" Gwen asked. "We came all this way. We can't just accept that getting in will be impossible."

"No," Roan said. "We're not accepting anything. My sister is the queen, remember?"

Gareth laughed. "I don't think she'll remember you."

Gwen lowered her voice. "And have you forgotten your mark? And mine? They will burn us at the stake like the demons they think we are."

"Maybe," Roan said thoughtfully. "Maybe not. We need to gather more information on just who my sister is."

They'd asked more than three-dozen people about Queen Rhea. And all of them agreed, she was the most holy woman to ever rule Knight's End. In fact, they called her Rhea the Righteous. She'd even carved a W into her own face to mark her as Wrath's servant, which explained the numerous similarly scarred faces they'd seen throughout the city. According to everyone they spoke to, Rhea's purity was so bright she'd singlehandedly defeated the largest northern army to sail against the west.

That news had rocked all three of them. The north had been defeated? How? When? Evidently it had been recently, within the last few days.

My sister, Roan thought, as they stood without the castle gates, which, strangely, stood wide open. *She rules differently. She invites the commoners into her stronghold.*

And hundreds of the people, if not thousands, were accepting her invitation, marching through the gates and into the large inner courtyard. "She will accept me," Roan said, glancing back at Gareth and Gwen. "I know it."

They'd discussed their options, and agreed to risk Roan revealing himself to his sister. If she was truly the good, honorable woman the westerners believed her to be, certainly she would speak with him.

"Just don't show her your mark," Gwen muttered, after grudgingly assenting to the plan.

He nodded. "Remember, stand outside the castle gates at dusk each day until I come find you," he said.

Gareth said, "Be safe." It was the most normal, serious thing he'd said to Roan in days, probably since they were trapped in the wood nymph's enchanted locket.

"I will." He longed to embrace them both, to hold them close, to let this moment linger a bit longer. Instead they clasped arms briefly and then Roan slipped into the throng.

He pushed and forced his way toward the front of the crowd, as close to the raised dais as he could get. There he saw her:

Her white purity dress flowed around her body covering much of her skin, but her face and hair were visible. Her hair was almost the exact color of his, her features soft, with high cheekbones, a delicate nose, piercing turquoise eyes, and…

Though he'd known to expect it, the scar on her face made him gasp, and several people gave him strange looks, moving away. The W carved into her face was the same as the ones he'd seen on so many faces throughout the city.

Sister, what have you done? he thought.

His next thought was similar, because that's when he realized why the people had been invited inside the castle, what they were gathering to watch.

It was an execution.

Thirty-Three

The Northern Kingdom, Castle Hill
Annise Gäric

Annise's breath was short, her heart beating too fast. This was different than the last time she'd commanded her army. The last time was a rushed, frantic burst of orders while they faced a stone-faced giant that was already killing her men at will.

Today, however, with the sun poking along the edges of the horizon, their enemy was not yet visible, hidden somewhere behind the tall, white walls of Castle Hill. Hundreds of soldiers stared at her, waiting for her to say something inspiring, something to get their blood pumping.

Tarin's voice was a deep whisper meant only for her. "Truth," he said. "Speak the truth."

She smiled thinly at him, nodding her thanks for him being there, for being her rock. She tried not to think that the night before may have been their last together, and though it was full of passion, she felt empty in its wake, like her soul had been sucked out.

She didn't want it to be the last time she felt his warmth beside her.

She took a deep breath. *Truth. Yes. That is the right way.*

"I am not my father," she said. A sea of eyebrows went up, dark arches beneath gleaming helms. It wasn't what they had expected her to say. "I will not force you to fight. I will not use fear as a weapon. For any who do not believe in our cause, you may go without repercussion, without punishment, without judgment." She gestured to the walls of the castle, which were dusted with snow. "On the battlefield, I am your queen commander, and you will obey me without question. But here, in the *before*, you have a choice. Behind those walls is an enemy of nightmares, ninety-eight monsters that will test our mettle to its breaking point."

Her voice changed, softened. "I am scared—I will admit it." Silence fell, and Annise swore she could hear each snowflake as it landed. The fear inside her felt supercharged, until it became something else. Excitement. Energy. Truth.

She lifted her voice, infusing it with strength, power. "But this is *my* home, and I will not abandon it, not to the likes of the Imposter King. That is *my* choice. Now it is time to make yours. Leave now, and go in peace. Or"—she paused again, letting that single word sink in—"fight with me. Stand with your brothers, your fathers, your sons! Stand for our great kingdom, a kingdom that has been shamed by my father's brother, by the unnatural army he has raised against us! Stand for me, your queen, and I will fight with you, side by side! What say you?"

Nothing. Snowfall. Sun breaking the horizon, shimmering across the falling flakes and gleaming armor. A pale city on a snowy hill, its impenetrable walls cloaked in years of mistrust, oppression and fear. Ranks of soldiers, some who'd fought in numerous battles, while others who'd never experienced a single one, joined in this shattered moment of truth, of choice, of—

"I will stand," a voice rang out, as clear and crisp as the morning. "I will fight." Sir Metz stepped forward, his armor as pristine as always, his sword raised in a sign of loyalty.

Silence fell upon his words as they floated away.

But then the echo came. "I will stand. I will fight. My sword is yours, as is my life." Sir Dietrich stepped forward, blade raised to the heavens.

More voices appeared, melding together until they were a single voice, a shout hammering like a drumbeat. "Stand! Fight! Stand! Fight! Stand! Fight!"

Annise turned away, her eyes meeting Tarin's for one bare moment. He nodded. Beside him, Zelda was smiling, and, for once, not eating. The expression on her face was unmistakable, filling Annise with warmth: pride.

She basked in the moment for three breaths.

And then she led her men into battle.

The city outside the castle was empty, or at least it appeared to be, though the occasional dark shadow could be seen peeking through a curtained window. She wondered whether the citizens were hiding because of Annise's army, or because of her uncle's monsters. *Perhaps both*, she thought.

A sea of foot soldiers marched ahead of her, armed with grappling hooks and rope ladders. Annise and her various cavalries rode behind, not in superiority to the foot soldiers, but because they would be like a spear thrust in the event the soldiers managed to breach the wall and open the gates.

As it turned out, none of that was necessary, for, just as the first line of soldiers reached the castle wall, the gates shuddered, snow cascading from the stone parapets above them.

Beside her, Tarin said, "They come to us."

Another shudder. And then another, the thick wooden doors cracking in the middle, where they met. There was a final crash, and the doors swung open, though the way was blocked by something as dark as night, a broad panel of flesh that was almost snake-like in appearance.

Several of the soldiers fell backwards, but were held up by the rest of the men. *Frozen hell below*, Annise thought. *What* is *that thing?*

Something shot out from the entrance, a long black rope, snapping at them from a fanged mouth. A man screamed as the tendril grabbed him by the leg, dragging him away. A brave young man leapt forward and hacked at the monster's limb, but it was already gone, the man sucked inside the castle, his scream cut off abruptly.

Annise's head spun, her thoughts scattering like sticks in a child's game of Pick 'em Up. *This is impossible. We are the walking dead. I have sentenced all these souls to death.* Despite the "choice" she gave them, she knew they would've followed her to frozen hell and back. Which might've been better than where they were now, the demon they were facing.

Tarin said, "Annise. Your command. Give it now."

The calm in his tone was like a warm broth pooling in her mind. *I can do this. I will die for this cause if I must.* "Sir Dietrich," she said. "Lead the assault."

Dietrich, who was no stranger to battles from his time defending Raider's Pass, didn't need further urging. "Men!" he shouted, raising his sword in the air and pointing it toward the black-fleshed beast. "Attack!"

The sea churned forward, an ocean of weapons and armor and lives. As planned, the foot soldiers swept to the sides, opening up a space for the cavalries to charge through. Annise spurred her horse forward, aware of Tarin at her side, his Morningstar already cutting wide circles around his head.

Grasping the reins with one hand, she drew her own weapon, the Evenstar Fay had given her. Nearby, she saw Zelda and Sir Craig raise their weapons together. Sir Craig leaned down to embrace his wife, pecking her quickly on the lips. The moment of tenderness was so out of place next to the monster blocking their path that it took Annise's breath away. Steeling herself, she refocused.

Up ahead, a dozen fanged tendrils shot out from the castle gates. Men hacked at them, slicing several off, but not before four other men were dragged away. Shouts of war surrounded her as the first cavalry rode through the gates, directly into the wall of black flesh. Sir Dietrich slashed at the skin while Tarin hammered it with blows from his Morningstar. Annise looked up to see what sort of monster they faced, and immediately wished she hadn't. The creature was like a black worm, with no arms or legs save the fanged tendrils that spilled from its eyeless, noseless, earless crown. Several were stumps, spitting dark fluid—those that had been severed by her soldiers—but there were still plenty intact. They shot down toward the riders.

Annise swung her Evenstar, hitting one just before it slammed into her face. The short chain wrapped around the tendril and the barbs sunk deep. The maw screamed and then flopped free, slapping at her horse's hooves with a wet thud that reminded her of the time she and Arch had been ice fishing in Frozen Lake and he'd landed a particularly large boarfish.

One of the other riders hadn't been so fortunate. He screamed as his horse was grabbed by two snake-like tentacles, carrying them both upwards to the other snapping mouths, which quickly pulled him apart. *Sir Morley*, Annise remembered, the name of the rider she'd forgotten during the previous battle.

Bile rose in her throat as her muscles threatened to freeze up. "No," she growled. She had to be strong. For her men. For her kingdom. For herself.

"How do we kill it?" she asked no one in particular. It had no eyes to blind, and the surface of its skin all looked the same. The only things they could fight were the fanged tentacles, and killing one of them seemed to have no effect on the overall beast.

Nearby, Tarin swept his Morningstar across another tentacle, cutting it off. Dietrich, his sword a maelstrom of slashes, severed two more. If nothing else, the monster was running out of tendrils.

Another rider pulled up beside her. "Even a worm has a brain," Sir Metz said. "If we can get to it, we might have a chance."

Annise nodded. "I'll do it."

"What?" Tarin said. "No."

So many were dying, and this was only the first of ninety-eight monsters they would face on this day. But Annise had already made up her mind. When the next tentacle launched itself toward her, she waited a beat longer and then wrapped her chain around it, clinging to either side as it lifted her into the air.

A weight clung to her heels, and her first thought was *Tarin!* but when she looked down it was Zelda clinging to her, grinning like a banshee. "You thought I would let you have all the fun?" her aunt shouted.

Something swooped from the side, drawing her attention away from her aunt. The tendril's jaws snapped at Annise as if it had a mind of its own, but she managed to kick it away. They rose higher and higher, until they were dangling above the monster's "head," which reached almost to the top of the castle's walls.

"Brace yourself!" she cried down to Zelda.

And then she released one side of the chain and dropped.

Frozen air rushed past her and she bounced off the slimy side of one of the tentacles, twisting in the air before landing hard on her shoulder. Zelda landed hard beside her, eyes wild. They started to slide, and Annise scratched at the side of the beast's slick skin to no effect. Frantically, she reached down and drew her sword, using a short thrust to jam it into the monster's flank and arrest her slide. Zelda did the same, stopping at almost the same position.

They hung for a moment, just breathing, looking around. This close to the creature's body, the tentacles seemed to have forgotten her, flailing downwards, searching for fresh victims on the ground.

"We have to climb higher," Zelda said.

Annise nodded, raising her Evenstar by the leather handle, whipping it overhead and slamming it down further up. The spikes struck, sinking deep into the monster's flesh. With a grunt, she wrenched out her sword, using one arm to pull herself higher. Zelda began doing the same, using her sword to clamber up the slick skin.

Next Annise jabbed with her sword, higher still, repeating the rhythm as they scaled their giant foe. Swing, pull, jab, climb, again and again, until she was at the apex, looking down upon the bloody battle, which had spilled into the castle courtyard in which she used to play as a child.

She was horrified to see that while she'd been scaling Mount Slimeworm, three additional monsters had arrived, and were now doing battle with the third and fourth cavalries, as well as several platoons of foot soldiers. The rest of her army were bottlenecked at the castle gates, trying to press forward into combat.

Of the new monsters, one was like a giant crab, its massive claws snapping men in half like individual pieces of kindling. Another had feathers and razor-sharp talons. It scooped up a handful of soldiers and flew overhead, dropping them to their deaths. The third had skin bristling with spikes, like a porcupine, and dozens of spearmen were trying to shove the tips of their long weapons between the quills to pierce its flesh. Four men were already impaled on its hide, dead.

Annise shook away the images and turned her attention back to the worm she rode, which was continuing to attack the first cavalry, though it was down to only a handful of tendrils. Still, simply by rolling over, the worm could probably squash hundreds of men. She needed to finish it now. Sir Metz's words came to mind: *Even a worm has a brain.*

"Dig," she said to her aunt, who had just reached the summit. Without an Evenstar, it had taken Zelda a fraction longer to complete the climb.

Her aunt grinned excitedly and raised her sword overhead.

Annise mimicked her movement, and then, in unison, they brought their blades down into what she hoped was the creature's head.

If the worm felt the blows, it showed no sign, nor made a sound. She yanked her sword free. Again and again they cut into the worm, digging a ragged chasm into its flesh, carving deeper with each strike. Annise grunted with each stroke, her arms burning from the effort. Something changed, the black meat becoming lighter toned, and then a pink liquid spewed forth, splashing across her face. She clamped her mouth shut, the blood bitter on her tongue, and continued stabbing. Up, down, up, down, up—

The world dropped out from under her, but she managed to slash down once more, her sword acting as a grappling hook as the monster fell. Screams assaulted her ears as howling wind provided accompaniment.

Deep in the monster's flesh, she rattled back and forth, bashing into her aunt when the beast slammed to the ground. She lost her grip on her sword, though Evenstar tangled around her as she shook loose, tumbling hard to the ground, banging both elbows and a knee.

Already, bodies littered the ground around her.

Dazed, she stared at the snowflakes falling into the courtyard. She blinked.

Young Tarin, just a boy, raced across her path, hurling a snowball. Expertly, she caught it in one hand, crushing it with her fingers. He squealed and tried to run away, but she launched her own snowball, catching him between the shoulder blades. He sprawled headlong in the snow, doing a full somersault and coming up wearing a grin and ice in his dark hair. "You win again," he said. "You are the queen of Snow Wars!"

Her eyes opened and Tarin was there, but he wasn't that small, skinny boy, but a broad-shouldered warrior in night-dark armor, no longer riding his stallion. "Annise," he said, kneeling beside her.

"I'm fine," she said, though she felt as if she'd been trampled by a horse and two oxen.

"You're incredible," he said. "Both of you."

"Tell us something we don't already know," Zelda said, already back on her feet.

Annise shook her head. Though Tarin's words warmed her from the inside out, they didn't have time to linger here. "We have to get back."

"The monsters are fighting each other," Tarin said. "It might give us a chance."

She looked past him and saw he was right. The creature with the claws snapped the giant bird's wings off as it tried to claw out its eyes. The porcupine-like monster tucked itself into a ball and rolled up against them both, poking holes in their skin.

"My fool of a brother can't control them," Zelda said.

Annise nodded grimly. But still, even with the monsters distracted by each other, they were losing soldiers in droves as side effects to the carnage.

Nearby, the worm's skin shriveled and fell away, leaving a half-naked man in the center. He was dead, his head opened by the two Gäric blades. Tarin strode over and retrieved the swords, handing the weapons to Annise and her aunt, and helping Annise to stand.

Side by side by side, they strode back into the battle with the monsters.

Annise was exhausted, slumped on the ground, her arms on her knees. She could barely lift her sword or Evenstar. Though they'd killed forty-six monsters thus far—Sir Metz was keeping the tally, shouting it out with each new victory—their foes kept coming, relentlessly. Her uncle had begun releasing one at a time, having realized very quickly that the monsters would fight each other if released together.

The cost of each victory had been steep. Annise didn't know the exact numbers, but she was certain she'd lost at least half of her force. The third cavalry was gone, as well as the sixth. All of them had taken significant casualties, and most of the horses were lost. In reality, they were all just foot soldiers at this point—even Annise, the queen, her title as worthless in battle as a dress constructed entirely of diamonds.

Another monster fell—a mamoothen as big as a small mountain that had been their toughest foe yet. Its wooly hide was bristling with arrows and spears, many of them broken. Sir Dietrich had done the most damage, carving a line across the beast's throat. Like all the other monsters, when its fur and skin peeled away, a dead man was all that remained.

"Forty-seven!" Sir Metz shouted, his voice easily discernible in the exhausted silence.

What nightmare will emerge next? Annise wondered.

The ground rumbled beneath her, as if in response. Something bellowed, a cry that sounded more anguished than angry. And then the monster stalked through the inner arch set into the courtyard wall on four legs, forced to duck its head, which reached to the top. Its fur was black, its snout long and gray, sitting above a large mouth. Its paws were big and padded and ringed with curved claws. The enormous bear reared up onto its hind legs and released another mournful bellow, revealing sharp teeth as it pounded its chest.

"Archers!" Dietrich shouted. After the initial wave of four monsters, the commander of the first cavalry had gotten into a rhythm. Archers first, then foot soldiers, then cavalry, if any remained. A three-pronged attack that worked in the end, though it took time and sacrifice. Too much sacrifice. "Fire!"

The archers unleashed a storm of arrows, which hit various parts of the bear, though none were shot high enough to hit its head. Several stuck in its flesh, but most bounced off of its strong hide. This wasn't unusual—most of the monsters seemed to have almost armor-like skin.

The bear roared again, and then charged, scattering the archers to either side. Dietrich cried his next command, and the foot soldiers bravely charged, an assortment of seasoned veterans and old men and boys no older than Archer. They hacked and jabbed. Some even launched grappling hooks, using them to try to climb the bear to get a shot at its head.

They are spectacular, Annise thought, watching. Another mid-battle decision they'd made was to have half the army attack a monster while the other half rested. That way the attackers were always fresh, or at least fresher than they would be. An added benefit was that the soldiers wouldn't get in each other's way. Tarin paced beside her, watching as the bear swept a claw across three men, slashing their throats open.

"Tarin," she said, but he ignored her, continuing to pace. As the battle had progressed, he'd grown more and more agitated, until she could barely get more than a growl of response from him. *"Tarin."*

Still nothing, his fingers flexing and opening around the handle of his Morningstar.

"Sit down," she said. "That is a command."

He stopped pacing, his chest rising and falling, but he still refused to look at her. He didn't sit, just watched as the bear killed two more men.

"Tarin," she said again. "Sit down. I command it."

He didn't sit. Though he'd become more distant over the course of the day, this was the first time he'd disobeyed a direct command. Annise grunted as she fought to her feet.

He faced away from her, those giant hands curling and uncurling, forever in motion. He was muttering something under his breath, but she couldn't discern the words. She slipped her hands around him, across his chest. She had expected him to stiffen, perhaps to try to pull away from her. Instead his elbow shot back, catching her in the temple, the hard armor like a battering ram, knocking her back.

Stars pulsed around her vision as it dimmed, her legs crumpling. She closed her eyes, willing the world to stop spinning, trying not to think about the fact that the love of her life had hit her.

The world blinked back into focus and Tarin stood over her, his faceplate lifted, his mesh covering pulled down. His mouth was wrenched into something between a snarl and a twisted curve of horror. "What have you done?" he asked.

Annise had no time to wonder whether he was asking her or the thing inside of him, the monster that had taken the beautiful boy he'd been, the compassionate, gentle man he'd become, and carved it into someone out of control, a creature of violence and bloodlust; she had no time because at that very moment, the giant bear reared up, turning in their direction. Its forepaws thumped down and it charged.

"Look out, Tarin!" Annise cried, but it was too late. The bear's monstrous strides devoured the space between them, and it swiped Tarin aside, knocking him into the air. His armor clanked heavily as he bounced off the stone wall before thudding to the ground. "Tarin!" Annise yelled, but he wasn't moving.

The bear stood over her, one paw on either side, its maw opening to reveal fangs dripping with black saliva. *This is it*, she knew. A prayer flitted through her, for Archer. It was his kingdom now, and he needed to recover to see it through, to take down their uncle.

The bear's mouth drew closer, stopping so close she could feel its hot breath on her face, see its eyes boring into her. *Those eyes.* Somehow, impossibly, inexplicably...those eyes were familiar to Annise, brown orbs as deep as the ocean.

And she knew.

She knew.

"Sir Jonius?" she said.

The bear seemed to startle at hearing the name, rising up slightly, clamping its mouth shut, blinking in confusion. In Annise's peripheral vision, she saw Tarin stir. *Not dead*, she thought, relief swirling through her stomach.

She refocused on the massive bear. "Sir Jonius," she said again. "Do you remember me? It's Annise, your little snow angel. I have returned." Sir Jonius. The man who had always been kind to her as a child, who'd brought her presents on her name day, who never failed to wink at her as he passed. The man who'd carried out atrocities for her father. The man who had imprisoned her brother, watched as her mother was executed. The man who had let them escape from Castle Hill.

The most confusing man Annise had ever met was now a monster.

"You are still in there," she said. "I have to believe that."

The bear unleashed another roar, so loud she was forced to cover her ears with her hands.

On the edge of her vision, Tarin rose, stalking toward the bear, swinging Morningstar over his head. "Tarin," Annise said. "Stop. I command it."

He stopped for a moment, continuing to swing his weapon. His face was a miasma of confusion, a river of blood streaming from a slash in his forehead. Anger, frustration, fear, sadness—she could see them all coalescing in his haggard expression.

He started forward once more.

"No," Annise said. "Don't. I know this man." Tarin stopped. This time he remained still, letting Morningstar fall to the ground.

She gazed back at the bear. "Sir Jonius, this is not you. You are no monster. You are a knight of the realm, and thus, you are sworn to obey the ruler of the kingdom. That is me. I am Queen Annise Gäric, come to reclaim my throne from the Imposter King."

The bear—Sir Jonius—reared up on its hind legs, raising its clawed paws, preparing to stomp down.

I tried, Annise thought.

To her surprise, the bear turned away, motioning with its snout toward the archway leading to the rest of the castle.

Annise rose. Her soldiers were approaching, their weapons drawn. Sir Dietrich. Sir Metz. She waved them down. "Men! This is Sir Jonius. He is one of us now. Do not harm him. Understood?"

The soldiers eyed the bear warily, but nodded. He roared once more and charged deeper into the castle. After only a moment's hesitation, the men followed.

"Forty-eight?" Sir Metz said.

Ninety-one. That was the latest count. Annise knew they'd all be dead already if not for Sir Jonius in all his monster-bear glory. Fighting beside she and her men, he'd helped them slay dozens of beasts. Another stone monster. A creature made of snow that reformed its limbs when they shattered. A bull the size of a catapult. On and on, monster after monster battled them.

Sir Jonius was leaking blood from numerous wounds, his dark fur matted and slick, red blood dripping behind him in the snow. But still he fought on, occasionally looking back to meet Annise's eyes.

Annise was still woozy from when Tarin had hit her, but the adrenaline had served her well, and she fought on, afraid to stop to rest for even a single moment. Afraid that if she did she would lie down and not get back up.

In between monsters, Annise tried to get Tarin's attention, but he was lost inside himself again, his helmet still off, his translucent cheeks crusted with rivulets of dried blood and bulging with black veins. When a new monster appeared, Tarin fought alongside Jonius, roaring and whipping Morningstar with all the force of a winter storm.

On one occasion he killed a monster—a twelve-eyed shell-armored monstrosity—by shattering its carapace and digging out its heart.

You're incredible, he'd said to her earlier. It felt like a lifetime ago. Though, in a way, he was incredible, too, but watching the fury with which he fought sent a dark wave of dread down her spine.

"Ninety-three!" Sir Metz shouted. Two more monsters had fallen, human bodies littered around them.

Five more foes emerged, all at once. It seemed her uncle, in his final stand, had abandoned his strategy of releasing one at a time. The first three were of the usual variety: a creature made of bone with long sharp shards for hands; a beast that seemed to be made of tar, which oozed behind it like a black stream; a giant caterpillar with thousands of legs and a maw filled with a dozen rows of pincer-like teeth.

But the last two were different. For one, they were even larger, stretching toward the sky. For another thing, they both took on the shape of men. One was formed from ice, and wore a crown of icicles. A long beard formed of snow blanketed his chin and chest. Annise recognized him immediately—the Ice Lord. The bearer of the icemark, a cruel man who'd murdered hundreds during his appointment as her father's weapon. Now he was as tall as the walls of Castle Hill. The second man was her uncle, Lord Griswold, the Imposter King himself, except now he was made of metal and wielding an axe the size of a tree.

He drank the rest of the potion, Annise knew. Half for him, half for the Ice Lord. Their final stand.

The two leaders waited at the back, watching as their last three monsters attacked. The caterpillar stampeded through the remaining men, swallowing several whole before being hacked to pieces by Sir Dietrich and Tarin. Annise fought alongside Sir Metz, who was as talented with the sword as anyone save perhaps Sir Dietrich, and Zelda, who was as fierce now as when they took down the very first monster. Together, along with the remaining archers and several spearmen, managed to dispatch the tar creature, though at least a dozen men vanished into its black slime in the process. Sir Jonius fought the last creature on his own, ripping off chunks of bone with his enormous paws. Even when a sliver of bone punctured his chest, he was able to bite through its spindly spine. The monster fell to pieces, revealing another dead man.

"Ninety-seven," Sir Metz said.

The Imposter King stepped forward and laughed, a hollow rumble that seemed to penetrate Annise's chest, rattling her heart.

He swung his axe. Annise dove to the side as it crashed into the ground, opening up a long slash in the earth. It took her uncle a moment to wrench the axe head from the ground, and Annise took advantage of the respite to race forward, slashing Evenstar across his ankles. The spiked ball rebounded without effect, glancing off thick metal boots. He kicked at her and his toe caught her midsection, picking her up and tossing her through the air.

The world spun and then she landed softly. Sir Jonius's soft brown eyes stared down at her as the giant bear set her back on her feet. And then he charged into battle, swiping his claws across her uncle's abdomen. Though his claws were sharp, they did little but score thin marks in the metal.

Lord Griswold slapped the bear away lazily with the back of his iron hand.

Her uncle stepped back to regroup, watching as the Ice Lord swept his hand across the last group of archers, who were firing fletched arrows into his icy skin. The second his fingers touched them, they froze into statues. When he swung his arm back the other way, they crumbled to ice dust under the blow.

Annise whirled around. There were so few of them left. Sir Dietrich was rallying a few soldiers to him, preparing for a final attack. Tarin fought on his own, bludgeoning her uncle with Morningstar while he looked down like a god, laughing.

Sir Metz had formed his own small pack, who now surrounded the Ice Lord, trying to hack his thick ice legs to pieces. She was surprised to see Sir Craig still alive, fighting bravely, a far cry from the staggering knight she'd known to fall first in tournaments.

Annise wobbled on her feet, trying to decide what to do. No option seemed right. Every path seemed to end in death, both hers and the few of her soldiers that remained. Somewhere in her battered brain she had a thought. An idea.

"To me," she said, but it came out as naught but a whisper. Another soldier was frozen by the Ice Lord. A spearmen was crushed under her uncle's metal boot. She took a deep breath. "To me!" she shouted, her voice rising over the clank of metal on metal.

All heads turned her way, and then, without hesitation, they ran toward her. All except for Tarin, who continued fighting her uncle, a tiny whirlwind in the midst of a tornado. Even Sir Jonius lumbered over to listen, though the other soldiers kept their distance from the bear, whose chest was ornamented with a bone shard.

Annise couldn't think about Tarin now, not when her last two dozen men and her aunt were staring at her, waiting. Every second was a risk. Every moment carried a weight: the potential to be their last.

"Let the Ice Lord kill the Imposter King," she said. "It's the only way."

At first all she got were confused looks, but then Sir Dietrich nodded in understanding. "Yes. Men, harry the Ice Lord from the side facing the Imposter King. When the Ice Lord reacts, flee toward Lord Griswold."

The men nodded, their weary faces armored with determination.

As one, they charged back into the fray. Tarin was dodging axe blows from her uncle, and though he was but an ant next to the giant he faced, Annise swore he stood at least a head taller than before, his armor looking awkwardly small. She shook off the thought and raced after her men, who were closing in on the Ice Lord.

He reached out to touch them.

"Ahhh!" Dietrich yelled, dodging the touch, slicing off one of the Ice Lord's fingers, which shattered when it hit the ground. The others shouted, too, and then Annise found herself releasing a war cry, swinging Evenstar wildly, hitting any piece of ice she could reach. One of her soldiers, who was no longer a man, but ice, crumbled to the ground. She accidentally brushed up against Sir Jonius's thick coat, but he barely noticed, so intent was he on raking his claws across the Ice Lord's legs.

"Retreat!" Dietrich shouted. The group turned sharply, like they were each a part of one creature, Sir Jonius included, and sprinted toward the Imposter King. Annise glanced back. As she had hoped, the Ice Lord, enraged at having had chunks of his legs slashed off, dove after them, long icy fingers outstretched, reaching for them. Reaching for her...

Annise threw herself to the side at the same time many of the others did. As she tumbled, she saw that one man had been a beat behind, turning to ice midway through his dive, shattering as his frozen body hit the ground.

Sir Craig.

A pang of sadness hit Annise, but she shook it away as she rolled to a stop. Now was not the time for mourning. Not yet.

She watched as the Ice Lord's momentum carried him toward his master, Lord Griswold himself. The metal giant tried to dodge out of the way, but his size became his disadvantage. He was too slow by half, the Ice Lord's fingers brushing across his calf.

Annise held her breath. Nothing happened, the metal gleaming in the sun. *No,* Annise thought. She was out of answers, out of ideas. How did one defeat a man made of metal, and a giant no less?

Her breath rushed out of her as she saw it: a streak of white appeared on his calf, spreading across the metal, rushing up his legs, along his torso, and into his chest. Her uncle stared down, his metal mouth gaping open in surprise. His arms froze, and then his mouth too, still open. The rest of his head was consumed last.

Tarin swung Morningstar across Lord Griswold's frozen boots, shearing through the ice like it was nothing but wet paper. His giant leg crumpled and the weight of the rest of him jerked to the side, snapping his other leg in half. When his body hit the ground, it shattered into a million pieces, a mountain of crushed ice.

The Ice Lord seemed so shocked by the turn of events that he didn't even bother to defend himself as Tarin smashed Morningstar through him next, bringing him to his knees before landing a final blow to his skull. He, too, cracked and joined the icy rubble that had once been his master.

While the few survivors watched, Tarin brought his weapon down again and again and again. No one tried to stop him. Annise turned and walked away, unable to watch the spectacle any longer, going to comfort her aunt, who was sitting on the ground cradling a chunk of ice resembling Sir Craig's head.

PART IV

Rhea ● Grey ● Raven
Roan ● Jai ● The Beggar
Annise

Though the fatemarked shall, at times, be pulled
toward their individual destinies with such force they
will feel powerless to stop their momentum, in the
end they will each have the same choice we all have: to
act for good or evil.
The Western Oracle

Thirty-Four

The Western Kingdom, Knight's End
Rhea Loren

Ennis had painted her into a corner, and though at times Rhea was a wildcat, there was no clawing and biting her way out of this one.

He had chosen death, and she would give it to him and her people.

She was no coward, not anymore. No, that girl was trapped in Rhea's past, a jumble of old crinkled fading memories: huddled in the crypts with the dead, cursing Grey Arris for abandoning her; sobbing as they ran through the castle, slipping on blood and tripping on corpses; quaking beneath the blade of the now-dead Fury who took her beauty and gave her strength; in the tower, just before the battle, soaking her dress with tears, feeling so utterly alone.

Never again.

Ennis had requested not to be bound, but to be free at the end, and she had not begrudged him this honor. He stood before her on the execution slab, his chest bare. "Do you have any final words?" she asked. A hushed silence fell over the audience, as they craned their necks forward to hear what the dead man would say.

Ennis looked at her without fear, without anger or malice. Only with sadness. "Only some advice, my queen," he said. *"Fire breeds fire and even a single spark can birth an inferno.'"*

Rhea immediately recognized the quote from a favorite book of hers as a child, *The Brave Mouse*. She remembered how many times she asked Ennis to read it to her, and though he must've been bored with the same old story, he never refused her. In the tale, the mouse was forced to choose between saving his one true love from a fire, or sacrificing her to save the rest of the mouse village. In the end, the mouse watched his love vanish into the flames while he ran to save the village with a bucket of water. Once the fire was extinguished, he drowned himself out of grief. A morbid tale, to be sure, but one that Rhea always thought was so romantic, especially because the girl mouse ended up surviving with very bad burns, unbeknownst to the brave mouse, who was already dead.

Appropriate for the occasion, Rhea thought, but she wouldn't let mere words pierce the armor she'd donned that morning.

"Wise words, Cousin Ennis," she said. "But in this story, I am the inferno." *Rhea the Inferno. Add that to your list of names for your great queen.*

The crowd grew restless as Ennis continued to meet her eyes, refusing to do the decent thing and look away. *So be it.*

Rhea raised her blade and plunged it into his heart.

His eyes widened and he gasped, clutching at the hilt, but Rhea didn't see him fall. She'd already slipped the knife—which was oozing with blood—inside her hip scabbard. She turned to face her people. A tear crept from the corner of her eye, rolling down her cheek. "Today my heart is heavy. My cousin was a good man, a servant of Wrath, but during the battle his actions were misguided. He believed my life was more important than the lifeblood of the realm." On the edge of her vision, Ennis's body stopped shuddering, going still. "To that I say nay. I am but one woman, a mere mortal, while the realm is eternal. Wrath is eternal, and God's will shall be done long after I am gone. So to all of you I say, serve me, yes, but only to the extent that in serving me you serve the realm. My dear cousin forgot that, and it cost him his honor and his life. The seventh heaven will be barred to him, but I am hopeful he will gain entrance later, and that one day we will meet again, in Wrath's holy presence."

"Wrath be with you, Queen Rhea," the people said as one.

She nodded solemnly, pressing her fingertips to her lips. She kissed them and then turned to close Ennis's eyes.

That's when she heard a voice carry through the crowd. "Sister, what have you done?"

The voice was too deep to be Bea or Leo's, and who else would call her sister? One of her cousins perhaps? But when she spun around, her eyes narrowing, squinting across the brightly lit courtyard, she saw someone else making their way through the human tide.

Her heart rattled in her chest. "Father?" she whispered.

But no, he was too young, without the streaks of gray in his hair nor crow's feet on the edges of his eyes. He was tall and built like a bowstring. His long hair reminded Rhea of her mother's.

As the man swam through the crowd, Rhea's furia crowded closer together to block his passage. The blond man with her father's features stopped. "Rhea. It's me. It's your brother, Roan. At long last, I've come home."

Rhea was just a suckling babe when her brother had vanished mysteriously, sixteen long years ago, at the age of only two. Three years after that, her mother had killed herself.

Her father had rarely spoken to Rhea of Roan or her mother. And when he did, the words had seemed to choke out of him. Thus, much of the information she had gathered about her lost sibling was gleaned from rumors. A particularly bratty lordling had told Rhea that Roan had run away from home because his parents were as cold as snakes. Rhea had been so angry she'd sputtered and fumed and, eventually, walked away from him. It didn't even matter that the story was clearly untrue—what two-year-old child could run away from home? That night, she'd hidden a beehive under the boy's bed. His screams could be heard throughout the entire palace. But the most popular opinion was that Roan had been kidnapped by a man from the south—a gray-skinned Dreadnoughter named Markin Swansea, who'd been a friend of her mother's. They said he was secretly a Southron spy who wanted to destroy the royal line by removing the eldest heir. There was even talk of murder.

As far as Rhea's mother went, some said Cecilia Loren had gone mad after her son's disappearance, becoming a raving woman with little control over her own actions. Others said Cecilia Loren had stabbed herself after receiving a message while in court. Rhea didn't know what to believe, and she'd long ago given up on knowing the truth.

Sometimes the truth is as impossible to reach out and grab as a star in the heavens, Rhea mused now.

She waited on her throne, alone, save for the blank-faced furia lining the walls. They weren't very good company, so Rhea remained silent, lost in her own thoughts. She'd only been three when her mother had died, so any memories she had of her were fuzzy around the edges, like a piece of parchment soaked in water and dried in the sun. But she'd always remember her golden hair, the way it cascaded around her shoulders like a sunlit waterfall. In her faint memories, her mother was an angel.

The door opened and she shook her thoughts away. *Mother is dead. Father is dead. I am alive. And this man claiming to be my long-lost brother, Roan? He is a ghost.*

And yet when she saw his lustrous blond hair, all she could think about was her mother.

She tried to focus as he was escorted through the court. As she'd instructed, he was not in chains, permitted to walk freely like any other petitioner. If this was truly her brother…

She shook away the thought.

One of the furia stuck out an arm to stop him when he reached the steps up to the throne. "Sister," the man said.

The furia kicked out the back of his knees, so he was forced to kneel. "Your Highness," she corrected. Rhea raised an eyebrow. Soon the furia would need to choose a new Fury, or even all Three, considering the other two still had not been heard from. The warrior with the thick red eyebrows had potential.

The man claiming to be Roan grimaced, but didn't cry out. He looked up at Rhea. "Your Highness, Queen Rhea, my sister, I implore you to listen to what I have to say."

"Implore me?" Rhea said. "You claim to be my brother, the lost prince of the west? How daft do you think I am?"

"If you will only hear me out. They say you are righteous, sister."

"Stop calling me that," Rhea growled. But those eyes, as blue and fathomless as the crystal-blue sea, just like her father's had been. They were unmistakable.

"You cannot fight the truth."

"I *am* the truth. I have conquered the northern armada and Summoned Wrathos from the sea."

"So I've heard. That is good. Lord Griswold is an evil man."

"I don't know you. Your opinion is of no import to me."

The man sighed deeply. "You are right. I have bungled this introduction, badly I'm afraid. Let me start at the beginning."

Though Rhea was tempted to stop him before he started, she didn't, and once he'd begun, she couldn't bring herself to do anything but listen as he told his tale. If it was a lie, it was well-spun. He told her how their mother had given him over to the Dreadnoughter, Markin Swansea, charging him with keeping Roan safe. How he'd grown up on the streets of Calypso after running away from his guardian at age eight. How he'd contracted the plague, but somehow managed to fight off the infection and escape Dragon's Breath, washing up on the eastern shores. Then came his chance meeting with Prince Gareth Ironclad—Rhea couldn't help but lift her eyebrows at that part—and his brief stay in Ferria, the Iron City, before marching to Raider's Pass and participating in a bloody battle with the Gärics in the north. Not Lord Griswold, but Archer and Annise, the son and daughter of the Dread King, both of whom were her cousins. And, finally, how he'd departed in defeat, fording the

Snake River and fighting through the Tangle to eventually arrive in Knight's End.

When he'd finished, Rhea brought her hands together in a slow clap. "Bravo," she said. "But if I'd wanted fiction, I'd have visited my personal library."

"You think I'm lying?"

"Either that or you were born with an addled mind."

"Please," Roan said. "I came here in good faith."

"Why?" Rhea said. "To claim the throne for your own? Even if you are my brother, you are no heir, not anymore. I am the anointed queen, Rhea the Righteous, defender of the west. You have no claim here."

"That's not why I'm here," Roan said.

Rhea stared at him, considering. "There was a crucial element missing from your story. An unanswered question."

The man nodded. "Yes."

"Why did my mother, Cecilia Loren, send you south with Markin Swansea? You said she charged the Dreadnoughter with keeping you safe. Why would you need to be protected when I did not? What made you different?"

Instead of answering directly, he said, "I came here to visit the Western Archives, not to steal your crown."

Rhea frowned. The faces of the two dead archivists floated across her mind. The burnt documents. *There are no coincidences.* "For what purpose? Tell me before I send you to the gallows."

"Research."

Her frown deepened. "Another vague answer. My patience is growing thin. Another one will be the end of you."

Roan sighed, his lips pursing. He seemed to be considering something. "Sister, I am tired of lies and secrets. So tired. All I want is answers. I want to know who I am, why I grew up in

445

Calypso while you were here in Knight's End. I want to know what my true purpose is."

"And you believe the Western Archives can tell you all that?" She was missing something.

"Yes. All I want is information on the Western Oracle."

It took all of Rhea's concentration to keep her expression steady, though underneath her skin her blood was rushing through her veins. "The Western Oracle was a dark sorceress. Why would you seek to read of her dark magic?"

"Because of the fatemarks," Roan said. His eyes were boring into hers, searching for something.

"You mean *sin*marks, I presume." *Fatemarks fatemarks fatemarks...* The word echoed in her ears.

"That is the name you give them now. But it wasn't always that way."

Rhea had discovered as much in her own research, but how had this man come to that same knowledge? "Let's say I believe everything you've told me, though that is an enormous assumption. What does any of it have to do with understanding your purpose? What does your quest offer me?"

He closed his eyes, holding them like that for a while, so long that Rhea wondered whether he'd fallen asleep. When he opened them, his eyes flashed with certainty. He'd made a decision. "Do you have a torch?" he asked.

She narrowed her eyes. "Why?"

"I want to show you something."

"Bring fire," Rhea said, and several furia rushed to obey her order.

A torch was lit and brought near. "Closer," Roan said. He unbuttoned his linen shirt, pulling the wings back to reveal a smooth, muscular chest. Something sparked, and bright lines began to form, curling, drawing themselves into his flesh.

Three leaves attached to a single stem.

He was marked.

Rhea breathed in, holding the air in her lungs, her eyes unblinking.

The mysteries of Rhea's past were connected, one by one, forming a single, clear picture. She released her breath and stood.

"Bring the sinmarked to my personal quarters. Leave us alone."

Despite the harshness of her words, she knew the truth:

He was her lost brother, Roan Loren, the true heir to the western throne.

My throne.

Thirty-Five
The Western Kingdom, the Dead Isles
Grey Arris

Grey's hand was sweaty, and, instinctively, he reached for his other hand, desperate for something to hold on to, to steady himself. When his fingers closed around the ruined stump of his arm, something bent inside of him. A part of him that used to be broken. Perhaps still was broken. It was hard for him to tell anymore.

Somewhere outside the stone building, wind howled. Rain pounded. Waves crashed on a dead and uncaring shore.

"Don't do this," Grey said. "Kill me, but not in front of Shae. She's been through enough."

"We have to know the truth," the Fury said, and Grey was surprised to get an answer from the hard-faced woman. She sounded different, somehow. More desperate. More urgent.

"Why? Why do you care about Shae's mark?"

"*Sin*mark," the Fury reminded him.

"She's just a girl. She's no threat."

The Fury whirled on him, grabbing his cheeks between her icy fingers. Squeezing. "You know nothing."

Grey couldn't argue with that. "Then tell me what you mean."

A thump resounded from somewhere above them. *Are we underground?* They must be, for the stone structure was only one level atop the cliff. The Fury's gaze flitted to the ceiling, boring holes in it. "Hurry!" she said, dragging him forward by the arm.

Somewhere further along the dim corridor, the other Fury also urged them to make haste.

Dozens of furia ran down an intersecting tunnel before flying up a steep set of stairs that winded away. They carried weapons.

Thump!

"What is happening?" Grey asked, trying to squirm away from the Fury.

Thump!

The Fury turned quickly, her arm lashing out and backhanding Grey across the face. Stunned, Grey spat out a glob of blood.

The other Fury ran back, grabbing him under his other arm. He kicked and fought every step, but they carried him down the hall, shoving him roughly into a room. Wall sconces blazed brightly from each corner, intersecting in the center of the space.

Where

Where she

Where she hung.

Shae. *Oh gods.*

The chains were clasped to each wrist, dangling from iron hooks pounded into the stone ceiling. The flesh around the

449

chains was puffy and red, her skin raw-looking. Her chin was pressed against her chest, her eyes closed, her strawberry-gold hair oily and stringy, covering part of her face. She was stripped to naught but a thin white slip, which was soaked, revealing her pale, skinny arms and legs. There were angry burns on one arm, and red slashes on the other.

The rest of the small stone prison was empty, save for a small table with a book lying on it, flipped open to a page littered with scrawls of dark, shaky handwriting. Grey immediately noticed a drawing of a symbol:

It was like half of a broken key—the end you would push into a lock first.

The same strange symbol had been drawn in ink on various parts of Shae's body—her palms, her knees, her feet. Which, he now realized, was also drawn next to the mark she was born with, clearly visible on her palm due to the torchlight illuminating her skin. What he'd always thought was a golden crown attached to some sort of broken scepter had really been something else entirely.

The other half of a broken key, now completed by the ink on her hand.

It was exactly the same as the key he'd imagined in the stars.

"Shae," Grey said, taking a step toward his sister.

Strong arms yanked him back. Held him. His sister didn't stir, motionless. *Is she already dead?* Grey thought, a slash of icy dread wrenching through him.

"Do you know how the Dead Isles got their name?" one of the Furies asked.

"I don't care about—"

"It was the original Furies," she continued, as if he hadn't spoken. "Do you think we were always the undisputed

450

priestesses of Wrath in the west? No. Nothing worthwhile is ever easy. There were those who opposed my sisters, the strongest of which was a group of men called the Seekers who believed women were inferior to men. Can you believe such a notion? Anyway, there was a battle, and those who came before me and my sisters *won*. They slaughtered the Seekers—all of them. But there were others like them, and the furia needed to send a message. So the first Furies brought the bodies of their enemies to these very isles, and called upon Wrath's blessing. Now the souls of the Seekers haunt this place, a warning to those who think to defy us."

Grey shook his head. It sounded like a bedtime story. A bad bedtime story. "What does that have to do with me?"

"Because from that day forward, when Wrath blessed these islands, any who died upon their shores was cursed to live on through eternity, chained to the second heaven, a fate even worse than the first heaven. When you die, you will receive the same fate."

Grey had had enough of threats. "Shae!" he shouted again.

His sister opened her eyes slowly, her eyelids fluttering. "I hate the dreams the most," she said. "I don't want to dream anymore."

She was clearly confused. How long had she been chained in this room? When had she last eaten, tasted water on her lips? "I'm here, Shae," Grey said. "I'm really here." Tears dripped from his eyelids.

Shae shook her head. "Go away. I don't want to hope anymore."

She's been dreaming of me, Grey realized. *That I would come to rescue her. I'm her hope.*

But what if I'm not good enough? What if I'm not strong enough? What if my parents were wrong to trust me with her life, her secrets?

Another heavy crash from above drew him away from his insecurities and back to reality. All his doubts didn't matter, not in this moment. He would save her or die trying.

"Tell us about your sinmark," the Fury instructed Shae. "Or your brother dies."

A hand wrapped around his neck, a blade pressed to his skin. He could feel his pulse pounding against the cold metal.

Shae blinked. "Grey?"

"I'm here."

"You came."

"I came."

"Your hand."

"They took it, but they couldn't stop me."

"I'm—I'm sorry."

Fresh tears bloomed. "No. You have nothing to be sorry about. This was my fault, you hear? You've done nothing wrong. Nothing."

"Grey, I'm scared."

Thump! Thump! Thump!

"Tell us what we need to know," the Fury commanded. The blade cut into his skin, and Grey felt warmth run down his neck.

"My mark doesn't do anything," Shae said, a plea in her voice. "It's never done anything."

"She's telling the truth," Grey said, trying not to move, not to press his skin further into the blade.

"One swipe and he's dead," the Fury said. "Would you let your brother die, Shae? It will be you killing him."

"No!" Shae screamed. "He didn't *do* anything. Let him go. I will tell you everything! I will tell you about the dreams."

Thump! Thump! Thump! CRASH!

Grey didn't have time to process his sister's words, as shouts poured from above. There was the sound of steel on steel, the clop of what sounded like hooves on stone, and then more thuds and thumps.

"Dammit!" one of the Furies yelled. "The door has been breached. We have to help our sisters. Leave them. We'll return."

The Fury holding the knife to Grey's throat growled her frustration, but then drew her blade away, leaving him gasping. She kicked him hard from behind and he sprawled to his knees. And then they were gone, slamming the door behind them. A key turned in a lock.

Grey fought to his feet, ignoring the screams of battle, the clash of metal, the cries of pain. Only she mattered. Only Shae. "We have to get you out of here," he said.

"They have the only key," she said. "They took it with them."

"There must be another way."

"There is," she said.

"What?"

"Pull me down," she said. "By the feet."

"Shae—"

"Do it, hurry, the dead are coming!"

The cries were closer now, and Grey swore he heard the whinny of a horse. The dead? What was she talking about? Surely she didn't believe the Fury's faerytales...

"They've been attacking for days, Grey. The dead horsemen. I've heard the furia talking about them. They're scared of them. But they've never gotten inside. Until now. We have to go. Now!"

Grey bit the back of his hand, shocked by the potency of his sister's delusions. He couldn't do this, could he? He knew he was out of options. It was the only choice. The shackles were tight on her wrists, but not *that* tight. She was all skin and bones. "I don't want to hurt you."

"You could never hurt me, Grey," she said, and he was shocked at how grown up she sounded. How strong. *Where has my baby sister gone?* Grey wondered.

He grabbed her ankles, taking a deep breath.

Something pounded on the door, hard. *Tha-thump!*

"Grey!" Shae cried.

"I'm sorry," he said.

And then he pulled.

She screamed, but when he stopped pulling, she shouted at him to "Keep going! Keep going!" He gripped her feet harder and yanked them down, shutting his mind off to his sister's cries, which were equal parts pain and determination. She'd been through hell and back already, but Grey couldn't give up on her now.

Her body stretched, and he feared he would pull her in half, but then she shot downwards like a dropped stone, crashing into him, her knee slamming into his abdomen, her head bashing his shoulder, her foot stepping on the inside of his ankle.

The pain was nothing as he held her, as he wept into her hair, as she cried into his drenched, filthy shirt. Her wrists were ripped and bleeding, as were her knuckles, but she was free.

Tha-thump!

The hit to the door was so hard it rattled the whole room, a stark reminder to Grey that they were far from safe. Clearly, it wasn't the Furies, who would've simply used the key to get in. "What are they?" Grey said.

Shae rolled off him and said, "Get behind me."

Who is this girl? "What? No." Grey stood and tried to push her behind him as the door shook once more. Whatever was out there was strong. Grey didn't know if they were dead horsemen or something else, but he knew they would need to move fast as soon as that door came down.

"Grey," Shae said, touching his hand.

He ignored her, his mind searching for a solution. When the door came down, which it certainly would, there'd be a moment of confusion. It might be the only moment they'd get. "By the side of the door," Grey said. "Get ready to run." Shae was barefoot, but it didn't matter. Getting away from whatever was beating on the door was the priority.

"Grey," she said again. This time she touched his cheek, steering his gaze toward her. "Trust me."

Trust her with what? He tried to pull her toward the side of the door, but instead she stepped in front of him. "Shae, what are you—"

"Make yourself as small as you can," she said.

Tha-thump!

This time, the stones above the door cracked.

Tha-thump!

Grey tried to grab his sister, but she was slippery, pulling away, maintaining her position in front of him.

Tha-thump!

Rock dust rained from the ceiling and the door released a mournful groan.

Tha-thump!

The hinges snapped and the door began to fall. Grey dragged his sister back by the waist, but she stepped on his feet so he couldn't swing her around. The heavy iron door slammed into the ground, the clang reverberating throughout the room.

They both froze.

Its skin was like stretched white silk, icy-looking, glowing unnaturally. Its head was that of a man, but with completely white eyes, like it was blind. Its hair was roiling waves crashing on its white-rock scalp. Its arms and torso were muscular, a long stone sword gripped tightly by white-knuckled fingers. Blood dripped from the blade.

Beneath its torso, its body transitioned to that of a pale-white horse, with a broad, horizontal back and undercarriage held up by four powerful hooved legs.

As Grey stared over his sister's shoulder in fascinated horror, he realized he could see right through the creature, faintly, like peering through foggy glass.

Not dead horsemen, he realized. Dead *horse* men. Suddenly all the ghost stories about the Dead Isles didn't seem so farfetched. Was this one of the Seekers the Fury had spoken of?

Without taking his eyes off the man…horse…thing, Grey tried to nudge his sister toward the side of the room. Perhaps if it really was blind, they might be able to slip past it and into the corridor. She reached back and grabbed his hair, pulling it. Her eyes found his, boring into him.

Get behind me. Trust me. Make yourself small.

Grey knew he owed his sister more than he could ever repay her. His life, yes. And certainly her trust. Slowly, he ducked behind her, bringing his legs together and squeezing his arms in front of him.

The horse man stepped forward, his hooves clopping on the stone. He stopped so close to Shae that Grey could have reached between her legs and touched its leg, though he wondered whether his hand would go right through it. The creature let out a breath that sounded more horse than man, one of its hooves pawing at the rock floor.

With a squeal, it turned and departed, charging through the doorway.

Shae turned, her face as calm as a flower on a spring day. "Now we can go," she said.

As Shae led him into the corridor, Grey didn't demand an explanation for any of it. There was no time, and anyway, he didn't know where to start. His sister was changing, becoming something...different...but then again so was he.

They ducked back into the room when they saw three dead horse men filling the hallway to the right.

Grey also saw the bodies. The furia, their red robes flung haphazardly about their bodies. Had any of them survived? If fierce warriors like them were defeated so easily, what would that mean for Grey and his sister?

Nothing, Grey thought. *We make our own path.* It wasn't until he thought it that he truly believed it. No longer would they swim with the current, nor against it. They would swim across it, and together they would reach dry land.

"The way out is blocked," Shae said.

"Then we'll find another way. A better way."

Shae's eyes locked on his and she nodded. "Follow me."

I will follow you anywhere.

She was about to leave again, when she paused, taking two quick steps over to the table. She picked up the book with the markings, tucking it to her chest, and then returned to Grey's side.

Gripping the book in one hand, she tiptoed out into the corridor and turned left, back toward where Grey had been held captive. Grey stalked after her, sidestepping a body. One of the Furies. The one who had taken his hand, who had threatened to slit his throat. She was missing both arms. A stone sword was buried in her chest.

Grey moved on, glancing behind him once as they turned the corner.

One of the horse men was looking down the hall.

He shouted something in a strange language, and dozens of hoofbeats rang out behind them.

"Hurry!" Grey said, pushing his sister in the small of her back, adding momentum to her strides. Ahead of them, the path seemed to dead end, but Shae didn't try to slow her strides. At the last second, she pulled him to the right, into a narrow gash in the wall. They were forced to shimmy side to side to make their way through.

An arm chased after them, leading with a stone sword. It flew toward Grey's head and he flinched back, but then it stopped with the point a fingernail away from his eye. The horse man screamed something nonsensical and jabbed again, but Grey had already moved further away, and again the sword came up short. His horse hips were too wide to breach the narrow space. Perhaps it was an intentional part of the building's design, by whomever had built it.

When Grey looked back, the horse man was gone, off to find another way to get to them.

Shae reached a thin alcove and turned right, disappearing. "Wait," Grey said, and her hand shot out. He reached for it and she pulled him onto a set of narrow stairs, which seemed to go up and up forever into darkness.

They climbed blindly, single file. With each step, Grey expected to hear the scream of the horse men, feel a stone blade in his back. But he knew his mind was his worst enemy—the dead couldn't follow them through this path. Somehow the stone stopped them.

Finally, when his legs were beyond exhaustion, they reached something solid. Together, they pressed all three of their hands against it and pushed as one. Slowly, slowly, the stone barrier slid away, revealing a crack of gray sky and swirling mist.

They stole onto the edge of a night-black cliff, high above the ocean. Below, angry waves smashed against the impenetrable island of the dead. The drop-off was sheer—there was no way to climb down. Grey realized it was the same side of the island he'd arrived on. He even spotted part of his small boat wrecked on a jagged rock sticking up like the claw of a sea monster. The only advantage was that this particular cliff hung out over the water, somewhat clear of the rocky shoreline. But was it far enough?

Horse men screamed from somewhere through the mist, and they whirled around, searching the rocky landscape. "They're coming," Shae said. "I can't hide you forever."

Grey still didn't understand exactly how his little sister had done what she had done, but he didn't need to. Not anymore. "We have to swim," he said.

A glowing white figure emerged from the mist, then another. Dozens more followed, screaming, brandishing stone swords.

They turned back toward the ocean, and Grey grabbed his sister's hand. There was no other choice; the overhanging cliff would have to be far enough over the water, else they were dead. "Ready?"

She nodded, her jaw set. Grey knew his sister was scared of heights *and* water. But that was a different girl. This version of Shae had been through so much more terror that a leap from a cliff into the ocean was nothing.

They leapt, their arms and legs wind-milling.

Wind and rain pelted their faces.

Waves roared, rushing up to meet them.

And then the sea swallowed them whole.

In the depths of the sea under the cloud-gray sky, Grey immediately lost all sense of direction. He also lost Shae's hand when they plunged underwater, and now he frantically searched, flailing his arms from side to side.

He thought he felt his fingers brush up against her, but then she was gone again.

On and on he searched, reaching into murk and gloom, his desperation growing as his lungs began to burn. He couldn't lose her now, not after everything they'd both been through.

For the first time in his life, he prayed. Not to Wrath—the vengeful god of the furia—but to whatever power created the sun and the moons and the stars. And the ocean. *Please. Release her. Give her back to me. Spit her out.*

He couldn't hold his breath any longer, and he kicked hard in the direction he thought looked slightly lighter, a muted shade of gray. Water threatened to tear open his mouth and pour inside. But still he kicked, even when he felt a dark shadow loom to the side and he was thrown against a rock. He clawed at the stone, pulling himself up, up, up, finally breaching the surface, his pale hand clutching the jagged stone like the edge of a lifeboat.

His lips murmured his prayer, even as the waves pounded him, crashing on his head, knocking him to and fro like a shattered piece of driftwood. *Please. Release her.* And then he spoke the two words he'd been thinking from the moment his sister was taken.

"Take me instead," he whispered to the wind. Louder: "Take me, not her!" Shouted at the top of his lungs, his voice rising over the pounding waves and howling wind and rainfall. "TAKE ME!"

Arms grabbed him from behind, clinging to his waist. He looked back and there she was. Shae. Wearing that same determined expression. "Don't go," she said. "Don't let them take you."

He wasn't ashamed to cry. Not now, not ever again. The tears poured from his eyes, mixing with the rain and seawater. "Never," he said. "You're all I've got."

And then he shoved off from the jagged rock, kicking as hard as he could against the current, which threatened to sweep them back toward the island. Shae clutched his waist, and he swam with one arm, fighting past the breakers, looking back only once the powerful current had released them.

High on the cliffs, the dead stood, watching. Waiting. There were dozens of horse men, and instinctively Grey knew they were unsatisfied, despite having feasted on the souls of the furia, who, according to the Fury's story, would rise again to haunt the isles. They were hungry, ravenous, because they had lost two souls from their shores.

Grey turned away and didn't look back again.

All Grey knew was that he needed to follow the sun. He wasn't sure exactly how far the Dead Isles were from the coastline, but thus far he'd seen nothing but endless ocean ever since the misty islands vanished from view. The sun had reached its peak long ago, and was now drifting toward the horizon.

Grey was chasing it, but he was swiftly falling behind.

At some point, Shae fell asleep, leaving Grey to drag her body through the choppy water. At some point, Grey became too weary to kick, to swim, letting their bodies drift with the current, which was moving swiftly south. He had seen maps of the Four Kingdoms, and he was fairly certain the Phanecian peninsula eventually jutted out, which could mean they would run directly into it. But that was almost certainly days away, if not weeks. They would die of thirst or starvation long before that.

So he conserved his energy for a while, and then swam again, pushing eastward. In her sleep, Shae's body was as heavy as a corpse, a thought that made Grey want to wake her up, just to be certain she was alive. But he didn't, letting her sleep. Anyway, he could feel her warm exhalations on his cheeks.

The sun stole the daylight, and night descended like a scythe. The moons appeared, first the one southerners worshipped as Luahi, a green fully-formed orb, and then Ruaho, the fierce red god, naught but a red sliver on this particular night. Regardless, neither moon was willing to do more than cast a shaky pathway of light in the wrong direction. Grey tried to keep his bearings, but soon became disoriented as exhaustion and fatigue set in. He stopped swimming, uncertain as to whether he was moving west, east, north, south, or, more likely, in circles.

His vision began to blur, and the thought of sleep was a powerful rope, gripping him, pulling him. Tempting him. *Can't sleep*, he thought. Sleep was death. *I'll just close my eyes for a few moments. Rest them.* He did, and it felt so good. The ocean was gentle now, rocking him, caressing his ears with a sweet lullaby.

When he opened his eyes he could see a face, distant at first, and then moving closer. It was familiar, her smile like a golden sunrise, her eyes like the bottoms of blue-crystal decanters.

Princess Rhea smiled at him, and he wanted to smile back, but his lips were too weary. He pulled back in horror as her lips turned to snakes, her teeth to fangs, her eyes to red beads ringed with fire.

He screamed, but his cry was lost in the water, which was all around his face, stinging his eyes, infiltrating his nose, his mouth.

His head burst from the water and he coughed, choking for a while until the ocean was dispelled from his lungs. *I fell asleep*, he realized. His vision of Rhea was a nightmare and he'd sunk under the water and—

Shae.

For a moment, he felt sheer panic, but it quickly subsided when he saw her. His sister, somehow, someway, was lying on her back, floating nearby. She was still asleep, her face as peaceful as a moonbeam.

Shaking the cobwebs away, Grey kicked over to her. She stirred when he tucked his hand under her knees and his stump behind her head, using his legs to tread water. Her eyes fluttered open, blinking several times before focusing on him. A smile creased her lips. "Grey," she said. Her eyes closed and she slept once more.

Grey stayed like that for a long time, watching his sister sleep. Though they were miles away from shore and might not even survive the night, he wasn't sad or scared or lonely. No, they were together again, and that was all that mattered.

He kept his sister afloat for as long as he could bear, until weariness took him and his eyelids refused to obey any longer, until his mind and the world spun in tandem, until an enormous shadow descended o'er him and he knew death had found them both, until he felt himself sinking, sinking, sinking, the water closing over his chin, his lips, his nose, his eyes, his head, until the angels of mercy murmured from the heavens and reached down their strong arms and scooped his soul up, lifting him higher, higher, higher to the sky above.

And, in the end, he smiled.

Thirty-Six
The Southern Empire, the Scarra Desert
Raven Sandes

Guta was still apologizing profusely as they departed Kesh. "She was with me for nigh on two years," he said. "She gave no indication of violence."

Raven whirled around and squeezed the man's arm. "We know. It's not your fault. You bear no blame."

His quick-to-smile lips were pulled into a tight line, his eyes fierce. "I have heard of those who cried tears of joy when they spotted Kesh in the distance, only to find it was a trick of the light, a desert mirage. Those men and women died wishing they'd found this place. Then there are others who could see our oasis, but fell before they made it. But thousands of others have eaten with us, slept in our huts, cooled themselves under our palms. We are a single candle of hope in an infinite sea of sand. Our

465

reputation is everything, and we have failed the most important women in the Four Kingdoms."

"You couldn't have known what that woman would do."

When questioned, Guta had been forthcoming. The would-be assassin's name, at least according to her, was Baj, and she'd been nothing but an excellent employee of Guta's ever since she'd arrived almost two years earlier, requesting a job.

And yet, she'd tried to stab Fire through the eye in the dead of night.

Guta said, "I will release my entire household and begin anew. Each new employee will be screened by my most trusted advisors in Calyp. I will earn back the trust I have lost."

"That's really not nec—"

Fire appeared just then, leading her guanik, and Raven stopped at the look in her sister's eyes. Stalwart. Weary, but alive. Fearless, despite what she'd told Raven only a day earlier.

I feel as if an arach is nipping at my heels and if I don't keep moving it will eat me alive.

Raven had made a joke in response, not taking her sister's words seriously enough. *She knew*, Raven thought. *Somehow, she knew.*

A roiling stew of guilt churned in Raven's gut. She was the one who'd convinced Fire to stay another night, despite her sister's instincts. She was the one who'd almost gotten her killed.

"Guta," Fire said now. "Thank you for your hospitality. It is unmatched in all of the south."

Guta offered a short bow. "A full investigation will be conducted. I am sorry for—"

"Enough," Fire said. "Your apologies are as unnecessary as they are sincere. I trust whatever actions you decide to take, but know that I believe Kesh will continue to be a torch of safety and hope in the Scarra." Guta opened his mouth to speak again, but Fire raised a hand. "Say no more. You have my blessing as we depart rested and replenished."

Finally, a thin smile found its way back onto the small man's lips, though it didn't carry the genuineness it had when they first arrived.

The guanero gathered in a protective circle around Fire and Raven as they mounted up and rode back out into the desert.

"I should have trusted you," Raven said.

"You have. You are here, by my side."

"But I advised you to linger when you believed riding on was the better option."

"Just because my paranoia was validated by the assassin doesn't mean it wasn't paranoia. That woman could've attempted to take my life the first night, had she wanted to."

"If not for Goggin refusing to leave her side, she might've."

Goggin overheard his name. "I should've throttled her rather than spun her," he said, shaking his head.

"Stop. Both of you. You're as bad as Guta," Fire said. "Like him, you couldn't have known what she would do."

"But *you* did," Raven insisted.

"I didn't. I only had a sinking feeling in my stomach. But I've had it since I made the decision to ride to war."

Raven recalled what her sister had said about feeling like she was born to be a weapon, and nothing more. Those words, even if they were wrong, made Raven want to protect her younger sister the same way she'd always protected Whisper.

The sun goddess stretched above them and they rode on, due west, carried on an endless tide of sand. The wind, thankfully, was at their backs.

"You saved my life," Fire said a while later.

"I'm a light sleeper."

"So am I, but I didn't awaken."

Raven shrugged. "You're my baby sister, so I'm obligated to protect you. And you happen to be the empress, so as an honorary member of the guanero, I am sworn by oath to save your life if I have the opportunity."

Fire's lip twitched. "Oh really? So it was just duty that drove your valor?"

"And Whisper would never forgive me if I let you die on my watch."

Fire's smile faded. "Gods, what are we going to do with her?"

"Survive," Raven said. "Protect her from this world. Defeat Faata and defend our borders."

"And what of the east and west and north? Long have they coveted the south. Eventually, they will come, whether it's the Ironclads crossing Dragon Bay or the Lorens from the Burning Sea or the Gärics sailing down the Spear. The Scarra can only protect us for so long."

"By then, our dragons will be full size. Our enemies will flee from us in fear. And if they don't, they will burn."

Fire nodded at that. Burning was one thing she understood all too well.

They rode on for a while longer without speaking, though it was a comfortable silence, as only one can be between sisters. Fire finally said, "I fear the assassin was one of our own."

Raven flinched at the notion. "You mean a Calypsian?"

Fire nodded. "There are those who long to sit on the Southron throne, to usurp the power our family has held for many generations. They could have assassins in various places where we'd least expect it, lying in wait. That woman was in Kesh for nearly two years biding her time on the slim chance that I might eventually pass through the desert. Our enemies are as patient as spiders."

Raven said, "She had the Calypsian look, but she could've been paid by anyone."

"Even Faata?"

"No," Raven replied quickly. "He wouldn't. Not like that. He will protect his lands, his way of life, but he won't murder his own daughter in cold blood." Raven hated the doubt in her own voice, hated that the man she'd grown up with had become a monster in her eyes.

For the next three nights, they marched until both moons were high overhead, casting dueling swords of light across the desert. They slept briefly, rising before Surai rose from the west.

No one grumbled or complained, not even Goggin. Nor Raven, though she could see the weariness creeping along the ragged line of soldiers behind them. When they did stop, everyone went straight to sleep, having filled their bellies during the march. As the heat wore them down and sand coated their tongues and lips, few words were spoken, save from Goggin, who seemed so steadfastly upbeat that Raven began to wonder whether he'd snuck some simpre into his waterskin.

On the fourth day, Goggin looked up and said, "The Spear."

Raven followed his gaze past the hundreds of dunes to a distinct line of silver in the distance. She thought it could be a trick of the desert light. "Are you certain?"

"Twice I have seen this sight," he said. "I'm as certain as anyone can be of visions in the desert."

Still, Raven dared not hope, not until they were closer. Fire said nothing, but from that point her eyes were trained forward, fixed on that shimmering line.

Goggin was right. The dunes became smaller and thinner, until they fell away completely, giving way to hard-packed dirt and then tufts of brittle, brown grass. And then, abruptly, there was green grass and small three-leafed plants. The sound of burbling water arose as the river fully came into view.

The Spear was aptly named, its slow-moving water a straight, narrow shaft of blue that shot northward, toward Hyro Lake, and southward, where its tip would eventually pierce the heart of the Burning Sea.

The guanik didn't need further urging as they sped up, pushing for the promise of water. When they arrived at the riverbank, the guanero dismounted and stripped down to their underclothes, bathing and laughing in the water, while their coarse-skinned mounts drank voraciously. Goggin entertained his men and women by launching himself off the land, landing in the water with a thunderclap that left a red mark on his chest.

For the first time since they'd left Kesh, Raven felt a swell of joy in her heart, though it was short-lived when she saw Fire standing on the riverbank, looking past the water to a barren land of red rocks and cracked earth. At the edge of the land something rose up like a mountain, running east to west, blocks of stone so large that it was beyond Raven's comprehension as to how they'd been stacked atop one another. It was a marvel akin to the pyramids of Calypso.

Despite the bounty of clean, blue water running before her feet, Fire was already looking ahead, to the Southron Gates.

Although Raven could see the impatience in Fire's eyes, an ever-burning flame not unlike the Burning Tree within their palace in Calypso, her sister was wise enough to allow her army a full day's rest and leisure on the flanks of the Spear.

Men and women lounged on the banks of the river, cleaning the sand from their leather armor and skin, sharpening their weapons, massaging their sore muscles. Slowly, grim expressions turned to smiles, especially when Goggin stomped through the sea of soldiers slapping backs and shouting words of encouragement. They'd conquered the Scarra, and he was determined to give them their moment of victory.

In truth, Raven knew they'd been lucky, their journey blessed by the desert god, whose name they did not speak. He had held back the great sandstorms to let them pass. His scorpions and pyzons had mostly stayed away.

All told, only eight had perished on the windswept dunes, and four of those were their reptilian mounts. Four soldiers out of three thousand, Raven mused. It was an enormous victory indeed, one worth celebrating.

When Goggin approached her, Raven said, "Thank you."

"For what?"

"For encouraging the soldiers. For being a spark of light in the dark."

Goggin snorted. "I fear your words are far too poetic for a simple man of few talents like me. I am only as loud and boisterous as I am to distract from my many faults."

"And yet you are loved by many."

"Most women are afraid I might eat them."

Raven shook her head. "You sell yourself short."

"There's nothing short about me."

Fire joined the conversation. "You are good at breaking things," she noted.

"Much to my mother's chagrin when, as an oversized youth, I tripped and knocked over her fine clay dishes," Goggin said.

"Tomorrow that will come in handy when we shatter the Gates."

"Indeed. I will aim my clumsiness at the wall and hope it breaks before my skull."

Fire laughed. "The Human Battering Ram. That should be your nickname."

"Beats Gogi. That's what my sister used to call me, before she could pronounce Goggin."

"I wouldn't say that too loud," Raven said, "or the guanero will grab onto it and never let you hear the end of it."

"That's where you're wrong," Goggin said. "They already know about that old nickname, but the last time one of them used it he ended up dangling from his feet with his head halfway down my guanik's throat. No one's repeated it since."

Though Raven wasn't sure whether the large man was japing or not, it was a stark reminder that the happy-go-lucky commander of the guanero was a warrior at heart, capable of fierce bouts of violence when necessary.

Like Fire had said, they would need him and his warriors on the morrow.

They crossed the river during the dark predawn threads, knitted together like a gray blanket across the Spear. Though the guanik were heavy beasts, they floated as well as wood, carrying their riders easily against the current with their powerful, churning legs. The rest of the army swam, carrying their leather armor and weapons above their heads and kicking ferociously.

When they'd all forged the river, the tiniest sliver of sunlight peeked over the horizon. The Southron Gates, however, were cast in an ominous shadow, making them appear as an enormous slumbering beast, a pyzon perhaps, without beginning nor end.

Would it swallow them whole? Raven wondered darkly. She shook her head. It was a foolish thought, for the Southron Gates were intended to keep intruders from the north from invading Phanes. As Fire had cleverly realized, an attack from the south would be completely unexpected. The element of surprise would serve them well on this day.

Like an army of ghosts, they crept northward, hugging the edge of the river. No one spoke, the only sounds whispered by the river and the gentle scrape of leathers against steel. The lights of the easternmost Phanecian war city, Sousa, twinkled to the west, far enough away that they were not an immediate threat, though Raven knew once the attack began that enemy soldiers would pour forth, charging for the Gates.

Raven tried not to think about that—the immediate concern was reaching the wall with minimal casualties.

The eastern edge of the great southern wall rose up like a black cliff. Atop the wall, backlit human slashes patrolled, looking northward, oblivious to the silent invaders sneaking up from behind. In the event of an assault by the west, the Phanecians would shoot flaming arrows, catapult heavy stones, and dump large vats of burning tar over the edge. In the half-century since their construction, the Southron Gates had never been scaled, never been breached.

Something tickled the back of Raven's neck. A feeling. Something wasn't right. "Fire," she said.

Her sister looked over at her, a grim expression masking her shadowed face. "The air is amiss," the empress agreed, without Raven having spoken a single word, other than her name.

"They should've seen us by now," Raven said.

"Their attention is elsewhere," Fire said.

That's when Raven realized those patrolling the wall weren't gazing northward, but to the southwest. And they weren't moving slowly, they were running at full tilt, away from the end of the wall.

"What in the name of the gods…" Goggin growled.

A shout broke the silence, then another. The line of guanero pulled to a halt, scanning the wall. Had they been spotted? Raven wondered. But no, the patrols were still moving away, leaving this portion of the wall unprotected.

She squinted into the distance, which was still cast in morning shadow, though the sun extended its reach second by second, its light gaining ground, revealing burnt redlands and then—

"Gods save us," Goggin murmured.

A sea of bodies churned in the distance along the base of the wall, like an insectile scourge pouring from a shattered hive. The forms were headed west, their path aimed at the exact point on the wall the guanero were targeting.

There were thousands, perhaps double the size of the Calypsian force.

Faata's slave army, Raven realized. *He knows we're coming.*

"Go!" Fire screamed into the wind.

Thirty-Seven
The Western Kingdom, Knight's End
Roan Loren

His sister's quarters, though lavish, smelled of fire. A charred mound of burnt books and papers sat in a corner next to a table and three chairs.

"Leave us," Rhea commanded the furia who had escorted them. Roan was still having trouble getting used to their dark stares and blade-like expressions. He wondered if the red-clad women were capable of smiling or laughing. He thought not.

The three women didn't seem to want to leave their queen unprotected with him, but they obeyed anyway. His younger sister wasn't what he expected. She was stronger, more commanding, though he still had difficulty looking upon her scarred face.

"Brother," Rhea said. "Roan."

He was surprised, and he managed to meet her crystalline eyes, which sparkled. "You believe me?"

"Yes. You and your mark explain so much. Too much. Your disappearance. Mother's death. The lies. Everything. I believe you."

"Then you'll help me?"

"Of course, dear brother. So long as you make no attempt to usurp the throne. We are kin, after all."

There was something off about her tone. Insincere. Then again, he'd only just met her, perhaps this was always how she spoke. "What of the twins, Bea and Leo?"

"They are safe," she said, which Roan thought was a strange answer.

"Can I see them?"

"Eventually, perhaps. But this will all be very difficult for them to understand. They're still children. I don't want to confuse them." She laughed lightly, though it sounded rehearsed to Roan's ears. "Wrath, it's confusing enough to me."

Roan gestured to her face. "They say you cut yourself. Is that true?"

Rhea raised an eyebrow. "You ask a lot of questions."

"I know. I'm sorry. It's just…I never thought I'd be here. I never thought I'd meet you."

"That makes two of us," Rhea said.

Roan nodded. A question burned in his throat. "That man you executed…" She'd done it herself, plunging the knife into his skin. She'd killed him without hesitation. He couldn't imagine doing something like that.

"Yes?"

"Who was he? What did he do to deserve such a fate?"

"Ennis Loren. Our cousin. He disobeyed a direct command from me during the fight in the bay. He almost caused us to lose the battle."

Oh gods. She killed her own cousin. No, our cousin, he corrected in his head.

Roan tried to keep his voice even. "Isn't sentencing him to death a bit drastic?"

Rhea sighed. She rubbed her eyes, and for the first time since he met her he thought maybe he was seeing the real her, the version that only appeared when she was alone, when her guard was down. Her eyes fell back on his, and there was great sadness in them. "I loved Ennis like my own brother. He was my most loyal supporter."

"Then why kill him?" Roan was trying to understand, trying to reconcile the compassionate girl he saw in front of him now with the fierce queen who'd stabbed her own cousin in the chest during a public execution.

"I gave him a choice. Banishment or death. The law gave me no other option," Rhea said. "Who am I but a hypocrite if I don't uphold the law? Ennis committed treason in wartime, a crime punishable by death. Offering him the mercy of banishment was as far as I dared go."

"And he chose death? Truly?"

Rhea nodded sadly. "Evidently leaving the west was a fate worse than death to Ennis."

"But there were no other witnesses, right? You could've pretended it never happened. No one would've known." And then he wouldn't be dead. *I wouldn't have had to watch you kill him.*

"*I* would've known," Rhea said. "I'd never look at him the same way again. I'd never be able to trust him. And I wouldn't be able to look my people in the eyes and pretend to be the righteous queen they believe me to be."

Roan, in a way, could understand that. His sister was a woman of principle, it appeared. He changed the subject. "Why did you burn these books?" He gestured to the charred pile.

"They're from the Archives. I asked for information on the Western Oracle, and it turns out my archivists were not nearly as obedient as I'd hoped them to be."

"They tried to destroy everything?" Roan felt sick. They came all this way and the very information they sought had been tossed in the fire just before he arrived. "Did anything survive?"

"I don't know. We can go through it in a moment. First I want to talk about your mark."

Roan worried he'd made a massive mistake in revealing his mark. He'd agreed with Gwen and Gareth that he wouldn't. And yet, as he had stood before his sister, his mark had pulsed in his chest. It had seemed to be telling him it was time. Still, he'd acted on instinct, without really thinking about the consequences. She could kill him on principle, as she had their cousin. The furia could force her to act. He needed to find out whether the decision was folly. "Don't you mean my *sin*mark?"

Rhea waved the word away. "I only said that for the sake of my furia. They expect me to act a certain way. I have a reputation to uphold. My people aren't ready for the idea that they've been lied to their entire lives."

Roan gaped. This was too good to be true. "But what about what you said earlier, about obeying the western law, about not being a hypocrite?"

"This is different. This law was based on a lie. The law needs to change."

Roan could feel his heart beating in his chest as he asked the most critical question yet. "So you believe the marks have a greater purpose?"

"You could say that." She explained what she'd learned so far. The marked girl, Shae Arris, who the furia referred to as *the key*, being taken south, in search of something; the symbols they'd found, matching known fatemarks; the map that showed the locations of other important documents.

"I read something about a Peacemaker," she said. "I wonder who that is? I've already met Kings' Bane, and—"

"You have?" Roan interrupted.

"Sort of. I haven't spoken to him. At the time, I was cowering like a pathetic little girl while he killed half the palace, including Father. I'm rather embarrassed about the whole thing."

Embarrassed? Her father had just been murdered and she was...*embarrassed?* Roan said, "I've met Bane twice. I've spoken to him. I stopped him from killing the heir to the eastern throne."

Rhea's eyebrows went up, and a flash of anger crossed her face. "Gareth Ironclad? Why would you protect him?"

"Because I could. Because he's my friend."

Slowly, slowly, the anger melted from her face. "You are a...good man," she said. "I can sense it. But what does your mark do? What does it mean?"

Suddenly, Roan felt like this was all wrong, like he was trapped behind iron bars, locked in a dungeon. He spoke slowly, considering each word. "I can heal people. That's how I saved Gareth."

"Hmm."

That's all she had to say? *Hmm?* He was about to speak when there was a knock on the door. "You may enter," Rhea said.

One of the furia came in, glanced at Roan, and then approached the queen, whispering something in her ear behind a cupped hand. As the message was delivered, Rhea's eyes snapped to Roan's.

When the woman had left, Roan asked, "What is it? What's happened?"

Rhea waved the question away. "It's just western business. Nothing for you to be concerned with."

Roan had been considering something since he saw his sister. Since he saw her face. "You know, my mark, its power…I can heal your face if you want me to."

The question seemed to freeze her, her eyes wide and unblinking, like a deer caught in torchlight. And then the moment passed, and she was the girl on the dais again, executing a man without hesitation. "Why would I want that? I cut my face in honor of Wrath. I am his servant."

Roan heard the determination in her voice. There was no point in arguing, not about this anyway. Perhaps later, after they'd become better acquainted. But there was another topic he needed to discuss with her. "Listen, Rhea, we have a chance to forge a real peace across the Four Kingdoms. With my mark and my alliance with Gareth Ironclad, and your reputation as a righteous queen, we can—"

"I've been told Gareth Ironclad is missing. His brother, Grian, has declared himself king. He's been amassing troops from all corners of the eastern kingdom."

"That may be true," Roan said, "but I know where Gareth is. We can talk to him together, create the first alliance between the east and the west in a hundred years. We can do it *together*." All the words he'd been thinking since he decided to finally return to Knight's End jumbled together in his head, seeking a way out.

He couldn't stop until he'd emptied his brain of them. "We can change the way westerners think about the marks. I can heal the sick and injured, show them the *good* things the marks can do. We can use my power to unite the kingdoms."

Rhea tapped her teeth with long fingernails. Roan was getting more used to the scars on her face now. They almost blended in with the rest of her, becoming a part of her. He might not understand why she wanted to keep her scars, but he couldn't deny the fact that they seemed to define her in an unexplainable way. "You sound an awful lot like a Peacemaker," Rhea finally said.

Roan couldn't hide it any longer. The truth was the only thing that could set him free. So he told her. Everything. Start to finish.

When he was done, she nodded, as if she'd known much of it already.

"You are the Peacemaker," she said.

It wasn't a question, but Roan felt like he should answer. "Yes. I think so. That's what Bane called me."

"The message I received earlier. It was from one of a dozen riders I sent south, to try to recover the marked girl and the map. The rest are dead. Would you like to hear what she has to say?"

This was why Roan was here. To learn. To solve the mysteries of his past. "Yes."

The woman was chained to a bed, her red clothing ripped, clinging to her skin, which was pale between the tatters, except where it was slashed deeply, all the way to the bone. She was convulsing, her eyes rolled back in her head.

Roan turned to the side and vomited.

Rhea stepped forward like nothing was wrong. She grabbed the woman's chin, forcing her face toward her. Eyes still rolled back, body still convulsing. "Tell me what you saw in the Dead Isles," she commanded.

The woman froze, eyes rolling forward, her gaze frantic and unfocused. "The dead, everywhere. Not men, not horses. Both. They killed them. They killed them all."

"I don't care about the dead," Rhea said. "What about the rutting girl? The one with the rutting mark? Shae Arris. And the map. Where is the Wrath-damn map?"

Roan wiped his mouth, shocked by the obscenity-laden outburst from his younger sister. How did she become this way?

"Gone," the woman said. "All gone."

"What about the girl's brother, Grey. Did you find him?" There was desperation in her tone, in her eyes.

"He found us," the woman said, spit dribbling down her chin.

"What happened to him?" Rhea said, grabbing the woman's torn dress, pulling her face closer.

The woman shook her head. "Don't know. Dead all around us. I ran. They hunted me. Everyone dead. I made it to the boats. Somehow. Somehow…"

Rhea's teeth were clamped tightly together, her breaths whistling between them. She seemed to be fighting for control of herself. "Is that all?" she finally said.

"No. Found something else. Swallowed it. It's inside of me." The woman's eyes rolled back and she convulsed several more times before going still.

Rhea reached out and placed her hand in front of the woman's mouth and nose. "She's dead," she said. Turning to one of the furia she said, "Cut her open. Bring me what she found after you clean it up."

Thirty-Eight
The Western Kingdom, Knight's End
Rhea Loren

Roan was alive *and* marked. And he was also the Peacemaker foretold by the Oracle's prophecy. And Grey had gone to the Dead Isles. He had found his sister. And now he was probably...

She refused to think it.

Has the world gone mad?

Rhea and Roan had been going through the burnt documents for a few hours, waiting for the contents of the dead furia's stomach to be brought up. Roan hadn't spoken much. *Good*, she thought. *Let him be scared of me. I may need his fear soon enough.*

I can heal your face if you want.

Wrath. The temptation was great. She could have everything she'd ever wanted back. Her beauty. And it wouldn't take away her power, would it? She would still be queen. Beauty *and* power—the combination would be unbreakable.

No. She knew it would change everything. Change her. Change what her people thought of her. It wasn't until her face had been mutilated, her beauty stripped away, that she realized she never needed it in the first place. It didn't define who she was and what she was capable of. The scars on her face were the best thing that ever happened to her.

"There's nothing here," Roan finally said, startling her away from her thoughts. He delicately closed another charred book.

"Unless the important parts were burned," Rhea said, thankful for the break in the silence. The break from her thoughts.

"Maybe," Roan said, sounding frustrated.

"Brother." Rhea softened her voice. "Roan. Like you said, we are in this together. We'll find something."

Her words seemed to placate him, and he went back to searching through the pile. *Wrath*, she thought. *My brother acts like a puppy. Peacemaker? Hah! I could destroy him with a word.*

A furia entered, carrying a strange object. She handed it to Rhea, turned, and departed.

"What is it?" Roan asked.

Rhea inspected the object, feeling the grooves with her fingertips. "A sliver of wood."

Roan frowned, shifting to look over her shoulder. "It has markings," he said.

"Words," Rhea said. "In WA you shall find the truth."

"WA?" Roan said. "Western Archives?"

Rhea nodded. What else could it mean? "It has to be here somewhere. The truth. A clue. Something."

"We've been through everything three times. There's nothing here."

Rhea considered the problem. "The Western Oracle had to know that years might pass before anyone went looking for information on her. She was an outcast, sentenced to be burned at the stake as a witch. Even speaking her name in the west is taboo."

Roan nodded, his eyes widening with understanding. "She wouldn't have hidden the clue in something that could be easily destroyed."

"Check the bindings. Look for false bottoms. Anything where something could be hidden."

Together, they searched, ripping books apart, tearing the bindings, cutting off covers. Rhea hit something hard, like iron. "Here," she said. She peeled away the cover of a book—*Fatal Prophecies: Volume I*—to uncover a small metal box with a basic copper latch. Her eyes met Roan's and he nodded.

"Open it."

She did, and a key rattled out. It was small, iron. There was nothing else inside the box.

Roan said, "Look for another box."

A while later, he said, "Got it." In his hands was another metal box, this one thicker, sealed with a lock.

"Give it to me," Rhea said. Roan handed it over, and she fitted the key into the lock and turned. The box sprang open. Inside was a single sheet of parchment, folded a dozen times to fit. She pushed down the corners and read what it said aloud:

Seeker of Truth, find the hoard of Knowledge,
And Find Me.
I am old, but I will see this land returned to Peace.
I will see Prophecy fulfilled.

485

I will die when it is Time.

Rhea had the urge to destroy the paper. "This is useless," she said. "It means nothing. More cryptic sayings that any soothsayer of the east could've spouted."

Roan didn't seem nearly as disappointed. "I don't think so," he said. "It says she's alive, the Oracle. She must be, don't you see? The land has not been returned to peace, and her prophecy has only begun to be fulfilled."

Rhea considered it, still skeptical. If this woman really was as powerful as everyone said she was, and she really had created the fatemarks, was it possible she'd found a way to extend her life well beyond a normal human's? Or was she human at all? It was said the Orians could live for two full centuries. "But she was burned to death years ago."

"Maybe not," Roan said. "Maybe she wanted everyone to think she was dead."

"If she is alive, how do we find her?"

"Simple," Roan said, grinning. "Find the hoard of Knowledge."

"We can search the Western Archives again, but I doubt we'll find some old half-burned woman hiding amongst the tomes."

Roan chuckled, and it made Rhea want to scratch his eyes out. She took a deep breath, letting the urge pass. When did she become this violent person? *When I killed Jove,* she thought. *When I realized how good it felt to hurt others, that strange mix of horror and excitement in the pit of my stomach.* "What?" she asked.

"The Western Archives are not the hoard of Knowledge, not even close."

"Then where?"

"Citadel," Roan said. "Calyp, not Knight's End, has the largest library in all the Four Kingdoms. And it might not be the Oracle herself that is still alive."

Rhea frowned. "Then who?"

Roan told her what had happened in the Tangle, about the shapeshifting man-bear who had helped save them.

"If Bear Blackboots really is the Western Oracle's son and is somehow still alive after all these years, we'll find him in Citadel."

Yes, she thought. *I knew there was a reason I didn't kill my brother the moment I found him.*

Rhea stood abruptly. "I will return soon," she said.

Rhea wondered whether she'd made a grievous mistake. If anyone discovered what she'd done...*my people will never trust me again.*

And all for what?

Love. It was a word she struggled with more and more each day. She loved her cousin, Ennis, so much that she could never have killed him. It wasn't the same love that he had for her, but it was just as powerful.

Ennis was motionless on the bed, his bloody shirt removed, leaving his chest bare. There was no wound, save for a tiny cut in the flesh of his left breast. The shirt would be burned, all evidence of what she'd done destroyed.

Before the execution, he'd watched her as she'd strapped the bags of sheep's blood across his heart. He hadn't asked what she was doing—he already knew. He had played his part as well as she could've asked, though she suspected his quote from *The Brave Mouse* wasn't part of the play.

The poison on the tip of her retractable knife was called falsedeath. It was extracted from the stem of a rare plant found only in the Tangle. She was surprised to find a small supply available from the apothecary, though she'd had one of her furia obtain it for "Wrath's business" so as to not arouse suspicion. The fast-acting poison stopped the heart and the lungs, sending the body into a strange stasis, neither dead or alive. A second dose provided within a few days of the first would usually reverse the effects.

That's what Rhea was counting on now, by Wrath's will.

She threaded a hand behind Ennis's neck, tilting his chin back. She opened his lips with two fingers and dribbled the remaining falsedeath on his tongue, then forced his mouth shut.

She waited anxiously. *Please*, she thought. *I will never ask for another thing. Never never never…*

He remained still. No breath passed from his lips or nose. She touched his chest, but there was no beating heart.

Rhea collapsed on top of him and wept.

His body jolted and he gasped.

Roan Loren

Rhea had left hours earlier, promising to send up food—which she did. Roan ate the steamed vegetables coated in white sauce and left the roasted quail. Dusk fell while he ate, and he wondered when he would see his friends again. Twice he tried to open the door to wander about the castle, and twice he found it locked. On the second attempt, a furia opened it, telling him to be patient and wait inside, for his own safety.

Who would hurt me? he thought. He laughed, realizing the foolishness of his own question. If the truth of his fatemark became known, *everyone* in the kingdom might want to hurt him.

He tried to be patient, rummaging through the burnt documents, but finding nothing additional of note. No more iron boxes or keys, maps or clues. He was certain everything pointed to Citadel. *We did it*, he thought. He couldn't wait to tell Gwen and Gareth. Gwen especially, who would be thrilled to know they would be journeying to find the woman who gave them their marks. *Our purpose.*

Roan was thumbing through a sheaf of parchment, mostly destroyed, when Rhea finally returned, still wearing her bloodstained armor. There was something more upbeat about her demeanor, a spring in her step. "I want you to go to Calyp and find the Oracle, or her son...this Bear Blackboots character," she said. "You are from the south. You know how to blend in, the customs."

"I will try," Roan said, feeling giddy. This was exactly what he wanted.

"When you find either of them, bring them back to me."

Roan hadn't expected that, but he thought it made sense. "So they can teach us? So they can show us the path to peace?"

"No," Rhea said. "Bring them back in chains."

"What? Why? They might hold the key to peace."

"Exactly, dear brother. Why would I want peace? I've decimated the north. And the east will never agree to an alliance, no matter what the Oracle or her son believes. The south? They are embroiled in civil war, ripe for destruction."

Roan could feel the horror on his own face, taste the bitterness on his tongue. A question formed on his lips. "Then why do you want them at all?"

"For their power, you fool. Maybe they can give me my own mark, a custom design with the power of my choosing. Perhaps they can even give me more than one. My furia should have powers, too. And if the sorcerer or her son are really still alive, then they also hold the secret to immortality. I wouldn't mind being immortal, would you? It's the only way I'll be able to conquer the Four Kingdoms. And if you're a good brother, I might let you live, though first I'll have the Oracle or her son wave their magic fingers and remove your mark. I can't have you healing people all the time."

The sick feeling he'd felt earlier returned. Who *was* this madwoman? He couldn't believe she was related to him, to his mother, even to his father, who never tried to conquer the entire Four Kingdoms. "Rhea, sister, this isn't right. There is no need for more violence."

"Oh, I know," Rhea said lightly. "But I like it too much to stop now."

A thought from earlier floated to the top of Roan's mind. "Rhea, where are Bea and Leo? You said they're safe, but where are they?"

Rhea smiled wickedly. "Chained in the dungeons. They've been naughty. Can't have little demons like them running around, can we?"

"I..." Roan had no idea what to say to her. *Why did I show her my mark in the first place? Why did I reveal myself to her? Why didn't I listen to my friends, who warned me against such brash action?* His fatemark pulsed in his chest, as it had before, calming him. Somehow, for some strange purpose unknown to him now, this was the path he needed to take. But that didn't mean he wasn't the master of his future. "I won't bring the Oracle back to you in chains. I will find her, but I can't do that."

"Dear brother, but I think you will. Bring them in."

Two forms were pushed roughly through the door by a group of furia.

Gwendolyn offered him a dark stare and mouthed *I'm sorry*, while Gareth only shrugged. Both were in chains, stripped of all weapons.

Roan shook his head.

"We found them loitering near the castle gates. My spies in the city had already informed me that a man matching your description was seen wandering the city, asking strange questions about me. He had two companions with him. I assume these are the two."

There was no use in lying. Roan nodded.

"This is the missing Gareth Ironclad?" Rhea guessed. "Your *friend*."

Again, Roan nodded.

"Then who is this beautiful witch of the iron forest? Another friend? Evidently this armor of hers is somehow fused over her skin, though we tried to remove it."

What was Gwen to Roan? A friend? More than that? Did the label really matter now? He said nothing.

"I see. Well, whatever she is, she put up quite a fight when we found her. King Ironclad, too. They killed over a dozen furia before we were able to subdue them. The witch killed ten of them. Apparently she moved like the wind. She wouldn't happen to bear a mark, too, would she?"

"Obviously," Gareth said. One of the furia backhanded him across the face. Roan stepped forward to help him, but two of the red women blocked his path. Gwen, even in chains, threw herself at their attackers, but two more furia muscled her to the ground.

491

Roan said, "No!" and tried to break through. Strong arms held him back.

Gwen raised her chin proudly, launching words between clenched teeth and a waterfall of silver hair. "I bear the heromark. Something you will never understand."

Spitting out a wad of blood, Gareth said, "Western hospitality is everything they say it is."

"Bravo," Rhea said, her eyes meeting Roan's. "Your friends are providing more entertainment than this city has seen in days. Isn't that what you declared your trade to be to my guard at the gates? Entertainers?"

Roan said nothing, his jaw clenched. He'd come here in good faith to be reunited with his sister in the hopes that together they could change things. Instead he found a monster sitting on the western throne.

"What do you want from us?"

Rhea smiled. "You have your orders. Travel to Calyp. Bring the Oracle or her son back. In chains, if necessary."

Roan could feel Gwen's eyes searching his face, but he didn't turn to look at her. "And if I refuse?"

"Then I kill the iron witch," Rhea said. "Slowly. Piece by piece."

"She is nothing to me," Roan lied.

Rhea raised an eyebrow, laughing lightly. "You may be entertaining, brother, but you are no actor. You are in love with her, I could see it on your face the moment she walked through that door."

Roan couldn't help but to look at Gwen now, to see her reaction. Her lips were tight, pressed into a line. Her yellow eyes a mystery. She said nothing. But Gareth's expression was unmistakable, as easy to read as a freshly penned stream message. Sadness. Anger. Betrayal.

Roan remembered their kiss, the way Gareth had reacted. He remembered their time spent together in the locket, how he'd awoken to Gareth sleeping in the crook of his arm. He remembered the way the beautiful Ironclad boy liked to hide his true feelings behind japes and an arrogant smile. And he realized:

He's in love with me.

And, despite what Rhea had assumed, it wasn't just Gwen Roan was in love with.

It was both of them.

Roan pushed down the thought, which made no difference to their present situation. "What about Gareth?" Roan asked, turning back to his sister. "What will you do with him?"

"The Ironclad will be ransomed."

"For what? He's already the lawful heir and his brother won't turn himself in."

"I don't want his brother. I want the ironmarked one. Beorn Stonesledge."

Gareth scoffed. "He won't fight for you."

"Then he will die. Either way, he won't fight for the east either. We all know he's your greatest weapon. Well, perhaps this iron witch *was* the greatest weapon, but she won't be much use anymore."

"You're evil," Roan said. It was a pointless comment, he knew, but he couldn't help it. He was still shocked by how quickly things had turned against him.

"Let Wrath be my judge," she said. "Take Ironclad to the tower cell. Give him a nice view of the east, so he can watch the destruction of his people. Haul the witch below. She can rot next to the twins."

"Don't do this," Roan said as the furia hauled his friends to their feet. "Please. This isn't you. This isn't what our parents would have wanted."

"You know nothing about me, what I've been through. You abandoned me, just like everyone else."

"Roan, I'm sorry," Gwen said, earning herself a final punch in the stomach. Gareth said nothing, though his eyes met Roan's.

And then they were gone.

Thirty-Nine
The Southern Empire,
the Southron Gates, near Sousa
Raven Sandes

Hot wind gusted against Raven's face as they rode full tilt toward the wall, Iknon's muscular shoulders undulating beneath her with each stride. She clung to the harness with one hand, her fingers aching, but strong and well-calloused from years of training amongst the guanero. Her other hand gripped her whip, trembling with readiness.

Fire was already holding her sword aloft, flames kissing the steel. The other guanero were equally prepared for battle, their weapons drawn and slashing through the air. Goggin rode no-handed, using his strong legs to clamp the sides of his steed, his hands clutching his dual scimitars.

Several of the wall's defenders had finally noticed their approach, shouting a warning. Even in the dark, their white-powdered faces were visible, almost glowing under the moon and starlight, like oval orbs of light. They dropped to one knee and fired longbows, but their arrows went long, splashing into the waters of the Spear.

They fired again, and one of the guanik released a cry of agony, tripping and tumbling headlong, the long shaft of an arrow protruding from its neck. Somewhere beneath the beast, its rider was crushed as it rolled. Raven and the rest of the guanero knew that stopping meant death; in any case, there was nothing they could do for their fallen sister—she had gone to meet the gods in the sky.

Without a command, the guanero closed ranks around their empress, creating a human and reptilian shield of leather and scales. Protecting her was the priority.

As arrows continued to whistle past, occasionally hitting their targets, Raven glanced to the west. The slave army no longer appeared as ants, their features coming into detail. Only a few rode horses, at the front, and their clothing appeared newer, cleaner. At least one was a Dreadnoughter, while the others were a mix of Terans and Phanecians. *Strange*, Raven thought. The rest ran on foot, their skin as red as rusty iron.

One of them fell, then another. *Who is shooting at them?* Raven wondered. She looked about her to see if any of their own archers had stopped to fire on the enemy. But no, they were all following Fire's command to charge the Gates.

Another volley of arrows flew from the wall, landing amongst the slave army. *They're shooting their own people!* Raven realized. That's when she noticed something else about the slave army heading on a collision course with them:

"They have no weapons!" she shouted over the pounding of guanik foreclaws. In reality, those on horseback were armed to the teeth, but the foot soldiers were clearly unarmed, being picked off by the archers on the wall. And the men had long hair, which was highly unusual for Teran slaves.

Fire shouted back, "They're trying to escape!"

The moment her sister said it, Raven knew she was right. This was no army, no threat. If anything, the thousands—whose numbers were decreasing under the barrage of arrows—were allies, in the sense that they had a common enemy.

"Do not attack the slaves!" Fire commanded, and several riders slowed to pass the message back through the lines.

"Bloody fools!" Goggin growled, staring at the slaves as he rode. "They cannot hope to breach the wall without weapons." Just as he said it, an arrow ripped past him. He flinched, and when he turned back to Raven, blood poured from his head. His ear was gone, ripped away by the force of the arrowhead. He grimaced and snarled, "I'll take a hundred enemy ears as retribution!"

Raven didn't have time to respond, as the wall was approaching, so close now she could see the faces of their enemy as they sighted down their arrows.

"Archers!" Fire shouted. The call went down the lines, hundreds of men dropping to their knees as the guanero and foot soldiers marched onward. "Fire!"

Though the empress's cry was lost amongst the screams of the approaching slaves, the archers got the message anyway, unleashing a flock of arrows toward the wall's ramparts. Several enemy archers were hit, one tumbling off the wall and landing face down on the ground, his body crushed under the trod of a guanik, snapping as it passed.

They rode along the shadow of the wall, the stone blocks even larger from close range, taller than any of them, even while mounted. The wall rushed past in a blur. From the left, the slave riders danced deftly between them. Wheeled carts clattered behind the horses, attached with short ropes. Raven was surprised to find all the riders to be women, their faces spotted with strange black markings. Except for one, a dark-haired young-looking man with white fear in his eyes, which were larger than most Phanecians. He rode behind one of the women, his arms roped around her stomach. And then they were gone, skidding to a stop near the foot of the wall.

The man dropped from the horse into a fighter's stance, while the woman landed lightly on her feet beside him. She screamed something, but her words were lost to Raven as Iknon thundered out of sight.

The stone gave way to a thick sheet of iron.

The first of four Gates built into the wall.

Protected by the guanero, Fire dropped from her steed and pressed her hands to the Gate.

Jai Jiroux

Everything had gone according to plan. Until it hadn't.

As Jai had suspected, none of his people had taken his offer to turn back. Even Joaquin had clasped his shoulder and said, "You may be a soft-hearted pyzon-killer, Jai Jiroux, but I will not leave you now."

The people were quiet as they exited the rocklands, moving across the desert plains like ghosts. Not so much as a single baby wailed in the night. The horses' padded hooves were mere whispers in the dirt, and Shanti's cart creaked so softly the sound was lost on the wind.

The lights of Sousa sparkled to the northwest, but they were well clear of the warcity, aiming their path for a point on the wall somewhat east of the iron gates. Jai led them, targeting the spot based on what his father had said: *The hollow in the wall is a hundred paces east of the easternmost Gate, northeast of the famed warcity of Sousa.*

Though he believed his father, his trust didn't stop a deep pit from forming in his stomach, growing larger with every step.

What if he was mistaken?

What if Vin Hoza had since had the wall repaired?

What if a fire arrow strikes our barrels of fireroot before we reach the wall, sending us all into the Void?

What if this journey was all for nothing?

What if what if what if...

This is my destiny. Right?

He didn't have the time for such thoughts, because they were approaching the wall. He saw fire to the right. The glint of steel in the light of the moons. Shadows moving. Some of them larger than others. "What the Void?" Sonika Vaid said, noticing the same thing.

"An army," Shanti said. "We have to leave the people behind and open the wall."

"Wait. Look!" Sonika said, pointing. A flag flapped in the breeze, displaying a sigil:

A dragon rising over a red sun.

"Calypsians," Jai breathed, incredulous. *How is this possible? What are they doing here?*

Before he could contemplate further, the wall's armed defenders began shouting, having realized what was happening. Arrows flew through the air, landing amongst his people. They dropped in droves, screaming. Running now, charging the wall in a mass of humanity, stumbling over the dead.

Shanti grabbed Jai around the waist and scooped him up onto her horse. She spurred her mare forward, while the other Tears did the same, charging for the wall. "I have to go back to my people," Jai cried above the pounding hooves.

"There's nothing you can do for them now," Shanti said. "The wall is all that matters." Truth burned in Jai's heel.

And then the Calypsian army was among them, flashing past. One of the soldiers held a flaming sword, her red leather armor smoking. She was surrounded by guanik, the reptilian steeds of their Southron neighbors.

But none of that mattered. Like Shanti had said, nothing mattered but the wall. If they couldn't breach it, they were all walking corpses.

Jai almost flew from the saddle when Shanti's horse skidded to a stop on command, but her strong arms held him back. He flung a leg over the side and landed naturally in phen lu defense stance on the ground, while Shanti came down lightly beside him, immediately untying the ropes wrapped around the barrels in the cart. "Help me!" she shouted, but Jai was already grabbing one side of a barrel, lifting it while she did the same on the opposite side. The other Tears gathered around them, firing arrows toward the top of the wall, picking off enemy archers.

They hefted the barrel into position. "Is this the right spot?" Shanti asked as they set it down.

"It's the best guess I have," Jai said. The knot in his chest grew thicker.

"Then it'll have to do." They went back for another barrel, then another, placing them in a neat row. One of the Tears had fallen, a Dreadnoughter, an arrow protruding from her stomach. Even still, she continued to fire from her knees.

"Get back," Shanti ordered.

Jai rushed back amongst the Tears while Shanti uncoiled a large length of twine, shuffling backward. Arrows rained down upon them, and another Tear went down. Sonika, the arrow's feather protruding from her shoulder. Jai knelt by her side. "Help Shanti, not me," she gasped. "She's our only hope."

"I won't leave you," Jai said, grasping her under the arms and helping her to her feet. Nearby, the other Tears were doing the same for their other fallen sister. As one, they fought their way back from the wall, reaching Shanti as she finished unraveling the twine.

"Light it," Sonika said between gritted teeth. An arrow flew past, narrowly missing Jai's hip.

Shanti struck her flint and sparks flew. One of them caught the dry twine, smoking for a moment before bursting into fire. The orange flames danced along the rope, running toward the pocket of barrels. More arrows soared down from above, but they were no longer aimed at them. They were aiming for the rope. Someone had realized what was happening, and they were trying to stop it, to break the twine with a pinpoint shot.

Those Tears still capable of shooting fired another volley of arrows at the top of the wall. The flames were halfway to the barrels.

Jai looked back at his people, who were still charging the wall, stumbling over bodies. *So few*, he thought, tears blurring his vision. Though there were thousands, it was like their numbers had been sliced in half. *The rest are dead or injured*, he knew. Women. Children. Men. Good people. *My people.*

Jai held out his arms as they approached, as if he was going to hug them all. "Stop!" he shouted. Somewhere behind him he knew the flame was still making its way toward the kegs of fireroot.

The people crowded against them, jostling from behind, driven by panic and fear. Those at the front tried to hold back the mass of humanity, but slowly it pushed forward. And then—

BOOM!

Compared to the blast that had caved in the entrance to Garadia, this explosion was an act of the gods, a giant hammer pounding the earth. The force of it was so strong it was like a shove against Jai's back, throwing him into the churning mob of people. They went down hard, a tangle of arms and legs, their cries swarming together like a hive of bees.

Stone shrapnel fell like rain, piercing their skin, bruising their bones. Jai covered his head with two hands until it was over.

Dazed, he fought to his feet, trying to make sense of the fog swirling around him. *Smoke*, he realized, the acrid stench curling his nose.

An arm grabbed his and he whirled. Shanti. She wasn't grinning this time, although the explosion must've sent a thrill through her gut. There was too much death and destruction to smile. Maybe ever again. But still, some of them were alive, which meant there was hope. Only a sliver perhaps, but better than nothing.

"Go!" Jai roared, pushing her toward where he thought the wall was. She looked back at him, surprised. "I have to stay with my people. You finish the job," he said. She nodded and turned away, off to find her remaining barrels hitched to her horse.

Jai reached down and grabbed the nearest person he saw, pulling her to her feet. Next he picked up a fallen boy, his face smudged with ash and blood. It was Jig, his eyes wide. "Follow the others," he said, giving him a shove.

More and more people charged for the wall, which was just coming into view as the smoke cleared. Jai couldn't believe his eyes when he saw it. For, amongst the shattered stone and mangled bodies of the archers who had fallen from high above during the blast, was the truth of his father's words:

The wall was like a cracked eggshell drained of its yolk, yawning open to reveal a narrow hollow in its center. A way through. Already Shanti and the other Tears were hauling the fireroot kegs into the stone corridor. "Run!" Jai shouted, reinvigorated, shoving bodies toward the gap in the stone.

A pair of forms materialized in front of him, as if born from the rising smoke itself. One was a boy wearing a dark cloak, his pale head shaved to the skin. The other wore a gray cloak that shrouded his face, not a shred of skin visible beneath the thick cloth.

The boy spoke, his voice deeper than his age would suggest. "Our plans have changed. You want peace? Infect the slave army," he said, speaking to the hooded man beside him.

The Beggar

It would be so simple an act: pull off his gloves, throw back his hood, and touch them. If he infected enough people, the plague would spread out of control, like a wildfire, burning Phanes alive from the inside out. The empire would fall. With one side of the Southron civil war destroyed, the fighting would have to stop. Peace would reign in the Southern Empire once more.

He would be using his power to *do good*. Right? That's what Bane told him.

My friend.

My brother.

All it would take was a simple touch, and then Bane could save his energy to kill another warmongering ruler.

Peace will dawn upon the Four Kingdoms before winter comes…

The Beggar pulled off his gloves and threw back his hood.

Though chaos ruled the night, smoke hanging in the air, mixing with the screams, one man stood watching him. His eyes were too wide to be fully Phanecian, and yet he was no slave like the others, his skin tanned rather than red like the Terans. He spoke: "Who are you?"

The Beggar glanced to the side, but Bane was gone. Had he abandoned him? *No*, he realized. *He trusts me to carry out the plan. He has other work to do.* The Beggar stepped forward, hand outstretched. "I am a friend," he lied.

The dark-haired man moved closer. He had a knife in his belt, but he didn't draw it. "I have to go," he said. "My people are escaping through the wall."

The Beggar frowned. *Escaping? But they are slaves—Vin Hoza's slave army. They are supposed to be fighting the Calypsian army, enacting violence. Threatening peace. I am supposed to stop them. But if they're not fighting, then why am I here?*

"Who am I?" he murmured, feeling empty inside once more.

"What?" the man said. "I don't have time to linger. Our window is closing."

"No," the Beggar said, and he wasn't sure if he was speaking to himself or the man. "I—I—" He took another step forward, so close now that if he were to lunge he would almost certainly make skin-to-skin contact.

Do it. He knew the voice was in his head, inexplicably, but still, he whirled around, looking for the source of the command. He cradled his head. "No no no no," he muttered.

Do it.

The man said, "Are you hurt?" His expression of concern was too much for the Beggar, especially because of what he was about to do. *What I have to do. What I was born to do.*

He lunged, and the man was so surprised by the move that he froze, not even trying to get out of the way. The Beggar snatched the knife from its scabbard.

Jai Jiroux

The unnaturally pale man had his knife, brandishing it before him. His grip was at an odd angle, but still, one cut and he'd be finished. There was something off about him...

"It's fine, I'm not going to hurt you," Jai said, casually falling into defense stance. He could easily take the knife away. Disarming a foe was one of the first lessons you learned in phen lu. Not to hurt them, but to subdue them. Somewhere nearby, there was a second explosion. *Shanti. She did it.* A swell of satisfaction rolled through him. Some of his people would escape. So many were dead, but not all.

Not all.

"I know," the young-looking man said.

"Then why are you doing this?"

"Because I must. Because it is who I am."

He raised the knife over his head, the blade cast in green light from Luahi shining from high above.

The Beggar

This was all the Beggar had left. *This is who I am.*

"I am no killer," he whispered. "Not anymore." No, he was a boy again, not scared of his shadow anymore, but innocent. He was the boy his mother had once named, the last word that passed by her lips before the evil inside him had killed her.

I am not the Beggar. Not anymore. This time he would truly kill to save thousands of lives.

"I am Chavos."

And he brought the knife down, stabbing it into his own gut.

Jai Jiroux

Oh gods, he's killed himself.

The man fell, blood dripping between his fingers, watering the dust with crimson rain.

Jai rushed to his side, preparing to put pressure on the wound, to do everything in his power to staunch the flow of life, to save this stranger, this—

"Stay back!" the man hissed, kicking out a boot.

So startled was Jai by the sudden attack that he stopped dead in his tracks.

"I am the Beggar of Calypso, the Plague Reaper, the Destroyer of Souls. I have murdered thousands in cold—" He gasped, his lips and eyes widening in tandem. *The Beggar,* Jai thought. *So it's true. He is the origin of the plague.* The man's voice weakened. "I am lost. Don't let him emerge victorious."

"Who?" Jai's voice was a whisper.

"The mad one. He will destroy us all."

"Who will? Emperor Hoza?"

The Beggar shook his head slowly, his eyes fluttering closed. "No. My brother. The Kings' Bane."

His body convulsed violently, his back arching, and then he went still.

He was gone.

When Jai finally managed to climb amongst the rubble of the wall and navigate the narrow passageway, the majority of the survivors were already through, as well as the Black Tears. Shanti waited, breaking into a grim smile when she saw him. "I feared you were dead."

"I survived a hungry red pyzon, remember?" Jai said. "Everything else is child's play."

Shanti hugged him fiercely, surprising him, and it took him a moment before he squeezed back. Together, they stepped over the final stone blocks and into the west, a land of freedom.

Jai's eyes darted to the top of the wall, but it was empty. There was no one left to stop them.

Jai's people were laughing and crying, celebrating their freedom while mourning those they'd lost. Jig ran up and Jai stooped to embrace him, spinning him around. Viola was next, and then Marella, followed by dozens of others. Even the Dreadnoughter twins, Gorrin and Orrin, came to him, though they clasped his arm rather than hugged him.

Jai forced himself not to count the survivors, but it was clear they were less than a thousand, a mere fifth of the number they'd left the Red Rocks with. The mix of joy and sadness was the most conflicting feeling he'd ever experienced.

Sonika approached, and he reached out to clasp her arm. She pulled him into a hug, whispering in his ear. "You did this, my friend."

Thousands dead, all to save so few. *Is this what I've done? Is any of this worth it?* Jai pulled back. "No. We did this."

She nodded, and Jai was about to embrace her again, when he heard a shout. Together, they turned, locating a commotion near the destroyed portion of the wall.

"Go back," someone commanded. Jai recognized broad-shouldered Joaquin. Just beyond him was another man, his brown skin sheened in ash and sweat as he stumbled over the blocks.

Axa. He made it.

The former master held his mirror aloft, talking into it, oblivious to Joaquin's position in front of him. Joaquin shoved him back when he stumbled into him.

"Wait," Jai said, stepping forward, between them.

"I'll kill him if he doesn't turn back," Joaquin said. "I swear it. So many of our people are dead, and *he's* alive. It's not right. What kind of justice do the gods give us?" The man's face, though stoic, was laced with sorrow, a miasma of anger and sadness and guilt and regret.

"I'm sorry," Jai said. "But more killing isn't the answer."

Joaquin dropped to his knees, all fight having left him. "Then what is the answer? Why must humans treat each other this way? Why must vermin like him survive when good men and women do not?"

"Only the gods know," Jai said.

"I'm sorry," Axa said from behind.

Jai turned, at first assuming he was talking to his mirror again. But no, Axa was looking directly at him. Slowly, he turned the mirror around. "Sorry," he said again.

"Jai Jiroux," a voice boomed from the mirror.

Subconsciously, Jai took a step back, because that voice...

That voice.

A powdered face appeared in the reflection, smiling. Diamonds sparkled from his chalk-white skin. His narrow eyes bore into Jai like twin blades.

Emperor Hoza stared at Jai. And then he said, "Slaves! Capture Jai Jiroux and the Black Tears. Bring them to me."

Jai whirled around, not understanding, trying to make sense of the senseless. "Yes, Master," the slaves said in unison.

Joaquin was the first to grab Jai, and he didn't struggle, not as dozens more piled on him, binding his arms and feet. Nearby, Shanti's eyes were wild as she was bound too. Sonika fought like a tigress, but was eventually subdued. The rest of the Tears were also captured.

Jai lay in shock, his cheek pressed against the ground. What had happened? What had Axa done? Was this his fault?

Axa turned the mirror back around. "You have done well, slave," Vin Hoza said. "I will consider reinstating you as a master."

"Thank you, Master," Axa said.

Jai closed his eyes.

509

Forty
The Northern Kingdom, Castle Hill
Annise Gäric

Annise felt numb. Bodies littered the castle grounds. Hundreds. Old men who should've been living out the last of their days next to warm fires. Young boys who should've still had their entire lives ahead of them. Seasoned warriors who had fought in, and survived, numerous battles, only to fall under her watch. Too many. She'd lost all but seven of her army. Utter annihilation. And yet they'd emerged victorious. No matter how hard she tried, she couldn't seem to reconcile the two conflicting truths.

Losing Sir Craig, her aunt's husband, hurt the most, especially because he'd been killed in the battle's waning moments, while carrying out *her* plan.

Is victory worth the cost?

She wanted to look away, to hide her eyes from the truth before her, but instead she planted her feet on the wall and stared down at the carnage, at her dead, at the remains of each of the monsters they'd slain. They'd fought *for her.* They'd died *for her.* She could've just relinquished the crown to her uncle and disappeared, and then all of these people would still be alive.

Why did you do this, Uncle?

There was no answer now, nor would there ever be. Sometimes men were just evil in the core of their souls, this she knew. Her father was one like that. Her uncle was another.

But if she had not fought, had not risen to the occasion, the kingdom would be doomed. She had to make their deaths mean something. She had to bring peace to the north for the first time in a century.

"I did as you commanded, Your Highness," Sir Metz said, approaching.

"Good," Annise said without looking away from the corpse-littered courtyard. "Thank you." Sir Metz, as always, had been eager for her orders, even after the long, exhausting battle. Annise had immediately sent him to the castle pond to send a stream to Blackstone with the news of the Imposter King's downfall, and that Annise had reclaimed the crown. The message ended with an order to cancel the attack against the west across the Bay of Bounty, and for nine-tenths of the northern army to withdraw. She hoped she'd been quick enough, and that an alliance with the west was still a possibility, regardless of Queen Rhea Loren's stubbornness. As queen, Annise's first order of business would be to refortify the borders at Darrin and Raider's Pass. From there, she wasn't certain what to do next.

Annise also had Metz stream a message to the east, informing the Ironclads of the change in northern leadership and warning them not to attempt an assault at Raider's Pass nor Darrin. She hoped it would work—it would take time for her troops at Blackstone to complete the journey to their eastern borders.

Tarin hadn't stopped moving since the battle ended. Annise watched as he strode from body to body, salvaging their weapons, which he knew they might need for the rest of the army when they arrived in Castle Hill. There was a pile for swords, one for armor, one for boots. The men kept their uniforms and personal possessions. From there he would throw a man over each shoulder, and sometimes one across his back, too, and haul them to a growing pile. Carrying three at a time, Tarin looked huge. Well, hug*er*. Though previously she thought her eyes might've been playing tricks on her—how could a man as large as him get any bigger?—now she was certain. He *was* bigger, at least by a head, maybe more, a mamoothen of a man.

What is happening to you, Tarin? For the first time since she'd known him, he made no move to replace his helm or to pull his mesh mask to cover his face.

Although she was certain he was aware of her gaze, he never looked up at her, continuing the work that would break a lesser man's back, heaping hundreds of bodies in a pile.

He's preparing a funeral pyre, Annise thought. In the north, the ground was generally too hard and frozen to bury a body, so fire was used, the ashes scattered in the Frozen Lake or on the wind. It was said that if the ashes were deemed worthy, they would be taken up into the clouds, becoming part of the snowfall. If unworthy, they were sent to frozen hell, where the person would form once more, only to live out a thousand lifetimes in misery.

Annise hoped both her father and uncle were enjoying the fruits of their labors.

Tarin, she thought, her eyes never leaving him. *Come to me.*

She knew he would not, not until the fire burning inside him had been extinguished, the voice quieted. Until then, he would use his aggression to carry bodies.

Dietrich and three of the four men he had left were off somewhere in the castle, searching for servants and other castle workers who might still be loyal to Lord Griswold. If any were found they were to be brought to Annise for interrogation.

The fourth surviving soldier had been sent to retrieve Archer, who had been left with a small contingent of guards.

Sir Jonius was still a bear, but he was growing smaller by the moment, resting against the wall beside the funeral pyre. Though his numerous wounds were serious, he wouldn't allow anyone to touch him. He, like Annise, refused to take his eyes from the desolation he'd been a part of.

Zelda sat in the puddle that used to be her husband, staring at something perhaps only she could see.

A sound finally pulled Annise's attention away from the yard. She looked back over her shoulder to where the city was spread out below her, a series of stone buildings connected by uneven cobblestone streets. Several soldiers, including the one she'd sent, moved slowly toward the castle. Behind them was a train of carts bearing the tradesmen and women who'd travelled with the army from Gearhärt. Annise immediately spotted the blacksmith cart, where Fay sat working on some new design, the next version of Evenstar perhaps. Her gaze moved on, toward the front of the line of carts, until she saw a horse attached to a cart laden with supplies.

For some strange reason, she expected to find Archer awake, and her heart leapt in her chest.

But no, he was unconscious, his form as still as the dead.

Annise sighed, making her way toward the steps that led down from the wall.

Sir Metz was still standing at attention, as if awaiting her next command. "At ease," she said. "I have no need of your service right now."

"Thank you, Your Highness. I will polish my armor as I await your call."

"As you wish, Sir," Annise said. For once, his armor *did* need a good cleaning. "Be sure to obtain sustenance as well."

He bowed and descended the stone steps.

Annise made to follow him, but then stopped when movement in the city caught her attention. It wasn't the guards leading Arch's cart up the lane, but behind them. Someone else, stepping from one of the buildings. A man wearing a thick coat and scarf. A woman crowded behind him, equally dressed for the weather. They peered after the soldiers and cart.

Others emerged from hiding, citizens of the north, gazing respectfully after their beloved prince. The one they always hoped would one day be their king.

Annise tried to take a breath but couldn't seem to get her lungs to work. Finally, the air shuddered through her throat. Despite all the people below her and the height from which she stood, she felt alone and small. It was as if now that she was back in Castle Hill, she was that broad-shouldered princess again, who preferred wrestling with the boys in the yard to dancing at the winter ball. Unlikeable. Unlovable. Destined to be Archer's awkward older sister, *What's her name again?*

And then Zelda was beside her, sticking her jaw out defiantly. A moment later Sir Dietrich appeared, along with his men. Sir Metz, his armor still unpolished, returned next. Sir Jonius, who was a man again, save for extraordinarily hairy arms and legs, strode up the steps and fell in line. His chest was laced with gashes and spotted with bruises, but his thick bearskin had protected him enough that he would survive. He couldn't seem to form a smile, but his eyes were the same, always the same, as he nodded to her.

Annise nodded back and then looked around, expecting Tarin to come next, but he was still toiling in the yard, sweat dripping from his brow.

She wanted desperately to go down those stairs, to meet Arch's cart, to shake him until he awoke, to beg him to tell her what to say to the people gathering outside the wall.

His people. Even now, even as the queen, she couldn't think of them as hers.

She gritted her teeth and stuck out her jaw and planted her feet on snowy stones, willing her toes to grow roots. *I will not leave this spot until these people are* my *people.*

The soldiers led the horses and cart train through the gate, but Annise didn't watch them. Her eyes were focused on the people milling about below, stamping their feet in the cold, their breath misting from their lips. Once they had stopped moving up the laneway and were gathered tightly together, she spoke.

"I am your queen," she said. "I will not fail you."

She had an entire speech planned out in her mind, all about how she would be better than her father, how she would listen to her people, how she would reduce their taxes and protect them from enemies both within and without their borders.

But she never got to give that speech, because it was after only those nine words that the people began cheering and stomping their feet. They raised their hands toward her, their fists clenched. "Queen Annise!" they sang. "Queen Annise!"

A tear trickled down her cheek.

Later that day, Annise sat beside Zelda. They stared at their reflections in the puddle, which had reformed into ice as the temperature dropped. The iced-over puddle was all that was left of Sir Craig.

"Aunt," Annise started to say, but Zelda cut her off.

"Did I ever tell you about your uncle?"

"Lord Griswold? What about him?" She frowned. Her uncle had never been warm toward her, and frankly, she didn't care. She wouldn't mourn his passing.

"No. Helmuth," Zelda said.

Annise shook her head, wondering where this was going. "All I know about Uncle Helmuth is that he left Castle Hill long before I was born, after Grandfather skipped over him in the line of succession." She also knew he had been born with a lame foot, which was why he was remembered as the Maimed Prince, a nickname that had always bothered Annise. Surely there was something more important to remember him by than a deformity from birth.

Zelda nodded. "That's correct. My father was a difficult man, but at his core, his heart was gold. It just needed a little polishing before you could see it. In the end, he regretted the way he'd treated Helmuth. He hated that he'd driven him away." She paused, seeming to collect her thoughts. "Unlike Griswold and Wolfric, I never despised Helmuth. We weren't friends, exactly, but we played together sometimes. Games of the mind rather than of the body. We were closely matched, but he usually won. Your Uncle Helmuth was clever. He might've made a good king in another world."

Although the story was fairly interesting to Annise—she'd never heard anyone speak a good word about Helmuth—she still didn't understand her aunt's purpose in telling it. And one thing she'd learned from spending time around Zelda was that she always had a purpose. "This isn't another world though. It's the only world we've got."

Zelda offered a toothless smile. "My point is, I mourned Helmuth when he left, just as I grieved for my father. We all mourn differently. I choose to remember all the good, because most of people have plenty of good in them, even if they do foolish things from time to time. Craig had the most good of any man I've ever met. He was the only man who looked at me and saw me. Really saw me. This thing is rare to find."

Annise nodded. She knew that as well as anyone. Tarin was the only one who'd ever made her feel that way.

Zelda continued. "Craig lived a good life. Half the time he was scared of his own shadow, and yet he refused to hide from the sun. He took chances he never had to take, risked his life for what he knew was right. He fought to the very end."

"I'm sorry I thought bad thoughts about him," Annise said. "I'm sorry I believed him to be a coward."

"Don't be ridiculous," Zelda said. "You couldn't have known. My husband was a talented actor. When he was Drunk Craig, he hid his honor in his false flask. When he was Sir Craig, he hid his fear behind his shield. He was one of a kind, and he always had affection for you. He told me many times how much he believed in you. As queen. As a person."

"He did?" The thought made tears well up, and Annise let them drip down her cheeks and splash onto the ice.

"We all do. Why the frozen hell do you think we're here fighting monsters? Well, besides for the fun of it!"

Annise laughed and hugged her aunt, who, despite her jape, was also crying. They held the embrace for a long time, remembering Sir Craig. Remembering his sacrifice.

Annise was worried about Tarin. Well, *more* worried. She was used to how he would pull within himself after a battle, but he'd never avoided her for this long.

Give him time, she kept telling herself, but after a week with no communication…

I'm losing him, she realized. *Enough is enough. No more waiting.*

So she went to him. Sir Metz insisted on following her around as her personal guard, and she was too exhausted to begrudge him the honor. "Wait here," she told him as she entered the small underground room. He didn't object, although he didn't seem that keen on leaving her side.

The room had once belonged to the potionmaster, old Darkspell, who Annise had been frightened of as a child. It was his potion that had created the ninety-nine monsters that had devastated her army. Unfortunately, when Sir Dietrich and his men had searched the castle, they'd found no sign of the hunched old man. His supplies were gone, too, leading them to believe that he'd fled as soon as the battle began, perhaps even earlier.

A wise move. Annise would've seen him strung up by his wrinkled old toes for what he did.

Now, Tarin had claimed the room for his own, spending hours in the dark, not even bothering to light a candle or lamp. It was here that she found him now, his back resting against the stone wall, his elbows on his knees, his head stuffed between them, eyes downcast. Though he still wore his armor, his helmet was off, his head and face exposed.

Despite his size, his strength, his armor, he looked so vulnerable it almost brought a tear to Annise's eyes.

"Leave me," he said as she shone her lamplight across him. His voice was a shadow of the man she knew.

"No," she said, still fighting back tears.

"I am dangerous."

"Yes," she agreed. "To our enemies."

He shook his head, looking away once more. "To everyone. To myself. To you. This thing inside me…I can't control it. I thought I could, but I was wrong. It controls me."

"You weren't wrong." Annise placed the lamp on the potionmaster's empty table, and strode to Tarin, grabbing his chin in a tight grip.

His eyes met hers. "I love you," she said, her voice trembling. Only as she said it did she realize it was the first time she'd told him. *Why didn't I say it sooner?*

A tear trickled from his eye, meandering down his cheek, changing direction each time it crossed one of his protruding black veins.

"Look, Tarin," she said. "Whatever is happening to you, we can face—"

His expression changed in an instant as he cut her off. "You have no idea what is happening to me," he growled. He reached up and touched her jawline, which still bore the long shadow of a bruise. His touch was too tender for the words he'd just spoken, and they made Annise shiver. "You say you love me? Then you have to let me go. I cannot put you at risk any longer."

"What?" *Let him go?* "Tarin, no. I won't. I can't. I am—"

"The queen," he interrupted. "And I am a distraction, and a dangerous one."

She'd had enough of this talk. "Do you love me?" she said.

"You know that I do, Ann—"

"Then what else is there to talk about?"

"It's not that simple." He raised his hand as if to touch her—she wished he would touch her—but then let it fall to his side. "I am the only one of my kind, and no one, myself included, knows what I'm capable of."

"You're not a monster."

"Tell that to the monsters I slayed during battle."

"We *all* killed them. We *all* became something other than our normal selves. That is war. It'll make monsters of us all."

"But I'm different and you know it."

"I've been told the exact same thing my entire life, but I'm not running away from you."

"But you're not—"

"Stop!" Annise grabbed his chin beneath her hands and kissed him. He hesitated for a moment, but then kissed her back, roping his hand around the back of her head, his fingers nestling against her scalp, pulling her toward him. Like he couldn't breathe without her. Like she was an addiction he couldn't get enough of. His other hand found her hips and maneuvered her against him, into his lap. She slipped her tongue into his mouth and, as her fingers traced hot lines down his jaw and along his neck, he groaned.

A quarter-hour later they were both warm and sweaty and, though still fully clothed, it didn't feel that way. Annise nestled into the crook of his arm, not even minding the hardness of the armor beneath her head. "Glad we settled that," she said.

Tarin sighed. "That was an evil trick."

She laughed. "But it worked, didn't it?"

"For now."

"We'll 'talk' later. And by talk I mean remove our clothes."

He shook his head again, but didn't argue further.

"Now I've got a few matters to attend to. Would you like to come?"

"No, thanks. I might soak in a cold bath."

She smiled. "Is that my fault?"

"Completely."

"Good. I'll have Dietrich melt some snow. See you later?"

He nodded.

Sir Metz seemed anxious when she finally emerged from the room. Well, more anxious than usual. "A stream has arrived," the knight said. "It's from Blackstone."

"Good," she said. "We need information."

Metz led her up the stairs and along the stone corridors. Though it had seemed like night in the dark potionmaster's room below, aboveground it was midday, white sunlight breaking through the thick gray clouds. It was in the throne room that Annise found her guardsmen and aunt gathered, standing in a semicircle around the throne.

Their stares found her, their expressions serious. She climbed the dais, but didn't sit. "Did you read the message?" she asked Sir Dietrich.

"Yes."

"And what does it say?"

He pursed his lips briefly, and then said, "Blackstone has fallen."

The words made no sense. "Fallen? But my uncle had thousands of soldiers there, the entire strength of the north. That simply cannot be."

"The truth is hard to hear sometimes," Zelda said. "That's why so many people avoid it."

"It is signed by six separate lords," Dietrich said, showing her the bottom of the letter. "As Lady Zelda said, it is the truth. Northern forces crossed the Bay of Bounty at full strength. Your uncle planned on taking Knight's End and then marching south. Hundreds of warships sank. No soldier was left alive, save for the ones Queen Loren sent back across the bay to tell the story of her victory. It is said a creature of the deep rose up and decimated our armies. It is said Rhea herself controlled the creature."

Frozen hell. First her uncle's army of monsters and now this? The Four Kingdoms had descended into chaos. *We have no army. I am looking at the entirety of our strength in this one room. Well, except for Tarin.*

Annise felt the room begin to spin. She took a step back and sank onto the throne. "All is lost," she said.

"Your Highness, if I may?" Sir Jonius stepped forward. He was completely back to normal now, the monster potion having worn off days ago.

Annise couldn't speak, but she gestured for him to go ahead.

He cleared his throat. "These are perilous times, and your uncle was taking drastic measures."

"I hadn't noticed," Annise said dryly. She wasn't in the mood for a recap of the carnage her uncle's monsters had wrought on her army, nor more talk about Blackstone.

Jonius soldiered on, unperturbed by her weary tone. "Toward the end, Lord Griswold was obsessed with an ancient scroll he'd found locked away in your father's private collection."

Annise frowned. "What scroll?"

"It was a map."

"What map?"

"A map to the Sleeping Knights."

Annise breathed out heavily. "They are a children's bedtime story."

"Your uncle didn't think so."

"My uncle was a fool."

"Now that is the truth," Zelda said. "But that doesn't mean he was wrong."

Jonius took another step forward. "He was an evil man, yes, like your father, and perhaps a fool, but he certainly believed in this…bedtime story, as you call it."

Anger swirled inside Annise. "If you believe my father and uncle were so evil, why were you their stepping stool for all these years? Why did you kill on their behalf? Why did you betray me? Yes, you helped us in the end, but do you think that makes up for everything you did? All the atrocities?" Annise realized she'd stood up at some point during her tirade, her hands fisted at her sides.

Jonius only looked sad. He said, "My wife was sick."

Annise paused, glancing at her aunt. Zelda shrugged; apparently she wasn't aware of this information either. Annise said, "I didn't know you had a wife. I never saw her in court."

"She was bedridden for many years."

"I'm sorry for that," Annise said, still wondering how she could've been ignorant to so much about this man's life. "But what does that have to do with your actions?"

He told her everything. About how years ago Darkspell had formulated a tonic that kept Sir Jonius's wife alive, how first the Dread King and then the Imposter King threatened to cut off the supply if the knight didn't obey their every command. Sir Jonius began crying partway through the story, and that was when Annise knew exactly how it would end.

"When did she die?" she asked. "Your wife."

Sir Jonius blinked, unshed tears sparkling in his eyes. "A fortnight ago. First I tried to escape, but your uncle's men caught me, imprisoned me. Then I tried to take my own life, but I failed. Or perhaps I was too cowardly."

"You are no coward, Sir," Annise said. "You proved that with your valor during the battle. I would be dead if not for you. We all would."

He shook his head. "I want to be tried for my crimes against the kingdom. I will admit to them all. I have not forgotten a single one."

Annise descended the steps one at a time, slowly. She placed a hand on his shoulder. She felt as if her heart was cloven in two, first by Tarin's words, and now by this knight's. "I will not try you for crimes you were manipulated into committing by my father and uncle."

As fresh tears bloomed, he shoved his knuckles into his mouth, biting down hard. When he removed them, he said, "My wife is dead. She was my life, my everything, as pure as freshly fallen snow. And I keep asking myself, why am I still alive? Is this my punishment? What is left for me to live for?"

"I don't know," Annise said. "But you *are* alive. And if you cannot live for yourself, Sir Jonius, live for me. Serve me and I will do everything in my power to rebuild our great kingdom, with you by my side."

He shook his head, but Annise knew it wasn't his answer. "Good," she said. "Now show me this scroll of yours."

Calling the scroll a "map" was being generous. Yes, it showed landmarks like the Mournful Mountains and Frozen Lake, but beyond that it was difficult to discern. Clearly, Sir Jonius was correct about its purpose: "Sleeping Knights" was written in flowery calligraphy near the top of the map, right above a spot labelled "Cavern of the Ancients," set deep into the Hinterlands, further north than anyone had ever explored, at least as far as Annise knew.

There was one great explorer, however, Heinrich Gäric, the same Crimean explorer who'd originally discovered the Four Kingdoms, who'd led a party far to the north in search of gold. No one really knew what had happened to him, and that was five hundred years ago anyway.

On the other hand, the legend of the Sleeping Knights was no secret. One of Annise's childhood nurses had told she and Arch the story many times, upon request. The one-thousand knights were said to have been the elite soldiers of the early northern kingdom, established shortly after the first Gärics had splintered off from western rule, declaring their independence.

Annise's ancestor, the fourth Gäric ruler, King Brown Gäric, was said to be a strange man, a superstitious recluse who dabbled in sorcery. After his elite squad was formed and trained, he'd supposedly found a way to grant them immortality, so they would always protect the north from invasion. However, what he didn't know was that once they were made immortal, they would leave him for the Hinterlands. According to the legend, they'd left because they were not truly needed, and only when they were called upon in the north's true time of need would they rise up again from their slumber.

"A bedtime story," Annise said again, sighing.

"Perhaps," Zelda said. "Perhaps not."

Annise looked to Sir Dietrich. "What do you think?"

He looked surprised to be asked for advice. "The only other option is to begin training new soldiers from the cities. It will take years, especially because we have so few knights left to train them."

Annise didn't have years. She might not even have days. The north was ripe for the taking, and as soon as the rest of the Four Kingdoms realized it, they would swarm through Raider's Pass and grab Castle Hill by the throat. "I don't know that we have any other choice," she said.

"I always wanted to meet one of the Sleeping Knights," Zelda said, brushing a finger across the spot on the map.

Hours had passed since she'd left Tarin, but finally Annise and her inner circle agreed to sleep on the choice of whether to pursue the supposedly immortal Sleeping Knights, and make a final decision on the morrow. Now, she sought him out once more, determined to talk some sense into him.

He wasn't in her quarters, like she had hoped. She asked several people, but no one had seen him. Grudgingly, she traipsed back down the steps into the darkest part of the castle, seeking him in the potionmaster's old room.

She scanned the room. Empty.

Memories flashed of Tarin sitting in the corner. How he'd kissed her, breathed her in. How he was like kindling to the fire inside her.

She frowned, and was about to turn to search elsewhere when she saw a sliver of parchment peeking out from beneath the table. Evidently a gust of wind had blown it to the floor.

She stooped and picked it up, the paper slightly crinkled, as if it had been splashed with moisture, only to have dried.

Her heart stopped. Her breath caught. Her fingers shook.

All she'd read was the very bottom, where Tarin's name was signed in neat lettering, just beneath the words "Goodbye, my love."

Hot tears splashed on the page as she read the rest:

My dearest Annise,

You are perfection exactly the way you are, while I am a broken man. This monster inside me has eaten too much of my heart, my soul, and I fear my every action. Being reunited with you gave me hope, with your every word, with your every touch, that I could be fixed. You made me better. But alas, it wasn't enough.

I continue to have hope for the kingdom, however, as I know you will be the queen you were meant to be, the queen the realm deserves. My greatest sorrow is that I will not be there to see you rule, to share your embrace, to feel the touch of your beautiful lips upon mine.

Our time together was too short. Too hell-frozen short. I would gladly die for one more day, one more night, but I will not risk your safety for my own selfish desires. I will cherish the time we had, the memories.

Do not seek me out, for you shall not find me. Perhaps in my solitude the monster will retreat into the dark hole it emerged from when I drank the witch's potion. But, please, do not wait for me to return, as I don't expect I ever will. Find a suitor who will love you the way I have.

Goodbye, my love,
Tarin Sheary, the Armored Knight

She placed the note gently on the table, using her dress to wipe it clean of her tears. Then she dried the tears on her cheeks. Memories flashed through her mind: building a shelter on the Howling Tundra together, sharing body heat all night; the first time they'd kissed, after the battle at Raider's Pass; his japes about her being the Bear Slayer; the pink hope flower he'd pressed into her hand; their first night together, the passion they shared, the love. Their embrace had felt like a fire that could never be snuffed out, but which was now a wet pile of ashes leaking smoke.

She remembered what she had thought while riding, how she would rather die than live without Tarin. Now, as she faced that exact scenario, she wondered if she'd meant it. Was she like Sir Jonius, her lifeblood connected to that of another person so deeply that without him she was lost?

She thought of the people of Castle Hill chanting her name while she stood high on the wall. Not Archer's name, but hers.

No, she thought fiercely. She was saddened greatly by Tarin's departure, almost as sad as she had been when her mother had been executed, but no, she didn't want to die. No, her strength, her life, was not tied to one man or to any man. It was tied to something inside her, an inner strength she never knew she had. Not until now, anyway.

I am the queen.

She didn't need some silly title after the traditions of her father and grandfather, like the Undefeated King or Dread King.

No. I am Queen Annise Gäric, and that is enough.

Forty-One
The Southern Empire, Phanes,
the Southron Gates
Raven Sandes

Fire had easily melted the first of the four iron Gates, the liquefied ore pooling on the ground, cooling rapidly and forming a metal floor. At some point, there had been an explosion, and then another, but from where, Raven knew not.

From there, Fire led their forces west along the wall, toward the next of the Gates, nearly a day's march away. They took heavy fire from the wall's defenders the entire distance. Arrows, heavy stones, and vats of boiling tar rained from above, killing many.

But still they marched, as Surai arced overhead, cooking them alive in their leather armor. It was almost as bad as the desert—worse perhaps—because they couldn't stop to rest. Twice Raven deflected arrows with her shield. Being on the enemy's side of the wall had its advantages, however. Thrice small forces of chalk-faced Phanecian soldiers sallied out from Sousa and attacked in the typical phen ru style—spinning wooden batons capped with blades on each end and using acrobatic maneuvers—but they were ill-prepared for a full-scale assault on their side of the wall, and Goggin and his guanero were able to repel them without taking a significant number of casualties. Also, Fire sent platoons of soldiers up the stone staircases, where they fought along the wall. Eventually, Fire and Raven took to the wall as well, using the high ground to move quickly across the borderlands. To the north were the four western border cities: Vinya, Sarris, Cleo, and Felix, the counterparts to the Phanecian warcities. Beyond them were the Forbidden Plains, an infernal stretch of uninhabited land meant as a buffer between Phanes and the west.

Up ahead, a large enemy contingent blocked their path, but Fire launched several fireballs, scattering them off the sides, where they fell to their deaths. Raven's sister's words came back to her.

I am a weapon.

Indeed, she was, Raven could not deny it. But still, it didn't mean Fire wasn't more than that, too. When they returned to Calypso, she would convince her of that, beating it into her head if necessary.

Their warriors and guanik were weary, but still Fire led them onwards, toward their goal of destroying the second of the Gates. With half of the four Gates destroyed, it would be months before their faata could gather enough ore to replace the enormous iron barriers, which had previously taken a year each to construct. By then, it was almost certain that the north would be in position to march on the south. Pincered between the north and Calyp, Phanes would surely fall.

As planned, they reached the second Gate just as the sun goddess slipped below the horizon, spraying the sky with her final gift—flowers of purple, red, and pink.

They descended the staircase above the Gate, and, once more, Fire placed her palms, fingers splayed, on the thick metal, which bore an intricate design of the four-eyed lioness. Her hands glowed red, the heat and color emanating outwards, superheating the metal until it began to drip red-hot tears.

Fire danced back, joining Raven and the rest of the guanero who were silently watching, many of them with their swords, scimitars, and whips raised high in support of the empress. "Arrrrr!" Goggin roared, a war cry of victory. Many echoed his call.

"We should retreat," Raven said. "We have accomplished what we set out to do and there are many leagues between here and the Spear."

Fire said, "Hemptown is due south of here."

"Exactly," Raven said. "The army at Sousa will have sent word already. They'll be preparing a counterattack. If we race along the wall, we may be able to escape before they cut us off."

Fire shook her head. "We haven't lost more than a twentieth of our force. We have marched far. I will not waste this opportunity."

"Waste it? You have destroyed two of the Great Southron Gates. The day is won. Accept victory where you have achieved it."

"Here is my command," Fire said. "I will ride south with the guanero. You will lead the rest of the army back across the Spear to the Scarra. May we meet again in Kesh with its famed hospitality."

"Fire, no," Raven said. "I cannot leave you. I will not."

"Will you deny my command, sister? That is treason."

"Then I choose death," Raven said without hesitation. Though she hadn't exactly grown closer to Fire on this journey, she felt she understood her more. She knew what her sister was doing, what she was risking. She couldn't let her do it alone.

Fire sighed. "You need to return to Calypso. If I don't return, you will rule. We cannot let it fall on Whisper's shoulders."

In the end, the decision was taken out of both their hands, as Goggin cried, "Incoming soldiers!"

Raven and Fire turned their gazes to the south, where an army was running northward. This was no small counterforce, but a formidable army at least twice their size. The soldiers wore armor plate painted black and red like the massive desert pyzons Phanes was known for. They ran, not in formation, but in small groups, weaving in and out of each other in a classic Phanecian manner designed to confuse the enemy. "Sister, hear reason," Raven pleaded. "We can still retreat. Our soldiers are made stronger from this journey. We can outrun them."

"I will not run," Fire said, her eyes dancing with flames.

Raven had known her sister long enough to realize when her mind was made up. "Then there is only one choice left."

"Yes," Fire said. "We fight."

"May I?"

Fire nodded.

"On my command," Raven said, raising her whip in the air. The wind seemed to stop, as if holding its breath along with the soldiers. "Charge!"

The foot soldiers, in classic Calypsian diamond formation, led the rush across the desertlands, the earth cracking under their heavy trod. The guanero filled in the hollow center of the diamond, holding back for the initial wave to make contact. Arrows fell amongst them, but even the Phanecians seemed to prefer a hand-to-hand clash, which meant most of the enemy were probably masters of phen ru.

And then, like two great waves colliding on an ocean of sand, the two armies came together, thousands of men and women locked in a battle that would be recorded by the survivors in the annals of history.

A blade of enemies burst through their ranks, fighting like wildcats in the typical Phanecian manner: furious and without abandon, powdered white faces flashing in the dying light. There were no slaves amongst them, which supported Raven's belief that her faata was building up his slave army in the heart of the empire—Phanea. The Phanecians performed phen ru backflips and frontflips and even sideflips, attacking acrobatically. Their thin boots were strapped with blades, and they aimed deadly kicks at throats and chests. Knives were tied to their wrists, and when they raked their fists through the air, steel flashed. Dozens of Calypsians fell under the onslaught.

Raven swung her whip, lashing it across the eyes of one soldier who tried to leap at her wielding a bladed staff. He howled, clutching his eyes and falling, where he was cut down by Goggin as the large man rode past. The guanik snapped and clawed at the Phanecian horses, which were mighty steeds at least twice as large as the typical western horses. The stallions, which were also painted red and black, kicked back, refusing to back down.

Fire was a tornado of fiery fury, slashing her enflamed sword at any who came close, while simultaneously launching fireballs into pockets of the enemy. A group of archers targeted her, but she melted their arrowheads and charred the wooden shafts as the darts flew through the air. Another fireball wiped out the lot of them.

Raven's reptilian steed, Iknon, barreled forward, trampling a soldier, who screamed as he was crushed underfoot, while Raven cracked her whip once more, curling it around the neck of a man, yanking him off his feet. With a quick snap of her wrist, she flung a knife through his throat.

As the battle continued, Raven lost sight of her sister, though evidence of Fire's power was everywhere: piles of human ash; half-melted swords and shields; fireballs arcing across the sky. Where Fire went, death followed.

Night fell, and still the armies battled, until there were more dead than living, a mixture of alternating dark and pale faces staring up at the sky with empty eyes. Raven and Iknon were forced to pick their way carefully across the killing fields, searching for enemy combatants. Her leg was bleeding profusely where she'd taken a slash from a rider's sword. Iknon was covered in blood, too, both human, horse, and guanik, though Raven wasn't sure whether any of it was his.

Raven pulled her mount to a halt, her eyes searching the gloom for any sign of Fire. There were many fires burning, but none moving. Occasionally steel rang against steel, and voices cried in pain and battle, but they died away more quickly, until they were few and far between. Other shadows moved across the landscape, some heading south—surviving Phanecians retreating to Hemptown or beyond.

Raven marveled at the fact that they seemed to have won, despite their much smaller force. It was a testament to their strict training regimen, as well as the advantage Fire's power gave them.

Goggin appeared before her, looking much like a monster with a long slash across his face and his missing ear. One arm dangled limply from his side, broken. Still, he held one scimitar in his other hand. For once, his expression was grim.

"Where is the empress?" Raven asked, dismounting.

Goggin shook his head. "Not sure," he grunted. "Last I saw her she was off yonder. She was battling many foes."

"And winning, no doubt," Raven said, her words far more certain than the fear roiling through her gut. *If she is dead, I would feel it*, Raven thought, assuring herself. "With me, commander."

Goggin followed her as she moved in the direction he'd last seen Fire.

"So many dead," Raven murmured.

"War is death," Goggin said.

"This was supposed to be a mission, not a war."

"These days, they're the same thing."

They found Fire ringed by dead enemy soldiers. She was lying on the ground, staring up at the stars; several of the red gods were blazing across the sky, much like they had on that night Raven had sat beside her in the desert. A blade was embedded in Fire's stomach, her fingers clasped around it as if in prayer.

"Sister," Fire said when she saw Raven kneel beside her.

"Don't speak," Raven said, her heart sinking into her gut. "We need to bind your wounds. Can you melt the sword from within?" Her hands trembled as she tore at her own clothing beneath her leather armor.

Fire shook her head. "I have no strength left." And then: "I'm glad you're alive. Keep Whisper safe. Defeat Faata. Reclaim the south. Honor me."

"You can honor yourself," Raven said.

"I go to the gods. Watch for me amongst the stars."

"No, I'm going to get you help. We brought healers with us for this very purpose." *If any are alive.*

"I have played my part, sister. Now it's time for you to play yours."

Raven cried out as her sister's skin began to burn. She stumbled backward, but Goggin caught her with one strong arm, picking her up and carrying her away. She screamed and punched and kicked at him, but he held her fast, his feet sure and steady as he weaved through the sea of dead.

Eventually, Raven stopped fighting, her body shaking with grief, though her eyes were dry. Finally, Goggin set her down, steadying her with his hand, preventing her from collapsing.

A fire blazed amongst the carnage, as high as a funeral cairn.

And then it exploded, the flames as white as the noonday sun, washing over the battlefield like a dust storm, licking at the bodies, consuming them in its heat. Instinctively, Raven and Goggin ducked, huddling together as the fire flowed over them, somehow never touching or burning them, an inferno all around. It was like being in a fire, but protected by some unseen force.

Unseen, but not unknown. *Fire,* Raven thought. *Fire protects us, even as she dies.*

"Oh gods!" she wailed. Because now she felt it. The hole inside her, the missing piece of her heart. The blank space in the world, where Fire used to be.

The tears finally came, dripping into the unburning flames.

The sparks soared into the night sky, thousands of fireflies spreading on the wind.
The grass of the Forbidden Plains caught first, the brittle plants tinder for the unnatural flames.
Next was the Tangle, which began to burn like a bonfire.
Though the east and the west had long been separated by war, hatred, and fear, it was now split in half by Fire.

Few of the enemy had survived on the battlefields south of the Southron Gates. The warcities of Sousa and Hemptown were decimated, depleted of their armies because of Fire's final act. Even in death she was the weapon she had promised to be.

As for the Calypsians, Raven and Goggin now led the survivors, a force of three hundred strong. *One tenth*, she thought. If she hadn't seen the bodies herself, she wouldn't have believed it. Of those three hundred, almost a third were too injured to walk, which meant every two soldiers had to carry another between them. The only positive was that the guanero had defied the odds, more than half of the guanik-riding warriors and their steeds surviving the battle.

It was slow going, the journey back to the Spear taking twice as long in reverse, especially because small bands of Phanecians harried them with arrows shot from the wall from time to time. Each time a band appeared, Raven and Goggin were forced to halt the retreat, fight to the top of the wall, and kill them. It was slow and gruesome work, and they lost another twenty-six lives while doing it.

Eventually, however, the Spear appeared, a gossamer thread of liquid steel.

On the other side, they rested, cleaned and dressed their wounds, and ate.

Raven sat on the riverbank with her head in her hands. She felt cold inside, like Fire had taken all of her warmth when she'd passed on to the next world. Goggin sat near her, not speaking, understanding her need for silence. The large man was proving to be far more perceptive than Raven had ever given him credit for.

She sat like that for a long time, thinking about her mother, about Fire, and finally, about Whisper. Thinking of Whisper hurt the most, because Raven knew she would be heartbroken. She wondered whether she should've fought Fire harder when they were planning this mission, persuaded her to wait, to consider other options.

But no. Once Fire's mind was made up, changing it was like trying to stop a storm.

I loved her for that, Raven thought. She never realized it until now.

The Spear burbled swiftly downstream, and Raven wondered what it would be like to jump in, to let the current carry her into the Burning Sea, never to return.

"Whisper needs me," she said aloud. It was a reminder to herself that though Fire's life was over, hers was not.

"We all need you," Goggin said. Raven flinched; she had forgotten the guanero commander was still sitting with her, his presence like a calming breeze.

Raven shook her head. "Calyp is broken."

"That's where you're wrong," Goggin said. "Calyp was not your mother, or Fire, or even you. Calyp is more than any person, even an empress. Calyp is a proud nation, home to thousands of souls who depend on us to protect them. And, just like your sister was, Calyp is as strong as ever."

Raven was about to respond, to thank Goggin for speaking the words she needed to hear, when a shout arose. She swiveled around, craning her head toward the side, noticing a shadow moving across the dunes of the Scarra. She squinted, gazing at the sky, where a bird angled their way.

Wait. It was too large to be a bird, and getting larger by the second. "Dragon," Goggin breathed, and Raven knew he was right. It was one of the largest in the brood, Heiron, a black sinewy creature with an addiction to bacon spiced with *mixa*. Raven had grown up with him—he was hatched when she was but five years old. Based on the side-to-side style of flight, Raven also knew who the rider was: Rider, the dragon master, her black cloak flapping in the wind.

While the entire camp watched, Heiron unfurled his wings and circled twice, finally swooping down to land with impressive grace beside Raven. She couldn't help the laugh that bubbled from her lips, though her eyes sparkled with tears. Heiron, who seemed to be grinning a razor-sharp grin, nuzzled against her hand when she held it out. Though the dragon was larger than any ten of the guanik put together, he was still at least a year away from full maturity. And the next year would be his biggest growth spurt yet, a thought that still made Raven marvel.

Rider slid off her mount, her dark eyes laced with concern. Unlike the dragon, she was not grinning. Without Raven needing to say a word, Rider strode up to her and embraced her. Raven's tears soaked the woman's cloak.

When Raven pulled back, Rider said, "I'm so sorry." Though the woman, who was twelve years Raven's elder, had a sharp, angular face, her expression was full of compassion.

"How did you know?"

"From your face. And from a distance I saw how small your force had become. I feared the worst."

"So Whisper doesn't know yet?"

"How could she?"

Raven nodded. "It is better that I am the one to tell her. Now, tell me Rider, why have you crossed the desert on dragonback?"

The compassion slipped from Rider's face, replaced by a frown. "Grian Ironclad has turned his attention away from the north."

Raven raised an eyebrow. "That surprises me. His father and brother were killed at Raider's Pass, his eldest brother injured. Surely he seeks revenge."

"We've received numerous streams in the last fortnight, since you've been gone."

"Saying what?"

"The north lost the bulk of its forces in the Bay of Bounty."

"Wh-what?" Raven had understood the words perfectly, but she couldn't make sense of them. Their entire plan to destroy half of the Southron Gates was built on the notion that the north would decimate the west and then march on Phanes.

Rider nodded. "It's true. Two other messages confirmed it. Evidently Queen Rhea is more formidable an enemy than anyone expected. It is said she Summoned a monster of the sea."

"So the north has fallen at last? What of Lord Griswold and Castle Hill?" Raven was still trying to process the news, what it all meant.

"The self-declared King Regent raised a final army of superhuman warriors using some kind of a potion. One hundred men who became monsters. But they were struck down by Queen Annise Gäric and her army of rebels striving to take back the crown. It seems they did."

Raven shook her head. Two queens, two mighty victories. She wondered what it might mean for her chances as empress. Other than her mother, the Four Kingdoms had long been ruled by men. "At what cost?" she asked.

"Annise lost all but a handful of soldiers, though her brother remains unconscious from the battle at Raider's Pass. If not for two great warriors, she might have lost the day."

"What warriors?"

"A giant known as the Armored Knight. And a great swordsman, a Sir Dietrich."

"So Queen Gäric has nothing left?"

"Correct. There are rumors that she fled north, into the Hinterlands."

"What is there?"

"Snow. Ice. Nothing. She is the least of your concerns."

Raven realized the conversation had come full circle, and that Rider had been holding something back the whole time, building to this point, or perhaps delaying the topic altogether. "You said King Ironclad has turned away from the north. Meaning what? That he's moving south?"

Rider shook her head. "Not *moving* south. He's already south, along with most of his troops. Without the north to defend against, he's shifted forces from Norris, Crow's Nest, and Glee."

Raven closed her eyes. She'd barely had a day to grieve the loss of her sister, and already reality was knocking at her door.

When she opened them again, she asked, "What are you not telling me?"

Rider grimaced, as if the next topic was too distasteful to broach. "We received a stream from Kesh as well. Several actually."

"Guta?"

She nodded. "He's completed his investigation into the assassination attempt on Fire."

"And?"

"The assassin was paid in iron shields. Hundreds of them were discovered in her personal effects."

"The east was plotting an assassination for *two years*?"

"It appears that way."

"Why us? Why not the west?"

"Perhaps they have paid assassins in many places. The Ironclads have always had a long memory."

Raven gritted her teeth. "So do the Sandes."

Forty-Two

The Crimean Sea, somewhere south of the Dead Isles
Grey Arris

G_{rey} felt warm and dry. He released a sigh of contentment. All the pain and fear were gone, swept away by death, and whatever came after.

He opened his eyes to sunlight spilling through a portal window. Beyond the window, there was blue sky. It was moving. No, *rocking*. He could feel everything rocking, swaying, gently moving side to side.

The bed beneath wasn't particularly soft. And the pain wasn't gone, after all. No, he could feel it in the aches in his joints and a strange numbness in his fingertips. He raised his left arm to find his hand still gone, but wrapped in fresh bandages.

"I'm not dead," he whispered.

Someone giggled, and he flinched, turning to follow the sound. A pair of sparkling brown eyes set in a cute brown face topped with a spill of unruly ringlets stared at him. "No, you're not dead, Grey Arris. Not today."

"Kyla? But how?" She sat in a chair by his bedside, an open book on her lap. And the way the sun was hitting her face…Grey lost his breath for a moment.

"We went back to find you," she said matter-of-factly.

"But your father…the captain…"

"It was his idea, believe it or not. We sailed south for half a day, and all Da did was pace the deck the whole time. Then, finally, he commanded the men to turn the ship around and make for the Dead Isles. I think half of them soiled their pants when he gave the order." She laughed lightly.

Grey shook his head in wonderment. He knew the captain's superstitions, how he believed bringing a ship near the isles would mean certain death. And yet he'd gone anyway. To help him. To save him.

Kyla continued. "Night had fallen, but he refused to sleep, manning the winches himself, steering the ship all on his own. I'd already had plenty of rest after…well, I wasn't tired anyway, so I kept lookout. I spotted you floating there in the water, and at first I thought you were dead, but then you lifted a hand…well, not a hand, but your"—she gestured to his stump—"arm, and so I shouted to Da who roused the men. They lowered him to the water with ropes and he grabbed you and your sister—"

"Shae!"

"She's fine. She's up on deck telling stories to the men. They're already very fond of her. She smiles more than you ever did…"

Grey swung his feet over the side of the bed and tried to stand up, but everything spun and he fell back down.

"Whoa there, hold on," Kyla said, resting a hand on Grey's chest to hold him back. "From the way Shae tells it, you've had a helluva ordeal. You need to rest."

Grey waited for the ship to stop spinning, and then placed his hand on top of Kyla's. It felt so…natural. So easy. Like the touch of someone he'd known his entire life. "Thank you," he said.

Kyla's lips parted slightly, an amused smile playing on their curves. "For what? It was Da who gave the orders."

"For being here when I woke up. For waiting for me."

Kyla smiled and leaned toward him. His heart raced as her soft brown lips opened further. She whispered in his ear. "It's a really good book and I didn't want to put it down," she said, pulling back and holding up the novel she'd been reading. "A love story, actually. There's this princess and this pauper, and, of course, they fall madly in love, but then everything goes wrong, and currently it seems they're both doomed to be apart."

Grey laughed and said, "Sounds like real life." He remembered what he'd felt for Rhea, but how he'd screwed everything up because of his selfishness and bravado. His arrogance.

"Perhaps. But I've read this one a thousand times, so I already know there's a happy ending."

Grey felt warmth on his cheeks and it wasn't because she'd told him the book's ending. No, it had nothing to do with the book, which was pure fiction. It had to do with the girl sitting in front of him, the feel of her hand in his, and what he knew he was about to do.

He leaned forward and kissed her.

At first she froze, her mouth flat and lifeless against his, and he wondered whether he'd made a grave mistake, but then she responded, her lips moving like gentle waves lapping against a shore. This kiss was so different to how it had been with Rhea— so much more tender, slower, like they had all day to finish it. And yet he could feel the passion like an electric current running through his veins, his heart galloping like a thousand horses.

Neither of them pulled away so much as there was a gradual, natural separation when the beautiful, perfect first kiss had finished.

Grey said, "I'm sorry."

Kyla said, "Never be sorry for that." Her hand was still on his chest. He weaved his fingers through hers.

"But Callum. He's waiting for you in Talis. I don't want to—"

"I loved Callum," Kyla said. "I could've been happy with him, but—"

"You still can."

"No," she said, shaking her head, her curls bouncing. "He was my first love, but not my last. I have changed too much. And I don't know if I could ever look at him again, not when he'll remind me of her."

Her daughter. Floating forever amongst the stars.

"But I have my sister," Grey said. "I don't know where my path will take me next."

"It doesn't matter," Kyla said, taking Grey's stump in her other hand. "Wherever you go, I will go too."

"But your father…"

"Went back for *you*," Kyla said. "He's a practical man. He doesn't take chances like that for just anyone. He will give his blessing."

Grey kissed her again, and this time they lingered much longer, letting the ship's rocking guide their movements, until they were both out of breath and laughing, holding each other closer and closer until their warmth melted together.

Grey found his sister holding court at the bow of the ship. She looked perfectly at home with all the attention, her eyes bright and wide, the breeze tossing her strawberry-blond hair behind her.

"And you say the dead had the legs of a horse?" one of the sailors asked.

"Aye," Shae said, spitting the word out. She was clearly mimicking the sailors, pandering to her audience. "Which is why they were so fast."

"But they couldn't pass through stone?"

Shae shook her head. "If they could, I'd be dead!"

The men laughed and slapped their knees. Shae's eyes found Grey's at the back of the crowd. She gave him a slight nod. "And my brother would probably have been turned into one of the horse men. But if you ask me, I think he'd be far more handsome with hind legs and a tail, don't you think?"

More raucous laughter, the men turning to greet Grey, slapping him on the back and pretending to stab him with their blades. Evidently his actions both on and off the ship had turned the tide of their respect in his favor. And yet, he noticed they still wouldn't look at Kyla, the shame of their sins clearly written on their faces.

Grey made his way through the crowd to where the captain sat on a barrel, watching but saying nothing, a pipe held between his lips. When Grey reached him, he stuck out his hand.

The captain looked at the offering for a moment, but didn't take it. Instead, he stood to his full height, looking down at Grey with narrowed eyes. Had he seen the way Grey had been holding his daughter's hand when they'd approached? Could he still see the slight blush on Grey's cheeks?

Just when Grey feared the barrel-chested man might shove him overboard, the captain pulled him into an enormous bear hug, slapping his back and squeezing. "Now yer home, son," he said. "Now yer home."

When the general hubbub had died down and the captain had ordered his men to "Git back to work, ye lazy dogs!" Grey sat next to Shae on the deck, their legs dangling between the wooden railing. Since he'd been gone, the deck had acquired a fresh layer of salt, and he was surprisingly tempted to give it a good scrubbing. But not now. The captain had exempted him from his labors indefinitely.

"Kyla is pretty," Shae said, the edge of her lips rising playfully.

"You think so?" Grey said, avoiding her gaze. "I hadn't noticed."

Shae laughed. "How are we here?"

"Let me tell you…" Grey said. And then he did, letting the entire story pour out of him like water from a bucket, unfiltered. He made no attempt to justify his choices and took complete responsibility for his mistakes, something he'd never have done while in Knight's End.

When he finished, Shae said, "I can't believe Princess Rhea would kiss *you*."

Grey shook his head. "After that whole story, that's your response?"

"Yes."

Grey laughed. "Fair enough. Sometimes I wonder what she saw in me too. I was a rutting fool back then."

"And now?" she asked. Grey noticed she hadn't even bothered to scold his swearing.

Grey smirked. "Still a rutting fool. But working on being better."

"Grey," Shae said, and her gaze was suddenly serious. "You *are* better. And you're forgiven. For everything. You might've made mistakes, but that doesn't change the fact that this was the path we were meant to take."

Staring into his sister's eyes, Grey wondered when she'd gotten so wise. However, a question still stood out in his mind. "Why did the furia take you to the Dead Isles? Surely they knew there was great evil there. Surely they knew it was a risk."

Shae nodded. "They feared they wouldn't survive, but they went anyway. They were constantly talking about 'the path of the Oracle.' She was a woman, I guess, like them, but they spoke of her like a god, the same as when they used Wrath's name. They said she'd gone to the Dead Isles and hidden something there, so they had to follow."

The Western Oracle, Grey thought. *But she is a myth*. Then again, he used to think the ghosts of the Dead Isles were a myth too. "What did she hide?"

"This," Shae said, and she slipped a tattered book from underneath her leg. Though the cover was grimy and breaking apart, the single word on the front was still readable, because it was carved into the wood, rather than written in ink:

Truths.

"While you slept, the sun dried it out, though most of what was written is lost."

Grey extended his hand and took it, idly flipping through the pages, which were wrinkled and torn, the ink smeared in illegible rivers of muck.

Grey remembered the way the book had stood open on the table in the room where Shae was held prisoner. He remembered the symbol drawn inside, the same symbol that had been drawn all over his sister's skin. He scanned her arms, her legs, her feet. The markings were gone, washed away by the sea.

As he moved his fingers through the ruined pages, the book fell open, almost naturally, to one particular page. Like the others, the words on this page had been lost to the ocean. And yet one marking remained untouched. Impossibly untouched.

It was the symbol the Furies had drawn on Shae, half her mark and half another mark.

When joined together they formed a golden key.

His fingers brushed over the drawing. "I don't understand what this means," he said. He remembered something from the island, when the Fury was moments away from slitting his throat and the dead horse men moments away from breaking down the door. Something Shae had said to the Furies in order to save his life.

I will tell you everything. I will tell you about the dreams.

Shae was staring at him, saying nothing.

"What have you seen in your dreams?" he asked.

Shae looked back at the ocean, squinting into the sun. "A man," she said. "A criminal."

Grey frowned. "What man?"

Shae fingered the spot on her hand where Grey knew her mark was hidden. "One of the marked. Like me. His mark is the other half of mine."

A fortnight ago Grey might've laughed her words away. A dream? Come on. A hidden book titled "Truths" with a weird symbol in it? He'd found more truth in his daily bowel movements. Messages in the stars? Hogwash. And the Western Oracle being a real person? That was the icing on the proverbial cake.

And yet, he knew exactly what this all meant, at least on the surface. "We have to find this man from your dreams," he said.

Shae said, "I know."

"Where do we start?"

"He's a pirate," she said.

"The Burning Sea."

"Aye."

"Pirate's Peril."

"Aye."

"I'll see how far the captain is willing to take us."

Grey started to rise, but Shae stopped him with a hand on his arm. "Grey?"

"Yes?"

"Thank you for never giving up on me."

"You're welcome," he said.

She released his arm, and when he turned to walk across the deck, he could see land in the distance, just before the point where the sky met the horizon. The air seemed full of plumes of dark smoke, roiling up like swift-moving storm clouds.

And he swore that, just below the smoke, he could see fire.

PART V

Roan ⬥ Jai ⬥ Annise
Raven ⬥ Bane ⬥ Roan
Rhea

Our heroes and villains must face fire and truth,
which, by the reckoning of the times we live in, are
forged of the same material.

The Western Oracle

Forty-Three

The Western Kingdom, Knight's End
Roan Loren
One week after capture

The door to Roan's quarters burst open, Rhea's scarred face filling the space. "To the tower! Now! Ironclad is going to kill himself!"

It only took him a moment to process the words before he was on his feet, rushing after his sister, simultaneously wondering if she was playing some kind of sick game with him.

Still, he couldn't chance it.

He flew down the corridor after Rhea. Furia were running, too, their feet pounding. They reached an opening cut into the wall with a metal platform. "Inside! Hurry!" Rhea hissed.

He stepped in beside her, breathing heavily, and several furia crowded in beside them. The platform began to rise as a couple of burly guardsmen cranked a wheel attached to ropes. If Roan could've stopped thinking about Gareth, he might've been impressed by the invention.

My fault, he thought. He had practically admitted to being in love with Gwen, while, the whole time, he'd missed the signs of Gareth's affections for him, reading them as a stalwart but complicated friendship.

And now his friend was going to kill himself.

My fault.

"He will only talk to you," Rhea said.

Roan's head jerked to the side, surprised. *He wants me to see him do it. Oh gods, I can't do this. I can't I can't I can't...*

After what felt like an eternity, the lift groaned to a halt and they stepped out into a tiny stone cubicle. A stiff wind pelted him. To the right, steps descended, curving out of sight. Dead ahead was a doorway, already open, two furia standing just inside. They looked back, their crimson hair blowing in the wind.

"Save your friend," Rhea commanded, pushing him forward.

Roan stumbled, but then regained his balance, stepping quickly inside the room, past the red-clad women.

His eyes shot to the large window, now shattered, which explained the wind gusting inside. A lone figure stood on the edge of the window frame, his back to Roan.

Gareth.

He's been up here the whole time, with no company but himself, his own thoughts eating him alive.

"Gareth," Roan said.

"This is for the best," Gareth said, not turning around.

"Let's talk. We can work this out."

His friend laughed without mirth. "Since when have you become the optimist?" he said into the wind.

"Since I met you," Roan said.

"Not Gwen?"

"Yes. Her too. Both of you have changed me."

"You've changed me, too, friend. But this isn't about you."

What? "It's not?"

"You are always so self-centered, did anyone ever tell you that? Yes, you broke my heart, but that wasn't your fault. Not really. A heart is not something that can be commanded; it chooses whomever it wishes."

"Then why are you doing this?"

"I am the Shield," Gareth said. "Remember?"

Roan frowned, trying to understand what he was getting at. "Not anymore. You tried to save Guy. You did your part."

"Are you the only one allowed a second chance? A third? I can still *be* the Shield. If my death can make a difference… I was born to do this, and I won't be used as a weapon for your sister. If she gets her hands on Beorn Stonesledge, the east will be doomed."

"Not necessarily," Roan said. "Your brother is strong, as is his army." He remembered the defenses Gareth had shown him in Ferria. "There is still hope."

Gareth finally looked back. "Yes. There is. Because of me. Remember me fondly."

Roan saw the look in his friend's eyes, the goodbye, and he rushed forward, stretching out his arms, his fatemark pulsing uselessly.

Gareth jumped.

Toolatetoolatetoolatetoolatetoolatetoolate

Too late.

Light shot from his chest, a sunburst of whiteness streaming through the window, capturing Gareth's falling form in a blaze brighter than the sun at noonday.

He stopped, his body frozen in midair, just outside the window.

He twisted his head back and his eyes met Roan's. *How?* his expression seemed to say. *Why?*

"Because I love you, too," Roan said. He extended his hands and pulled at the light, hand over hand, like he was hauling a rope toward him. Face full of awe and surprise, Gareth floated back inside the tower, until he was able to step down, gaining his feet once more. Standing in front of Roan.

"You love me?"

Roan nodded. "I have for a while. But I love Gwen, too. I'm sorry, I never intended this to happen. It has to be enough for now."

"I'm crying on the inside," a voice said from behind. Rhea stood watching, her furia crowded behind her.

Roan turned back to Gareth. "Stay strong. And never stop fighting. You are not the Shield, not anymore." He extended his arm.

Gareth looked at it for a moment, and then grabbed it, pulling Roan into a hug. Seconds later, Roan was being dragged away, the door slamming in his face.

Yet before he lost sight of Gareth's face, he saw the change in it.

He saw the recognition.

He was looking into the face of a king.

Forty-Four

The Southern Empire, Phanes,
Garadia Mine
Jai Jiroux
One month after capture
at the Southron Gates

The backbreaking labor was nothing to Jai. After all, he'd toiled alongside his people in Garadia for years. The only difference now was that he didn't have a choice.

He was a slave, no different from the other slaves except for the strange fact that he didn't bear the slave mark. Emperor Hoza had tried again and again to enslave him using his powers, but every time, Jai's justicemark had flared on his heel, somehow protecting him from being marked.

Instead, Jai dragged a heavy ball of iron everywhere he went, chained to his ankles, which were chained to each other. His hands were free, but only so he could work. At night the mine masters cuffed his arms together and then into a bolt hammered deep into the stone. Escape was futile.

Because of Shanti and her fireroot, it had taken Jai and the other slaves a fortnight to dig out Garadia, but eventually they'd succeeded. Now diamonds were flowing the same way they always did.

Shanti. Just thinking her name was a dagger to his heart. He didn't know where she was, or even if she was alive. The other captured Black Tears had been enslaved and sent to Garadia, too. He saw Sonika and the others from time to time, but like any other slave they had black eyes that seemed to stare right through him. For all their efforts to save slaves, they couldn't even save themselves.

Shanti hadn't been brought to Garadia, for obvious reasons. She was an escaped slave; somehow, like her father had, she'd broken the mark she'd been given as a child. The emperor wouldn't risk her escaping again.

You can't command them to be free.

Her words from that star-speckled night on the cliffs came to him often these days. At the time, he hadn't taken much notice of them, but now they were a truth that haunted him. In the end, all he'd been to his people was another, kinder master.

What if he'd never commanded them to be free? he wondered. What if he'd never met the slaves of Garadia? Would more of them be alive? Had his very presence in their lives been a death sentence? Was that what Shanti was trying to tell him?

Jai shook his head, willing her face from his mind. He raised his pick, glancing around. Hundreds of black-eyed slaves

560

worked, chipping away at the stone, searching for the next diamond. Some were familiar, faces he'd known for the last few years, faces he'd failed—Jig and Viola and Marella and even Joaquin, who had warned him about Axa; and others were new, replacements for the thousands of his people who had been killed trying to reach the Southron Gates.

What was it all for? Jai had always believed that a great sacrifice could save his people. By them. By him. Perhaps he would have to die for them, but as long as his death bought their freedom, he was a willing sacrifice.

This was supposed to be my destiny…

Instead, so many had died and he had lived.

He had failed.

Gritting his teeth, Jai hammered his pick into the rocks, over and over, until the impact was like a distant memory, fading into the background of the mine, a dull noise lost amongst the cacophony of his thoughts.

Why? was one of the unanswerable questions that kept popping up. He hated that question, because it was like asking the gods why they allowed evil in the world, or why they created a monstrous creature like a red pyzon, or why storms blew across the sea, swallowing ships whole.

How? was the other question, and Jai believed he had a pretty good handle on that one. He'd been tricked by the emperor. When he'd been "given" Axa as a new slave, the emperor had already enslaved him, had already commanded the former master to pretend to be Jai's slave, when really he was a spy the entire time. But why hadn't his justicemark warned him? *He is not the enemy. Not anymore.* Those were the words that filled his mind as his mark pulsed.

I've been a fool. Jai had thought he was doing the right thing, giving the man a second chance. Instead he'd played right into the emperor's hands.

The mirror trick was harder to understand. Clearly it was enchanted, though Jai had never heard of such magic. Certainly it wasn't of the gods. Perhaps the emperor had a dark sorcerer in his employ, specializing in magical mirrors. Whatever the case, it had given Hoza the power to follow Jai and the slaves as they fled Phanes.

He smashed the pick into the rocks so hard the impact vibrated into his bare chest.

"Why did you wait until we were through the Gates?" Jai said aloud. The question for the emperor had churned through him for days on end. And though the answer was obvious, he kept on asking it, until it was all he could think of. Emperor Hoza had made an example of Jai, of his people. He let them get close enough to taste the fresh air of freedom on their tongues, only to snatch it away at the last second. "Bastard."

None of the other slaves seemed to hear him, their focus entirely on their work. The hardest part of this Void he was in was being surrounded by people he loved and having them not know him from a spider on the wall.

Crack! His pick hit the wall hard enough to break free several large chunks. A few of the slave children scrambled to pick them up, setting them on a flat stone and using smaller, more precise tools to break them to pieces.

Jig was one of them.

"Jig," Jai said.

The boy chiseled at the stone, as if Jai didn't exist. His scalp was bald, his long hair hacked away after he was recaptured, as was the hair of all the men.

"Jig,' Jai said, louder. "It's me, Jai Jiroux." Jai wondered if he was going mad. The fact that he continued to try to speak to those he once knew seemed to suggest it. As if they would magically recognize him, offering a wink and a "Hullo Jai!"

A whip cracked and Jai flinched, arching his back as the sting of the blow crackled down his spine. He felt the warmth of blood rising to the surface of his skin. "Back to work, *slave*," the master growled, his powdered face giving him a ghostly pallor in the dim lighting.

Jai fired a scathing look at the master, a man named Carvin, brought over from one of the other mines. Word was he'd coveted a spot in Garadia for a long time.

"Ease off him," another voice said.

Jai stared at the wall. He didn't want to see the face of his failure. His weakness.

Mine Master Axa spoke again: "Carvin, back off. We need him unbroken if we're going to meet our quota."

Carvin reluctantly moved down the line, off to harass other slaves. Jai raised his pick once more, but a strong hand caught it on the backswing.

He froze, still refusing to look back.

"Jai," Axa said.

Jai said nothing.

A sigh, heavy, like a thick blanket.

"Why didn't you kill me when you had the chance?" Axa asked.

The man had asked the question a dozen times, but Jai had yet to answer him, and today would be no different. He hated the question, because it reflected everything he longed to forget back at him.

I was trying to do the right thing.

I promised to leave no living slave behind.

I thought I was being noble, giving you a second chance.

I should've killed you. Maybe then I wouldn't have failed.

Despite that last thought, Jai knew that if he had the chance to do it all over again, he still wouldn't have been able to kill Axa.

Jai longed to hate him, but he couldn't manage even that. After all, the man had acted on Emperor Hoza's command, as a slave. He'd had no choice in the things he'd done, regardless of how awful they were. Jai couldn't fault him for that.

And ever since…he'd been a different man. Though Emperor Hoza had returned Axa's freedom and given him Garadia, he didn't act like a master anymore. He wouldn't give the slaves their free will back, as Jai had once done, but he treated them with respect and often protected them from the whips of the other mine masters. He didn't even powder his face any more, not while in Garadia at least, a detail that was not lost on Jai.

Typically, when Jai ignored Axa, the mine master would move on. But not today. This time Axa leaned closer, until Jai could feel his hot breath on the back of his neck. "I have a plan," Axa whispered in his ear.

Jai didn't move. Didn't breathe. Didn't speak.

"Ever since I was…since I felt what it was like to be controlled, to be *owned*, I can't get the memories out of my head. They're like waking nightmares. I can remember *everything*, and yet it's like it was happening to a different person, some stranger."

Jai said nothing.

"I will save you," Axa said.

Finally, Jai spoke. "I don't want to be saved." *I don't deserve to be saved. I deserve to be here, slaving for the rest of my days, until I die.* "Save the rest of them if you want your conscience to be clean."

Axa backed up a step and Jai felt like he could breathe again. "My conscience will never be clean. But I will do this thing. I will do what I can for the slaves in Garadia."

Jai raised his pick and swung it as hard as he could.

Forty-Five

The Northern Kingdom, Castle Hill
Annise Gäric
One month after retaking the castle

The decision had been made a fortnight earlier, and now finally it was the eve before their journey north, into the unexplored Hinterlands, chasing after a legend.

Annise felt alive, ready, and she was sorely tempted to leave immediately, in the dark of night. Of course, she wouldn't, for, with no sunlight, the cold alone would do them in within a few hours.

Castle Hill would be left under the rule of Queen Regent Zelda, who had Annise's full authority. She knew the kingdom was in good hands. Annise only hoped her aunt wouldn't be forced to face an invasion in her absence. Though Sir Dietrich, Sir Metz, and Sir Jonius had begun a soldier training academy, the soldiers-in-training, most of whom had never held more than a spatula or hammer before, were still eons away from being battle ready. The number of volunteers, however, was staggering, especially since Annise had allowed women to enroll. Only a tenth of the trainees were women thus far, but she was certain the proportion would rise.

Annise thought of Tarin often, especially at night, when she huddled under the covers trying to stay warm. Sometimes she imagined him tucked against her, his lips close enough that she could feel his breath on her skin. Sometimes her heart ached so much she thought for certain it would shatter, closing off her airways. But it never did. And when she awoke each morning, she cast the memories away along with her quilt. Her love for him was still as bright as a flame, but she wouldn't let it consume her to the point where it would hurt her ability to rule, to care for her people.

Tarin, as he'd promised in his letter, had not returned, and Annise suspected he never would. She couldn't hate him for leaving her, not when his reasons were so pure, so full of love for her. He'd sacrificed as much as she had. If anything, they were both martyrs.

Besides his goodbye message, she'd found a stack of parchment hidden in the chamber. On it was written stories in Tarin's handwriting. Stories about his life, from the point after his parents had faked his death. Just as he'd promised.

Annise had them tucked away in a box under her bed. She had yet to read any of them. She wasn't certain when she would be able to do so without shattering.

Now, Annise rose from her bed and shuffled across the cold stone floor to where Archer slept peacefully, a candle lit by his bedside, slowly melting down to just a nub. As she'd commanded, one of the castle maids would come by to replace the candle *before* it was completely gone. Although the ritual sometimes made her feel silly and superstitious, she refused to abandon it, not while her brother remained alive, as if he would pass into the night the moment his candle went out.

For a while, Annise watched Arch breathe, his face so calm, so undisturbed. She wondered whether it was better that he'd slept through all the bad that had happened. At least she could protect him from the pain.

He stirred in his sleep, as he often did. Annise used to feel a leap in her chest, but not anymore. Now she just watched as his lips twitched, his eyelids fluttered. She reached down and held his hand. "Brother, tomorrow I'll be leaving. I don't know if I shall ever return. But you will be safe, I promise. Aunt Zelda will care for you."

She paused as his face went still and peaceful once more. "Archer, I love you."

His hand squeezed hers and she froze for a moment before letting out a breathy laugh. He'd never done that before, and for a second she thought he might—

His eyelids fluttered opened. He blinked. His lips opened. "I love you, too, Annise," he murmured. And then his eyes closed and his chest rose and fell as if he'd never awoken in the first place.

Forty-Six

The Southern Empire, Calypso
Raven Sandes
Four days after the battle
at the Southron Gates

Raven had ridden Heiron all the way back to Calypso, stopping only twice for the dragon to rest and eat. Now, as she watched Whisper emerge from her quarters, Raven almost wished she'd taken more time, delaying this reunion so she could think more about what to say.

She's so beautiful, Raven thought. *So pure.* Whisper wore a pink, ankle-length dress with a silky red lumia flower stitched into the shoulder. *She doesn't deserve so much heartache in her life.*

The moment her sister's eyes rose from her feet and she saw Raven approaching, Whisper raced across the courtyard, flinging herself into Raven's arms. Raven held her to her chest, squeezing as hard as she dared. Breathing. Crying. Kissing her cheeks.

Whisper was crying, too, and yet she said, "You're crying." Raven had never cried in front of her before. The youngest Sandes' head craned to look past Raven. "Where is Fire? Couldn't she have met me at the same time?"

Raven bit her lip.

Whisper's eyes darted back to meet hers. "Raven?"

"I'm so sorry. I did everything I could to—"

Whisper squirmed out of her sister's arms, backing away, her eyes wild. "I knew it. I knew it from the moment you left." There was the sharp bite of anger in her voice, which also trembled with sadness. "And when the tree burned down..." She whirled around and raced back to her quarters, flinging herself through the door of hanging bones.

Raven started after her, but stopped when the last thing her sister said came into focus. *What about the tree?* Her eyes darted left, to where the Unburning Tree should've been. "No," she breathed.

The tree was gone, like Fire, burned to ash.

One month later

As Raven sat upon the dragon throne, streams continued to arrive from the northern edges of Dragon Bay, as well as from the northeastern dunes of the Scarra.

None of the reports were good. The eastern army was killing and pillaging Calypsian nomads at will. Twice Raven had sent platoons of peacekeepers, but none had returned thus far.

Raven was empress now. As before, Whisper had not challenged her, content to pass her days reading stories of faeries and sprites written on parchment bound into books, painted with bright, gay images on their leather covers. Whisper had paid a fortune to have them written just for her by a famous Dreadnoughter storyteller. Though Raven had encouraged her to come to court on numerous occasions, her sister had yet to stray far from her room. Nightly, Whisper awoke screaming, terrified by the nightmares that now plagued her. Raven had taken to sleeping in her bed to provide as much comfort as possible, but she knew it wasn't sustainable, not forever.

"Empress?" Goggin said, snapping her away from her thoughts.

"How far into the desert have the easterners sallied?"

"Half a league. Perhaps a little further. Not far enough to be of concern just yet. But they grow bolder by the day."

"Ships?"

Goggin shook his large head. "None that we have seen thus far. They seem determined to wage this war on foot."

Raven soaked the information in. This kind of news was bad for everyone. If she did nothing, she would appear weak, and her people might lose confidence in her. Then again, Fire had chosen to be aggressive, and where had that gotten her?

She bit the side of her mouth, using pain to chase the memory away. Though a month had passed since her sister's death, the sting was still there. Sometimes the pain was as distant as a star, and other times as near and hot as a flame pressed to her skin. Fire had been a lot of things, but forgettable was not one of them.

Lately, however, she'd fought the sadness with anger, rage, letting it coil inside her like a snake. *Why can't the easterners just leave us alone? Why can't Calyp remain an island, cut off from the rest of the Four Kingdoms, living in peace?*

"We must strike back," Raven said.

Goggin nodded. "I agree. My only concern is that the new guanero are not yet trained."

"Double the training hours. Dawn until dusk until they are ready."

Goggin blinked, but then said, "As you command."

"And the dragons?" Raven asked.

The dragon master, Rider, stepped forward. "None will be mature until next year."

"But can they fight?"

Rider's eyebrows dipped. "Empress?"

"You heard me." Raven couldn't believe that a month ago she had been on the opposite end of this argument, siding with Rider against her sister. Now she finally understood how hard a decision it had been for Fire to leave the dragons in Calypso while they rode to war. *If you hadn't listened to me, sister, would you still be alive?*

It was thoughts like that that made her want to scream and throw things.

"Yes. They can fight," Rider said. "But I would advise wait—"

"Good," Raven said, cutting her off. "I will attend dragon training on the morrow, and make a final decision by sundown."

Raven couldn't meet Rider's eyes, couldn't bear to see the disappointment in them. "As you command," she said, spinning on her heel and leaving the court. Goggin had already left. None remained but the ghosts of Raven's past.

A noise made her turn. Whisper stood in the shadows of the curtain blocking the exit into the courtyard. A single tear rolled down her cheek. "You're going to leave me, too, aren't you?" she said. Though her eyes sparkled, the predominant emotion in her tone was anger, much to Raven's surprise.

"Whisper, I—"

"Don't apologize. Don't you dare apologize."

Raven closed her mouth, standing. She parted her lips once more. "I won't apologize. I have a duty to protect our people, our lands."

"What about me?"

"Yes. You too."

"Then don't leave me."

"It is tradition that—"

"The empress rides to war with the Calypsian army," Whisper finished, wiping the tear tracks from her cheeks with the back of her hand. "I know. I was tutored by the same scholars as you, *sister.*" She spat the last word. Raven had never seen such ferocity in her youngest sibling. Then again, she *was* a Sandes, an heir to the dragon throne, so it was inevitable it would eventually come out.

"What would you have me do?"

"Stay."

"I can't."

"Then call off the war. Then no one has to go. We can wait and see what happens. Let the other kingdoms destroy each other. That was what Fire wanted, wasn't it? That was her big plan?"

"Only partly," Raven said. "Once our enemies were weak, Fire wanted to march on them. She wanted to go to war. Before the battle in which she...she called herself a weapon. She said that was her only purpose in life."

"But you're different. You're not like Fire."

Once Raven would have agreed with her sister. But now...she wasn't as certain. Sometimes she felt like she *could* summon fire at will, as if flames lived in her veins the same way they had in Fire's. "No, I'm not Fire. But I am the empress now. And I will not sit on the dragon throne while the guanero ride to war."

"Then I challenge you for the throne," Whisper said, defiantly.

"Whisper, it's too late for that."

Whisper backed up a step, the curtains swirling around her, the Calypsian sigil shifting over her head. "I hate you," she said, her mouth a snarl. And then she slipped between the curtains, vanishing like a stone dropped in a dark pool.

Raven sighed and slumped back into the throne. She banged her head on one of the dragon's teeth that roared from the back of the royal seat, but she didn't have the energy to rub the spot, which was now throbbing fiercely.

You can hate me, she thought. *But I will protect you until death, just as Fire did.*

Forty-Seven

The Southern Empire, Phanes, Phanea
Bane Gäric
One month later

As he watched Emperor Hoza sleep, Bane considered whether to kill him.

Vin Hoza seemed so peaceful, his diamond-studded skin sparkling in the candlelight, as if violence was a cloak he pulled on when he awoke each day, not a part of the man himself. Bane almost laughed at the absurd thought, but managed to stop himself.

In the end, the Beggar had been wrong. Taking one's own life was never the answer—Bane now knew that better than anyone. Though the hooded man hadn't spoken much, at least he was a companion. A friend. Unfortunately, however, the one marked with the plague had tried to take his own life before carrying out the mission Bane had given him.

Though he hadn't been tired, Bane had rested with his friend for a long month, nursing him back to health. A month wasted, although it didn't seem that way. Another month without peace. His mark had left him alone, and for a while he'd wondered whether the prophecy was done with him.

He'd wondered whether he'd failed his creator, the one Bear Blackboots called the Western Oracle.

During this time, Bane, like his friend, had once contemplated suicide, but that was a distant memory now, as fuzzy as the snowfields of the north. No, he was once more determined to fight for peace to the very end.

I should kill Hoza in the name of peace, Bane thought. Now that Empress Fire Sandes was dead—he could feel her death in the very marrow of his bones—three more true monarchs had to die, one way or another. It was the only way there would be peace.

And yet two had already died in the south. Only two rulers in each of the Four Kingdoms were supposed to die. The south was finished. He should be going elsewhere, targeting a ruler in one of the other realms.

But he wanted this so badly…

Needed it like water on the lips of a man dying of thirst in the desert.

Bane raised his knife over the slumbering man's head, the blade hanging in the air like a trembling icicle. *Why am I hesitating?*

He knew the reason. The Beggar hadn't killed. Well, he *had* killed, in the past, but after meeting Bane he tried only to take his own life. *Why?* Bane wondered. If someone born with a mark meant to kill, like his, was able to resist his very nature, should he do the same?

The answer came in the form of a growl in the dark, from his own throat. "No. I am Death."

Hoza's eyes flew open at the sound, his lips opening to utter his command, to make Bane his slave.

But he never got the words out, never uttered a single syllable, his windpipe severed in half by Bane's knife. Bane wrenched the blade out, cleaned it on Hoza's bare stomach, and then slipped it back in its sheath.

Six, he thought. His father, the Dread King of the North, King Wolfric Gäric. King Gill Loren, his uncle. King Oren Ironclad, Juggernaut of the east. Empress Sun Sandes, the dragoness. Empress Fire Sandes, the firemarked. And Emperor Vin Hoza, the Slave King. Six steps closer to peace in the Four Kingdoms. Two to go.

He felt a fire on his scalp as another section was filled in. Strange. He hadn't expected it to do that when he'd killed three southern rulers. The fire continued, growing, *different* than usual.

Surprised, he moved quickly over to where a tall, thin, looking glass rested against one wall. He dipped his head so he could see his own scalp.

How? he wondered. For there, on his skin, his mark had changed, grown. The circle was larger now, and split by five arrows rather than four, creating ten sections. Two more than before. Six were filled in. Four remained. *Four.*

How is this possible? Bane wasn't certain how to feel, but the overwhelming emotion that coursed through him was, to his horror, excitement. He'd thought he was getting close to fulfilling the prophecy, but he wasn't. There was still much work to do. He was still needed.

And there were so many monarchs left to choose from, warmongering rulers who deserved to die. *Who is the most deserving?* Bane wondered. Queen Rhea Loren had wiped out the northern army using a sea monster. But was she really the queen? Her brother, the Peacemaker, Roan Loren, was older than she, the lawful heir to the western throne. And what of the north? The Dread King's brother had fallen, but now there was word that his niece—*my sister*, Bane reminded himself—Queen Annise Gäric was traveling to the Hinterlands to regroup. *I should've killed her when I had the chance...* And then there was the heir to the east, Gareth Ironclad. He may have handed the ore-throne to his brother, but he was still a threat. In the south another Sandes might have to die; there was talk that Empress Raven Sandes was considering an attack on the east. *Or*, Bane thought, *I could just stay here, in Phanes, and kill the Slave King's heir, Falcon Hoza, who will soon learn that he's the new emperor.*

Would his mark grow even larger with more sections if he did that? The thought excited him. No, *thrilled* him.

Decisions. Options. *There's no hurry. I have time. And I must rest after my latest kill.*

After all, the Four Kingdoms had waited more than a hundred years for peace. They could wait a little longer.

Suddenly exhausted, satisfied that his work there was done, Bane reached down and picked up the dead brown pyzon, which he'd killed when he first arrived in Hoza's bedroom. Gently, quietly, he placed it on the bed next to the dead emperor, letting the snake's blood mix with Hoza's.

All across Phanes, slaves startled awake, rubbing their eyes.

Though they'd only been sleeping a few hours, it felt as if they were waking up from a decades-long sleep.

One by one they realized:

I am free.

Some wept.

Some screamed at the top of their lungs.

Some laughed, like it had all been a bad dream.

But Jai Jiroux did none of those things. When he awoke in Garadia, chained to the wall next to the hordes of rejoicing slaves, he felt only horror at having led most of his people to their deaths just before they would've been free.

Forty-Eight

Unknown location

Chavos (previously known as the Beggar)

Unknown time later

I am Chavos.

He sat up quickly, half-blind, his mind spinning. Where had those words come from? Who had spoken? *No, no, no.*

Instinctively, his hands probed his stomach, exploring the rough stitches where he'd plunged the knife into his abdomen. He winced at the pain—the wound was still tender.

I am Chavos. That voice again. *It is my own,* he realized, but from the past.

"I am the Beggar," he said, but that wasn't right either. The fact that he could speak wasn't right. The fact that he could feel his heart beating in his chest, hear his ragged breaths slipping between his lips, wasn't right. He was supposed to be dead.

"Hello Chavos," a voice said from nearby.

He twisted his head to the side too fast, his head pounding. "Who's there?"

"Your friend. Your brother." That familiar voice.

"Bane." Though he spoke the word like a curse, he felt relieved. He wasn't dead, but maybe there was a reason for that.

Maybe this was a second chance.

"You made a mistake," Bane said.

Chavos knew he needed to lie. "Perhaps I did."

"There's work to be done still."

"Yes. There is."

Chavos lay back down, his pulse racing. One of them was going to die, that much was certain. And it wouldn't be him.

Forty-Nine
The Western Kingdom, Knight's End
Roan Loren
One month after Gareth Ironclad's suicide attempt

Roan was finally leaving Knight's End. The delay was a strategic one, as Rhea had received word of some unrest in the south. Something about a slave revolt and an attack on the Southron Gates by the Calypsians. It was better to be patient, she had counselled.

Not that Roan had any say in the matter. He'd been locked in a room since Gareth's suicide attempt. It was a nice room, but that didn't change the fact that it was a prison. He hadn't been allowed to see Gareth, Gwen, or even his younger siblings, Bea and Leo, though he'd requested visits on multiple occasions.

Rhea sometimes came to see him, but only to remind him that if he didn't obey her that Gwen would be hurt, killed if necessary. She never threatened Gareth; no, he was far too valuable.

Roan had given up on trying to understand his sister. Obviously bad things had happened to her, but he didn't know which tragedy had turned her into this cruel creature she'd become. The death of her father perhaps. Or maybe it was seeing the palace littered with bodies after Bane's murderous rampage. Or it could've been the murder of her eldest cousin, Jove, just after he'd become king. One of the guards had told him that Rhea had witnessed it. A trail of blood seemed to follow his sister. Roan wished there was something he could say to bring her back, to convince her this path she was on was wrong. Unless, of course, she was always this girl. That was a possibility, too, though he hoped not.

Roan blinked away his thoughts, refocusing on his one opportunity to see a friend before he departed the west. The dungeons were dark and moist. Trailing Rhea's long white purity dress, Roan's footsteps echoed in the stone corridor. They passed several cells on the left. In each was a prisoner; although, hunched and cowering in the corners, they hardly looked human anymore. In one cell there were two curled up forms, so small they might've been children.

Roan felt sick. Would he find Gwen in a similar condition? He wished he'd never come to Knight's End, wished he'd never left Calypso. *If this is my fate, if this is what it means to be the Peacemaker, I don't want it.*

Rhea stopped at the next cell. A voice said, "What in Orion's name do you want?" and Roan's heart leapt in his chest. He rushed the last few steps and looked between the bars. "Roan?"

Her silver hair was knotted and greasy, hanging in limp vines. Her face was smudged and dirty, her form-fitting armor dull and in need of a good polish. But, unlike the other prisoners, she was still standing, still strong, her golden eyes alight with a mixture of anger and surprise.

"Gwen," Roan breathed. "I'm so sorry." He'd been wanting—no, *needing*—to say that to her for weeks.

"No one forced me to come with you," she said. "I wanted answers, too."

"But I trusted my sister. I fell into her trap."

Rhea laughed, but they both ignored her.

Gwen said, "It's not your fault. We didn't stick to the plan either. Yes, we came to the meeting place at dusk, but when you didn't appear, we caused a scene. We banged on the doors. We shouted."

Roan didn't know that. He'd wondered how they'd been caught so quickly. He'd always just assumed it was his fault. Regardless, none of them would've been there if not for him. But there were worse things still to talk about. "Did you hear about Gareth?"

Gwen nodded. "*She* told me."

Roan glanced at Rhea, who smiled cruelly. "As Gareth's friend, I thought she should know."

"She came to hurt me with her words," Gwen said. "She said you saved him though."

Roan shook his head. "It wasn't me. It was my mark."

"Same thing."

He shook his head harder.

Gwen said, "Don't start doing this again, feeling sorry for yourself. You don't get to do that, not while I'm stuck in here."

"I'm getting you out."

"I don't want you to get me out. I don't want you to save me."

Her words shocked him. He moved forward, gripping the bars. "Don't say that."

She took a step forward, but remained far enough away that he couldn't touch her. Her voice softened, and yet took on a stinging quality. "Roan, I will never love you like that. So you should stop loving me. Gareth, too. He only loves what he can't have, it has always been his way."

Roan blinked rapidly. "I won't." He wasn't certain who he meant, Gareth or Gwen.

"Then you're a fool."

He knew what she was doing—trying to push him away so he wouldn't do what Rhea wanted. So he would escape the first chance he had, disappear and never return to Knight's End. Right? Or was there truth to what she said? He'd seen her demons; he knew they haunted her. Perhaps they wouldn't let her love, not ever again. Or maybe she could just never love him as more than a friend. Perhaps Alastair had taken her heart when he died, all those years ago.

Sadness washed over him as he realized: *I never even got to kiss her the way I wanted to.*

"Enough," Rhea snapped. "Reunion over. Time to leave."

"Wait," Gwen said.

"No one tells me to—"

"Just let her speak!" Roan said. Rhea flinched, surprised by the outburst. Despite everything she'd done to him, Roan had never let his anger take control around her.

Rhea said, "Very well. Say what you have to. It's the last thing you'll say to him for a very long time."

Gwen took another step forward, but was still out of reach. "Leave the west and never return," she said.

When Roan finally looked back, Knight's End was a smudge of gold on the horizon. They'd ridden hard for a long time, and he'd trained his gaze forward until now. He didn't want to think about who he was leaving behind.

He was surrounded by red-clad furia, who would escort him as far as the Snake River. He wasn't certain whether they were there to protect him or guard him. He didn't care either way.

Gwen's words kept coming back to him, how she would never love him the way he loved her. That Gareth didn't really love him either.

He didn't think of her words because they hurt. No. Quite the opposite. The more he listened to them playing over and over in his mind, the more he could hear the truth written in them. Or, more correctly, the opposite of the truth. Gwen was lying. Though she'd tried to mask it with harshness, it was there, as obvious as sunlight reflecting on a pool of water.

She already loves me. I know it. Gareth too.

At least that's what he kept telling himself, over and over. It's what he needed to hear. He spurred his horse on faster, determination coursing through his blood. He would travel to Calyp, to Citadel. And if the Western Oracle or her son, Bear Blackboots, were there, he would find them. And yes, he would bring them back to Knight's End. But not in chains. No, they would come with sword and spear and marks of power.

He would save Gareth. He would save Gwen.

Nothing will stop me, because it's my destiny.

Fifty

The Western Kingdom, Knight's End
Rhea Loren

Rhea tugged her purity dress over her head. For the first time in her life, she was glad to wear it. The dress's bagginess was coming in handy for her current situation.

She tossed the dress on her bed, her hands automatically coming down to rest on her belly, which was a lot rounder than it had been even a few weeks ago. Her small breasts had grown, too, ample bulges on her chest that reminded her of her old nursemaid, Selma. The nausea came and went, and was usually the worst in the morning. Food helped a little, when she found time to eat.

Rhea rubbed her fingers against her smooth, pale skin, as if trying to feel the life growing inside her. *My child*, she thought, her mind going back to that night with Grey Arris. A night that had changed everything, in more ways than she'd realized at the time.

But no, it wasn't Grey's child, would *never* be his child, regardless of how it was created. Just as Ennis could no longer be her cousin, but one of her many guardsmen, his face shrouded beneath his helm. She would never be able to tell her people the truth about him.

But she *would* tell her people the truth about how she would soon have an heir. At first they would be in shock. How could Rhea the Righteous, Rhea the Pure, Rhea the Brave, be with child? How could she have committed such a grievous sin out of wedlock? And with whom?

And that's when she would make the declaration that would secure her place in history, more so than even her momentous victory in the Bay of Bounty.

"I am a virgin," she said now, practicing her facial control. "My child is born of Wrath."

And they would believe her, raising her pedestal even higher, all the way to the heavens.

Yes, she would have her war, and they would be her pawns as she seized the Four Kingdoms by the throat.

Want to know more about your favorite characters from Fatemarked? Grab *Fatemarked Origins Volume I* and *Volume II* for eleven short stories from the Four Kingdoms, featuring the origin stories of Gwendolyn Storm, Tarin Sheary, Shanti Parthena Laude, and Bear Blackboots!

And keep reading for a sample of *Soulmarked*, Book 3 in the Fatemarked Epic, available NOW!

A personal note from David...

If you enjoyed this book, please consider leaving a positive review on **Amazon.com**. Without reviews on **Amazon.com**, I wouldn't be able to write for a living, which is what I love to do! Thanks for all your incredible support and I look forward to reading your reviews.

THE FATEMARKED

(d)=deceased

***For a complete online listing of sigils, symbols and fatemarks from The Fatemarked Epic:
http://davidestesbooks.blogspot.com/p/fatemarked-sigils-symbols-and-fatemarks.html

 Lifemarked- Roan Loren (the Peacemaker)

 Deathmarked- Bane Gäric (the Kings' Bane)

 Halfmarked- Shae Arris

 Swordmarked- Sir Dietrich

 (d) Icemarked- the Ice Lord

 Ironmarked- Beorn Stonesledge

 Heromarked- Gwendolyn Storm

 (d) Firemarked- Fire Sandes

 Plaguemarked- the Beggar

(d) Slavemarked- Vin Hoza

Justicemarked- Jai Jiroux

ROYAL GENEALOGY OF THE FOUR KINGDOMS
(three generations)

(d)= deceased

The Northern Kingdom (capital city: Castle Hill)

(d) Wilhelm Gäric (the Undefeated King)
(d) Ida Gäric

Born to Wilhelm and Ida:
Helmuth Gäric (the Maimed Prince)
(d) Wolfric Gäric (the Dread King, political marriage to western princess, Sabria Loren)
(d) Griswold Gäric (usurper)
Zelda Gäric (childless)

Born to Griswold:
Dirk Gäric

Born to Wolfric and Sabria:
Annise Gäric
Archer Gäric
Bane Gäric (The Kings' Bane)

The Western Kingdom (capital city: Knight's End)

(d) Ennis Loren
(d) Mira Loren

Born to Ennis and Mira:
(d) Gill Loren (married to Cecilia Thorne Loren)
(d) Ty Loren
(d) Sabria Loren (political marriage to Wolfric Gäric)

Born to Ty:
(d) Jove Loren
Sai Loren
Wheaton Loren
Gaia Loren
Ennis Loren

Born to Gill and Cecilia:
Roan Loren
Rhea Loren
Bea Loren
Leo Loren

The Eastern Kingdom (capital city: Ferria in Ironwood)

(d) Hamworth Ironclad
(d) Lydia Ironclad

Born to Hamworth and Lydia:
(d) Coren Ironclad (Thunder)
(d) Oren Ironclad (the Juggernaut, married to Henna Redfern Ironclad)

Born to Coren:
Hardy Ironclad

Born to Oren and Henna:
Gareth Ironclad (the Shield)
(d) Guy Ironclad
Grian Ironclad

The Southern Empires
Empire of Calyp (capital city: Calypso)

(d) Jak Sandes
(d) Riza Sandes

Born to Jak and Riza:
(d) Sun Sandes (the First Daughter, marriage union to Vin Hoza, emperor of Phanes, now severed)
Windy Sandes (the Second Daughter, childless)
Viper Sandes (the Third Daughter, childless)

Born to Sun and Vin:
Raven Sandes (the First Daughter)

(d) Fire Sandes (the Second Daughter)
Whisper Sandes (the Third Daughter)

Empire of Phanes (capital city: Phanea)

(d) Jin Hoza
(d) Dai Hoza

Born to Jin and Dai:
(d) Vin Hoza (marriage union to Sun Sandes, empress of Calyp, now severed)
(d) Rin Hoza
(d) Shin Hoza

Also born to Vin and Sun:
Falcon Hoza
Fang Hoza
Fox Hoza

Acknowledgments

When I finished Truthmarked, it was the longest book I'd ever written. The third book in the series turned out to be longer, but it doesn't change the fact that Truthmarked is the book that taught me how much stamina as a writer I truly have. And that's a necessity when writing an epic fantasy series.

That being said, I had A LOT of help along the way.

First and foremost, to Piero, my cover artist, your covers are absolute perfection. It's like you're in my head! Well done and thank you. (Secretly I believe Piero is artmarked, so technically he cheats.)

To my loyal beta readers, Laurie Love, Elizabeth Love, Karen Benson, Kerri Hughes, Terri Thomas, Abalee Cook, and Daniel Elison. I keep feeding you longer and longer books and you keep sending them back my way with more and more red ink on them. Thanks for fixing my own foolishness.

A very special thank you to Beverly Laude, who won a character naming contest, and came up with Shanti Parthena Laude, a beautiful name that just happened to be perfect for one of my characters. You truly are a Peaceful Maiden of Highest Honor!

Last and most definitely not least, to my readers, gah. You surprise me at every turn in the best of ways. Thanks for supporting me, my family, and my dream. I write for you.

The saga continues in other books by David Estes available through the author's official website: http://davidestesbooks.blogspot.com or through select online retailers including Amazon.com.

<u>High Fantasy Novels by David Estes</u>

The Fatemarked Epic:
Book One—Fatemarked
Book Two—Truthmarked
Book Three—Soulmarked
Book Four—Deathmarked (coming soon!)
Book Five—Lifemarked (coming soon!)

Fatemarked Origins:
Volume I
Volume II
Volume III (coming soon!)
Volume IV (coming soon!)
Volume V (coming soon!)

<u>Science Fiction Novels by David Estes</u>

Strings *(also available in audiobook)*

One of "15 Series to Read if You Enjoyed The Hunger Games"—Buzzfeed.com
The Dwellers Saga *(also available in audiobook)*:
Book One—The Moon Dwellers
Book Two—The Star Dwellers
Book Three—The Sun Dwellers

Book Four—The Earth Dwellers

"Fire Country is a fast, fierce read."—Emmy Laybourne,
author of Monument 14
The Country Saga (A Dwellers Saga sister series)(*also available in
audiobook*):
Book One—Fire Country
Book Two—Ice Country
Book Three—Water & Storm Country
Book Four—The Earth Dwellers

"The Walking Dead for teens, with ruthless witches instead of
bloodthirsty zombies."—Katie Reed, agent at Andrea Hurst &
Associates
Salem's Revenge:
Book One—Brew
Book Two—Boil
Book Three—Burn

"Someone must die before another can be born…"
The Slip Trilogy:
Book One—Slip
Book Two—Grip
Book Three—Flip

About the Author

David Estes was born in El Paso, Texas but moved to Pittsburgh, Pennsylvania when he was very young. He grew up in Pittsburgh and then went to Penn State for college. Eventually he moved to Sydney, Australia where he met his wife and soul mate, Adele, who he's now happily married to.

A reader all his life, David began writing science fiction and fantasy novels in 2010, and has published more than 20 books. In June of 2012, David became a fulltime writer and is now living in Hawaii with Adele, their energetic son, Beau, and their naughty, asthmatic cat, Bailey.

A sample of SOULMARKED, Book 3 in the Fatemarked Epic by David Estes Available NOW!

One

The Hinterlands, beyond the bounds of the Northern Kingdom
Lisbeth Lorne

She arrived in the midst of a storm, in the deepest throes of night.

Born of thunder and lightning and howling wind and needles of sleet, she was a spell incarnated, the product of magic and faith and a power beyond human understanding. She was the daughter of Absence and Wrath and Surai, the many-named gods of the south, the Creator, the One responsible for Life and all those who claimed it.

You shall be Lisbeth Lorne, a voice said. It wasn't a shout, but a whisper, nearly lost on the wind.

"Lisbeth Lorne," the girl tried. She laughed at the way it sounded on her tongue. She laughed at the coolness of the snow settling on her face and hands. She laughed at how the fabric of her pale blue dress felt against her smooth skin. She laughed because she was, inexplicably, alive.

Unlike the other humans that walked the face of the planet, she remembered the time before; a time when she was naught but a soul, a ribbon of light, free from the bounds of gravity and human nature, free from deception and violence and disappointment and foolish decisions. In those days, those eternities, she sang with the stars, spoke with the sun, slept with the moons.

She was free.

And yet now, trapped in this body, held fast to the ground, there was something liberating, astonishingly exciting—a giddy feeling in her lungs and chest, the simultaneous cold of snow against the warmth of the blood running through her veins.

I am alive.

The truth of the thought echoed through her, and she took off, stumbling over the drifts at first, her new knees knocking together, her new arms awkward at her sides. As the wind splashed against her smile, she fell less and less as she learned, as she found her balance.

Instinctively, she knew she saw the world differently than others. Some would call her blind, but that wasn't exactly true. She might not be able to see the outward physical nature of her surroundings, but what she saw held far more truth; for she saw the *soul* of every living thing, pulsing, alive, the truth behind a wall of lies, a single grain of sand amongst billions.

She relished the joy of dancing across the soul of the world, feeling it breathe beneath her feet.

Hours later, the night began to fall away, and she stopped, tumbling to the snow, breathing ghosts into the lightening sky.

A wolf howled. Then another.

She sat up, looking around. They weren't wolves—for they didn't have the cool blue souls of wolves, ever stalwart—but something else, something larger, their inner beings red slashes of lightning, hungry, ever hungry. There were ten, twenty, a hundred, a sea of predators racing over the snowy hills, cresting one and descending another, starting up the final slope to where Lisbeth sat catching her breath.

Riding each beast were other souls, a combination of light and dark, bold and fearless and intense. They were violent shadows that had tasted blood.

Something pulsed through her: Not fear, exactly; more like curiosity.

The first of them reached the hill's apex, skidding to a halt. Though blind in the typical sense, she sensed the weapons: spears raised, shoved forward, their blades surrounding her.

"Uz nom nath kahlia!" one of them said, a grunt that seemed to come from the deepest part of his throat. *You have broken the pact*, Lisbeth understood.

"Iz nom klar," she spoke, the rough words hurting her throat. *I have just arrived.*

The one who spoke, perhaps the leader, cocked his head to the side, his soul displaying the gray tide of confusion. "Uz Gurz hom shuf? Cut?" *You speak Garzi? How?*

"I don't know," Lisbeth said, instinctively reverting back to the language that felt more comfortable.

"Filth language," the creature said. "Now you must die."

He raised his spear over his head just as the sun appeared, orange rays reflecting tongues of flame across the blade. This

Lisbeth could see, though it was naught but flashes of light on the edge of her vision.

Lisbeth closed her eyes. She wasn't ready to die; she had only just arrived.

Bright blue light burst from her forehead, piercing the vision of the multitude gathered before her, both riders and beasts. The Garzi cried out, their voices raised together, their weapons dropped as they tried to cover their eyes.

In that moment, she revealed their souls at all their extremes. The darkness. The lightness. The pain. The betrayal. The fear. The joy.

The light died away, revealing the mark on Lisbeth's head: a single, blue eye.

The Garzi warriors crashed from their mounts, screaming, scrubbing at their ears, at their eyes, at their heads. The beasts fled, abandoning their masters, knocking into each other in their haste to escape.

Rivulets of blood streamed from noses and ears, streaking the snow.

Even once it was over, the fallen warriors continued to shake, wracked with shivers though they were not cold.

Lisbeth opened her eyes. Her other eye, marked on her forehead, vanished, leaving her skin as pristine as freshly fallen snow.

She saw what she had done—hundreds of souls, cracked, wracked with pain—placed her face in her hands, and wept.

Two

The Northern Kingdom, Castle Hill
Annise Gäric

The night was a snow-haired queen wearing a crown of stars.

The queen's eyes were the moons, one green, half open, and the other red, just a sliver peeking out from behind a dark eyelid.

Annise sighed, wishing that being a real queen was as magical as the false one in the sky. Instead it was full of impossible decisions, unbearable sacrifices, and a lifetime's worth of heartache.

Frozen Lake stretched out in front of her, disappearing on the horizon, reflecting moon and starlight. *What secrets do you hold?* Annise wondered to the night.

The urge to relinquish the crown back to her younger brother, Archer, and depart Castle Hill to find Tarin still arose from time to time, but she tamped it down. That was something the old Annise would do. The new Annise would fight for her people, her kingdom. The new Annise wasn't selfish.

Then why do I have to keep telling myself?

She turned away from the night, shivering despite the warm blanket wrapped around her shoulders. The temperature had dropped the last few days, ever since that night when Archer finally opened his eyes. With his awakening, it seemed, winter had awakened as well.

Annise slipped back inside, closing the door to her balcony behind her. Warmth from the hearth instantly unfroze her bones, causing her skin to tingle.

Archer was sitting up in bed, staring at her.

She couldn't help it—she flinched. Though, for the last three days, her brother had been waking up more and more and for longer periods of time, it was still a shock whenever he did. It was like she'd grown so accustomed to his unconsciousness that him sleeping seemed more natural than him being awake.

"Does my face truly scare you, sister?" Arch said, smiling weakly.

I remember when his smile used to light up the entire kingdom, Annise thought. *Now it doesn't even light up his face.*

She released a breathy laugh, pulling her blanket tighter against her skin. "Only the awakeness of it." In truth, his face *did* scare her a little. His skin was far too pale, save for the dark half-moons under each eye. Worse, his cheeks were too skinny, the bones protruding at sharp angles. This sum total of the changes was that he looked even more like their youngest sibling, Bane, than she'd like to admit. *Bane, the same brother who'd sent Archer into unconsciousness in the first place*, she reminded herself, not losing the irony.

He yawned. "Shall I go back to sleep?"

"No," Annise said quickly. "Well, yes. That is, if you're tired, you should sleep." The healer was strict in her instructions: Archer should continue to sleep for long periods in order to let his body fully recover from the injuries suffered at Raider's Pass.

"I'm tired, but I don't want to sleep ever again," Arch said. "I've got bedsores all over my body—my back, my legs, my—"

"I'm sure your many admirers will rub a soothing balm on them for you," Annise cut in.

"If you'd let me see them," Arch said, and Annise was glad the quickness was returning to his mind. He'd always been one of the few in the castle who could rival the speed of her tongue.

"It's for your own good. We don't want you to overexert yourself."

Archer narrowed his eyes and chewed his lip, not looking convinced. His tone turned serious. "What I really want to know is: How did I get knocked out in Raider's Pass and wake up in Castle Hill?"

Annise cringed. It was the question she was hoping he wouldn't ask for a good long while. She'd received a three-day respite, as he'd been too weak to do more than slurp soup, sip water, and sleep, but now there was no dodging it. She decided to face it head on.

"Well, there was a horse attached to a cart. And you were in the cart. The horse pulled the cart, and here we are."

"I see you haven't lost your sense of humor, sister."

"It's a permanent attachment to my body, lest I fall into despair."

"Annise."

"Archer."

"I'm the king, I need to know what I missed. I'm ready to lead again. To rule."

"About that…"

She was saved by a knock on the door. "You may enter," Arch said, sounding kinglier than he had since reawakening.

Sir Metz entered, bowing at the waist. As usual, his silver armor was so well-polished Annise could see her wobbly reflection in it.

"Good evening, Sir Metz," Annise said. "Allow me to formally introduce you to my brother, Archer. Archer, this knight was responsible for your protection many times while you slept. May I present Sir Christoff Metz."

"Well met, Sir," Archer said. "Thank you for your service. Now what can we do for you?"

"Do for me?" Metz asked. "Nothing. I serve the kingdom."

Arch cocked his head to the side and glanced at Annise. She shook her head. She could explain the knight's eccentricities later. "What my brother meant was: Why have you disturbed us so late?"

"That's a rude way of putting it," Arch muttered.

Metz looked right at Annise when he said, "Apologies Your Highness, may I have a word?"

Frozen hell, Annise thought. *Could he be any less subtle?* The answer, of course, was no. Sir Metz was about as subtle as a stampeding mamoothen trying to cross a frozen lake.

"Of course," Arch said, sitting up straighter. Annise saw a flash of pain cross his face, but then it was gone, hidden behind her brother's calm, confident expression. "Whatever you need to say, you can say in front of my sister."

Metz looked at Arch, then back at Annise. "Yes," Annise said, hoping to salvage the situation. "Speak freely in front of both of us."

The knight raised an eyebrow, but then said, "A stream has been received from Darrin. There is a storm gathering strength in the east. It looks to hit Castle Hill directly."

"We have weathered many of storms before," Arch said. "Why are you telling us this?"

"Because we have delayed depart—"

"Thank you, Sir," Annise said. "That will be all."

The knight, seeming almost relieved, bowed again and departed the way he'd come, leaving them alone once more. Annise avoided Archer's stare as it bore into her from the side.

"Why did he stop answering my question upon your command?" he asked.

Annise said, "There is much I need to tell you."

"Then tell me."

Just like ripping off a bandage…

"I had a name day, Archer. I'm eighteen now."

"And?" He still didn't get it, still hadn't thought things through enough to understand. *I guess that's what happens when you're brought up assuming you will be king someday.*

"And you've been unconscious for more than a fortnight."

"A fortnight? That long? I suspected, but I couldn't be certain. I think I understand what you are saying."

"You do?" Annise was surprised at the lightness in his tone.

"Of course, sister, my injury didn't dim my wits. You've been leading my soldiers, haven't you? Knights like Sir Metz have been obeying your commands while I slept. They're in the habit now, and we haven't formally returned the torch to its rightful place."

"Archer—"

"Tell me everything. The sooner the details are filled in, the sooner I can return to the throne and decide the next course of action."

"It has already been decided. I will be going north, into the Hinterlands, along with Sir Metz, Sir Dietrich, Sir Jonius, and maybe some others. We are going to find the Sleeping Knights."

Arch frowned. "Enough japes. I'm no longer in the mood."

"It was no jest."

His frown deepened. "The first thing I will do is revisit this decision. On whose authority was it reached?"

"On mine," Annise said, rising to her full height and jutting out her jaw. "Under northern law, you have not yet reached the age of rule. I have. I am the queen now."

SOULMARKED by David Estes, available NOW!

Made in the USA
San Bernardino, CA
29 April 2020